PANGAEA: UNSETTLED LAND
By Jarrod D. King

Pangaea: Unsettled Land

for Aunt Valerie

PART ONE

CHAPTER ONE

I

The little girl's vision was blurred with tears and she could barely see anything but the white of snow as the man returned. The boy sitting next to her did as he was told and continued to watch her. She wiped her eyes on the man's big coat wrapped around her freezing, wet clothes and looked up as he spoke.

"There are no cracks in the ice," he said, dusting snow off his shoulders. "Nobody could have fallen in the lake."

The girl didn't respond. She knew what she had seen. What she'd heard had been an entirely different matter.

"Dad, are we gonna be able to skate today?" the boy asked.

"Don't you see your neighbor practically freezing to death? No, son, we're taking her back home." He offered a hand to the girl. "Come on. Let's take you back to your grandma."

She grabbed his hand and was hoisted into his arms. Her wet sleeves clung around his neck as she looked back at the lake. That horrific episode replayed in her mind over and over.

II
Moments ago…

"Gisela," a woman called to her young child with arms wrapped at her waist. "We're here." Dressed warmly in white parkas, they both sat atop a pale horse. Its hooves kicked up snow as it trotted out into the open. It was winter in the Northern Third, where the winters were always the harshest. As the woman gazed out at their destination, she saw light snow falling onto a frozen lake. The sun hid behind the clouds, but peeked through from time to time as if watching events unfold and anticipating a scene it did not wish to witness. Tall trees surrounded Lake Maesus with branches that trembled with the air's light breeze before going still. The woman pulled the horse's reins and it came to a stop as they approached the edge of the lake.

Two beautiful green eyes looked up at her. "Yay! Can we have fun now, Mama?"

She chuckled at her younger reflection. "Yes, we can have fun. First, let me make sure the coast is clear. Come on, hop down."

Gisela slid off the side of the horse and stuck her landing like an acrobat. Her mother followed and secured the horse by tying its halter to a small metal snap in a nearby tree. They came here so much that she had decided to install it herself last summer. She looked into a small sack attached to the saddle and pulled out a pair of binoculars to peer through.

Gisela huffed, "The lusae don't even come here, Mama."

Her mother tuned her out and continued surveying the edges of the vast lake for any sign of movement. The fact that the lusae hardly ever approached the lake was a strange phenomenon, but this was what made it safe for travelers. Even so, Gisela's mother wanted to be sure the dangerous creatures were nowhere to be found. In fact, this was why she had rode in on horseback. If there were the slightest chance a lusae were about, her wheeler's loud engine would have stirred them, and she didn't need the threat they posed. As she gazed through the binoculars, she pressed a button, making the electronic marks and measures on the lens disappear. Her eyes caught sight of an animal on the opposite side of the lake. "Ah! Gisela, come look!"

Gisela trotted over with a puzzled expression and accepted the binoculars from her mother. She turned wildly as she looked through trying to see what all the fuss was about. "Hold still," her mother said. She put her arms around her daughter and steered her gaze in the right direction. "Look."

Gisela gasped. On the opposite side of the lake was a ceffyl, or water horse, with its head hanging towards the frozen solid lake. Its coat was the purest of white. Its mane and tail dripped with water. The creature simply tapped its hoof on the frozen edge of water then lifted its gaze towards the sky as liquefied water spouted up into the air and down into its mouth. After a few gulps, its gaze rested straight ahead as if knowing it was being watched. Startled, Gisela pulled the binoculars away, feeling like quite the intruder. She peered through again and saw the ceffyl had fled and the spot on the lake was frozen once more. "It's gone," she said.

"It's okay, we're safe," her mother replied. The creature they saw had been on the far side of the lake. The distance between them was enough for them not to worry. Plus, the ice was always thick enough for them to skate without concern. As a mother, she always took precautions, but nothing ever happened out here. She grabbed the binoculars and sat them back in her pouch and gave her daughter a wide smile. "Now, let's have some fun." She went around to the other side of the horse and untied the laces of two pairs of ice skates hanging together from the saddle. Gisela eagerly held out her hands for her pair and sat on the snowy ground to change. Her mother walked to the nearest picnic bench and dusted off the snow-topped seat before sitting down. When she looked up, she saw Gisela stomping off in her ice skates towards the lake. "Gisela, don't go too far," she called. She didn't answer, but her mother knew she'd heard her. She was constantly amazed at her daughter's lack of fear in a world where people feared so much. The lusae, Ethereans, the elements themselves, even the people of the other Great Nations. Gisela saw none of it as abnormal or scary and had, in a sense, embraced it. She supposed that was how a lot of kids these days saw things. Times certainly were changing.

***

For an eight-year-old, Gisela moved on the ice with the grace of royalty. She'd gotten much better since they had started skating together last year. Her mother saw she had a love for the water. She picked up swimming even faster than she had ice skating and loved to come to this very lake during the summer for a dip. Gisela swayed back and forth, up and down. The furry hood of her parka flew back and her long, dark brown hair went traveling in the wind as she made her turns. Suddenly, she skidded to a stop.

She always listened to her mother and she never strayed far from the edge of the lake, but something caught her attention this time and she couldn't shake her curiosity. What was that she heard? It couldn't have been her mother, for she was still on the bench lacing up her skates. Again, a soft voice in a hushed tone: "Gisela."

"Mama?" she asked. She looked further down the open lake, back towards her mother and back again. It sounded like her mother, but how could that be? She called to her mother at the bench a few yards away, "Mama. Did you call me?"

"No. Wait for me. I'll be right there."

Gisela turned away from the direction of her mother and began to skate further into the lake. "Come, Gisela. I'm here," the voice said again.

***

Sitting by the table, her mother had nearly finished tying her second skate when she looked up and frowned. "Gisela," she called. "Gisela, don't go out any further without me." She looked down at her unfinished laces and quickened her pace. Louder, she called again, "Gisela, wait for me!" As she finished with her skates, she looked up. She was alarmed by how her horse had begun neighing and jumping wildly. As the metal snap broke, she reached for the horse in vain as it kicked up snow and disappeared in the opposite direction. She looked back at the lake and completely lost her breath at the realization that Gisela was no longer there. "Gisela!" she yelled. She fought the onset of panic as she scanned her surroundings for any lusae. As expected, none were around. Perhaps Gisela was playing a trick on her – blending into the snowy ice with her parka as she had done many times before. She trudged her way on the ice skates to the lake and cried, "Gisela, that's not funny. Get up–" but her words were cut short as she looked ahead. She lost her battle with panic as she saw an opening in the lake. Had her mind been clear, she would have noticed that the hole was not cracked and jagged, but oddly wide, smooth and deliberate. She only saw Gisela struggle to pop her head out of the water once for a quick breath, but then swiftly return below, unable to keep herself afloat. She had no time to think of anything but her daughter, so she skated forward.

She slowed herself as she neared the hole in the ice and began to remove her parka. After tying a knot in both sleeves she held on to one end and tossed the other into the water. The cold grew more intense against her body as she lie flat against the ice. She shivered in a mix of cold and fear with a silent prayer running through her mind. *Oh, God! Oh, God! Oh, Elao, please! Please!*

Almost as if her pleading was answered, her daughter's head popped up out of the water once again. "Grab on, Gisela! Grab it!"

She watched Gisela grab a hold of the knotted sleeve and wasted no time crawling backward and pulling her out. She got this far, but worried about cracks forming under their weight so close to the hole. *How could this happen?* she thought. She knew how thick the ice was and they came here to skate all the time. There had never been an incident. As she pulled Gisela to safety, she saw that the ice did not shift, nor did any more cracks form.

The ice seemed just as thick at the edge of the hole as it was on the entire lake. It didn't make any sense. It was unnatural. Something was definitely wrong here.

She grabbed Gisela and pulled her close as she sat upright. She held on to her so tight, unsure if she'd ever let go again. It took a moment, but she finally felt relief. "Gisela, can you walk?" Her daughter nodded. "Okay, get back to the bench."

***

Gisela's body shook fiercely, desperately trying to recover. She knew to listen to her mother and mustered enough strength to get to her knees and stand up. As her mother began to do the same, she started toward land and only made a few steps before hearing that voice again. Was it laughing?

"I'll be waiting for you, Gisela…"

She thought she heard something, but it was more like a whisper. She couldn't be sure. Then, she heard a splash. Frightened, Gisela turned around and saw that the hole in the ice had moved just inches away from her feet. She tried to catch her balance, but felt the thud of solid ice on her bottom. Her mother was gone and the hole gradually froze over. She looked back and forth trying to make sense of how the opening in the lake had inexplicably resealed itself. The only heat she felt rolled down her face in the form of tears as she screamed and begged for her mother to return.

CHAPTER TWO
Thirteen years later

The snow finally melted, marking the year's beginning of spring in the Northern Third. Slade took a deep breath of the clear air while leaning on the rail of his thirty-fifth-floor balcony. He exhaled deeply. He was disappointed and still unhappy about what lie ahead. It only worked for actors in the movies he guessed. A day of classes at Burrow University loomed over him like a dark cloud. He hadn't completed his assignments and hated to go unprepared. There was no choice but to go; however, he still hoped he could skate through what was sure to be a long day.

He saw the university not too far off in the distance. In the early spring scenery, even he couldn't deny its beauty. Its main tower stretched high with stone, reaching to scrape the sky. The tower was flanked by an east and west wing that was just as intimidating as it was enthralling. Just ahead of it were yards of freshly sprung green grass protected in spots by full trees swaying with the wind. Slade looked at the other students below walking to and from class. Some had almost tumbled out of one of the surrounding dormitory buildings trying to get to class on time. Others just enjoyed the scenery, walking hand-in-hand. Slade felt a pang of envy as he saw this. They found love and were just fine

7

with where life was taking them. How? He quickly turned his attention back to the scenery of the campus in an effort to free his mind of negativity. He especially loved the view of Lake Maesus to his far left.

The tinny chime of his communicator snapped him back to reality. He turned from the balcony and reentered his apartment. The glass sliding door closed behind him, giving the thin, white drapes on either side one last flap of air. His black, silk pajama bottoms were his only source of covering and he felt the snap of cool air against his brown, toned back. His shoulders sat back, perfectly straight, as he walked barefoot on the cool wood floor towards the side of his bed. The sensation on his feet found relief as they touched the thick carpet on which his king-sized bed sat. He glanced at the face of his comm. and smiled as he saw who was calling. He grabbed the device, put it to his ear and spoke in a smooth tenor, "Hi, Mom."

"Good morning, Slade. Is everything okay?"

"Yeah, what do you mean?"

"Well, I just haven't heard from you in a few days."

"Mom, there's no emergency if I don't call you."

"I know. I just know you weren't doing so good a few days ago and I haven't spoken to you since."

Slade sat down on the edge of his bed. "I'm good," he began. What was really on his mind and what had caused him to be unprepared for class was the end of a hard-to-define relationship he'd experienced a few weeks ago with his friend, Mason. They were drawn together by their commonalities. Both were from the same hometown, and before Mason transferred back home, they both attended Burrow University. Mason was very popular back home in Reor as well as in Burrow. What had started as a friendship began to evolve into something more intimate, or so Slade thought. Mason would touch Slade on the shoulder, obliterate his personal space and hold long eye-contact when talking. When discussing their aspirations, he'd even make promises like, "I'm taking you with me." Once, he even asked Slade to comment on his looks. All of this from Mason with no steps to take it further confused Slade. He constantly began to wonder, Are we just friends, or something else? So, when Slade asked him and Mason withdrew his friendship, he got his answer: neither. Slade tried reaching out, but Mason never spoke to him again, and now he was back in Reor. Slade closed off his feelings a bit after being hurt like that. He figured Mason's flirting was just a type of mind control to keep a loyal follower. And Slade did not appreciate being fooled. He had mentioned this situation to his mother once when it happened but tried to move on by not speaking about it.

"Okay," his mother said. "When you find the right one, you bring him to me first."

Slade saw he couldn't fool his mother.

She continued, "You know I don't like it when you get down on yourself. Get through this last year and come home."

"Yeah. I will."

"Speaking of coming home, we are going to see you during spring break, right?"

"Of course; I can't wait." This was only half-true. He treasured the time he spent with his family, but it was the only choice he had. It was his last year and he'd never experienced the fun of spending a vacation with friends. He settled on the fact that it would never happen. With the exception of Mason and one other friend, he never really got close to anyone. His status as a noble was a barrier between him and most of the other students for any connections beyond surface level.

"Your sister called me the other day. Even she's going to come this time. Crazy girl. I think she's bringing her mystery boyfriend along with her."

"Good for her. How's Dad?"

"He's good. He just left for work. How's school?"

He groaned. "Fine, I guess. I have to go to class in like twenty minutes."

"Okay. Well, I'll let you go and get ready."

"I don't wanna go," he said feigning dread.

His mom laughed. "I'm letting you go, Slade. Get to class. You'll never be able to work for the queen if you don't pass. Bye, baby."

"Bye, Mom." He dropped his hand to his lap and stared at the comm. Working for the queen in any capacity was regarded as a great honor and was something the Maxwell family had done for generations as nobles. It was because of his mother's work with the queen that he had all that he had: the big penthouse, the most expensive technology, and the nicest clothing. He was next in line to find a position as part of the government of the Middle Third, but he constantly questioned whether that was what he wanted. He wanted something new, some adventure, to experience different cultures all around the world. Working at a desk for the queen wasn't going to do that.

He looked at the time on his comm. Class began in fifteen minutes. He sighed and found enough willpower to slowly push himself off of the bed and get ready to go to school.

CHAPTER THREE

I

Slade entered the auditorium-style classroom relieved to see his philosophy instructor had not yet appeared. Maybe class would be cancelled and he wouldn't show. That would be one class Slade could scratch off the list today. He began to do some philosophizing of his own and wondered why exactly he was here. Slade could have decided to go to school in Reor, as the rest of his family once did, but the call of something new and extraordinary allured him here. He'd only been to the Northern Third once as a child, but he enjoyed the idea of staying in another country, long term. He could immerse himself in a culture completely different from his own and learn what life was like outside of the safe little bubble that was Reor. He thought being away from his family would give him the space to grow into who he wanted. He fought his mother for her blessing and she finally gave in, but what he once considered a new adventure as a student slowly turned into an act of tedium as the days and years went by. It was nice getting to know students from all walks of life, but neither they nor his studies satisfied his hunger for emprise. He knew there was more to the world than what he had been shown or taught, but for some reason he just couldn't break through the surface. He wondered if it was a mistake ever coming here. Had the pulling inside of him steered him wrong?

11

Slade began to climb the stairs and look for a seat. The classroom, like every other classroom Slade visited, was brightly lit and clean. After only four years of the university being erected and populated by students, everything including the stationary cushioned seats was in perfect condition. He could see most of the students already arrived and were seated and talking amongst themselves. Except, of course, for one girl who usually sat in silence. His friend, Gisela, had been saving his seat. After spotting her, he continued his climb, but paused when he noticed the guy sitting in a front seat on the far side of the room. His massive arms were folded in front of him. He chatted with a couple of classmates, but Slade knew when class started, he would never speak up unless called on by the instructor. Slade thought he was kind of arrogant, actually. It seemed like he thought he was above things like school and learning. Who did he think he was? Slade's eyes stayed on him too long – his classmate looked back with eyebrows lifted in a concerned expression. Slade blinked and forced his attention back to getting to his seat, currently covered by a textbook.

When he got to his row in the middle of the room, the girl he sat next to smiled and removed the textbook. "Hi, Slade." Her straight brown hair was tied into a bun and she adjusted the placement of the oval glasses framing her green eyes.

"Hi, Gisela." He sat down as she studied him, running her eyes up and down, up and down. Finally, he said, "What?"

"You're in rare form today. Jeans and a hoodie? That's not usual for the prince of BU."

He chuckled at his new title. "I had a late start, okay? And I'm nobody's prince. I *wish!*"

"That's not what everyone else says. I hear it every day: 'Slade's got a hover car, all the nicest clothes, everything'." She mocked in a nasally voice, "'He doesn't even live in the dorms. He's got his own tricked-out penthouse with the *latest* from the Middle Third'."

He shrunk back in his chair a little and asked, "Do they think I'm a snob?"

"Yes, but you are, so own it," Gisela teased.

Slade rolled his eyes but secretly appreciated the banter. As clingy as she could be, Gisela was the only one who accepted him for him and not for the things he had. He relaxed and studied the map on the front wall of Pangaea – their home. One big mass of land surrounded by a never-ending sea. Despite having traveled to a few different cities, Slade knew there was so much more out there he hadn't seen. The land was divided into three Great Nations: the Northern Third, where Slade was now; the Middle Third, where Slade was from; and the Southern Third, where he had yet to visit. He promised himself right then that he would get there someday. That feeling of hope was snuffed as the instructor entered the room. So much for a cancelled class.

The instructor stood straight at the front of the room and addressed his class, "All right, everyone, let's get started." In his crisp white shirt, colorful bowtie, and tweed blazer, he stared at his students, eyes leading his head from side to side, watching and waiting for the final murmurs of conversation to end. "Since the beginning of civilization there have been stories that help us explain who we are and how we got to this point in time. Some historically accurate and others...a bit more unbelievable. We're going to explore some of these stories today. It was your assignment to come in prepared to talk about these things, so let's start. Who would like to go first?"

The class fell into an awkward silence for a moment while everyone waited for a brave soul to step up and break the ice. Slade pulled his hood around his neck and tried to hide amongst the crowd of students. He tried his best not to look into his instructor's eyes, but mistakenly made eye contact with his stare. The instructor began to open his mouth and Slade could feel the dark cloud of disappointment creeping over him as he prepared to say, "I don't know." Just as the shadow was almost completely cast, a glimmer of light broke through in the form of a raised hand in the front row. *Thank Elao*, he thought.

Surprised, the instructor said, "Yes! Douglassaire. What is it you would like us to discuss?" He was talking to the guy Slade had all but stared down as he came in. Slade was just as surprised as his instructor to see Douglassaire speak up.

He was leaning back in his chair with his long legs stretched out in front of him. His deep voice carried clearly to the back of the room, "I looked at Ether the other day…"

The instructor nodded in polite, but feigned understanding. Did he mean he researched the story of Ether? Did he actually see Ether? Knowing his students and knowing the fact that the fabled isle of Ether didn't exist, he figured both were impossibilities and implored his student for more information. "Yes, Doug. What have you found? Tell us."

He shrugged his broad shoulders. "Well, I just think it's cool to think that our world was created from one place – a place we can't see or get back to."

The instructor addressed his class, "It's been years for some of you who have heard that story I'm sure. Could anyone give us a refresher?"

Slade remembered hearing the story but had forgotten some details. In any case, now was a good time to speak up and participate. He felt all instructors kept a mental note of who took part in the class discussions. If he could answer an easy question like this, the instructor may not bother him for the rest of the class. Then Gisela raised her hand. Just great.

"Yes, Miss Benitez," called the instructor.

"The story is that Ether is on the other side of world and protected by the ethereal spirits. It's said to house the Djed Key at its center which, if removed, would grant its holder the power of God."

"Very good, Gisela. Thank you. Now, does anyone actually believe this story?"

A bunch of students shook their head and some murmured, "No." Slade watched as Douglassaire was now sitting up and leaning forward in his seat. He seemed to be getting into it. "Ether's been disproven," said Douglassaire. "I mean, we've had people search all over the globe, but there's no island. If any place outside of Pangaea existed, we'd know about it by now."

The instructor began to pace in front of the room. "True, Mr. Hart, but how do you explain the existence of the lusae, these creatures with the power to control the elements? They've been around forever and the danger they pose prevents us from venturing further out into our lands. Then there are the Ethereans – humans, like us, but with the power to control the elements in the same way. Centuries ago, many of us would have denied their existence as well."

Douglassaire furrowed his eyebrows and thumbed his trimmed goatee, "You sayin' that we should actually believe this story?"

Slade perked up in his seat. The discussion unexpectedly drew him in and he awaited his professor's response.

"I'm simply proposing that you do not close your mind to the things which you cannot yet see. Perhaps in another decade we will have discovered this island just as we discovered the existence of Ethereans, however rare they are. And thanks to Queen Aeothesca displaying her ethereal talents years ago; however, mistakenly, perhaps the confidence she's instilled in her kind will show us that there is an even bigger population of Ethereans among us than we know."

II

The instructor dismissed everyone from class for the day and the normal everyday chatter commenced. Many already forgot what they had just talked about and moved on to more pressing issues like the next party they'd attend. Slade and Gisela rose from their seats and motioned toward the end of the aisle. Slade successfully dodged looking unprepared for class, but he was still intrigued by the conversation about Ether. He glanced ahead at Douglassaire wondering what made him bring it up. Slade left his row with Gisela following closely behind. As they descended the stairs, Slade said to Gisela, "That was interesting, huh? I didn't know you knew so much about that stuff."

She blushed and lowered her head. "My mother used to teach me all about Ether and its stories."

"Oh," Slade said as they turned and left through the classroom door. He knew that Gisela losing her mother in Lake Maesus must have been hard. She told him the story once – and about how a swimmer came upon the body the summer after the incident. He couldn't imagine what it must be like to walk past the lake every day on the way to school and be reminded of it all. Out of respect and a desire to keep things light, he ended that trail of discussion.

Slade and Gisela paused, suddenly feeling a presence towering behind them. They turned around to face a tall, dark brown figure.

"Interesting talk, huh?" Douglassaire asked. He smiled at Gisela. She didn't smile back. He looked at Slade who felt his gaze a split-second longer than usual. Slade was a few shades lighter, a couple of inches shorter, and slender. Complete opposites. Douglassaire looked back at Gisela and his deep voice spoke up, "You seem to know about Ether."

Slade responded, "She's an expert of sorts—"

"I'm not an expert," Gisela interrupted. "I just know the common stories. Nothing else."

Slade smiled. "Don't let her fool you. She knows more than most. You're Douglassaire, right?" He smiled and stuck out his hand.

"Just Doug," he replied, grabbing Slade's hand for a firm shake.

"Slade." He nodded his head to the side. "This is Gisela."

Doug nodded at Gisela. Her response was to stand still with her arms crossed and not say a word.

Sometimes her awkwardness annoyed Slade. Whenever something or someone new entered Slade's awareness, Gisela was always there as a shield. He could understand if it was just her way of being protective, but it was more like she wanted him all to herself. His patience ran thin as he waited for the chance to show Doug that there was always room for more friends.

Doug said, "I never knew much about Etherean lore, but what I looked up was interesting."

"What have you found?" he asked.

"Well, a lot of it ties in with religious beliefs. Something about an ancient fight involving Elao... I didn't really read all that much of it."

"Elao and Calamity," Gisela said. "The story's about an ancient battle between good and evil that gave birth to the magic the lusae and Ethereans use."

"Right," said Slade. "But why are you so interested, Doug?"

"You know how Ethereans are really rare? I've got a feeling about someone. He goes here."

"Wait, wait," Slade said in disbelief. "You think there's an Etherean here at Burrow? Who?"

Doug sucked air in through his teeth. "I don't think I should say. Not just yet anyway."

"Oh, come on, you gotta at least give me a hint, now."

"Slade," Gisela said nudging him with her elbow, "...that's not his secret to tell. And from the sound of it, he doesn't even know if it's true."

"Okay, okay, I get it, but I'm gonna keep an eye out. I think that's really interesting."

Doug smiled. "Yeah, me too. Well, I gotta go meet my group to train some more. I'll see you guys later. It was nice meetin' you."

"Same here," Slade said. As he watched Douglassaire turn and walk out of the building his impression from seeing him in class had changed. If he was being honest with himself, there was something about Doug that Slade really liked.

CHAPTER FOUR

The grassy field at Burrow University's athletic facility was freshly cut. Five young men stood atop the lawn practicing their sword skills against one another. Douglassaire was among them. He had inhaled the calming scent of the grass when he arrived, but now as he swung, dodged, and blocked, his adrenaline rushed and his sense of smell was limited. Of course, they didn't practice with real swords, which were outlawed on the campus. Instead, they used the school's provided bamboo swords. The people of the North had an aversion to war that permeated all aspects of their culture. Hardly anyone carried a weapon even in their own homes. So, it was understandable, but still a disappointment to all of the warriors of the South who enjoyed the sword's technological enhancements. While purely cosmetic, all swords were able to be customized from weight to color. The Middle Third had swords that were even collapsible. If a scholarship hadn't been offered to these guys for their outstanding fighting skill, they probably wouldn't be here at all.

The stretchy black material in which they were all outfitted felt light against Doug's skin. It was form-fitting with sleeves that stopped just below his shoulders and the bottoms just above his ankles. While it was a similar fit to what warriors wore under their armor, the lack of protective gear allowed him to enjoy the freedom of movement it gave him. It would keep him cool despite the intensity of the exercise. Atop his shoulders sat rounded spaulders with layers like the wings of a ladybug, an adornment used specifically for this activity – training for the Power Battle. It's a fight between the Southern Third's forty best warriors and all any of these men cared about – especially Doug. This battle would decide the next leader of the Southern Third – the next Southern Commander. Some wanted to fight for the fame while others wanted the power. For Douglassaire, winning the Power Battle meant freedom. He left his orphanage as a teenager to join the military. With no money and no family, it was the only way he saw he could survive. He'd been training for the Power Battle ever since, anxiously awaiting the chance to fight and win. This was his way to leave behind his life of poverty and begin making his own life choices.

Douglassaire's muscular frame was a favorite among two onlookers at the sideline who whistled their approval. He ignored the ladies, too focused on his training to bother, but his peer (who was busy taking the role of drill sergeant) did not.

Lesech paced back and forth with his hands folded behind him, scrutinizing each move the men made – a thrust here and a parry there. He shook his head and sucked his teeth in disappointment, none of it satisfactory. Douglassaire practiced with another, but kept notice of Lesech out of the corner of his eye. Lesech smirked and said, "You look horrible, Douglassaire. You'll die minutes after the doors open if you don't get it together." He stood the same height as Doug, but was much thinner. His olive-skinned, angular face was framed by a bush of big white curls, and his piercing hazel eyes were enough to command the attention of anyone.

The two ladies on the sideline cheered for Douglassaire once again. Lesech glanced back at them and then stood behind their idol as he continued his exercise. He stuck out his foot at just the right time and sent Douglassaire falling face-first. Trying to stave off embarrassment, Doug quickly recovered and broke Lesech's personal space with a glare just inches away from his face. His would-be fans had already laughed and walked away.

"Yes, that's it," Lesech said, "get mad."

"You're taking this too far, Lesech," said Doug, trying to decide whether to drop the bamboo sword and use his fist.

"What are you going to do about it? Huh?" Lesech stepped back and spread his arms, yelling, "What are any of you going to do about it?"

The others in the group stopped their exercises with puzzled expressions, nervous laughter, and anticipated what was coming next. "Beat his ass, Doug," one said. "Someone needs to be put in his place," said another. These Southern men didn't have the luxury of a real structured training like they would back home, so they mimicked the exercise on a much smaller scale to keep their skills sharp. With all of the fighting going on, it was commonplace for a duel to break out. And just like home, all training stopped to watch and take notes when two warriors got serious.

"What do you say, Lesech? Me and you. Right now." Out of the three duels he and Lesech had, Douglassaire defeated him twice. He was itching to add another win to his record.

Lesech simply stuck out his hand and caught a bamboo sword thrown by one of the other men nearest him. He lowered his eyes and grinned. "You ready for this?"

Without warning, Doug leapt ahead for the first downward swing to his rival's face. He anticipated the block and followed up with a surprise punch to the gut. Lesech's eyes opened wide as he doubled over clutching his abdomen. Doug struck him on the right shoulder with his sword as he went down. He lifted his sword and went for the left, but Lesech blocked and shoved Doug away.

"That was a cheap shot!" he exclaimed, rising back to his feet.

Doug caught his balance and hopped back to his stance with a grace that almost seemed out of place for his stature. "No rules in the Power Battle."

"Oh really? Says the man who's going for the pauldrons instead of the kill." It was true. Doug could have simulated Lesech's death with a simple blow to the head, but instead hit his shoulder, more in line with the official rules of the Power Battle.

The rules were simple. The warriors would all be outfitted with armor including two big pauldrons on each shoulder. Once the fight commenced, if both pauldrons were removed, you were eliminated. Some saw this as the more honorable way to win, but in the Southern Third, a warrior's death in the midst of battle was the more honorable way to lose. The kills are what kept the world watching, and Lesech always wanted to please the crowd. "Let me show you what the Power Battle will be when I'm involved."

Lesech ran forward and began swinging. Doug successfully blocked a barrage of attacks and tried to counterattack by swinging at what would be Lesech's one remaining pauldron. Lesech was already fast, but his speed seemed to increase with each dodge. The day was clear and the air still, but Doug suddenly felt stray gusts of wind blowing in front of him. The air resistance increased his difficulty in fighting. He couldn't make sense of what was happening. *How is Lesech not affected?* He tried his best to counterattack, but Lesech parried Doug's last swing and thrust his bamboo sword into Doug's chest. Doug fell hard.

Lesech stood over Doug, straddled with one leg to each side. He brought the point of his weapon down hard onto Doug's chest, just above his heart. "The record is 2 – 2. Now, we're even, orphan! If you still plan on joining the Power Battle, I hope you enjoy these last few years, because that is where you will die."

The rest of the group stood there in awkward silence. Doug always knew Lesech to be a bit on the eccentric side, but at that moment something had changed. He looked into Lesech's eyes and believed the intent behind every word. What was once a petty rivalry had now evolved into something more. Doug was never easily rattled until now. He just remained on the green grass looking up at Lesech – staring into the face of insanity.

CHAPTER FIVE

I

The sun was setting in the distance. As Gisela came walking down the path to Lake Maesus, she took in the vivid imagery. It was as if the red sky was fighting with the blue of the lake for her attention. The scene was as beautiful as it had always been. Tall green trees outlined the lake in a horseshoe, much unlike it had been years before. A large brick path was carved in recent times leading to the school it now served. Away from the lake sat a fork in the road. The two directions led to Burrow University or Ankor Village, where she called home. She had just come from her final class for the day and sported a light-blue book bag on her right shoulder. She was glad she brought her black fleece jacket with her, which protected her from the cool air. The temperature always seemed to drop around the lake. The scenery escaped her mind as she neared the lake and she began looking ahead as if in a trance. She badly needed a friend and this was the closest she was going to get tonight. She was going to speak to her mother.

Since her mother died at this lake, Gisela lived in an old house with her grandmother who was downright mean. Her grandmother hadn't always been that way, but her affections turned bitter after the incident. Home was not as comfortable as

23

it used to be. After the tragedy, her grandmother kept her away from the lake, saying it was too dangerous. The younger Gisela agreed, but the older Gisela went against her wishes. Ever since a path had opened up, she ran out of excuses as to why she shouldn't visit her mother's final resting place. She visited the lake every night since starting school at Burrow University four years ago. The shock of what happened to her mother was too much for so little a child and Gisela found it hard to find camaraderie amongst her peers. Then she met Slade. Suddenly, her loneliness had been lifted and the mere thought of being in his presence excited her. He was so different, and so handsome. His friendship gave her the bond she sought at the lake. Little by little, she lessened her visits until they numbered once every month, but tonight was unusual. She had just been to the lake the night before, but something happened to make her revert back to old habits.

Her slow trot came to a halt as she approached the edge of the water. She smoothed her dark blue skirt against the back of her legs and sat at the slope. She rested her chin on top of her knees while hugging her shins. The whole time she stared out into the calm blue of the lake. She reminisced about how she once was so happy to arrive at the lake to swim or ice skate. Now, she wouldn't even think about touching the water.

She spoke in a subdued, melancholy tone, "Hey." She didn't know where to start, but her pressing issue was with Slade. "You'll probably think I'm being stupid. And I'm a little ashamed to say it, but I feel like I'm losing my friend. Nothing happened, but…I just have this feeling. I love him, but I guess it was crazy to think I ever had a chance." She paused and searched for the words that would express her true feelings. "I'm just so lonely, Mama. Sometimes it's so hard living without you. I wish you were here."

She felt eyes on her and suddenly looked to her right at a group of students who approached the lake. They stole quick glances as if they could fool her into believing they weren't looking. She knew what they were thinking. She was quiet but not ignorant of the stories that were spun about her. They were whispering now, probably saying, "There she is. She just sits there and talks to herself." They grew silent as Gisela turned her head to look and began to walk away from her further down the side of the lake. *They don't know anything*, Gisela thought. She had grown used to the scrutiny. *They don't know what I know.*

Another reason she kept coming back was that she felt something...a presence. She hoped beyond hope it was her mother watching over her from the lake. The voice that spoke out to her when she was little girl sounded like her mother, but her mother was still alive when it spoke. She always wondered what that voice was and questioned whether what had happened was just an accident. It was this mystery that formed the other half of why she always visited the lake. Aside from speaking to her mother, she hoped that someday the lake's secrets would be revealed.

Gisela never stayed long. The sun was fading fast and there was no way she would stay here without daylight. Gisela grabbed her backpack and slung it over her shoulder as she got up. "Goodnight, Mama." She turned and walked down the alternate path in the road back home to Ankor.

II

Gisela turned the brass knob on the wooden front door of her two-story house and quietly stepped inside. She hoped she wouldn't be noticed. Sometimes her grandmother was asleep when she returned, halting any conversations that would take place and allowing Gisela to peacefully re-enter her home and go to her room. Those moments were few and far between, however, and tonight was not one of them.

Gisela felt deflated at the smell of chicken, roasted peppers, and other spices that greeted her as she entered. Her grandmother was awake…and *cooking*. Gisela slowly closed the door behind her and quietly removed her shoes. She managed to tiptoe up the first of fourteen creaky, wooden stairs without being noticed. Before her foot touched down on the second, her grandmother, grey mane wild and face flushed, swung out from behind the door leading to the kitchen. Her navy blue house dress printed with small red flowers wrinkled as she crossed her arms and her whole face became taut with disdain. "And where have you been?" she asked.

Gisela remained quiet and looked at her grandmother pleadingly. She really didn't want to argue.

"Look at this place! Look at this place!"

"It's clean."

"Damn right it's clean. I had to do it all myself because someone was out doing God knows what when she should have been here doing the cooking and cleaning," she huffed, catching her breath. During her tirade, her hands found her way to her hips. "Honestly, sometimes I don't even know why you're here. You're useless."

"I'm sorry."

"Sorry, my butt. Now, go upstairs and get ready for dinner."

"I'm not hungry." Gisela turned and quickly jogged up the stairs. She neglected to turn on the light as she entered her room. She slammed the door behind her and flopped face-first onto her bed. She could still hear her grandmother ranting downstairs.

"That's fine, you little bitch, but whatever you don't eat tonight's going in the trash."

Gisela was so used to these interactions that she didn't even cry over them anymore. That didn't make her grandmother's words any less hurtful. Her mother's death shattered their relationship. She was the glue that held their little unit together. Gisela remembered a comment her grandmother made to her soon after her mother died, when she was still very young: "If it wasn't for you, she'd still be here." It stuck with her for years. After much thought, Gisela concluded that that comment only hurt because it was true. All she could do was try to make up for it by stepping into her mother's role and take care of her grandmother and the house. But none of it was ever enough. She couldn't bring her mother back.

She closed her eyes, trying to forget she was even there. She thought about the joy in her life and how it was so fleeting. In fact, the only time she was truly happy was when she was with Slade. She thought about him now – wondered what he might be doing. Had his nights always ended on a note of sadness like hers, or was his life as perfect as she'd imagined?

CHAPTER SIX

Slade's unpreparedness for his remaining classes hadn't been an issue for the rest of the day. That night, Slade entered his suite with an excitement he hadn't had for a while. As his fancy, automatic door slid open, the lights turned on eliminating the shadows of night from his room. His brown leather messenger bag was heavy with books for school and he threw it to the floor. He briskly walked to his desk where he sat, hunched, with his two forefingers supporting his head at his temples. Slade shifted his weight and swung in his chair back and forth just taking everything in. Thoughts about the content of his philosophy class's discussion today were unshakeable. Furthermore, Douglassaire had mentioned that an Etherean may be hiding in plain sight at BU. That wasn't too hard to believe. Ethereans are humans, so they would look like anyone else. Also, according to science, if it weren't for some unknown genetic or neurological difference, they wouldn't have any special powers. Nor were those powers passed through a bloodline. A student here could be hiding their ability to control one of the elements: earth, water, fire, or air. Slade found that fascinating.

Slade turned to the monitor on his desk as he brought the toe of one foot to the back of his opposite Achilles heel and dragged his foot free of his sneaker. He did the same for his other foot and began typing away while studying the screen. Slade's curiosity knew no bounds as he searched for information. Sometimes his attention would shift and lead him to find radical theories from other people. For example, some believed in the existence of other dimensions, other gods, and whole worlds living right beside them that they had no knowledge of. There was even a name for one: Earth. Where they got that from Slade could not fathom, but his mind was charged and focused tonight. He wouldn't veer off track.

His inquiry into Ethereans led him to the story of Elao and Calamity. Most of the people of the Middle Third were deeply religious, and as one of them, Slade had been taught this story as a child. He remembered the story as a creative way to explain the inexplicable existence of magical animals called the lusae and powerful humans called Ethereans. But as he re-read the parable, he saw it through a new lens wondering, *What if this is true?*

A small island in a sea of blue
Populated only by two.
Nothing else existed outside of their view
And they wanted to create a world brand new.

The man, Elao, of righteous blood
Struck down his sword into the mud
His blade of fire, water, earth, and air
Created land where none was there.

He then gave breath to beings more
With legs of two and some of four.
He favored those that looked like him
And gave them control of all the land.

Flagitious fiend, Calamity,
Disliked the station of his race,
At once as Elao turned his face
Gave his power to kindred beasts.

The beasts began to war with man,

29

With powers they did not understand.
They fought until they gained terrain
And Elao vowed to stop their reign.

Against his will he gave away
Some power to the human race,
But much unlike his feral friend
Kept most of that power just for him.

He infused just a select few
With magic that they never knew.

Magic with a complex mind
Proved to be enough in time
For those few men across the world
To stop the beasts and live divine.

Calamity flew and soon proclaimed
"I vow to end Pangaea's days,"
But Elao wrapped his legs in chain,
And brought him back to ground again.

Elao and Calamity both enraged
Fought and fought for forty days.
And after each tenth day had passed
Ethereal spirits escaped their path.

Each spirit announced, nay, they swore
"Three of four to open the door."

Ether was lost from the world of men
And Elao grew tired of fighting then.
Without his full power he knew all too well
Calamity was one he could never fell.

He did what he could to put him to sleep
And banished Calamity, caged in the deep.

PANGAEA: UNSETTLED LAND

Elao, alone on the island now,
Sought more companions and soon found how.
He rose to a rest away in the sky
And watched his people from on high.

It was a nice story, but it couldn't *all* be true, Slade decided. Growing up in the Middle Third meant everyone believed in the goodness of Elao and the potential damnation of Calamity, but most, including Slade, separated parables like this from the bulk of their belief. As far as he knew, this story was written only to make a point. While Iusae and Ethereans did exist, there was no such thing as ethereal spirits, whatever that was, and there was no island. Certainly evidence to this would be available somewhere, too, but there was none.

Slade turned his attention to a video on the screen. It was old footage of a news profile on the Middle Third's royal family. He pressed play and saw wooden double doors fly open to an inner-garden area in Lorelei Castle, enclosed by brick walls. With no ceiling, the sun shone down on Queen Aeothesca who was standing there in a small garden of flowers with her back turned. She lifted her arms as the bricks that constructed the walls began to crack. The ground shook with fury and spurts of dirt shot into the air – the work of a furious witch. Suddenly, Queen Aeothesca turned her head in a miserable frown to the voice behind the camera as it spoke up, "Behold–"

Slade paused the scene and answered his ringing comm. "Hello?"

"Hello, son." It was his mother calling. Again.

Slade sighed, "Hi, Mom. I just spoke to you this morning."

"I know. I'm just checking to see if you're asleep by now. It's late!"

Slade took a breath to speak, but stopped himself to think. He opened his mouth again and said, "Mom. I got this."

"Okay, honey. Go to sleep. Have a good night."

A thought came to Slade. "Mom, wait. What's it like to work for the queen? I mean, what's she really like?"

His mother exhaled heavily, something she always did when thinking of the best way to say something. "The queen

31

is…complex. You know, sometimes I suspect she uses us advisors as a way to pretend like there's a balance of power, but the truth is she's the only one in charge. And nobody really trusts her because she's an Etherean. She just has too much power that goes unchecked."

"How can you work for someone and always look over your shoulder?"

"You're not getting second thoughts about your future are you?"

Slade paused perhaps a second too long. He hoped his mother didn't notice his hesitation. Working for the government of the Middle Third was expected of him, but what he really wanted was some excitement and adventure. How he would go about pursuing that he had no clue, but the mysteries surrounding Ethereans seemed like a good start. He decided his mother didn't need to know this, so rather than disappointing her he settled for a simple, "No. Of course not. I'm just curious."

"I compare Queen Aeothesca to a bee. If anyone were to ever go after her, they'd have to make their blow lethal, otherwise she'll return with a heavy sting. You always know her potential, and that's what keeps you alert."

CHAPTER SEVEN

I

Today, Slade lunched alone. The day's classes wore on his energy and the break was welcome. The glass walls of Burrow University's cafeteria allowed for plenty of daylight, but none of it reflected harshly on the grey tables. Slade approached a free spot with a tray of food in hand and sat down hard. For a moment he panicked, hoping his food wouldn't jump too far off the tray. He stayed up too late researching what was known about Ethereans. At that moment, all he wanted was to fulfill the promise of nourishment that lie before him. Then *he* showed up.

"Hey, Slade," said Douglassaire, flashing his white grin.

Slade looked up, surprised. "Oh! Hey, Doug. What's up?" Slade unknowingly sat up straight and began correcting the way his shirt sat on his shoulders. Every time Doug came around, Slade would feel his nerves set on edge and get the strangest urge to impress.

"Just in the neighborhood. Mind if I sit down?" Doug asked as he pulled the chair under himself.

It appeared to Slade that he didn't have a choice in the matter, but he welcomed the company. And the energy he was lacking certainly returned with force. "Yeah, sure," he said.

The table shook as Doug plopped down with his tray. Slade

just watched as the man sat there staring back, hulking over his food with his elbows on the table. In the back of his mind he always knew one thing about Douglassaire that he refused to acknowledge. He'd rather leave that knowledge alone than open himself up to disappointment. For what could he, with his posh, high-class ways, possibly have in common with a warrior from the Southern Third? Now, as he studied Doug's bright eyes, full lips, and square jaw, it felt like his brain completely stopped working except to breathe and accept his own impression. Douglassaire was gorgeous.

"You gonna eat?" Doug asked.

Slade shook himself from his stupor and looked down at his tray. "Yeah," he said, laughing nervously. He grabbed his fork and took the first unsatisfying bite of his now lukewarm entrée. "So…"

"What you been up to?" Doug asked as he took the first big bite of his food.

"Oh, you know, classes and stuff. Boring. Lunch couldn't come any sooner."

"Yeah, I feel you."

"So, um…" Slade searched for something – anything – to make this less awkward, "what brought you to BU?"

Douglassaire gave a *just-a-minute* nod as he finished the bite of food in his mouth. After washing it down with his water, he said, "I transferred here last year from a military school in the South. I got the chance to finish up school here and I took it, like all the other guys I train with."

"Oh, okay. How do you like it up here?"

He shrugged. "…s'okay. The school is nice, but the Northern Third is a little too cold for me. And there's not much to do around here."

"Tell me about it. I'm from Reor, so it took a lot of getting used to. But it's quiet, so it's a nice change of pace sometimes."

"Wow, Reor! And I heard you're a noble, too. That is a big change. What made you leave all that?"

Slade shrugged and began to poke at his lunch. He hated that word…noble, like he was somehow supposed to act different from everybody else. "I don't know. I just needed something new. I wanted to see some more of the world, you know?" He expected the usual response he got after his explanation: somebody telling him he's crazy, saying that if they were him, they would stay put.

Instead, Doug smiled and nodded. "Yeah. I'm the same way."

Doug's smile challenged Slade's brain to reenter its stupor, but Slade successfully fought it off. He felt a mix of emotions: he was relieved he didn't have to explain himself, happy that they actually did have something in common, and curious as to what other interests they shared. Slade felt the restrictions of his words come undone and started to speak with a renewed enthusiasm. "Actually, I've been looking into the story of Ether lately. It's pretty fascinating. By the way, have you found anything out?"

"About what?"

"That guy you said you think is an Etherean."

Doug paused. "Yeah…"

"And…?"

"We train in the same group for the Power Battle. I've just noticed some things about him."

"Like what?" Slade asked.

"Sometimes when we duel, I get close to beating him, then something happens at the last second. It's like a wind will pick up from outta nowhere, then he's faster and I can't read his moves anymore. It's weird, man."

"So, he might be an air Etherean?"

Doug nodded.

Slade sensed an opportunity to help. If he did, maybe he could get closer to Doug. He hadn't felt this urge before, but every minute he spent sitting there with him, his desire for friendship grew. "Well, if you're training for the Power Battle, don't you want to make sure?"

"Yeah, but I can't just ask him."

"I'm not saying that, but you can have a few more eyes on him. Catch him in the act. Who is this guy? I'll keep an eye out."

Slade noticed Douglassaire nervously shift his weight as he let the suspected Etherean's name escape his lips. "His name is Lesech. Tall guy with the white, curly hair."

"Wow, really? I think I've seen him around before."

35

"Don't tell him I told you."

Slade shook his head, "No, of course not. I'll let you know if I see anything."

"All right, but be careful around him."

"Why?"

"He's not wound too tight."

II

"Gisela, what do you want to be when you leave here?" Slade asked.

Slade and Gisela sat opposite one another at a picnic table on campus. The sky was grey and not as inviting as the previous day, but still pleasant enough to sit outside. Slade sat with his back to Gisela, leaning against the edge of the table with his elbows propping him up for support. Burrow University lie stretched before him with its paved pathways that carved small hills of grass and trees where students gathered. Gisela had her nose in a textbook and fidgeted with the grey scarf around her neck. The air was having mood swings between placid and disruptive. Every time it decided to pick up with a slight breeze, Gisela slammed her hand down to her textbook to save her place.

"I don't know. I haven't really thought about it much." She returned to her reading and stroked a stray hair back behind her ear.

"Really? We don't have much time left. This is our last year."

She looked up and frowned. "Is something the matter, Slade?"

Slade turned his body to face Gisela. He folded his hands on the table and leaned forward. "I'm just done feeling stuck. Let's just move on the next big idea that comes to our minds. Don't you want to do something special?"

Gisela briefly lowered her eyes as she searched for an answer, but her thought process was interrupted by the look of concern on Slade's face as he looked past her. Her eyebrows came together in curiosity and she turned to see what grabbed his attention.

Slade asked to himself, aloud, "Isn't that him?"

She searched the scene for a moment before settling on the tall figure with white curly hair and a black duffle bag in his hand. "Who, Lesech? What about him?"

"I think that's the guy Doug thinks is an Etherean. He's part of the same training group Doug's in, right?"

Gisela shrugged, readjusted her glasses, and turned back to her book.

"I think we just found our something special. I'm gonna go see what he's up to."

"What, you're going to make a career out of spying on people?"

"No, Gisela. Ethereans are still a big mystery. We should see what we can find out."

"Slade, please. He's not an Etherean."

"How do you know?"

"Somebody would have noticed something by now."

"Doug noticed something."

Gisela jerked her head as though she were offended at the sound of his name. "Since when does his opinion matter so much?"

Slade ignored this. "I have a feeling, Gisela. This is the adventure we've been waiting for." He got up from the table and said, "I'll be back." He could feel Gisela's eyes following him as he walked around the table and passed her.

"Seriously?" she said, exasperated. She dog-eared the page in her textbook and quickly threw it into her book bag. After slinging the bag around her shoulder, she called to Slade, "All right. Wait up," and trailed behind.

Now just a few yards away, Slade watched Lesech walk across the campus, away from the crowd of students on the grass. Lesech waved at a few friends along the way but seemed in a hurry and had no time to talk. With Gisela following closely behind, Slade blended in among the crowd and continued his pursuit. The crowd of students got less and less dense as he reached the brick path that led to the lake, and he realized that at any second Lesech could look back and see them trailing him. So, he grabbed Gisela's hand and pretended to be lovers on a slow walk down a scenic path. He smiled and looked up into the trees, out at the lake, and at Gisela, all the while watching Lesech in his peripheral view. This served him well when Lesech unexpectedly stopped at the fork in the road. His nerves began to stir as he saw Lesech look left, then right, and then turn to check behind him. But when Lesech moved on, taking a quick left into the woods, Slade felt proud of his perfectly executed ruse.

"Maybe we should go back, Slade," Gisela said.

She might be uncomfortable, but Slade had come too far now to stop. He let go of Gisela's hand and jogged after Lesech, down the brick path some more and into the woods. Slade felt bolder knowing they could hide among the trees. Gisela followed. Slade lost sight of Lesech for a moment, but followed Gisela's hand as she tapped him on the shoulder and pointed ahead. He stood behind the closest tree and peered from behind. The bag Lesech brought over was now on the ground and open. In his hands was a black estoc – a long, thin sword which he masterfully swung in an array of different postures. Slade was blinded to the fact that Lesech held a real weapon on school grounds, for what Lesech did next took him by complete surprise.

Lesech held on to his sword and closed his eyes as if meditating. Suddenly, he jumped and miraculously stood on what seemed to be an invisible platform of air just a few inches above the ground! Lesech fought to keep his balance as he slowly rose higher and higher. He got as far as two feet above ground before falling on his backside. His sword flew out of his hand and slid on the ground in Slade and Gisela's direction. They both shot their gaze away, trying to hide behind the tree and escape Lesech's sight. They were too late.

"Who's there?" Lesech yelled.

Slade and Gisela froze. This mischievous spying almost caused Slade to laugh nervously. Even if he got caught, he knew Lesech wouldn't really do anything. He hoped Lesech would just chalk it up to his imagination. That dream died as a blade sliced into the tree, nearly separating Slade's skull at the eyes and sending pieces of bark flying everywhere. Slade felt a jolt of horror and belted out a short scream as he fell away from the tree. On the ground, Slade turned his head to see Lesech holding the hilt of his sword and trying to yank it out of the tree's side. Boy, was he wrong. He remembered Douglassaire saying something was a little off about Lesech. He saw that now.

Slade took the opportunity to quickly jump up. Gisela motioned towards Slade, ready to leave, but their attempt to get away fell short as Lesech pulled the sword free and pointed the tip to Slade's neck. Slade threw his hands up in surrender.

Calmly, Lesech asked, "What did you see?"

Slade shook his head, "Nothing. We saw noth—" Slade suddenly found it hard to breathe. For a moment, he was confused. It wasn't fear that stopped his words. The air was simply not available. That's when it dawned on him that it was Lesech's doing. Just as he manipulated the air to rise above the ground, he made it scarce around Slade's mouth and nose.

"You do realize I could kill you and leave no trace of my being here?" Lesech cut his eyes to Gisela who was still breathing perfectly fine. "I'll ask again. What. Did. You. See?"

Slade started to feel lightheaded and dropped to his knees. Gisela knelt to grab him and said, "We saw you flying, okay. That's it. Please! Leave him alone."

Lesech released his captive, releasing his power over the air, and dropped the point of his sword. Slade drew in a huge audible breath and began panting.

"Flying!" Lesech said, amused. He began inspecting his blade for damage. "Hovering is more accurate."

Slade finally caught his breath and asked, "And you're an Etherean, right?"

He gave a cold look to Slade. "What do you think? Imbecile. If by Etherean you mean a more evolved human – yes! If by Etherean you mean persecuted by the lesser race – yes! If by Etherean you mean that I can control an element of nature...then yes, I am a *proud* Etherean."

"How does it work?" Slade asked as he got back to his feet.

Gisela shot him a look and said under her breath, "Slade, are you as crazy as him? He almost killed you and you're asking questions?"

"Funny! Coming from the girl who talks to the lake," said Lesech. Gisela recoiled. "Oh, I only speak of common knowledge. You've nearly become legend." He turned his

40

attention to Slade: "But you ask how our ether works and if I told you, I'd have to kill you." He paused and his lips curled into an evil grin. "Very well, I'll tell you.

"There are four elements: earth, water, fire, and air. And each Etherean can only control one. As you have so rudely spied, I can control air. In order for us to use our power, the element must be in our immediate presence. I'm fortunate because air is all around us."

"And you can just do whatever you want with it? Like fly? Or make a tornado?"

"I could, but it would require much training to achieve such things. It's like building muscle. If I were to create a tornado or a hurricane, I'd need a lot of power and strength. If I were to fly, I'd need finesse and control of air down to the molecular level. I'm not quite there...yet."

"You're not going to kill us are you?" Gisela asked.

"Will you be able to keep knowledge of my abilities to yourselves?"

Gisela nodded emphatically. "Yes, yes, of course. We won't tell anyone. Not even Douglassaire."

"Douglassaire!" he nodded, knowingly, "I see. Then, no. It would be like crushing ants. There's no need and no challenge in ending your lives. I can't say the same for Douglassaire. If I were you, I'd leave before I changed my mind."

Slade watched Lesech with caution. Just under the man's egotistical veneer he could sense a darkness. Lesech meant what he said. Slade knew he had to go – he'd even dragged Gisela into this; however, he couldn't shake his curiosity. "Okay. Just one more thing. Do you know more people who are Ethereans like yourself?"

"Of course. There are far more of us than anyone even realizes. Most of us keep our powers a secret to escape the disrespect of you lesser people. Some people have powers and don't even know it. If I had my way, you'd all die and leave Pangaea to us. Come to think of it, I'm beginning to change my mind. Leave me. Now."

Slade said nothing more as Gisela grabbed his arm and led him back to the brick path. As they walked back to the main grounds of Burrow, they remained silent, eyes straight ahead seeing everything and looking at nothing. Slade stopped and barely escaped his trance to say, "We just saw an Etherean. Here! Gisela, this is amazing!"

"Slade, I'm just glad we got away. I don't think I want to ever see him again." She studied his face. "You're really into this, aren't you?"

"Doug was right," he said aloud to himself.

Gisela scrunched her nose. "Well, you can't tell him. Not after that."

"I know, but maybe we can keep it just between the three of us."

"Slade, are you serious? Who knows what'll happen if you tell him? He could spread it all over the campus."

"Yeah," Slade said with a sigh. He was disappointed he couldn't tell Doug, but he didn't want to be on Lesech's bad side.

CHAPTER EIGHT

"Doug!" called Slade, fast-walking down the hallway of the university. He traversed the marble floor and dodged other students who were shuffling to their next class. Natural light momentarily blinded him as he passed by each window, but he managed to keep his eye on his target. Douglassaire heard his name and turned to see Slade hurrying to catch up.

"What up, Slade?"

"Hey. Where are you headed?"

"Political Science," Doug replied as they began to walk together.

"Fun."

Doug laughed at his sarcasm. "It's actually not so bad. It's funny how three completely different forms of government were able to form a truce."

"The democracy of the North, the Middle Third's monarchy, and whatever the Southern Third's government is."

Doug smiled. "I see you know some things. I'm just glad your queen doesn't abuse her power, otherwise that wouldn't work out so well. If anything changes, we're screwed."

"You're talking about the queen, but what about your government? Being ruled by the strongest warrior is no different."

"The Southern Commander has the most power, but he's

balanced by his Deputy-Commander and Lieutenant. It's a triarchy. Not quite the same."

"But you want to get into the Power Battle and win the top spot."

Doug, who kept his gaze straight ahead this whole time, stole a quick glance at Slade. "Yeah."

"Why?"

"Freedom."

Slade twisted his face. "Freedom? Are you *not* free?"

"Is doing what you have to do, instead of what you want to do, in order to survive called freedom?"

Slade had no idea from what Douglassaire was trying to survive, but he did understand the confinement of duties unasked for. He decided not to pry and attempted to end the conversation's turn into deep waters with, "More power to you."

"Yeah, thanks. That's exactly what I need, actually. Ethereal power to be precise," Doug joked.

Slade's walk came to a halt and his cheerful expression dropped. His run in with Lesech the other day had stayed on his mind ever since. He wanted badly to tell Douglassaire like he promised, but Lesech was dangerous.

Doug sensed his uneasiness. "What's wrong?"

"Nothing," said Slade. "Did you ever find out anything about Lesech?" He tried to continue walking, but Doug didn't budge. He must have sensed there was something Slade wasn't saying.

"No. You?"

Slade exhaled and looked over his shoulder. He had to be sure Lesech wasn't around. "I met him the other day."

"Okay. And what?"

"I can't... I can't say," Slade's eyes darted around the room and he was still looking for any sign of Lesech in the building. A sudden calm came over him as the heaviness of Doug's hand covered his shoulder. He felt himself being pulled to the side of the hall, but hardly noticed as he stared into Doug's eyes.

"Slade, did he threaten you?" Doug waited for an answer, but when none came from Slade he said, "Listen, as long as I'm here, you ain't gotta worry about him, okay?"

The look of sincerity and concern on Doug's face let Slade

know he was telling the truth. Doug would protect him. That was all Slade needed.

Slade nodded and Doug let go of his shoulder. Slade immediately missed the feel of his hand. It was like a piece of armor had been removed. "You were right about him," he finally said. "He was levitating. Like, he was literally in midair for a whole minute. Doug, I was in shock. I'd never seen anything like it before."

"He was flying?" Douglassaire asked. "Are you serious?"

"Yeah, not flying, though. Levitating. Hovering. He said there was a big difference."

"Whoa." Doug leaned against the wall for a moment to let it all sink in. "Lesech can control air. That explains a lot."

"What do you mean?"

"Well, remember what I said about what happens when we train together? I'll have the advantage, but then his sword starts swinging faster and faster."

"How does he do that?"

"If he's an air Etherean, like you're telling me, he's probably removing the air resistance from his sword and his body and transferring it to me to slow me down."

Slade gave a slow nod. He wondered what the different applications of such a power could be – the countless possibilities for total control of any of the elements.

"He must really hate to lose," Doug continued. "He'd really risk being found out just to beat me."

"Be careful, Doug. You were right; he's dangerous."

Doug smiled and tapped Slade on the shoulder. "Like I said, don't worry."

With each of Doug's smiles, Slade felt his heart going into dangerous territory. He feared getting himself into the same predicament he was healing from with his estranged friend, Mason, so he tried to deny it, but it just felt so good. He refocused his mind and said, "It would be cool to have power like that."

"Yeah, it would help me out, too," Doug said. "Thanks, Slade...for telling me."

"Anytime."

Doug looked at his watch. "All right, I gotta go or else I'll be late." He started to leave, but then hesitated. "Are you doing anything for spring break?"

Slade thought of the promise to his mother and the time he planned to spend with his family, but this was Douglassaire. He wanted to see where this led. "No. No plans."

"I'll be going back home. You should come, though. You can even bring Gisela. We'll have fun."

Slade was surprised by the invitation but delighted, nonetheless. His heart bounced at the idea, but he tried to keep his cool. "Oh, okay, sure. I'll be there."

With a nod, Doug turned and walked away. Slade was excited, but accepting Doug's invitation brought up a new problem. His nerves stirred in the pit of his stomach. He didn't know how he was going to break the news to his mother just yet, but he knew he would have to figure something out. He always wanted to do what the other students did and take a trip somewhere together for spring break but never had the opportunity. Now, of all people, Doug gave him the option to do something different. His invitation caused Slade's admiration of Doug to spike. As much as he denied it to himself, Slade felt an urge to join Doug and see if this budding crush went both ways.

CHAPTER NINE

I

Catherine, enjoying a moment to herself, walked down the west wing hallway of Queen Aeothesca's castle. She looked out the window to her left and began to study the geometric outlines of the different districts of the Middle Third below. The metropolis had some areas zoned for parks, but most were of tall buildings and residential structures. It had only been three weeks since she started here, but the view from the castle as it floated in the air never got any less awe-inspiring. With her hands and nose pressed against the cold glass, she started to catch a case of vertigo before being snapped back to reality.

"Off the glass!" one of the queen's maids exclaimed. She came walking quickly down the hallway towards Catherine with a spray bottle in one hand. Her hair was tied back by a white scarf and she proudly wore her uniform: a perfectly fitting white blouse and khaki trousers that hugged a little too tightly to her wide hips. "I just cleaned that. We all have to be mindful and do our part, Catherine."

Catherine backed away from the glass and watched the woman tug at the rag hanging at her waist. "*Our* part?" she asked. "I've no part in cleaning the windows, Annbeth, much less anything else in here. I believe that part's all yours."

Annbeth glared daggers at Catherine for her snobby remark, but went back to work. She pumped the spray bottle twice at the window and let out a loud gasp as all that she sprayed arched back and doused her face. It was as if she had sprayed at the turning blades of a fan, but there was none – only Catherine's powers. Annbeth frowned at Catherine, who had just retracted a raised finger. She muttered something to herself about Catherine having witch powers, but Catherine had long ago learned how to tune out slurs. Instead, Catherine giggled, then made an about-face as she heard her name through the speakers in the hall.

"Catherine! Catherine, dear, I need you in the study."

The queen was calling and she was always answered.

Catherine, her chin held high and hands folded in front of her, traversed the marble floor beneath her. She was happy to be the queen's new lady-in-waiting, but lately, the luster of such a high title wore off. Making friends with the other staff was hard because nobody would welcome her in. She was too high on the work ladder for the other maids to feel comfortable around her, and the queen's advisors were higher still. Her immediate reaction to being closed out was rebellious mischief, much like splashing Annbeth in the face. It was uncontrollable. There were no other ladies-in-waiting, so her only option for companionship was the queen whom she was almost always around. However, despite Catherine's attempts at learning more, the queen never opened up. No matter. Catherine would give it another go today. The queen would be a good, and powerful, friend to have.

She reached the wide opening provided by the double doors of the study. The bottom of her long, faded brick red dress hit her ankles with every step. And her short black hair, cut just below her earlobes, made a subtle bounce as she stepped into the room and stood straight. "My queen. How may I be of service?"

Queen Aeothesca sat at a great wooden desk below a large window overlooking the endless ocean made golden by the setting sun. She raised her head from the cluttered desk of documents and turned in her chair to face her Lady-In-Waiting. Much a woman of the present, she wore a cozy, off-white sweater and blue jeans. Her torturous-heeled shoes were kicked off to the side. She occasionally wore a dress as a reminder to her staff that she was, indeed, in charge, but mostly she left the traditional looks in her past along with her passed mother.

She smiled warmly. "Catherine. I need you. You see all of those books over there?" She pointed to her left at the table sitting next to the bookshelf. "I need those put back in the appropriate places on the shelf, and if there are any duplicates, please take them to the library."

Catherine nodded and replied, "Certainly, my lady."

"Thank you, dear." Aeothesca turned back to her desk and drew all of her thick red hair over to one shoulder. Catherine began studying the titles of the books on the table and placing them one-by-one in their alphabetical spots. She couldn't help but look over at her boss and steal a couple glances at what she revealed on the back of her, now, bare neck. She saw a black upside-down triangle – a sharp contrast against the queen's smooth skin. She noticed it every morning as she got the queen ready for her day and it always perplexed her. Perhaps the queen would open up to her about this. Catherine thought it a good enough time to ask.

"Your Majesty, might I ask you a question?"

"What is it?"

"That mark on the back of your neck… What is it?"

The queen paused and looked up through her window at her beautiful view. "Let's just call it a gift left by my mother before she passed away."

Catherine silently accepted she was no closer to learning anything about her superior. Her uncontrollable penchant for mischief reared its head. She dug some more. "And what about your sister? Did she get the same?"

Aeothesca's eyes darted at Catherine at the mention of her sister. Catherine tried to hide her smirk, feeling successful in getting a reaction. The queen removed her reading glasses and turned her chair to face Catherine. She leaned back and crossed her legs. "Close the doors, Catherine."

Catherine's amusement fell away from her face and she felt the seriousness of her lady's words. Perhaps she pushed too far in bringing the castle's gossip to the queen's ears. She complied and crossed the room to close the double doors. She could feel the queen's eyes watching her every move and grew more nervous with each second. She turned around from the closed doors and faced her queen with the feeling of impending doom.

"How long have you known you were an Etherean, Catherine?"

"All my life, my lady," she stammered.

"I, too. Well…nearly. I find that those who have known since birth of their gift with the power of Elao often mistake themselves as all-powerful. Would you not agree?"

Catherine nodded, her heart racing.

"I also find that those who live long, prosperous lives often learn the error of their ways for fear of finding another who is more practiced than they." Her stone cold glare turned only lukewarm with a cunning grin. "Hold on to that fear, Catherine. For dear life."

Catherine nodded again, drawing in a few short breaths and trying her best not to appear beaten.

"You see, I have a rather disagreeable reputation around the castle for a lack of care in the lives of anyone other than myself. For, in my view, if one ends, another is just around the corner to take its place. Your behavior tempts the revelation of whether or not that is true. No person alive, save for my sister, knows the true story of what happened between us. And after I tell you, there is a big chance that fact remains. Are you still interested?"

The breathing didn't help. Catherine's speech stammered and her face was flush. "No, Your Majesty. I apologize most sincerely. Please forgive me."

"Nonsense, dear. You would miss an opportunity to bond? I have not had this much fun since…well, since I told my last lady-in-waiting, God rest her soul. Please say yes."

Catherine knew she didn't have a choice. She would listen. Perhaps she could find some way to change the queen's mind to see her as an ally. This felt like a test. She was about to find out her chances of being the only person alive to know the queen's story. "Yes, of course."

"Fabulous! In all sincerity, dear, to have somebody know all about me and really understand me would be a dream come true.

I have not enjoyed such an understanding since my sister left. I sure hope you are that person. So!" Queen Aeothesca clapped her hands and looked to the ceiling while figuring out where to start. "Growing up here in Lorelei Castle, the famous floating palace is…different. Understand, dear, I would not ever trade it for living on the commoners' land below, but we certainly had our share of troubles. Some triumphs. I was blessed to grow up with my sister by my side. We were close, she and I. Annonymn was two years younger than I and we had a bond that only two princesses could understand.

"One of my fondest memories happened right outside in the back field. We had yards and yards of green land on which to run and play. And we did every day. Sometimes, we would run all the way to the edge and stop just before the railing. You know, where one of the big crystals stands that allows this place to float? Oh, we nearly gave the guards and our governess heart attacks each day, but we were children. Our gardener was always pleasant, but I am sure she held some hatred in her heart for us. After our races, we would sit and pick the flowers she had so dutifully planted by the crystal. Anyway, one day, it was the day after a terrible storm. Annonymn and I ran to the edge as usual. I started to slow down as I saw this red rose wrecked by the wind and rain and barely standing. Annonymn broke her speed at the rail and began celebrating her first victory over me in our race, but I paid her no mind. For some reason I was just fixated on that flower. A few petals had been blown away and the stem was bent. Unlike the other flowers by the edge, which had blown to the common land by then, it was still there, all alone. Down, but not out.

"Annonymn asked me, 'What is wrong, Ayo?' That was a nickname she called me. I was Ayo and she was Anna.

"'This flower. It looks so sad,' I said. I had just learned from our governess that plants are technically alive and, well, you know how children are. My little mind took that fact and ran with it. I suddenly felt horrible about all of the flowers I had picked. It was as though right then at that moment I could feel the loneliness in that flower and its need for care.

"Annonymn came over, her brown hair wild from running,

51

and snapped the flower in two so quick that she left half of the stem still in the ground. 'No!' I screamed. She did not know – could not have known how I felt. I snatched the flower from her hands and bent over the severed stem wishing I could do something. I heard Annonymn start to cry. I said, 'I am sorry,' and she quieted down, but I was not talking to her. I was speaking to the broken rose. Suddenly, something amazing happened. What I saw made the whole world go silent. I stood up with the top half of the flower in my hand and gave it back to my sister.

"'Here you go, Anna' I said.

"'No, you can have it,' she said.

"I shook my head. 'I do not need it. Look.' I pointed to where she pulled the flower and watched a huge smile cover her face as she realized a new rose was born and bloomed in its place.

"'Did you do that, Ayo?' she asked, bewildered.

"I nodded. I did not know what to think. I was scared and confused. Annonymn was not bothered one bit. She just began to skip and dance and sing, 'It is a miracle! A miracle! A miracle in Reor!' After a while I, too, could not help but smile. It was the first time I discovered my ability. It was also the only time I ever felt good about it.

"We soon went to tell my mother, Queen Jacqueline, and that was when I found out that my initial feelings of fear were accurate. Upon hearing about this, my mother's face dropped and her voice rose. She was in near panic. 'Did the guards see you?' she asked.

"Annonymn and I shook our heads. 'No, Mother.'

"'Who was watching you? Who was with you?'

"We told her the governess was nearby, but she was reading a book.

"'I see. You girls do not speak a word of this. Ever! Understand?'

"My sister balled her hands into fists and sat them firmly at her waist. She cocked her head to the side and asked, 'You mean we have to *shoosh?*'

"'Yes! *Shoosh!*' my mother responded, putting her finger to her lips. "The last thing I need is word getting out of a monster living among us."

"We both nodded, frightened out of our wits. We were confused as to why Mother was so upset. It never dawned on me that would be the last day we ever saw or heard from our governess. A week later, we got a new one. Knowing my mother, I suspect my old governess was hanged, but I never found out for sure. Oh, I cried and cried, thinking I was the reason something bad happened to her. I started to hate myself. I began to believe my mother's words. I thought I was a monster. Then Annonymn came to my rescue. She hugged me and said, 'Do not cry, Ayo. I think you are beautiful. And if we have to *shoosh*, that is okay. It is our secret!' It was then that I knew whom I could trust most in this world.

"Mother died of a rare illness and I became queen of a country at war at age ten. Two years later, we were able to end the war, but it was very taxing. Mother told the general and her advisor about my abilities before she died and instructed them to use me as a last resort. I hated being used as a weapon, but Annonymn was always in my corner and helped me feel better. Hidden in my royal aircraft high above the battlefield, the general made me use my power. I did as I was told and the earth shook and cracked, swallowing many soldiers at the front most lines of the Southern army. We did the same against the North and succeeded in scaring both countries to no end. They had no idea it was me, but it ended the fighting. This allowed us to strike a deal of peace, the Nomiso Agreement. I was so happy when that war ended."

Catherine was shocked at what she was hearing. She couldn't help but interject. "Your Majesty, if I may. There were always rumors about your involvement in the end of that war, but to think it all true! Are you truly that powerful?"

The queen was taken aback. For a moment she saw that her intimidating effect on Catherine wore off in exchange for something else. "Catherine. Are you envious?"

"I can only dream of that much control over my ability."

The queen smiled. It was the first time anyone had ever responded to her story without fear. For anyone else, their fearful response was when she knew they would be executed for their new knowledge. She knew that anyone afraid of her could never be a true ally. Catherine showed promise. "Have a seat, Catherine."

She pulled out the small chair next to her that was tucked beneath the table and sat. Catherine was still nervous about what fate awaited her after the queen's story, but she began to admire the queen a little more.

"I learned a lot about Pangaea at just twelve years and I felt swept along in a current I could barely handle. But I got through it. A big part of my success was having my sister by my side. She knew the whole truth, just as I am telling you. And while I felt like a fraud, she convinced me that I was doing the right thing. She always stood by my side, and she continued to…until an unfortunate incident occurred between us as women."

Catherine fondled the raised text of a tome that rested on the table with her fingers. She listened intently to the queen's story. *What happened?* Catherine wondered. She sat still, completely enraptured by the tale.

"I can see the wheels turning in your head, dear," the queen remarked. "I must say, having another Etherean in the castle is just so freeing. I feel like you could be the only one to truly understand me. I hope you do. I can trust you, can I not?"

"Of course, Your Highness. I've known nothing but rejection my entire life, and to hear of your acceptance—"

"Is it really acceptance, dear Catherine? With the exception of my sister I felt that same rejection that all of our kind feels. As a young girl, I was no more accepted than I was a weapon to be controlled. And people only try to control that which they fear."

Catherine absorbed this for a moment. Then she asked, "What happened to Annonymn?"

"It is not what happened to her, but more a question of what happened to us. Twelve years after the start of peace, we both stepped into womanhood, and with that came many suitors. All of which vied for power of some form. There was but one man who seemed the most genuine. His name was Orleone.

"I oversaw a celebration of my sister's twenty-second birthday. Nobles and politicians from all over were invited to join the festivities. Annonymn and I sat at the head table overlooking the ballroom floor with a trusted guard standing by just below. Our guests numbered in the hundreds and they danced, ate, and drank happily. Our table drew the lustful eyes of many men, and the envious eyes of the women. I sat there satisfied with what I was able to pull off for my sister. I asked her, 'Is this not wonderful, Anna?' To which she smiled and nodded, but quickly returned to a distant look in her eyes. I knew then that my poor sister had grown bored. I always suspected life here in the castle would not be enough for her. She was too adventurous a spirit to take the confines of this place for long. I watched as her face suddenly came to life at the sight of a man who pushed his way through the crowd to address her.

"'Princess,' spoke the man, 'may I have this dance?'

"How bold he was! The guard standing by nearly had a fit. 'How dare you address the princess without going through the proper channels?' the guard yelled. 'You speak to her lady-in-waiting and you will be contacted should you get the privilege of her interest!'

"Annonymn stood up and surprised our guard. 'Stop your bellowing! You're making a scene.' I must admit I was quite shocked as well. She addressed the man that had been berated. 'Sir, what is your name?'

"He looked as though a dragon were flying about the room. 'Orleone. My name is Orleone.' He managed to remember what little manners he had left to bow his head. My sister stepped down to greet him. By now the whole room quieted down, save for the sounds of our musicians. Everyone gazed at Annonymn and this man to see what would happen next.

"She curtsied and took his outstretched hand. 'Orleone, I am Annonymn.'

"'He knows who you are, dear,' I called out, mischievously. I flapped my fan open to hide my utter delight and said, 'Go play.'

"Orleone led Annonymn to the center of the floor and joined the other dancing guests. His timing was perfect as they moved with the beginning of a new melody. They both could not help but smile from ear to ear and their energy was infectious. How so simple a man from the North could make my sister so happy confounded me. I had never seen anything like it. I wanted it.

"From that moment on, they were inseparable. Orleone had become a regular at our castle. Looking back now, I can see that I was very envious of my sister. She had all the glory of being a royal, yet all of the work fell on my shoulders. It was easier to manage when we were growing up, but when Orleone came into her life we began spending less and less time together. She and her new beau enjoyed each other's company while I was left to my own devices. I had all the world's eyes on me, yet I was alone. Not only that, but as a queen I was intimidating and had little chance of ever having the carefree life of dear Annonymn.

"That same war that brought our nation so much glory covered me in the stench of paranoia. Word got out among the Northern and Southern Thirds that when their armies were defeated by what seemed to be acts of God, I was present. Historically, the only leader of a nation that appeared on the frontlines of battle was the Southern Commander, and to see my aircraft present at both cataclysmic events was a fact that even the terrified survivors could not ignore before their flight. Our army was sworn to secrecy, but they certainly knew of my presence and were never told why. I was scary to everyone – still am. And I will never be able to shake that.

"Yet, at one point, with Orleone, I thought I had a chance. What I had grown to admire about Orleone was his ability to see the world so simply. No doubt, he was the perfect match for Annonymn. They shared an innocence about life that you only see in our children's animates and books. To him, my dark cloud of suspicion had been lifted and he saw me through my sister's eyes. Before then, all of the other men who had come into my life never truly saw me; they only saw an open throne next to mine. Orleone was different, and if I were ever to have a true companion, I knew that he was my only chance.

"Oh, I felt guilty, but I was also justified. I knew Annonymn would feel hurt, but I told myself she would survive and surely find another man as a replacement. She already had so many suitors! Also, *I* was queen, and not she. And she would, in time, understand that he was my only hope for a king worthy of me. You do understand, Catherine?"

She nodded, "Yes, my queen." She was uncertain whether her

natural answer was enough, but it seemed to work so far. Catherine never expected to have so much in common with the queen. "With so much against you, how else would you find the appropriate mate?"

"Exactly. It is only reasonable. And I held on to my reasoning with the firmest of grasps that one day in the courtyard...alone with Orleone. He requested an audience with me and I obliged. We walked in the vast field of grass in which my sister and I played so often all those years ago.

"'Your Majesty,' began Orleone.

"'It is just us, Orleone. There is no need for formality. Aeothesca is just fine,' I replied.

"When I said that, he laughed at me. At first I thought his laughter came from a place of discomfort, but then he would not stop. I started to blush nervously. 'What is it?' I implored. 'Have I said something untoward?'

"He wiped a tear from his eye as his jollity subsided. 'No, no. It's just I've never seen you be *informal*. It's just...refreshing, is all. It's nice. You're not so different from your sister after all.'

"'I, too, can have my moments of extempore.' His face revealed great puzzlement at the use of my vocabulary. I decided to switch gears...he was such a simple man. 'How are you and Annonymn faring?' We approached the jagged edge of the terrain bordered by the railing my sister and I raced to as children.

"'She's precisely the reason I requested to see you. You see, as you know, I love Annonymn with all my heart. I'd like your permission to ask for her hand in marriage, and I want you to know that I will do everything in my power to make her happy.'

"My insides went hollow as I caught the railing with both hands. I looked out on Reor and said, 'You speak of power. You speak of that which you do not know. You will be a princess's husband, and that is all, for true power lie with me. A king lies with me.' The devils of temptation completely devoured my soul and I could not help but continue. I looked at Orleone. 'How would you like to be King?'

"A look of shock crossed his face. He stammered, trying to find his way out of the position in which I placed him. He quieted down when I pressed my finger against his soft lips and said, 'Think about it.'

"It did not take him long to decide. You see, dear Catherine, Orleone was still a man. No matter how different his ways were from others, his thirst for women and power was still ever present. They are like sharks, and when they smell blood, they attack.

"A knock came to the door of my bedroom that night. One of my previous ladies-in-waiting, Marigold, entered with her head bowed followed by Orleone. My lady left, no doubt knowing the circumstances, but sworn to secrecy. Orleone and I were alone. That is all you need to know. We lasted in secret for weeks. I struggled with how to tell my sister, but eventually fate handled that situation for me.

"I was on the far side of the palace one day in the inner garden, the same area where my mother used to train me, and I was practicing my delicate magic. Earthquakes came easy to me and I could re-grow single flowers that had been destroyed just like when I was a child, but to have the precision to control which way a stem bends or the swaying of each petal had both intrigued and eluded me. I tried this on the flower bed that day and was failing horribly. No matter how hard I tried, the earth kept shaking, holes opened up in the floor, and cracks formed in the walls. I tried hard not to overdo it so as not to alarm the staff, but apparently I gave my position away, for who else but Annonymn came bursting through the doors with a crew of cameras and reporters announcing, 'Behold! The Demon Queen!' You have seen the video, I am sure. Everyone has. I was stunned. The people with her were stunned. And the look on Annonymn's face was one I had never seen before. She was cold. Expressionless. Her chin was up, her chest was out, and her hands rested at her hips – royalty addressing royalty.

"She was doing an interview for the *people* and I mistakenly assumed that I would be left alone. Her actions showed that something had happened, and she was out for blood. My ethereal powers had been displayed and chronicled – a turning point in history and validation for some about theories on what or who ended the war. That even sparked murmurs of a new one. I entrusted everything to Annonymn, yet my deepest secret had been betrayed!

"I yelled to the crew, 'All of you! Go!' They quickly scurried away escorted by my lady-in-waiting who looked at me with tears in her eyes as she closed the double doors behind her.

"All that was left was my sister and I. We were alone. The silence in that room went on for an eternity as we locked eyes. I am well-practiced in holding back my emotions, but she always had a way of cutting through. I began to break first. "How could you? Annonymn!'

"'How could I? *How* could *I*? How could I!' She began to shake her head. 'Is that really all you have to say?'

"'What are you talking about?'

"She pointed her finger at me like a dagger. 'You know damned well about that which I am speaking, sister!'

"'That damned Marigold. Was she the one who told you? She must have been.'

"'This is not about her, Aeothesca.'

"'Regardless, it was time you knew. Better sooner than later. Orleone and I are to be married,' I said. 'Oh, do not look at me like that, Annonymn. You will find someone else. And this is no excuse to do what you did!'

"'No excuse? After what I did for you? I was there for you, Aeothesca. I was your biggest support when you had none, and you go and do this to me. Now you have lost the only person in this world who *thought* you were a true queen.'

"'Annonymn...'

"'Save it! Orleone is gone. He fled, a victim of his guilt. And now, I will go. Enjoy your grand life in Lorelei Castle, Your Majesty.' She bowed and turned to leave.

"Just before she reached out to open the doors I called to her. 'Very well, go! But if I ever find you again, just know that you will be killed for treason.'

"Her back was turned to me as she said, 'Thank you for the consideration of at least allowing me, your own sister, to leave alive.' She opened the doors and stepped through. Without ever turning around she said, 'Mother was right. You are a monster.'"

Catherine sat staring at the queen with her mouth open. The room was darkened by nightfall and the lights were dimmed.

Aeothesca chuckled, "My dear, you look as though you have been struck dumb."

Catherine corrected her appearance. She remained seated. The end of the story had come and with it returned her worry. She hoped she could leave with her life. "I apologize, Your Majesty. That was a very...fervent story."

The queen waved this idea away with her hand as though it were an annoying fly. "Oh, what is life, but a series of misfortunes with a few sprinkles of light? I glossed over so much, and I am sure there is more to come. Thank you, Catherine; that is all." She turned back to her desk in dismissal of her lady-in-waiting.

Catherine felt a jolt of disbelief. That was it? Had she managed to escape her punishment? She stood up and neatly tucked her seat under the table. The two books that belonged in the library were held to her breast by both arms. Relief swept over her as she made her way to the door. Then, the queen's voice stopped her in her tracks.

"As you now know, our family has a history of letting go of those whom we do not trust. My old governess, each other... It is also very hard to hold on to a lady-in-waiting who can keep a secret. You can keep this all a secret, I assume? I like you, Catherine. I would hate to see you end up like Marigold and all the others."

"What happened to Marigold?"

The queen's mouth curled into a smile.

II

The queen suggested Catherine take her first visit to the dungeons below the castle. Catherine took the queen's advice. The lights were dim and she felt her way along the brick wall barely able to make out what was in front of her. She stepped down the stairs and onto the concrete floor of the dungeon. On either side of her were the iron bars of cells that protected the world from the criminals they contained. She continued all the way to the back wall where a single guard stood watch. He was perfectly still and dressed in form-fitting chrome armor with the crest of the Middle Third on his chest. The design of the crest was actualized on the wall behind him in a literal torch lit with a white flame.

Catherine ignored the guard as she lightly stepped through the dungeon, wary of the prisoners and their grunts and cries of agony. She kept her finger under her nose, trying to block the smell of excrement and body odor. She was surprised to find that her own admiration for the queen continued to grow. The design of the cells was delightfully wicked. The prisoners all had a long rope wrapped around their necks. She also saw the glass floors in each cell – a constant reminder to the prisoners that they could, at any point, be released to their watery grave below with just the push of a button. Waking up to a bed of clouds and the sea would drive anyone completely mad.

As she continued her journey, she kept the queen's words in mind: "Marigold told my sister what she should have kept in confidence to me. She was promptly taken to the dungeon and relieved of her duty. Orleone fled the castle, but being the simple man that he was, he could not hide for long. The poor man never made it back to the Northern Third. He, too, was brought back to the castle and imprisoned. I recommend you take a trip to the dungeon and see for yourself the conditions in which they slept before their cell buttons were pushed. For days they awoke to the sight of clouds or, on a clear day, the deep blue waters of the Tethys below."

Catherine smiled at her queen's capacity for due discipline. Of course, she would keep the queen's secrets. As much as Aeothesca hated the term, she really was a monster, and Catherine finally felt at home.

CHAPTER TEN

I

The view of the Northern Third from the booth seats of Slade and Gisela's flight grew more and more obscure the longer they looked. Gisela remembered the days when she would watch aircrafts like these fly through the air and wonder what the world looked like from so high. The crafts were called supertrops and Gisela would watch their stingray-like design 'swim through the air' as the ads always said. While sitting across from Slade, she looked for the buildings of the North's capital, Septentrion City, but saw nothing but the white clouds that stretched out for what seemed an eternity.

An attendant came down the wide aisle. Slade was dozing off and Gisela braced herself for an interruption to her sky gazing. The table she'd drawn between herself and Slade from the wall was normally a signal to the attendant that a passenger wanted food service. Otherwise, the attendant would assume them satisfied.

"Can I help you, Ma'am?" the attendant asked.

Gisela raised her hand and pointed at the book on her table. "No, thank you. Sorry. Just reading."

The attendant smiled, nodded, and moved on. Gisela really had meant to read, but the book remained closed, trumped by the breathtaking view.

The clouds passed by her window as she bid farewell to her home and hello to a new place in which she had never been. Spring break had finally arrived and Slade had convinced Gisela to join him and Douglassaire. This was no easy feat. Gisela was wary of Doug's intentions. She barely knew who this guy was. However, she was swayed with the promise of seeing the imperial city of Reor as well as having fun in the Southern Third. She had been to neither place in her whole life and was relieved that her worries about her friendship with Slade were misguided. She was happy they had grown to the point where he would invite her on such an extended stay. Gisela glanced across the table at Slade who was now asleep. Perhaps this trip would be the time when their relationship took that fabled step into something more.

Hours later, the sky transitioned to dark and cleared up enough for her to take in the view of the Middle Third. She saw a small farm town bordered by wildlands left uninhabited by man. No doubt countless numbers of lusae lurked among the trees and tall grass. She looked out into the distance and wondered what the uninhabited western coast of the Middle Third would look like from this high up. Supertrops were restricted from flying over that area, for if they did, she and her fellow passengers would be most unnerved. A great, big active volcano to the far west of the Middle Third marked the land that fierce dragons called home. Gisela shuddered to think what one looked like up close. Thankfully, they hadn't bothered human land since ancient times. She tried not to think of encountering one while in the sky.

***

The aircraft emerged from the sky and finally landed safely on the ground in the Middle Third. If it weren't for the chime in the cabin's speaker, the supertrop's soft landing would hardly cause a stir. Slade heard the sound and sat up. His roomy seat felt as tight as ever. It offered no comfort against the thoughts running through his head. He was worried. It was unlike him. He usually always knew exactly what he was doing, where he was going, and the consequences of his actions. He usually had Mom and Dad to back him up. This time was different. He continued to tell his mom he planned on visiting for spring break, but he had yet to tell her his plans of leaving early. He wasn't looking forward to that conversation, but it was one he had to have if he wanted to see the Southern Third for the first time and spend time with Douglassaire.

The passengers all began to stand and exit the aircraft. Gisela waved her hand at Slade. "Hey, Slade, can we go?"

Slade was shaken from his daydream. "Oh. Yeah, let's go." He grabbed his small bag from under the table and slid out into the aisle followed by Gisela.

Gisela's ride in a hovering taxi was her first. As she and Slade quietly zoomed along the streets, she learned that there was no lack of fun in Reor as the lights of the metropolis invited permanent activity. As she gazed into the sky, she could even see that some cars flew high above the ground in some unseen path. Slade mentioned to her that only government workers had the privilege of using air cars for local air travel.

Although this was nothing new, Slade couldn't help but enjoy Gisela's excitement. What was just home to him was another world to her. For a moment he regretted making that promise to meet Douglassaire. He already stayed away from the exuberant life of his hometown for too long while at school. Now he would cut his time short. He would miss the hustle and bustle of the city. This was his place of complete comfort. *Maybe I should just stay*, he thought, but he knew he wouldn't. This was his last year in school and the last chance to do something fun. Plus, Douglassaire would be waiting for him. He wasn't going to let him down.

The flashing lights of the city were passed by and all that showed the way was the orange hue of the street lights on the highway. The taxi took an exit that brought Slade and Gisela to the quiet, suburban outskirts of Reor, and finally to their destination of the Maxwell family home. While the taxi slowed to a stop, Gisela grew incredibly silent. She gazed upon the expansive three-story home on top of the green hill in front of them. "That's your house?" she asked.

Slade nodded. "Yep. We're home."

"Wow…" she muttered in amazement.

Slade pressed his thumb against the fingerprint reader on the taxi's partition and confirmed his credit payment on its screen. They retrieved their bags from the trunk of the hover car and began to climb the stairs as it sailed away into the night. Gisela marveled at everything from the opulent shrubbery of the front yard to the large windows that ran the length of the house, and began a quick comparison to her home. Sure, she had a nice home, but the pristine white siding and tall, curved design of Slade's home was in a different league to her two-story home's brick walls. Slade spoke his name into the front door and it swung ajar without him lifting a finger. Gisela grew slightly envious at what seemed to be the Middlers' lack of a need for keys and currency cards. As they both entered the house, the lights flickered on, illuminating the wide, open rooms. A voice sounded from the floor above, "Slade?"

A sturdy, older man with glasses came walking down the stairs to greet them. He smiled and spread out his arms. Slade hugged him and said, "Hey, Dad." With one arm still around his father he made an introduction. "This is my friend, Gisela."

He stuck out his hand, "Hi, Gisela. Welcome."

She shook his hand and said, "Thank you, Mr. Maxwell. Your home is amazing."

"Thank you, thank you. I'm sure you'll have a fun week down here."

"Well, Dad," Slade started, "the thing is… we won't be staying all week."

"Oh…okay. You're not. How long are you staying? Are you going back early?"

"We'll be here for a couple of days, but I think we're going to meet a friend in the Southern Third."

"Okay… Did you tell your mother?"

Slade shook his head, "Not yet."

"All right, well, if that's what you want to do, I can't stop you…but *she* can," he laughed. He saw Slade's worry and changed his tone. "Oh, you'll be all right, son. Just don't wait too long to tell her." He grabbed Gisela's bag and changed the subject. "So, let me show you to your room, sweetheart. I'm sure you guys are tired after that flight."

Slade and Gisela followed him up the stairs. Slade continued on to his room after saying goodnight to Gisela who was then directed to a room of her own. The room he'd had since childhood exhibited a small bookcase, a clean desk, and a large window to the front yard. Everything was in its proper place. As Slade lie down on the bed, he looked at the ceiling with a strange mix of nostalgia as well as a longing for what his future may hold. He envisioned living in different cities all around the world, enjoying the different cultures, and learning more about Ethereans and their history. And as much as he tried to deny it, in each of those visions he saw Douglassaire by his side. Slade shook his head and thought, *Douglassaire probably does this to everyone – draws you in and pushes you away as soon as you get close.* Slade knew the type. He was still getting over the betrayal he felt from his flirtatious ex-friend, Mason, who dropped all communication when Slade asked for clarity on their relationship. He was determined to not get hurt like that again. Doug was just a friend – nothing more. He continued trying to convince himself of that as the waves of fatigue washed over him and slowly lulled him to sleep.

***

Gisela awoke to the smell of freshly baked sweet buns, coffee, and even more than her sense of smell could accurately detect. She rose from her bed and took a quick glance out of her window at the colorful scene. The deep blue of the large swimming pool at the back of the house wonderfully complemented the gorgeous green grass. Suddenly she felt stuck. She so wanted to go enjoy the treats that tickled her nose, but the house was so big and foreign. Plus, she didn't even know Slade's family. She started to wonder if she were underdressed. Sure, it was just breakfast, but everything about this place just screamed *fancy*. She thought about changing out of her white T-shirt and navy blue fleece pajama bottoms, but figured she'd find Slade and ask him.

Barefoot, Gisela quietly made her way down the hall feeling like an intruder. She desperately hoped not to run into any of

Slade's family. She finally made it to Slade's room and saw that his door was open. After knocking, she poked her head in calling, "Slade?" No answer, no Slade. Everything in her tightened as this feeling of dread overwhelmed her. She absolutely hated being abandoned. Just then she faintly heard a voice speaking downstairs.

"How can you justify killing anyone?" It was Slade. Gisela exhaled a sigh of relief and walked towards his voice.

"I'm just sayin'. If that's what they wanna do, then that's on them. We can't tell the Southern Third what to do." This was a female voice. As Gisela made her way down the stairs, she wondered if who she heard was Slade's mom. She almost crept around the stairs to catch a peek at what everyone else was wearing, hoping her attire wouldn't alarm them. The first person she saw was the woman to whom Slade was talking. Instantly, Gisela hated her own decision to remain in her pajamas as she saw that this woman had on a flashy pair of red heels, an expensive skirt, and blouse. Gisela mistakenly caught her eye and the woman asked Slade, "You brought company?"

"Gisela, in here," Slade called. Gisela had no choice now. She prepared to face her embarrassment. As she walked into the room, she saw Slade sitting at a small round table with the woman. She was greatly relieved to see Slade was still in his night clothes – a tank top and comfy, plaid bottoms. She also spotted another woman cooking the food in the kitchen a few feet away with her pajamas on as well. "Good morning," said Slade.

Gisela replied, "Good morning."

"This is my big sister, Samantha."

"I know you did not just call me big," Samantha teased.

"Would you rather I call you old?" Slade quipped back.

Samantha feigned shock. "Superior would be more appropriate," she laughed. She reached out and shook Gisela's hand. "Hi."

Gisela nodded with a smile. She evaded the shock of not dressing the part, but still felt intimidated by the girl's presence. Everything about her was loud and bold – even her hair, which she wore in a mass of black, soft, fluffy curls.

"Gisela's from Ankor in the Northern Third," Slade

mentioned.

"So, you're from a whole different world, huh? How do you like it down here?" Samantha asked.

"I haven't seen much yet," Gisela said, "but it's different...really different."

Samantha chuckled at this. "I'm surprised you made it out, girl. A lot of Northerners don't have time for the rest of the world."

"What she means is..." Slade began, in response to Gisela's puzzled expression, "she noticed a lot of Northerners don't travel beyond their borders. But we weren't even talking about the North, Sam, we were talking about the Southern Third."

"Yes! And their crazy Power Battle," Samantha responded with renewed interest.

The woman in the kitchen called out among the sounds of clanging metal and sizzling pans. "Are you going to offer her a seat, Slade, or just make her stand there all day?" Her jet black hair was pulled into a short ponytail and she wore a deep lavender silk robe.

"Sorry, Gisela. Here." Slade got up and pulled out a chair next to him. He jerked his head in the other woman's direction. "That's Mom."

Gisela made her way around the small table to her seat. As she did, Slade's mother came over, and warmly greeted her guest. "Welcome, Gisela. Have a seat."

"Thank you for having me."

"So, what do you think, Gisela?" Samantha asked, quickly getting back on topic. "I've only seen clips of the last one that took place, what...twenty...six years ago? I mean, it looks exciting, but I don't know if I'd like to see people hurt each other."

"I agree," Gisela said. "I'm not a big fan of violence."

"But what about making it a rule that the soldiers shouldn't kill each other? There's a lot of talk in the Middle Third about it. Do you think we should have a say in what goes on there?"

"There's nothing anyone can really do about it. That's their culture."

"Right. Thank you." Samantha turned to her brother: "For

them, dying in the pursuit of power is honorable. Plus, nobody died last time, so they're obviously past killing each other, too."

"Well, I think the whole thing is foolish," Slade said.

"It doesn't really matter what we think. That decision's up to the queen," said Slade's mom. "And she's not going to do anything about it."

Slade shrugged, "Why not, though? Doesn't she care that her people are up in arms about this?"

"Mmm, yes and no. She's very shrewd, that one. All she really cares about is keeping enemies as weak as possible..."

"Says the queen's advisor."

"Your mom's the queen's advisor?" asked Gisela. She knew Slade's family was well off, but having such a close link to the queen was surprising.

Slade nodded, "Well...one of them. After the last war, the queen got rid of her advisor and created an advisory board to help her make big political decisions."

"And how does the Power Battle keep the South weak?"

Samantha jumped in. "What Mom's basically saying is that Queen Aeothesca won't do anything, because the strongest army in the world ends up killing some of its best soldiers to see who's going to be in charge. Why keep them all alive?"

Gisela glanced at their mother who remained silent and went back to plating some of the food she'd been cooking. She supposed a woman with the queen's ear knew more than she could actually share.

Slade's mom came over and sat down plates of food for her children and Gisela. "Enough about this. It's so morbid. What's on the agenda for you guys today?"

Samantha's comm. rang and she held up a finger and got up to answer it in the next room.

"I promised Gisela to go sightseeing," Slade said.

"Oh? First time here, huh?"

Gisela nodded, "Yeah. I'm hoping to see most of it before we leave in a couple days." Just when Gisela began to feel comfortable, she suddenly felt the mood drop. Slade got silent as his mother shot him a look.

"*When* are you leaving, Slade?"

Samantha trotted back in with her heels knocking against the hard floor. "I'm sorry guys, I have to go," she said, grabbing a sweet bun off of her plate. "I'll come by for dinner tomorrow, I promise. Bye." She kissed her mom on the cheek, walked around the table, did the same to Slade, and left through the front door.

Seeing his sister come and go as she pleased gave Slade enough courage to answer his mother. Why couldn't he do the same? "The day after tomorrow," he answered. "We're going to the Southern Third for the rest of our break."

Slade's mom huffed in disappointment. "We planned to spend the week together. What changed? What's in the Southern Third?"

Gisela sunk in her chair and quietly nibbled at her breakfast wishing she could disappear from this awkward scene.

Slade remained silent, not knowing quite how to answer. Finally, his mother ended the conversation. "Fine, you know what, we'll talk about this later." She walked past her husband who had just come down the stairs and proceeded upstairs.

Slade's dad noticed the downcast expression on his son's face. "Don't worry, son. She'll be fine. Go enjoy yourself today."

"Thanks, Dad," Slade responded. "Gisela, are you ready to get dressed and go?"

Gisela nodded as they began to rise from their seats. She was happy for a break from the tension.

"Oh, Slade," his father called. "You got a call yesterday."

"Who was it?"

"Somebody named Mason."

II

What could Mason possibly want? This question ran through Slade's mind as he and Gisela rode a lift up to a local eatery on the rooftop of a building. When returning Mason's call, after a few courteous lines, Mason said, "Meet us at the High Lounge," and hung up. With little room to respond or ask questions, as per usual with Mason, Slade felt instructed. Even though meeting Mason would be uncomfortable, Slade saw this as an opportunity to get closure. He promised Gisela it would only be a short diversion to their day of sightseeing.

When the elevator doors opened up, Slade spotted Mason at the bar surrounded by three women. He stepped off and Gisela followed as he began to walk toward them.

"Slade," Gisela called.

Slade's tunnel vision was broken and he turned to see Gisela stopped by the bouncer who put his hand out in front of her.

"Nobles only," the bouncer said, pointing the way back to the elevator.

"She's with me," Slade called. The bouncer immediately let her through.

"Nobles only?" Gisela asked Slade. She took a look around the room and asked, "Am I even dressed for the part?" Her faded jeans and graphic tee were a stark contrast to the blouses and skirts of the other girls. Slade fit in just fine with his expensive button-up shirt with the cuffs rolled up.

"Just act like you belong. You'll be fine," he responded. He smiled and said, "Take it as an exclusive sightseeing stop."

Mason turned from the bar upon their approach. "Hey! Slade!"

Mason knew he was pretty. His baby-blue eyes could be seen a mile away, and his spiky dark brown hair was the perfect frame for his oval-shaped face. He used all of this to charm a slew of people into just wanting to be around him, and tried using it now.

Slade remembered, however, what Mason had put him through and ignored his enthusiasm. He stuck out his hand for a cordial handshake, but was surprised to get an embrace.

"How've you been, man?" said Mason.

Slade kept his arms to his side and broke away. "What do you want, Mason?"

"Give us a sec, ladies." Mason put his arm around Slade's shoulder and they walked to the glass wall with a sweeping view of Reor. "I knew you'd be in town, and I just wanted to reach out to an old friend."

Slade shrugged off Mason's arm. "We're still friends?"

"Of course we are!"

"Mason, cut the act. You stopped talking to me."

"I had to come back here."

"That's not what a friend does." Mason cocked his head and put a hand on Slade's shoulder, but Slade slapped it away. "And could you stop touching me? God! This is what you did last time. You look at me with your...eyes and think I'm just going to fall in line like everybody else. If you want to be friends, you have to stop leading me on and treat me like one."

Mason smiled and folded his hands behind his back. He gave a sympathetic nod and said, "I'm sorry."

Slade didn't expect that. Even though he thought Mason looked rather pleased for someone who had been told off, his anger began to weaken at the apology. Slade thought he probably only heard the part about him having pretty eyes. He wouldn't put it past him. Regardless, Slade got what he wanted, and now all he wanted was to leave. "Okay," he said. "Listen, I have to go."

"All right, but wait. I want to make it up to you. Meet me at Gnosh across the street tonight. Eight 'o clock. Just us."

A part of Slade wanted to leave things as they were right now, but he still had one unanswered question. Was Mason only interested in being friends or was there more? Gnosh was a popular restaurant for dates. Instead of straight-out asking him like last time, Slade decided to go and see. "Okay," he said.

"See ya then," said Mason. And with that, Mason turned and rejoined his group at the bar.

Gisela came up to Slade and saw the puzzled look on his face. "Are you okay?" she asked.

"Yeah, I'm fine. Let's go."

III

Gisela didn't know what to make of Slade's earlier meeting with his old friend. That Mason guy gave her a bad vibe. Whatever he said to Slade threatened to dampen the day, because Slade was distracted for a while after. She was going to fix that. Gisela was going to show Slade that all he needed to be happy was her. This day of sightseeing between friends could easily be turned into the date she'd always wanted with Slade. Gisela could also tell that her efforts worked.

They returned from their tour of Reor in great spirits and Gisela hadn't remembered a time when she was so happy. As they entered the door to Slade's home, she wanted to give her cheeks a rest from the slight pain they experienced from her smiling so much. They explored all of the shops, enjoyed tasty treats, and even took in the sight of the amazing Lorelei Castle. It hung in midair like a carrot dangling on a string – far enough away to seem majestic yet close enough to feel its power.

All the while, she turned up the charm, held on to Slade's arm, and explored his hometown with enthusiasm. She could see herself in this world – in Slade's world.

***

Slade closed the front door behind him and saw his mother sitting on the couch in the living room. He and Gisela shared a look of understanding and she went upstairs. The plan was to come home and enjoy a dip in the pool. So, while Gisela went to get changed, Slade thought it a good time to address the pressing issue.

He walked over to the couch and sat down in the available spot. His mother grabbed his hand and leaned in to kiss him on the cheek.

"I'm sorry, Mom," Slade started. "I just…want something else, you know?"

His mom waved a nonchalant hand in the air. "Oh, Slade, stop it. I wish I could have you here longer, but you're grown and independent. You'd think I'd have gotten used to it by now from dealing with your sister." She turned to look Slade in the eye. "You do whatever it is you think you need to do. Okay? I'll just have to enjoy you while you're here."

"Okay. Thank you, Mom." Slade smiled, but for some reason he couldn't shake his uneasiness, nor could he understand why. For the first time in his life, he felt like he was truly on his own.

"I hope you find whatever you're looking for in the Southern Third, sweetheart, but if you don't, just know you always have that Maxwell name…and a position to go along with it."

Gisela came back down the stairs with a towel wrapped around her shoulders. She proceeded outside to the pool. Slade called after her saying, "I'll be right there." As he got up to go change, he saw Gisela unwrap the towel, sit it on the ground outside, and sit on top of it next to the pool. She was wearing a black one-piece swimsuit and hugging her knees to her chest. She wouldn't even dip her toe in the water.

***

An unexpected thought occurred to Gisela as she sat by the pool. She was reminded of her talks by the lake back home, which inevitably led to thoughts about the day she lost her mother. Swimming used to be something she enjoyed very much, but she had stopped after that day. As irrational as it was, she still felt the water had betrayed her once. She wondered if she could even swim again.

Her deep thinking was shattered with a loud splash from the pool and cool drops of water hitting her skin. Slade had jumped in and they shared a laugh as his head rose above the surface. Gisela followed and let the water rise to her neck. It cooled and comforted her body. All of her fear disappeared when she saw him. She began to swim as though she never stopped at all. She knew as long she was with Slade, everything was going to be fine.

IV

Slade arrived at the restaurant on time to meet Mason. Before he left home, he told Gisela he was meeting up with an old friend and should only be about an hour and a half. He didn't want to leave her alone for too long. As far as he could tell, she was fine with that.

He came in from the street that was teeming with activity as the various establishments prepared for the nightlife crowd. Upon his opening the glass door, the hostess greeted him. "Welcome to Gnosh. How many in your party, sir?"

"I'm waiting for someone," he replied as he sat on the cushioned bench by his legs. The burgundy walls of the restaurant and the low lighting made for an inviting, warm environment. As he looked to the staircase across from him, he wondered if he could get a seat on the upper level. He returned a friendly smile to a server who passed with a sizzling plate in her hand. The steak and onions smelled exactly like what he wanted to order. He was ready to get the night started.

Despite all that Mason put him through, he anticipated seeing him again. Maybe they could get things back on track. Tonight, Slade was sure that Mason would give him the answer he'd been looking for. And if he wasn't willing, Slade would make him.

Ten minutes passed. Slade began to think maybe Mason came early and was already seated. He got up and took a look to the left and the right sections of the restaurant. He looked straight back at the bar. No Mason. He was probably just running later than usual. He sat back down on the bench and awakened his comm., found Mason's number and dialed. He heard it ring a couple times, and then:

"Hi, this is Mason–"

"Hey, Mason, where–"

I can't reach my comm. right now, but if you leave your info, I'll get back to you ASAP. It was just his recording.

Slade waited for the beep then said, "Mason, it's me. I'm here." He searched for something to say. "Call me."

He returned his comm. to his pocket and leaned forward with his elbows on his knees. Mason was probably caught in traffic. Slade heard the clanging of pots, pans, and plates in the kitchen and smelled the alluring aromas of the dishes prepared for other guests. He started to feel hungry, but it was balanced by the joy of getting his friend back, in any capacity.

The clock on the wall read 8:20. Twenty minutes late. *Come on, Mason,* he thought. Still in his seat, he leaned back. He didn't like this wait.

Maybe he missed him. He got up and walked to the hostess. "Did you see a guy come in? About my height, brown hair, blue eyes?"

"No, not since I've been here."

"Thanks." Slade pursed his lips and returned to his seat.

Ten minutes later, his knee began to bounce. He looked at his comm. No missed calls. He hoped what he thought was happening was really not happening. *No,* he thought, *Mason will show up any minute.*

8:40. *I'm definitely not waiting past 8:45.*

8:46. *Seriously, Mason?*

9:00. No call. No Mason.

Slade saw movement at the door, but it was just a family walking in. He sighed and everything inside of him went numb. He felt the pitying gaze of the hostess on his neck – one she quickly pretended not to have when he returned it. Slade felt embarrassed, angry, and stupid all at the same time. He awakened his comm. once again, found Mason's number and wiped its existence. He felt his face getting heavy and fought back his tears of frustration. He dared not look at the hostess as he got up and left.

V

The next night, Slade's sister rejoined the family for dinner as promised, along with her boyfriend. As they nibbled on dessert, they all showed their competitive side with a fun board game. Slade soon found himself to be eliminated and excused himself from the table. "I have to go finish packing," he said. "We'll be leaving in a little bit." However, after what Mason did last night, he wasn't sure if he wanted to see Douglassaire. What he envisioned for himself, all of the adventures he had by Doug's side, seemed like silly dreams now. As he ascended the stairs, he thought about his other option – his birthright as a Maxwell. A cushy desk job working for the Kingdom of the Middle Third. He walked into his old room which greeted him with a warm, golden light. His eyes darted between his perfectly tidy room where he slept since he was a child, his suitcase which lie open on the bed, and the window beyond which lie the distant lights of the city. He asked himself, *could I really live here for the rest of my life?*

"What's up?" Samantha asked, sneaking in.

Startled, Slade drew in a quick breath, but wouldn't dare let his teasing sister know her effect. "Just packing."

"No, I mean, what's up with you? Your attitude's different."

She always knew when something was wrong with her little brother, and while he pretended to be annoyed, he was always glad when she came to talk about it. "Sam, you had a good life here. You had a job waiting for you out of college, just like I do. Why didn't you stay?"

Samantha made her way further into the room. "I guess I just wanted something different." She moved Slade's luggage out of the way and sat in its place on the bed. "I didn't want to feel trapped, you know?"

"But it doesn't make any sense. Who gives all this up to be a fledgling fashion designer?"

His sister made a face that read, *watch it.*

"I'm sorry. But weren't you happy? Weren't you content?"

"Content, yes, but not fulfilled. I could go through the motions that Mom and Dad have set in place, but I'd feel like an empty shell. I chose to do something different, and while I might not have the bucket loads of money that our parents have, I'm doing what I love with who I love. I know someday it's going to work out for me and that's enough. What do you want to do, Slade?"

Slade crossed him arms and sat next to his sister. "I don't know. I just know it's not this."

"You do know, Slade. And whatever it is you want, you need to drop the 'poor me' act right now and go for it." Samantha reached her arms around Slade and gave him a hug. "It might be scary to let go, but sometimes you have to risk it all and just jump through the fire. You might get burned – heck, you might die, but what's worse? Having died trying to live, or living and just waiting to die?"

VI

The next morning, after giving their goodbyes, Slade and Gisela took off in a cab back to the airport. The sun had just barely broken and the traffic was light. The lights of the big city had all been turned off in what seemed to be Reor's only hour of rest. Gisela rested her head in her hand as she looked out of the hover car's window in a melancholy gaze. "I want to come back here someday, Slade." She felt her words had fallen on deaf ears and looked over at Slade to see he was deep in his own thoughts. She looked back at the passing architecture and even spied Lorelei Castle off in the distance. As she did, she thought about family. Not since she was a little girl had she felt anything remotely close to what she did when she was around Slade's family. She almost lost a little respect for him these past few days. He had it all, yet he still dared to be unhappy. *How could that be possible?* she thought. *What more could he need?* As she thought about it, she could see he was missing love in his life. That's what he needed. Their sightseeing day hadn't been enough. She decided a big gesture was in order. Once they reached the Southern Third, she would make him hers.

***

Slade looked back at Gisela thinking he'd heard her say something, but she remained still. He was unsure of what lay ahead, but what his sister said to him last night rang true. He'd rather die trying to make a life of his own than live somebody else's.

They boarded their flight and waited for takeoff. As Slade

waited patiently in his seat, he began to feel more at ease. He finally began to shake off what Mason put him through and looked forward to meeting up with Douglassaire. He wasn't going to let Mason ruin his trip. Maybe Douglassaire was different.

CHAPTER ELEVEN

I

Douglassaire arrived at his hometown, Probuston, in the afternoon. The once prosperous city had seen decline over the past decades and its architecture and buildings fought a losing battle to retain their former glory. The air was humid and dry – normal for most of the Southern Third. He stepped out of the bus wearing a simple black tee and jeans with a backpack strapped around his shoulders. While kicking away some debris left by a previous wanderer, a clique of teenagers stood a few feet away paying close attention to every move. He looked them in the eye and won the psychological game of chicken. They probably noticed the dagger in the small pocket on the strap of his backpack. Warriors never walked around alone and unarmed. He knew he could have taken them anyway. Once the clique moved on and decided not to cause trouble, Douglassaire took in the sight the building in front of him. After all these years, The Full Hart Home still looked the same. It sat on the corner of the street and its recently repainted brick walls were even more recently vandalized with graffiti – an 'A' with a circle around it, all in red. Who knew what that meant?

He hadn't been back in years. Doug hated that he ever had to come back here, but he felt he was long overdue a visit to an old friend. After knocking firmly on the door three times, the door opened and a woman looked out. Her silver hair was pulled into a bun that revealed her oval face. Her searching eyes widened as she realized who was standing in front of her. "Douglassaire."

"Hey," he said.

"Oh, Douglassaire!" she said as she wrapped her arms around him. "Oh, come in, come in!"

Doug walked through the doorway and looked on what used to be his home. "Not much has changed, Editra." The sound of children laughing in the backyard was muted by the closed back door in the kitchen. He looked at the small couch adjacent to an end table with its shelves filled with old children's books. Further back was the staircase to the bedrooms. There were only five bedrooms, but Editra managed to have up to eight children living there at a time. On the ratty area rug in the middle, a small boy sat reading what he could. As Editra closed the front door behind him, Doug studied the boy for a moment. The boy knew he was being watched and looked back, his eyes full of a fleeting hope. Doug averted his gaze to the wood floor below, hating himself in the process. He knew that look all too well.

"He reminds me so much of you, Douglassaire," Editra said. She sighed, "I worry about him. Though, seeing you now...I suppose I shouldn't worry about him so much. You talk about things not changing – look at you!" She grabbed him by the shoulders and looked him up and down. "You sure have changed. And for the better it seems." She clapped him on the shoulder and began walking towards the kitchen. "Come. Sit down. I'll make tea." She was as lively now in her old age as she had always been. Doug followed and dropped his backpack as he took a seat at the table in the black folding chair. He left the sturdy wooden chair with the cushion for Editra who was busy pouring water into an old kettle. She pulled out two chipped cups from the cabinet and sat in each of them one tea bag. Then, she made her way over to the open seat. "So, tell me, what has Douglassaire been up to?"

"Well, I'm in college now–"

"College! Oh!" Editra clasped her hands together at her mouth in excitement then waved this outburst away. "Go on, go on!"

"And I'm also training…for the Power Battle."

Editra smiled and was in awe. "No!" she whispered. "Oh, I just know you'll do great. I do hope you'll be careful, though. I'd hate to see anything happen to you." Editra just shook her head in disbelief. "You could soon be called Commander…" She couldn't quite finish the title. "Did you ever pick a last name, Douglassaire?"

"Hart."

Editra began to tear up. "Oh, Douglassaire," she said, wiping away the first tear to roll down her cheek, "there are so many of you kids who just don't make it. When I go out, sometimes I see them on the street making nothing of their lives, but I never saw you out there. When you left, I always wondered where you went. It makes me so happy to see you doing well. And I am honored that you chose my name for yours."

"I'm glad. I'm sorry it took me so long to come back–"

"Nonsense."

"…but I came back to say thank you."

Editra reached out her hand to touch Doug's as the kettle whistled loudly. She patted Doug's hand and got up to prepare the tea. "I almost forgot," she said, pouring the water into the prepared cups. "I found something for you. I've had it for a few years now. I held on to it not knowing if I'd ever see you again, but hoping." She walked over and sat two hot cups of tea on the table.

"Really? What is it?"

"I'm not sure… I never opened the package. It was with you when you were dropped off here as a baby. Silly me – I lost it among my own things and didn't find it again until after you left. You fix your tea. I'll see if I can go grab it." She stepped out of the kitchen.

Doug's eyes followed her as she kneeled over to nudge the small boy who had been reading but was now asleep. He stirred slowly and Editra motioned him upstairs, no doubt to continue his sleep in a more appropriate location. He complied, and as kind as ever, Editra rested a hand on the boy's shoulder, gently rubbing with her thumb as he walked in front of her up the stairs.

Douglassaire took a sip from his cup. He didn't really care for tea, but he at least wanted to make an effort.

He began to think about his old life here. He had always been alone. That's how he learned to survive. Some of the kids were mean, other adults could be mean…he had to protect himself. From the crime-infested town to the boring walls of the orphanage, he hated every aspect of this place. Editra was the only ray of sunshine he had.

He heard her footsteps on the floor upstairs slowly make their way down and saw in her hands a large brown envelope. Editra handed the package to Doug who looked it over. "It says: 'To Douglassaire'. I have no idea where it came from or who."

Over the years, Douglassaire practiced not to get the same look of hope that he saw in the young boy's eyes moments ago. This time was different. He saw his first name printed clearly on the front of the envelope and for the first time ever he felt that someone specifically reached out to him. Editra stood by and readied herself to shoulder Doug's disappointment as she had many times before.

He tore open the seal, reached inside the envelope and pulled out a small brown book. He sat the envelope on the table and studied the front and back cover. Nothing special, save for an elastic band stretched around the length of the book to keep it closed. He slid the band to the side, and when he opened the cover to the first page, a small square of folded paper fell to the ground. He bent over, grabbed the piece of paper and dusted it off before unfolding it to read the contents:

Douglassaire,

If you're reading this it means I was not fortunate enough to see you again. I wish I could have been there with you for every step – the way a father should. Unfortunately, for circumstances beyond my control I could not be the man that I wanted to be. The details of my findings about Ether, and the reason you are where you are now, are all in these pages. It is likely I have died for what I uncovered, and I am sorry. My only legacy to you now is this book, and I hope it helps you, in some way, to become the great man that I know you will be.

Love,

Douglass Heuresyt

Douglassaire stared at the letter and re-read it almost a hundred times. The world around him disappeared and all that was left were the words of the letter. ...*the way a father should*, it read. The back door to the kitchen opened and a group of loud children came in and became silent at the sight of a giant stranger sitting at the table.

"Go, children, go. Up to your rooms," Editra commanded. As their footsteps on the stairs echoed through the house, Editra asked Doug, "What is it?"

Douglassaire successfully avoided an emotional outburst. He folded the letter and stuffed it back in between the cover and the first page of the book. "It's a letter. From my father."

"Oh!" Editra gasped, putting a hand to her mouth. "Douglassaire..." Thoughts of those rare moments when a child had a chance at reconnecting with their parents started running through her head.

Douglassaire sat there staring at the book. Of all times, he received information about his identity now, when his determination to put his life on the line to win the Power Battle was unshakeable. He was grateful to learn he belonged to someone, but he hated his father at the same time. He began to feel his resolve to participate in the Power Battle rattle and knew that it stood a chance at completely crumbling should he open that book.

Editra was well prepared for moments like this even if they were few and far between. "You should read it," she said. "Every word."

Douglassaire opened his mouth to try to talk himself out of it. He was curious, but he wanted to stay strong and leave the past in the past. Editra raised her hand to stop him. "No," she said. "Always listen to those who love you. Listen to me. Listen to your father. Read the book."

II

Old habits resurfaced as Douglassaire took his old seat at the couch. Ready to finally find the answers about who he was and where he came from, he opened his father's journal and began reading:

2833.III.X

I'm excited. My work has finally gotten the recognition it deserves from Commander Azure and I actually met him in person! He told me that I'm being stationed at the observation facility in Nan-Tur, but didn't give me specifics. All I know is it's a long way away, deep in the jungle. I have to get back to packing soon because I leave first thing tomorrow morning. Whatever the mission is, my success would mean a handsome reward and an honorary warrior's medallion. That's the next best thing in the Southern Third to the recognition and respect that comes with actually being a warrior. I literally do not know what I'm getting myself into, but one does not say no to the Commander.

This is a strange world we live in and I'm happy to have made the right choice in exploring all of its mysteries. We call the lusae dangerous, but where many see danger I see beauty. The lusae are amazing creatures and there are many, I believe, that we haven't even seen yet. Hopefully, during this expedition I can come across one we have no knowledge of.

2833.III.XIII

At long last, I've made it to Nan-Tur. I barely have enough energy to make this entry due to the arduous journey. We left early in the morning and set up camp in the wilderness each night. I, along with a group of eight other warriors, set off in a caravan of three, wheeled trucks. We all donned the Southern Third's signature black, obsidian armor. I wish we had the hover technology of the Middle Third, but the silent engines of our military's vehicles did just fine as long we rolled slow. If not for them, we'd have to face off against more of the lusae than we did. And it was unfortunate, but we did have to dispatch of some of these magical creatures.

Even if for survival, it deeply saddens me to have been a part of killing any lusus. Save for the few aggressive types, they're hardly a threat if we show no threat first. This is why we make use of horses or silent engines and slow driving when traversing the wilderness. Our job is to communicate to them that we're simply "passing through" their territory, but mankind always has a way of overstepping their boundaries.

Our travel was going well until our second day. We made a stop for refueling in an area seemingly unpopulated by the lusae. We parked in a clearing where only tall grass stood and two of our group went into the woods to keep an eye on our surroundings. Not 20 minutes into our rest, the loud pop of a BAC rifle sounded off in their direction. I was speaking to the leader of our excursion when it happened. It was strange. The use of Bolt-Action Cannons is rare. The advancements we've made with the blade is preferable to the single shot of a primitive rifle that requires aim and loading all while in the midst of danger. And there is no honor in using it – unless you're hunting criminals. Yet, there I was hearing the crack of the gun in the distance. The leader said they were probably just having target practice – a little fun before getting back to work. I mentioned my concern, but he was un-phased. After some pushing on my part, he proceeded to use his radio to talk with his men in an effort to comfort me. He asked his two lookouts why they were using their guns. He received no response. He asked again with the same result. I tried my best to keep calm, but I already feared the worst. He sent two more of his men out to check on his lookouts. It was only a moment before the radio at his waist began blaring with a warrior's voice saying, "Urgent! We need backup! We need backup!" The leader sprang into action and the rest of his troops followed. I was told to stay put, but my curiosity got the better of me.

I traveled a short way into the woods, but lost sight of my protectors. I could feel panic creep into me as I looked around at the thick brush and endless stretch of trees with no sight or sound of the warriors I was with. Then, suddenly, I heard a loud roar off in the distance. The soldiers quickly ran towards me from the direction of the noise with one of them being carried on the back of another. It was one of the lookouts and he was injured. As they ran past me, yelling at me to get a move-on, I couldn't help but look behind them at what some of the fiercest men in the Southern Third were afraid of. Even with all of my experience with the lusae some of the things they were able to do never ceased to amaze me. The trees around me did the most unnatural thing and I knew instantly what we were up against. They began snapping at the bottoms and tipping over sideways making a way for this overgrown monster that was charging us. When I saw it I made no attempt at study and ran fast along with the warriors. We managed to dodge what seemed to be spears of tree bark that the monster shot at us and hid behind more trees hoping it would soon forget we were there. The leader to my left asked me, "How do we get rid of this thing?" I was glad he was finally willing to listen to me.

"Draw it away from its magic source," I said. I took a peek around my hiding place and saw it was an atlas – a huge bear with wooden quills that served as its fur, its protection, and its weapon. "He's an earth type with a favor for trees. Get him away from the trees." He didn't like hearing that. It meant drawing the thing closer to our vehicles in the clearing. He yelled at everyone to get back to the clearing, and as they started to move out, he stepped from behind the tree, aimed his BAC at the atlas and fired. This only further enraged the creature as the bullet bounced and merely chipped a piece of its wooden armor. I began running along with the leader back to the clearing.

We made it in one piece and the soldiers had their swords in hand, ready for a fight. I could barely breathe from all the running, but I managed to tell them, "Aim for the underbelly. That's the only way." The atlas slowly stepped out of the shadow of the forest and into the clearing. The leader reloaded his gun and decided to draw its attention by shooting it off, allowing the other soldiers the chance to cut the atlas down from underneath.

I couldn't just stand by and watch. Honor be damned, we needed to get away. So I grabbed a free gun from the truck next to me and shot it off in the direction of the atlas. It was an intense sight. The atlas's quills were flying towards the leader and I as the rest of the team slid on their armored shins to make deep slices in the creature's soft area. They successfully slid away and began to calm down as the defeated atlas fell, but I sensed all was not done. The quills on the beast began standing upright. I notified the team to get in the vehicles so we could go, for we needed to evade the creature's final attack. They showed that I finally had their respect by immediately listening and loading up. The engines were taken off of silent mode and roared to life allowing us to speed away, but not before needing to swerve left and right to avoid the rain of every last wooden quill on the atlas's back.

The injured lookout sat next to me while another soldier tended to his broken leg. I asked the injured warrior what happened to the other lookout. He said he tried to shoot a bird standing on a rock and the rock began moving. While I hated that they found sport in killing other animals, that did explain why we didn't detect any lusae nearby. Atlases, when sleeping, protect themselves by curling into a ball and lying still. The gray bark on their backs closes together giving them the appearance of a boulder. The warrior continued speaking, saying that the gunshot was what awoke the creature resulting in his partner getting impaled by one of its wooden quills. They didn't have time to retrieve him. He, on the other hand, managed to dodge the quills, but got his leg crushed by one of the falling trees.

I let his comrades continue to work on his injury and tried to rest as well as I could. I needed all of the rest I could get after that harrowing ordeal.

2833.III.XIV

I met with the director of the observational facility here. The mission was finally spelled out for me, but it wasn't what I expected. I thought I was to merely observe the lusae in their natural habitat, but for some reason, they want to know how to tame them. I hardly believe the government wants the lusae as pets. Could their intention be to use the lusae as weapons of war? I shudder to think of their destructive capabilities against other people. I take solace in the fact that the mission seems nigh impossible, but simultaneously I don't want to disappoint Commander Azure. I'll give this my best shot and hope I don't die in the process.

2833.III.XXX

It's been weeks since I've been out in the field. There were a couple run-ins and close calls with the lusae, but no progress on getting them to listen to me at all. Taming these creatures – no – controlling them in any capacity seemed impossible. Today, I found myself at my wits' end. I was ready to quit and watch my career fall to shambles and face the Commander in failure.

At times like this I usually try to take a deep breath and decompress. This time was no different. Unfortunately, I was in the middle of a jungle so true peace could not be found as I had to stay on guard for my own safety. I took a walk until I found a small river and sat next to it on a big rock. I listened as the water trickled and bounced over the rocks and drew in breath as the sun broke through the trees to hit my face. I was beginning to feel more *like myself, but that quickly came to a halt.*

I made no sudden movements as I saw the small creature with its beady eyes slowly walk towards me as if stalking its prey. I had seen one of these before – it's called a jaculus. It had the appearance of a snake, but walked with the talons of a bird. Its head slithered back and forth with each step. Deep inside I hoped and prayed it would leave me alone. Thankfully, its scaled wings were withdrawn to its side, for they could easily control small currents of air to literally cut down its opponents with just a flap. Those small cuts wouldn't be enough to kill me, but jaculi still had the venom and bite of any normal snake. It looked ready to use just that.

It stepped closer and closer, then suddenly jumped to land on the rock on which I was sitting. I couldn't help but flinch as it did this, causing what I knew would be my demise. It opened its mouth and made this terrible hissing sound as its wings spread, ready to jump at my neck and end whatever threat it sensed. I knew I couldn't outrun the blasted thing, so I waited for any possible chance at counterattack.

As it made one last step towards me, I felt a sudden gust of wind from behind so hard that I nearly fell on top of the creature. The jaculus flinched and prepared to attack again, but was surprised at yet another sudden gust of wind. It backed away slowly, but still hissed, seemingly at something behind me. I turned to look over my shoulder and saw an old man with a big white beard standing by the edge of the river. He had long, wiry hair and wore a dirty hooded poncho and baggy slacks. The jaculus jumped down and began charging the old man. His appearance betrayed the amount of power he had. Once again, he raised his hands and directed a strong gust of wind at the creature, knocking it on its side. It got up and walked away.

"You're an Etherean," I said. He simply looked at me blankly and nodded. As he started to turn away I told him I was eternally grateful to him for saving me. He pretended not to hear and began to walk away, but I couldn't help but feel that I was finally close to a solution to my mission. He just stopped a lusus from attacking – no bloodshed. It was as if the jaculus changed its mind.

I caught up to him and said, "How did you do that?" He ignored me and walked on around the bend in the river. I saw a small cottage, and asked, "Do you live out here?" It seemed ludicrous to think that anyone would be able to live in the same environment so close to the lusae. "Sir, I need your help," I implored.

"You just received my help," he said. His voice was raspy and sounded as

93

though he were on the verge of a cough. "I have no more to give. Go away."

"I just need to know how to tame the Lusae—"

"Tame them?" He said, swiftly turning to face me. "You must be some form of idiot."

"What you just did I've seen nobody else do. The lusae don't just turn and run."

"Nor are they pets!"

"Please, sir. Show me what you did. Tell me how you can live out here and not already be dead." He must have heard the desperation in my voice, for he gave up the fight. After staring me down in what I suppose was some contemplation of the pros and cons, he invited me inside his home.

The inside of the cottage looked like a perfect match for his wardrobe. Dirty, dusty, and cluttered. It was very small. Just a few feet away from his bed sat a small wood-burning stove. He told me to sit and I sat across from him at the small table by the window – also a few feet away from his bed.

"What brings you out into the middle of nowhere?" the old man asked.

"I'm here on behalf of the government. I have a mission."

"The government wants you to tame the lusae... I wonder what they would need that for..." He stroked his beard and thought upon it for a long while. I almost began to speak up until he said, "I should throw you out now. I want nothing to do with your corrupt governments."

"I'm not a warrior."

"That is obvious. You want to know how I survive out here? It's because I can show strength."

"How is your show of strength any different from everyone else who enters the wilderness?"

"It's different because I'm on their level. The lusae don't respond to you brandishing your sword. They respond to what they know. Ether. If you show that your ethereal power is greater than theirs, they back down." I asked how someone like me could make them back down, to which he replied, "You can't. You're not an Etherean, and they will always know your weakness."

I realized that making the lusae back down from a fight was far from taming them, yet that does not stop me from believing that there is a way. Half of the solution is that an Etherean needs to be present. The other half maybe I can handle. The money and recognition doesn't seem so far away after all.

2833.IV.XV

Taming the Lusae is no easy feat. Thankfully I have such a powerful sorcerer to help me. I've been to see the old man every day since first meeting him. His name is Zarius. I think he's gained a liking towards me. He showed me that once you show the lusae that you wield power greater than them, they respect you. It reminds me of training a dog. You have to be the pack leader. It's so simple, it makes me wonder why I haven't thought of this. Perhaps I had, but my failure was in overlooking the need for an Etherean — and the access to one.

Once you have the respect of a lusus, taming them becomes the same process as taming any other wild beast. They could never be domesticated, but it's become clear that some can indeed become controlled.

I can finally go back to the Commander with this knowledge, however I fear how he will take it. Ethereans are a rare breed and rarer still is the respect they seek from their peers. I'm surprised at my own disinclination to go home. I feel that Zarius has much more knowledge to be obtained and my thirst for it since meeting him has become unquenchable.

2833.V.II

I just realized I haven't made an entry in a while. I'm quite sure I've gained Zarius's trust. I suppose he sees my love of the lusae as endearing, for he, too, feels the same way. He has confided in me some of the secrets of Ethereans. I found every word fascinating. For one, he told me that he came upon a boost to his power. He didn't tell me how, but he did say that listening to his "new spirit" granted him knowledge beyond human comprehension. Mainly, that Pangaea has many different versions of itself that is outside of our reach — one where land is scattered across the sea. He calls it Earth and he seems so sure of himself, but like I said, it is beyond my comprehension.

I've successfully completed my mission, but feigned ignorance to my superiors in an effort to extend my time here and hear more of what Zarius had to say. The Commander has grown impatient and I'm afraid I cannot stay here any longer, but after what I learned I will most certainly return.

Zarius has shown me wondrous examples of his immense power — flight, destructive winds, even sharpened blades of air much like the jaculus we encountered, but much more powerful. He even told me a story that, if I hadn't witnessed his power, I would have found hard to believe. I asked him about his basket of crystals underneath the table in his cottage. He levitated one out of the basket and drew it to his hand, saying, "Crystals serve as a storage container. A sort of battery, if you will. You can store your ether inside and call upon it in times where your element is not present."

"What benefits would one have for doing that?" I asked.

"Suppose you are a fire user but have no fire around. You're useless. But with a crystal charged with your power, you could still use it if you needed. In my case, if I stored air into one of these I could swim deep underwater and use this to breathe, at least until the crystal were depleted. Now, my body is far from its days of strenuous swimming, but you get the point. And only the owner can use the power stored in the crystal – no one else."

"That makes me think of Lorelei Castle. They say Elao himself made it miraculously float one day."

"Do you believe it?" he asked me. I said I did not, but have heard of no other explanation. He then began to tell me about the castle:

"Lorelei Castle was built in Crystal Park, as you know, which is the reason for the presence of the two huge crystals in the back. What nobody knows is that it was not Elao, but an Etherean who lifted the castle with the help of the crystals. I was commissioned by Queen Jacqueline for the project. I was that Etherean."

I was in shock. The man had powers beyond my understanding, yes, but a display of power to that scale was unimaginable. He must have seen the look on my face, for he said, "It's true. The size of the crystals allowed me to store immense amounts of air ether inside and levitate the castle grounds straight into the air. It was a proud moment for me, and when I thought credit was due I learned that I would get none. We Ethereans accepted the truth, but most everyone else believed Queen Jacqueline's religious propaganda. Soon after, she banished me and promised me harm if I ever showed my face in the Middle Third again."

"Surely you could have used your power to fight," I said.

"Indeed! I could have removed my ether from those crystals and have the castle fall right out of the sky, but for what? There was no point in shedding any blood. I understood perfectly. Our world sees Ethereans as demons and in no way would the queen be associated with the likes of me."

"Is that how you ended up here?"

"I came to learn that humans have many faults and I made the choice not to live within their rules. In the wake of great power they become afraid and ready to fight, where the lusae bow down and show respect. I like it here just fine."

I couldn't imagine what it's like to have to hide who you are to the world for your acceptance. "Have you met any others like you?"

"Other Ethereans? Yes, of course. I stay away from them as well."

This surprised me. "Why?"

"Ethereans are humans, too, and just like those without their powers, they're always ready for a fight. They call me a genius. I have more power than most other Ethereans will ever wield in their lifetime. And because of that, every guild I have come across sought only to use me as a weapon in a proposed revolution for upper-class status, acceptance, and recognition. But you tell me, how can one who is already deemed a monster be seen as an equal through monstrous actions?"

He seemed dead-set on his philosophy. Maybe forcible means were not a complete answer, but in the case of his people, surely something could be done. He mentioned something interesting that I almost overlooked. "You said there were guilds? Guilds of Ethereans?"

He confirmed there were indeed groups of Ethereans who have banded together for the sake of camaraderie and training. One was not too far away from here in a city called Tybaltsburgh. It seems the more I learn of these people, the less interested I become in their animal counterparts. I know now, that as soon as I get the chance I will visit that city and learn more about their culture for myself.

2833.V.V

My trip back home to the capital has been much less eventful than my trip to Nan-Tur, thankfully. I spoke with the Commander yesterday and received my reward, and today attended a short ceremony where I got the warrior's medallion. I did it! My previous studies of the lusae have already granted me some measure of public favor, but to have the Commander's acknowledgment means so much. It's definitely a step up in my social standing. Whatever happens, I hope the government puts this knowledge to good use. They need Ethereans to tame the lusae, and I hope they treat both parties appropriately.

I hardly know what to do with this sum of money I've accrued. I never had this much to spend. However, as I sit here writing and thinking about the possibilities, something's drawing me back further south to Tybaltsburgh. I want to see if this guild of Ethereans really exists. If they do, they've done a good job of maintaining secrecy. I think that'll be what I do next.

2833.V.XIV

All of the planning has finally led up to this moment. I've finally settled in Tybaltsburgh and I'm ready to explore. Upon first impression, this city is ancient and has plenty of history. I had to park just off of the main road of the city (the only road for wheelers) and walk along the hills paved with streets of cobblestone. Stone houses lined the streets and formed small alleyways that are all somehow connected to the main plaza at the center. I could have easily found myself lost in this maze if it weren't for a woman I met on my way to the inn. Her name was Isabelle, and she is without question the most beautiful woman I've ever seen.

My interest in her grew with each moment as we walked together. Her smile and her brown, almond-shaped eyes captivated me. Our conversation revealed that she was born and raised here, but I figured as much from her proud gait and knowledge of the city. She helped me navigate the confusing new territory with ease and I quickly found the inn. She told me about the humble, easy-going culture of Tybaltsburgh. I could see the truth in that statement from the city's quiet, un-crowded streets. And the people seemed very nice and never in a hurry. It was much different from back home. I asked if she would join me for lunch, but she respectfully declined. At least I tried.

I may not have been lucky with her, but I hope it turns around when searching for clues of this secret guild. I start tomorrow.

2833.V.XV

I sat by the big fountain, the centerpiece to this town located in the plaza, not quite sure what to look for. The people were friendly enough, but I drew some stares and didn't know why. I thought we were dressed similarly enough, so perhaps it's just that everyone is so close to each other that they know an outsider when they see one. I sat with a cup of coffee from the cafe just steps away and this journal pretending to read and take notes, and all the while my eyes wandered aimlessly around the plaza searching for any clue to the guild.

Then I saw her again. Isabelle. Her long braids swung at her back with every regal step she took. She saw me and politely nodded her acknowledgment. Then she stopped at the cafe to give her order. The nod was nice, but I wasn't going to let it end there. I think she was surprised to see me at her side by the time her server came back with her coffee. I wanted to pay, but she rebuffed my offer and paid herself. I then played the role of the lonely tourist and said, "At least come sit with me, just for a moment. I'm new here and have no one to talk to." She hesitated, but finally accepted.

What began as a simple conversation stretched into two hours of lost time. Her thirst for knowledge and love of history rivaled my own need to know as much as possible about the lusae. We just had so much in common. However, that was not why I was here, and I felt she could sense that. I could tell she was beginning to grow comfortable in my presence, as she asked, "What really brings you to Tybaltsburgh, Douglass?" Her accent made her even more alluring. Almost every 'r' she spoke was rolled and when she said my name... Doe-glass – I almost fell in love. She continued, "There's nothing here for fast explorers like you."

"On the contrary. I believe there's much to explore. Do you know of any guild for Ethereans based here in this town?" As soon as I asked, I knew I lost her. Her expression changed and she quickly got up from her seat, ready to depart. I grabbed her hand before she could. "Isabelle–"

"Thank you for the conversation, Douglass." She shook her hand free of mine and began to walk away. It seemed I had struck a nerve and, ever the explorer, I wanted to know why.

"I spoke to Zarius," I called. That stopped her in her tracks. She turned and swiftly walked towards me.

She whispered, "What do you mean? And keep your voice down."

"I just wanted to learn more about Ethereans. Zarius told me about a secret guild here in Tybaltsburgh."

"And what would you have to gain by learning about Ethereans?"

"...my God. Are you one?" My mouth spoke the words on my mind against my will. This made her even more uncomfortable. "It's fine if you are, believe me," I said, trying to comfort her. "I just want to learn more."

"Come," she said, and she began walking towards the more secluded, gated park not too far off. I followed and when we got there she said, "What is your element?"

"Excuse me?"

"If you are an Etherean, you have an element that you control – what is it?"

"I'm not an Etherean."

"And the great Zarius spoke to you? I don't believe it."

"But he did." I knew this would probably be my only chance to get closer to the guild. She knew something, so I had to prove that I was telling the truth. "He's the one who lifted Lorelei Castle. Not anyone else, not Elao

like they say."

She paused, but slowly let her guard down. "You are true. I am sorry for doubting you. Still, allowing a non-Etherean to even know about our guild is…well, it has never happened before."

"Is there any way I could visit?"

"I'll have to talk with the guild master. They've never allowed a non-Etherean admittance, but if you know Zarius there may be a chance."

"Words cannot describe how grateful I am." Although, 'nervous' would be a more fitting description. I have no idea what to expect, but at least I have a friend in Isabelle.

2833.V.XVI

I had my first visit with the guild. They call themselves the Servants of Elao. Their whole philosophy is rooted within old religious teachings and the creation story in particular. They believe that it's their job to restore Elao to power. How they would go about doing that is a mystery to me.

This was my only shot at getting a peek to the mysteries of Ethereans. If I couldn't make progress here I would have no other leads. I know other guilds exist somewhere in the world, but finding them and finding a way in would be much harder without another's help. I'm very grateful to Isabelle for looking out for me. She informed me that it took some persuading, but the guild master agreed to see me. We left from the park through some strange alleyways and turns I could not remember and came upon a small downward staircase that led to a dark doorway. The opening was blocked by a wrought-iron gate with a lock. Isabelle produced a key from her pocket and unlocked the gate, making sure to lock it again behind her before we moved past. Small lights along the floor lit the dank tunnel allowing us to barely see our way, but I stayed close to Isabelle. I began to feel unsure and even more of an intruder. I tried to tuck away my feelings of nervousness and focused on learning the secrets of the Ethereans.

The tunnel finally opened up into a hall. It was still dark, but much easier to see here than in the tunnel. The dingy chandelier at the center of the room illuminated the dark brick walls that housed the empty tables and chairs. It all reminded me of an old pub – in fact I would swear that's what it was if it weren't for the absence of a bar. In the center, towards the back of the room sat what looked like a wooden stage. Three small stairs led up to the platform with an ornate chair. In the chair sat the guild master.

He was a small man with an awkward, but foreboding presence. His jet black hair dropped to the tops of his shoulders and he sat with his arms and legs crossed. He even wore this ridiculous pointed grey hat with a large red feather on the side. "Isabelle, thank you for bringing him. You may go," he announced. Isabelle gently bowed her head and left the room through one of the doors to the side, leaving me alone with this strange man.

He introduced himself and began his inquisition of me. He asked me to recount my story of meeting Zarius, no doubt to validate whether my knowledge of him measured up to his, and he also asked me my goals with joining the guild. I told him the truth — that society already had a firm opinion of their kind and I wanted to see their perspective. At this point he had begun to pace back and forth on the platform, rocking and nodding his head to my words as if listening to a song. Finally he stopped, and I suppose he decided to put a small bit of faith in my words, for he vaguely summed up the goal of the guild and offered me an honorary position among them. The only condition was that in the guild halls I had to always be accompanied by Isabelle. I didn't mind that at all.

2833.V.XX

Isabelle and I have grown close. It took a day or two for her to get used to the guild's requirement of being my chaperone, but I can tell she's warmed to it. She's very strong-willed and stubborn. I like the challenge.

Days ago, when leaving the guild together, I convinced her to give me an example of her power. She mentioned she was an air user and I badly wanted to see.

She said, "Ethereans aren't spectacles, Douglass. We're not here for your entertainment."

"Please. Just once, and I'll never ask you again." The street was clear and day was turning dark. It was the perfect time.

After a huff, she grabbed hold of my arm and I could feel a subtle change in the air around us. She lifted her foot and stepped up above me, inches off the ground. I was amazed. Seeing someone use their ether never gets old. She said, "Come on." It's a strange sensation to lift your foot and put your weight onto a plane of nothingness below, but I did. I nearly lost my balance, but Isabelle held on and corrected me. It was incredible. We took another step up, and then another. I'd never experienced anything like this and I could tell by her smile that she found amusement in my awed reaction. Her smile almost made me forget I was standing in midair. My words, "You're absolutely beautiful," came from my mouth without any forethought. I could feel our lips growing closer, but our moment was spoiled. A drunkard came walking down the street, leaning from one side to the other and yelling "Witch! Witch!" Isabelle released the air and the ground quickly met our feet.

He was infuriating. How dare he call someone like Isabelle a witch? I ran up to him and shook him from the front of his shirt. "Call her a witch again! I dare you!"

The strong stench of liquor turned my stomach. He grinned and his lips began to form the word again, but I wouldn't allow it and threw him against the nearest wall.

Isabelle grabbed my arm and said, "Let's go." As we walked on she said, "You know, Douglass, you didn't have to do that. I'm able to defend myself."

Still coming down from a high of adrenaline, I responded, "You mean with your ether? You shouldn't have to use it for defense. As long as I'm here you won't have to use it." Now, it may have just been my imagination, but I swear I could feel her grasp a little tighter on my arm after that.

2833.VI.I
Much like Isabelle, the members of the Servants of Elao were cautious with me at first, but after many meetings they've come to accept me as one of their own. I'm glad to feel a part of the group and I also find it quite maddening that Ethereans are shunned if they display their powers openly. They are people just like anyone else and most never seek to use their powers to hurt or kill other people. Of course, the operable word is "most", for there are some that do cause harm, and those few threaten the advancement of them all.

I've come to learn more concretely the main objectives of the guild, and this is the only side of them that I find completely foreign. I'm not a religious man myself, but these people certainly are. I suppose I shouldn't be surprised with a name like the Servants of Elao, but they take their mission seriously. They allege that the isle of Ether exists and that there's actually a way to get there. It all goes back to the creation story and the many tales thereafter about regular people who have a unique relationship with one of the four elements. They believe that four spirits of Ether exist somewhere in Pangaea, each representing one of the four elements, and that if they are somehow collected and brought together, the pathway to Ether would be clear. This would then allow them to remove the Djed Key and offer it to Elao restoring him to power so that he would correct the place of Ethereans in the world. Now, I have no clue as to what the correction would be ...more power? ...all humans become Ethereans? ...no other race, but Ethereans? The prospects would be awfully frightening to any normal humans. I must admit, I feel uneasy about all of this business myself. However, I doubt any of this is true.

I now have the title of Finder and have been tasked with actually charting the locations of these spirits. The guild master told me about the discoveries of their last finder and recounted them to me in an excited tone while wildly gesticulating with his hands:

"He said that you don't choose a spirit — it calls out to you. Also, that humans without powers could occasionally get the calling as well. He only ever charted one spirit, which unfortunately led to his end. It was quite obvious after he mentioned its location, and many of us here wondered why we never suspected it in the first place. You've heard of the Incaen Forest?"

I said, "I have, but I've never been. They say it's the work of an Etherean."

"I believed that story once as well. The Incaen Forest is a perfectly green wooded area that remains alight with flame both day and night. For an Etherean to keep that up religiously for years without any reward seemed unbelievable to me, but the mere idea that it was the location of the fire spirit made everything fall into place. Our last finder, a fire Etherean, heard the call of the spirit on his first visit. He thirsted for power so that he couldn't stay away. He returned to the forest and we haven't heard from him since. The fire still burns amongst the forest so we're quite sure he perished, failing to collect the spirit as he wished."

It all sounds too grand for my taste. I don't even know where to start, but I suppose I'll go along with it for now. Whatever I can learn I am open to, and I'll do whatever I must to stay close to Isabelle.

2833.VI.III

I lie here awake in the morning after the most magical night. My dear Isabelle finally sleeps besides me. The downpour last night gave us a reason to run to shelter, and my room was closest. I was almost certain she would have turned down my offer to stay, but to my surprise she accepted. And so ensued a night of anatomical mischief that I dare not chronicle in these pages.

I always wondered if I'd find someone as special as this woman, and now that I have, suddenly all of the things I've been searching for don't seem to matter anymore. All of the knowledge of the lusae, the Ethereans, none of it holds a candle to the happiness I get when I look into her eyes or see her smile. *All I want now is to just live happily and have her by my side. She is headstrong, but I will do all that I can to have her as my wife. Life really isn't all that difficult.*

2834.III.IX

I have neglected my logs for some time now. I've been in a state of bliss for much too long, and it appears that it will only keep extending. Today marks a most special day. My son was born! I am so elated at the moment, I can barely write down these words without thinking of the time I'm wasting not holding him. My wife, despite her rough day, is all smiles and to see my complete family together makes my heart burst.

We hadn't planned a name, but inspiration took over once our son looked at us for the first time. I asked Isabelle what his name should be and she said, "Douglass."

"Oh, that name doesn't nearly do him justice," I said. "It is you who brought him into this world."

"Well, we can't name him Isabelle!"

Then it came to me. A way to pay homage to the beautiful air Etherean who was his mother. "Douglassaire."

Isabelle gave me a puzzled look, then understood and said, "Douglassaire Heuresyt. I like it."

2834.VIII.XXIII

Seeing my child grow up before my very eyes is a miracle unto itself. He is only a few months old now, but already I see such intelligence, such promise. His constant smile is one that will light up the world someday.

My words may seem cheerful, but right now my despair is great. It kills me to have to leave that boy for any period of time, but I must. The guild has finally found what they think is a lead into the whereabouts of its second ethereal spirit, and I have been put on assignment to the Middle Third to confirm and chart its location. It's supposedly the earth spirit, and the guild master thinks I may even hear its voice. He sees my previous travels and love of environment as signs that I have an affinity for earth. Even if I do, I would hate to begin hearing voices in my head.

I didn't refuse this task because I've hardly done anything since I gained admission to the group, and this could be a parting gift of sorts. Isabelle and I agreed to leave the guild and move back to my hometown once I get back. We desire the best for our boy and ourselves, and getting away from the demands of the Servants of Elao is a good start. I'll do my best to find this spirit and return as soon as possible so that my family can move on.

2834.VIII.XXVII

All of the guild's digging has led me here to Sabulton, a small town by the edge of the Middle Desert. They've heard stories about a haunted mirage that all seems to originate from this area. Hopefully I can find something of substance to bring back to them.

For such a small town, Sabulton sure is busy. When I arrived, it seemed everyone in town was working. Some were sweeping the streets, others were setting up tables of their goods, and strings of lights were hung over the main street between the small stone buildings. I visited the only bar in town to get some more information on the earth spirit. The room was dark and the only sunlight came in from the windows on either side of the door. I could feel the subtle crunch of sand on the bottom of my boots as I came in. Some of the staff cleaned as well as they could, but all the sweeping in the world wouldn't stop the fact that this city bordered the desert. I spied only 3 customers. A couple was sitting at a small table and a man with graying hair was sitting at the bar chatting up the bartender. Whatever the commotion was about outside the people here apparently didn't care enough to join them.

I sat next to the man at the bar and his conversation with the bartender revealed an explanation for the city's activity. Apparently the town is usually very slow and quiet, but they'll soon be getting a visit from Queen Jacqueline, herself! Now, they are just finishing up preparations for a royal welcome. What could the queen possibly want in a town like this? That's the question I wanted to ask, but it was not the reason I was here. My face must have shown that I was listening in because the man turned to me and asked, "What brings you here, son? Here to catch a glimpse of the queen?"

"I'm looking into the haunting in the desert."

The man next to me paused for a moment and then laughed heartily. "You don't actually believe that do you?"

"I don't really even know the full story."

The bartender looked less comfortable with the conversation and said, "If you're not equipped to cross the desert, don't go out there."

"Oh no, son," the patron said, "not you too?"

"What can you tell me about it?" I asked.

The bartender firmly planted both hands on the bar and recanted the story: "A mirage is something you see after being in the desert for days without food or water. But this one… some say you can see it within minutes. It looks like a paradise — a beautiful lake and the greenest grass you'd ever seen. Then you hear a voice telling you to come, and you can't help but check it out. The next thing you know, your paradise disappears and you along with it."

"Have you ever seen it?"

"Me? No. I just hear some of the things these customers tell me."

"But you believe it," the man said. "You sure you're not drinking too much of your own whiskey?" He laughed and slapped the bar.

"I've heard the same story from a few different people. It might not be exactly as they say, but something's definitely out there. Be careful."

Like the man at the bar, I found the story hard to believe, but I hoped for the sake of my family that I could find something. I'd hate to go back to the guild empty-handed.

I hear cheering in the street outside. The queen must have arrived. I hope the excitement dies down soon so I can get some sleep.

2834.VIII.XXVIII

I saw the mirage in the desert and that has changed everything. I wish I had never gone out there. I'm back in Tybaltsburgh now, but who knows how long I'll be safe. I've done what I set out to do, and it's time to get my family out of here. I feel like a fool. I've brought danger to my family and the guild.

I set out for the Middle Desert early in the morning. I had a guide with me so I didn't get lost, but I didn't plan on venturing out too far anyway. I was out there walking for almost two hours. Then I saw the mirage. It was just as the bartender said. It was a beautiful oasis in the middle of the desert. It seemed to appear out of thin air. One moment there was nothing, and as I continued to gaze into the distance it slowly appeared. I was in shock, and my guide asked me if I was alright. At that point he hadn't seen what I was seeing, so I said nothing and began to walk towards it.

I vaguely remember my guide yelling after me, "Sir, you shouldn't go that way. Sir!" I didn't listen. I didn't hear a voice calling me, but my curiosity had been piqued, and that was enough of a pull for me. I had to investigate. The mirage grew closer with each step until suddenly I saw a little girl with red hair running towards it. The mirage didn't disappear as I expected. In fact, the little girl stepped on the grass and I saw it wasn't really a mirage at all! It was real. I stood at the edge of the grass, knelt over and plucked a few *blades, trying to make sense of everything. As I let the blades of grass fall to the ground, the little girl looked at me and demanded, "Who are you?"*

I don't know what was more confounding, the realness of the mirage or the sight of this girl. It dawned on me that the queen was still in town and I was looking into the eyes of her famous daughter, Aeothesca. All I could say was, "Princess?"

My guide caught up to me and said, "We must go, sir. We must—" and then he saw her too and bowed. "Your Majesty!"

"You must go, before they come," she said.

My guide and I were both startled by a gunshot close by. A man yelled, "Back away from the princess!"

"Run!" the girl said.

And we did. I panicked as I realized that we were being hunted by the guards of the Middle Third. I ran closely behind my guide until Sabulton came clearly back into view, but I was stopped by the sound of a shrill scream and looked back at the oasis. The mirage twisted and turned and sunk into the sand as if entering a funnel. It really was Princess Aeothesca who was standing there, and I watched as she was swallowed by the desert. The guide pulled at my arm begging me to come on. I began to run again as a barrage of bullets rang through the air. My guide fell, victim to two of them in the back. He was lifeless, and through my fear I hoped and prayed that I would be able to see my family again.

Thankfully, my wish came true. I am here now with Isabelle and Douglassaire and we will leave tomorrow. I managed to escape the guards. I suppose chasing me came second to a dead princess, but I know I won't be safe here for long. I know this without a doubt because of two things:

1. The princess is dead and a strange man (me) was last seen with her.

2. The only reason she was out there in the first place must mean she had the same information we did. The princess was an Etherean. And that's a secret I'm sure the Middle Third monarchy wants to keep to itself.

2834.IX.IV

I sit here a broken man. My dear Isabelle is dead and my son will never know his father. I am so tired of running. I've only wanted the best for the world, but it seems the world wants the worst for me. I curse my decision to even look for that damned spirit. This will be my final entry, and in it I leave all secrets I have left to tell.

First, the princess lives. I almost fainted to see reports of Queen

Jacqueline and her two daughters alive and well after a successful trip to Sabulton. I was positive my face would be plastered on warning signs throughout Pangaea. If only I were so fortunate. That left only the other possibility for Princess Aeothesca's survival. The stories of the four ethereal spirits were true, and she succeeded in collecting the earth spirit. If she wasn't already an Etherean, she certainly has some abilities now. This fact alone would throw the Middle Third, maybe Pangaea, into pandemonium. So now, instead of facing arrest and trial as the scapegoat for the death of a princess, I am simply being hunted for my information.

The next pieces of information they undoubtedly want to keep to themselves are the locations of the other ethereal spirits. The fire spirit still exists in the Incaen Forest. The air spirit remains as untraceable as air itself. Perhaps, like air, it is accessible from anywhere. Who knows? I have no clue as to the whereabouts of the water spirit.

I feel I could bear this burden more if it were only me who was being preyed upon, but the Servants of Elao had to endure the weight as well. And for that, I hate myself. My acceptance to find the earth spirit was my way of only doing what I thought was courteous to people who have been like family to me. Instead of bringing them information, I brought death, and in their own pride they vowed to defend themselves. Even Isabelle. The Middle Third must have tracked me back to the guild, for they found us and unleashed a surprise attack. It was a massacre. The fools thought they could stand up to trained knights with their own powers. I knew it was folly, but the Servants of Elao were like soldiers themselves, and could not run. The knights, abandoning their code of honor, withheld their blades and instead used their BACs to shoot at everyone in sight. I barely missed a bullet myself and saw that they were different than any I'd seen before. Why would they use bullets made out of crystal? The Middle Third never fails to confound me.

I begged Isabelle to run away with me, we had even planned to leave that day, but she couldn't leave her people behind. Amongst the mayhem, she told me to take Douglassaire and go. She kissed me for the last time and I grabbed our son and made a decision that will haunt me for the rest of my life. I left.

I cared for my son as best I could while running away. I began to hide in Probuston, a city on the decline. It certainly wasn't the environment I was used to, but I hoped that would be what made it the best place to blend in. I also hoped that I would hear from my wife – that by some slim chance she had survived the onslaught. I never saw her since. And now, I know I will never see my son again.

Just last night I returned to my room in Probuston and noticed something was amiss. Douglassaire was sleeping and strapped to my chest and instinctively I put a protective arm around him. The light in the room played tricks with my eyes. For a moment I was sure I saw movement, but then all was still. Then I heard the quickening of footsteps in front of me. I thought I was paranoid or going crazy, but there was a knife on the counter next to me and I grabbed it and swung in the air anyway. I made contact with something and my heart raced as blood shot out from some unknown place. The trail of blood began to fall backward and I heard a loud thump on the ground. All at once I saw a man outfitted in grey body armor on the ground with a wound at his neck. I was so distraught that I just fell to my knees. How did my life come to this? What have I done to deserve this misery?

I struggled back to my senses and searched the man lying on the ground. On his shoulder were the letters M.3.A.N. The reason I couldn't see the man before became clear to me. These men are known to have a cloaking ability on their armor — some advanced tech only the Middle Third know of. At that moment I realized that I am as good as dead. I'm now the target of the Middle Third Action Network or "mean", as they call it. They have ventured way out of their jurisdiction and into a major city of the Southern Third just to find me. I have no options left at saving myself.

I currently write this entry in Probuston's chapel. I just finished praying to whoever or whatever is up there for the safety of my son. I will leave him in the care of the local orphanage, and I will head back home to Pelagus to await my death. The Middle Third will not take me quietly.

III

The ride to his next destination was relatively smooth, save for a few bumps in the road. The bus stopped and the last passenger got off towards the front, leaving Douglassaire alone. He stared into the night, tightly clutching his father's journal as the lights of Probuston zoomed past. He remembered leaving the orphanage at sixteen thinking he'd make a life for himself in the military. He decided then that he would always be strong. Editra was his only close relationship during childhood, and he overcame what he thought of as the common weakness of wanting to be loved and taken care of. This was no small feat for an orphan. From then on, he took care of himself.

Yet, he looked at the journal in his hands and began to feel the vulnerabilities he dispelled so long ago. He couldn't explain it, but he suddenly wished he had someone sitting next to him on that bus. An image of Slade came to his mind. He always thought Slade was attractive, but it meant so much more that he stuck his neck out for him to get information about Lesech's powers. Slade would be more than welcome to ride by his side. Doug was looking forward to seeing him soon.

By his father's words, Doug got the answer to the question that every orphan has: *Why?* Now, a new question emerged: *What next?* Lesech's ethereal power was daunting, but now he realized that it was possible to gain the same power by collecting a spirit of Ether. This would give him the edge he needed to beat Lesech at the Power Battle. He also learned something else – the Middle Third killed his parents. Douglassaire no longer *wanted* to become Southern Commander. He needed to.

IV

It was midnight and the bus reached its final destination just before the border of Probuston and the tourist suburb of Lotus Valley. Douglassaire stepped onto the dirt road. He took a deep breath of the fresh air and let go of the heaviness of the day. He was ready to meet his friends at the hotel and needed only to walk a few minutes before reaching the next station that would take him there. He could feel a breeze pass his neck and begin to pick up. He took only a few steps before the breeze became a gust of wind that carried a whisper of his name, "Douglassaire…"

He paused and looked around. He saw no one, but was certain he heard something. Cautiously, he continued his walk while bringing his hand to his chest. He lightly clenched the dagger tucked away in the front strap of his backpack. Another gust of wind pushed past him and again he heard, "Douglassaire…"

He planted his feet and swung his dagger with the swiftness of a trained killer. The wind was stronger and continued to blow past him flapping either side of his shirt. "Who's there?" he commanded.

The whisper morphed into a booming voice as it said, "You lose yourself, boy. You are speaking to a king!"

Douglassaire's eyes darted all around him searching for source to the voice, but still could find none. He yelled, "Who are you? Show yourself!"

The wind swirled around him and Douglassaire felt watched from every angle. He shuddered, almost sure he could feel fingers digging into his shoulders.

"I am showing myself, but I am much too powerful for any human's eyes. I've had many a human name, Beaumine, Cystro, Zarius…but I believe you would recognize me as a spirit of Ether."

The dagger in Douglassaire's hand began to shake. He couldn't get a hold of his nerves.

"You have nothing to fear, Douglassaire."

"I'm not scared–"

"Lies! You pretend you are strong, but at this moment you know you are weak."

"What do you want?"

"The question is yours to answer. You called to me."

"What do you mean?" Self-consciously, he surveyed his surroundings. He felt crazy and hoped no one would see him and conclude that he indeed was. "I never said anything."

"Your voice need not sound to summon us. Your spirit has cried out, and as a spirit, that is all I listen for. You need my power, but are you prepared to do what is necessary?"

"What is that?"

"Become my vessel. Surrender yourself to me."

Doug drew in a breath to speak, but the words did not form. He wanted power, but would not surrender to anyone.

"Perhaps your spirit is as weak as your body. Goodbye, Douglassaire."

The wind died down and grew still again. Douglassaire yelled out, "Hey!" No voice returned his call. He called out again to no response and felt he made a terrible mistake. This fate was unfair. His whole life he felt he never needed help for anything. So, how was he to know that now would be the time to accept it? All that he wanted could have been made possible with the spirit's power, but he blinked. He dropped his dagger and fell to his knees. "Okay! Okay, I surrender!" He waited, but heard nothing.

Doug sat there by the road in the dark for a moment with his head hung low. He grabbed his dagger, lifted himself up, and walked silently to the next station.

CHAPTER TWELVE

I

The taxi sped away as Slade and Gisela walked through the front door of the hotel in Lotus Valley with bags in hand. Slade handled the check-in while Gisela stood very still, blinking slowly and fighting off sleep with every last ounce of energy.

As they boarded the elevator to their rooms, Slade stole a glance at his reflection in the metal backing of the elevator's buttons. He hated that his stylish button-up shirt had wrinkled from the long flight. "I wonder if he's here already," he said.

Gisela's only reply was a yawn.

They stepped off the elevator and found the doors with their room numbers. They each waved their keycard at the lock and stepped into their separate quarters. Slade was sure that Gisela was soon to collapse on her bed, but strangely enough he wasn't tired. Slade was eager to see this new city. He dropped his bag and stood in front of the glass door that led to the balcony. He waited for the door to slide itself open, then reached out to pull the handle after it dawned on him that he was no longer in the Middle Third.

The balcony was dimly lit as Slade walked out. He took in the view of the town, or at least what he could. Unlike Reor, the landscape was dark at night. With the exception of a few street lights and the outline of the amusement park in the distance, Slade couldn't make out much of what was out there. If he stayed home, his week would have been laid out before him, but now he felt that his week, and maybe even his life, was as dark and unknown as the view of Lotus Valley.

He looked over at his more immediate surroundings. As he expected, Gisela's balcony light was off and the area remained untouched. Then, he looked at the balcony next to hers. The same dim light illuminated a familiar figure hunched over the balcony rail.

Slade whispered, "Douglassaire."

Doug jumped at the sound of his name and scanned his surroundings.

Slade waved his hand and called, "Hey! Over here."

Doug exhaled and shared a laugh with Slade. "Slade. Sorry."

"Are you okay?"

"Just a rough day."

"You too, huh? You want to talk about it?"

Douglassaire looked at Slade for a moment, then turned and left the balcony without a word. Doug's balcony light expired and Slade was left all alone outside, the only light in the world shining on him. Slade's insides turned with despair. He got a flashback to how Mason treated him. All at once he became angry with himself and with Douglassaire. *Why did I say that*, he thought. He wondered what he could have said to get a different reaction. He also wondered, *Who does Doug think he is to just ignore me?*

Suddenly, a knock came to the door of his room, and Slade began to feel the strange sensation of despair turning to hope. He walked back into his room and picked up the pace with every step. Despite the small size compared to his apartment in Burrow, it seemed as though each step took a lifetime. He smiled as his eyes met Doug's. "Hey," he said. "Come in." He closed the door behind Doug who seemed cheerful enough, but something was off. His arms were crossed and his head was down, quite different from the confident classmate he came to know at Burrow. "So, how is your spring break so far?" asked Slade.

Doug got to the bed and sat down. "So far so good...I guess. I learned a lot about my father."

"What do you mean?"

"I didn't grow up like you. I never knew my parents. Never lived in a real home. So, when I found what my father left me, I was happy to get some info."

"Really? That's good! What did you find out?" Slade asked. He leaned against the wall next to the bed.

"For starters, my real last name is Heuresyt."

"Wait a minute. How do I know that name?"

"He did a lot of research on the lusae. Kind of a big shot in his day, I guess."

Slade nodded. "Okay, yeah, Douglass Heuresyt. Wow! How did you find out?"

Doug pulled a small booklet from his side pocket and handed it to Slade. "This. It was his journal. He wrote details about his life and how I ended up where I did. And he gave me even more."

Slade began to thumb through the pages, not reading anything in particular. "What do you mean?"

"Remember when you told me Lesech was an Etherean? I started to doubt myself. I wondered if I'd ever be able to beat him in battle. That journal says there are ways even a regular human can get powers."

Something in the journal caught Slade's eye and he read it aloud, "The four spirits of Ether..."

"Exactly."

Slade felt the gravity of this revelation as he sat down next to Doug. He planted his feet in the ground to stop himself from sliding down the small slope in the cushion made by Doug's weight. "There's a way to become an Etherean? Doug, this is huge. How do you do it?"

Doug finally uncrossed his arms and leaned back on his elbows. "Based on what I read, you find a spirit of Ether, and if you survive the encounter, you get their power. That's how the queen did it. Though, I'm not sure if that's everything."

"Okay, hold on. Back up. The queen?"

"My father wrote that he ran into her at the same time he found the earth spirit. He thought she died because she got swallowed into the ground, but she's alive and well."

"That would explain why she's so powerful. But, wait a minute, was she born an Etherean or is she just a normal person with the earth spirit?"

"I don't know, but her power is ridiculous. I try to imagine someone like Lesech with the boost of an ethereal spirit. That's just as scary."

"And why don't you think just surviving the encounter is all there is to it?"

Slade watched closely as Doug shot back up and leaned forward. His elbows were now on his knees and he folded his hands. "Can I trust you, Slade? Don't repeat this to anyone – not even Gisela."

"Of course."

"It's because I just encountered one myself."

Slade blinked and said nothing.

"I know it sounds crazy, but it called out to me – on the way here. Or, I guess it would say I called out to him."

It did sound crazy. Slade knew how important the Power Battle was to Doug, but was he just making this up out of desperation? He laid a hand on Doug's shoulder and asked, "Are you sure?"

Doug stood up and shook off Slade's hand. "Don't do this, Slade, I'm not crazy. I need someone to believe me. I need *you* to believe me. I survived meeting one of the spirits."

"Okay, but do you have any powers now?"

"No, but I don't think it's just survival. It wanted me to surrender myself. To take over."

"But you didn't."

"And I think I missed my chance. Slade, I don't have a chance at winning the Power Battle if I don't do something. I'm already frustrated as it is. Don't make it any worse."

"Well, is there anything you can do? Can you call out to it again?"

Doug shook his head. "I don't know. I think it only came to me because I was desperate. I'd have to feel that again. I'd have to do something crazy. But I don't want you to *think* I'm crazy."

Slade was touched. This was the most he'd ever heard Douglassaire reveal about himself and he realized that his opinion actually meant something to him. He came all this way to be by Doug's side, and while he feared what it would mean, he wasn't going to abandon him now. He stood up, face-to-face with Doug, and made his decision. "Okay. I believe you."

Slade fought to catch his breath as he stood there, mere inches away from Douglassaire's face. He badly wanted something to happen right then. He imagined feeling the warm touch of Doug's hand around the back of his neck. And for a moment he was confused, until he realized what he imagined was actually happening. He closed his eyes as he was pulled into Doug's world. He caught the smell of Doug's skin and felt the warrior's tongue slide over his in a passionate exchange, then was released. He lost his mind. It completely stopped working as his body took over, craving everything.

Doug swiftly pulled off his T-shirt and threw it to the floor, exposing his years of hard work. They just stood there looking at each other. Slade licked his lips and grew conscious of each breath he took. Douglassaire pulled Slade's small waist into his, giving him a preview of all he had to offer. They felt their lips touch again and Slade moved his fingers across the ridges of every one of Douglassaire's muscles, then held on as he was lifted into the air. He wrapped his legs around Doug's waist until he landed softly on his back in the bed.

Slade felt the warm pressure of Doug's hand against his chest and was shocked at the sensation of his shirt being ripped down the middle in one quick motion. Buttons flew everywhere. Doug noticed the concerned look on Slade's face and said, "You can afford it." Slade offered no contest and allowed himself the pleasure of exploring Doug's body while his own was devoured inch by inch.

II

Douglassaire's baritone voice caused Slade to stir. He squinted, shielding his eyes from the sunlight that flooded in as Doug held open the curtain to the balcony door. Doug was busy talking on the comm. About what, Slade didn't know, nor did he try. Slade, desperate for a continued period of rest, turned and buried his head under the covers. They both fell asleep much too late and the day broke much too soon. Slade felt himself drifting back to sleep, but not before hearing Doug say, "Yes, to Cloudswell Peak. Thank you." Slade wondered what he was up to, but before he could ask, his body fully accepted the invitation of sleep from the mattress below.

***

Gisela could hear birds chirping outside signaling the coming of a new day. She was used to getting up early at home to complete some of the chores around the house. She shuddered. She didn't want to think about her house, much less her grandmother. The fight they'd had over this trip was colossal, but Gisela finally won her grandmother's permission to go. It was nice to wake up and have no responsibilities or drama for a change. Without those responsibilities, she had time to come up with a plan to finally win Slade over. She figured she'd take him out to breakfast this morning. She'd have to find a way to separate from Doug, but when she did, she and Slade would enjoy another great afternoon exploring a new place. Then at nighttime, she'd top it all off by wearing some sexy underwear she bought in Reor and visiting his room. She'd let his hands take care of the rest. She chuckled and felt giddy about the whole thing. It would work, though. And she was looking forward to it.

She treated herself to a long shower, and after, got dressed in a tank top, shorts, and some old sneakers. She looked at the clock and figured she was probably still too early to bother Slade if he was sleeping, but she was excited and ready to go enjoy herself. *Forget Slade*, she thought, *I'll just have to wake him up.*

She closed the door to her room behind her and as she stepped into the hotel hallway, she saw Douglassaire coming out of Slade's room. Her enthusiasm for this trip began to wilt. She remained unnoticed as he tried closing the door without making any sound. Once he turned the corner towards the elevators, Gisela moved to the big window in the hallway overlooking the front lot and watched. After a few minutes, a taxi rolled up and Doug got in. As it drove away, Gisela walked to Slade's door and began knocking. She surprised herself at how hard she knocked. She had only planned a polite, soft knock that would wake up a, perhaps, half-asleep Slade, but seeing Douglassaire gave her the wrath to wake the dead.

The door swung open to a bewildered Slade. "What?"

Gisela tried her best to save face. "...I just wanted to see if you were awake."

"I am now," Slade growled, holding the door open. He was still trying to fight off his fatigue.

Gisela entered the room and propped herself against the small kitchenette counter. She would have told Slade to get ready for a day of fun, but said nothing. She denied the suspicion and anger bubbling just beneath the surface. *Nothing happened,* she told herself. She noticed Slade's eyes searching around the room, completely oblivious to her distaste. Dryly, she answered his obvious question, "He's gone, Slade."

"You saw him?"

"Creeping out of the room like a thief." The word used to describe Doug resonated with her as she said it. "Slade, do we really need him around?"

"He invited us, Gisela, we can't just leave and do our own thing."

"Well, he's certainly doing his."

"What do you mean? He's two doors down." Slade made his way back to his bedside and picked his destroyed shirt off the ground.

Gisela followed closely behind. "I mean he's gone. He didn't go back to his room. He left." She digested the mess of clothes on the floor and the bed that looked used on both sides. She knew what happened in here when she saw Doug leave the room, but it wasn't made real until now. He *was* a thief. And she couldn't stand him. She could feel her emotions welling up and asked, "Slade, what did you two—"

"Shit…" Slade muttered, picking up a piece of paper from the nightstand.

"What is it?"

Slade handed her the slip of paper and she read the message from Doug:

Going to do something crazy. Don't stop me. If I don't come back, I'm glad you believed in me.
- Doug

"What does this mean?" Gisela asked.

Slade thought for a moment and a hazy memory that seemed out of reach suddenly became clear. "Cloudswell Peak."

"What?"

"I think Doug's gonna jump!"

CHAPTER THIRTEEN

I

If Slade could control the driver's mind to make him drive faster he would. He told him to take them to Cloudswell Peak as fast as possible, but the speed wasn't enough to calm his nerves. This was an emergency. Slade wiped sweat from his forehead, fearing the worst had already happened. He hated Gisela's calm demeanor as she sat next to him.

The tall hill known as Cloudswell Peak overlooked a small lake. The base was lush with perfectly manicured green grass and tall trees that dwindled in number the higher up one climbed. The scene grew closer and closer until, finally, the cab stopped just before the peak's dirt path that led upward. Slade jumped out and began running up to the highest point of the hill where it reached a cliff. Gisela begrudgingly handed the driver some cash and darted off after him.

Slade followed the beaten path through the trees that obscured his view of the top. As the altitude climbed, his view became clearer and he stopped just beyond the point where the last trees stood and gazed out at the stretch of land before him. Gisela caught up to him and gasped in disbelief at the sight of Douglassaire falling over the edge of the peak.

Slade bolted and screamed, "Doug!"

Gisela kept up with Slade and held him back from falling over, himself, instead bringing him to his knees in despair. She held on to him from behind with her arms wrapped tight around his chest. With her head rested against his back she felt his body shiver in silent anguish. She stared blankly into the open sky feeling nothing, as her mind replayed a scene that took place years ago on a frozen lake in the Northern Third.

II

"You again?" said a booming voice. Douglassaire could feel the air pass through his body as he traveled downward. The air spirit conversed with him once more, "What is it?"

"Will I be the same?" Douglassaire asked.

"What?"

"If I surrender myself. Will I still be me?"

"That all depends on the strength of your will. If you think you can suppress me, then give it a go. But I should tell you, I am a conqueror by nature."

"You're speaking to the future Commander of the Southern Third. We'll see who's stronger."

Suddenly, everything went black.

III

Slade was finally able to stand. With Gisela's arm wrapped around his shoulder they began to walk back down the hill.

"Slade," Gisela began, breaking the silence, "why would he do that?" She waited for an answer that never came. "Slade, you still have me." She saw only a look of pain in his eyes that transferred to her as he removed her arm.

As Slade broke free of her grasp, he saw the sky darken and felt a strong gust of wind push past him. He shuffled his feet to regain his balance and saw Gisela had fallen over with her palms to the ground. They could feel it coming from all directions. They remained still, bracing themselves from the gale as their minds worked to figure out what was happening.

Gisela had to yell over the loud, hollow whistling of the winds. "What is this?"

Slade looked up in horror as he saw the air swirling into a tornado just past the peak. The mass of dark grey was closing in on the peak and would soon touch down and obliterate everything in sight. Gisela was able to stand and fight her way over to Slade. "We've got to go!" she said.

"Wait!" Slade's horror transformed to awe as the winds died down. The sky began to brighten up again and the tornado dissipated revealing a sight that set Slade's heart at ease. "It's Doug. He did it! Doug!" Slade called, waving.

Douglassaire slowly drifted to the ground, carried by the gentle winds that were once furious. He was nearly tackled by Slade's enthusiastic embrace. Slade had much to say, but could not find the words. Instead, he stared at a mark on the back of Doug's neck and wondered if it had always been there. It looked like a black triangle with a line of skin at the top separating the apex from its base.

Gisela stood back watching the reunion. Exhausted, she said, "Could somebody please tell me what's going on?"

CHAPTER FOURTEEN

I

The travel time to the Incaen Forest lessened as Gisela, Douglassaire, and Slade rode north, and the afternoon was slowly turning to night. Gisela sat alone at the window seat of the tourist bus, while the other two rode in front of her. She had always wanted to see something as spectacular as the ever-burning Incaen Forest, but now she seethed at the idea. Ever since that day in class Slade had seemed obsessed with ethereal powers – not to mention Doug. Now, miraculously, Doug had powers of his own, and suddenly Slade wasn't as interested in her friendship anymore. She thought this trip would turn her and Slade into a couple, but Slade seemed farther away than ever. She wasn't giving up, however. Maybe what she thought happened between Slade and Doug didn't really happen. She hadn't actually seen them in the act after all. In that case, she still had a shot and she would keep her eye on Douglassaire to learn the truth. She also had to figure out Slade's true feelings for her. Hope kept her holding on.

She was finally clued in on why Doug jumped off of a cliff, and how he survived. Apparently risking your life and allowing yourself to be possessed by a spirit of Ether gave one the powers of an Etherean. Outvoted, the boys decided to visit the Incaen Forest to see if a spirit called out to Slade or herself. Slade didn't say it, but Gisela knew him well enough to tell that he thought it was his turn now – a sure sign to Gisela of how bad an influence Doug was. She didn't care for any of this. It certainly wasn't worth risking her life.

She did notice that Doug was his usual self. He didn't seem possessed. Nor could he summon a tornado or fly again like he had at Cloudswell Peak. He gave some weird explanation that he subdued the air spirit inside of him allowing him to keep his wits about him. He could still manipulate air a little bit, but it would take either years of practice or complete surrender in order to do things like that again. It was all too outlandish for her taste.

***

The night sky full of bright, twinkling stars finally overtook the landscape. As the bus got closer to its destination, the stars became less and less visible. The bus slowed to a halt as everyone inside gasped at the sight of the burning forest surrounded by a high ridge. Around thirty people, some with children, had their cameras ready as they unloaded from the bus to get a closer look. The tour guide cautioned them all not to get too close. Slade, Doug, and Gisela were the last three to step out. They felt the heat and took in the amazing sight of a forest with flames that refused to spread beyond its own border.

The expected scent of burning wood was nowhere to be found. As the group looked closer, they could see the flames didn't destroy anything; they merely covered the leaves and the trees like an armor.

Douglassaire felt the air spirit inside of him react. He felt heavy, almost as if gravity pulled on him like a magnet. He also got a sense of familiarity…like he was meeting an old friend he hadn't seen in years. "This has to be it," he said. "You guys ready to find out?"

Gisela's attitude remained unchanged, but her curiosity was piqued. "We'll have to get away from all of these people first."

They separated themselves from the group and walked to the far edge of the forest. Slade was already distracted by a raspy voice: "Oh no, not another one."

127

"Gisela, did you just hear something?" Slade asked.

"What? No," she replied. She saw him take a small step toward the forest and started after him, but was stopped by Douglassaire who placed his arm in front of her.

Douglassaire recognized that sense of wonder and fear in Slade's eyes. "Let him go," he told Gisela.

"Who is that?" Slade called out into the forest. He ventured closer, out of earshot of his friends.

The voice continued, "You know exactly who I am, Slade Maxwell. You called to me, didn't you? But I don't have time for weaklings. Go away."

Slade could feel his heart begin to beat faster. Just last night he doubted Doug's claim, but here he was now speaking to a real spirit of Ether. "I want your power."

"Ha! Why, so you can impress your friends? Taking me on requires more than just vanity. Come, I dare you. You'll be burnt to a crisp – just like the countless others who have tried these past centuries."

Slade's fascination with Ethereans suddenly came to a head. Never had he thought it possible to be one. His body felt charged and the warm light of the flame was enchanting. He thought of how Douglassaire made it one step closer to his goal, and he wanted badly to be a part of that future. This was a way...and Douglassaire was watching. There was no way he was going to let him down here.

Ready to take the risk, Slade took a deep breath and walked faster toward the Incaen Forest. Just as he got to the edge, he heard Gisela screaming, "No!" He felt her arms wrap around him and fell backward on top of her, just in time to dodge a ball of flame that shot out just over their heads and into the sky.

Slade could hear the spirit as it laughed, "You are unfit for a vessel. And, quite frankly, you bore me."

"What are you, crazy?" Gisela exclaimed to Slade.

"Dammit, Gisela," Slade said, hastily getting up.

"You would have died."

"You don't know that. We just saw Doug do it this morning."

"Well, you're not him. Doug's special."

Slade shot her a look of disgust. He wasn't special to her? It was one thing to be rejected by Mason, even by the fire spirit, but his own friend, too? "Oh yeah? Well, guess what? You're not special to me either."

The verbal jabs left them both breathless. Slade's desire for a different life was his attempt at being special. Hearing Gisela say this just confirmed his fears that he would never make it. Really, who was he to even remotely think about any kind of relationship with someone like Douglassaire? He figured Doug would eventually reject him too. Once again, he opened himself up to people who let him down. He decided right then and there, never again.

With his spirit crushed, he started walking back to the bus. He averted his gaze from Douglassaire as he walked past.

"You okay?" Doug asked.

Slade stopped and looked back at Doug. "We're just too different, Doug. I realize that now." He turned his back and walked to the bus.

II

The ride back to their hotel was long and silent. Slade sat in the back of the bus surrounded with other tourists sitting on either side while Gisela and Douglassaire sat in separate seats further ahead. He knew his only chance at surviving his encounter with the fire spirit was complete resolve, intention, and a lack of fear, but Gisela shattered that for him. He regretted bringing her along, he hated himself for not being able to go through with it, and worst of all, he couldn't face Doug and not be as special as he was. Gisela was right. Doug was too adventurous and spontaneous. Slade figured himself to be too timid. Eventually, Doug would get bored and move on. So, Slade sat in the back of the bus, alone, determined to accept the inevitable sooner, rather than later.

Gisela had never felt so abandoned since the day her mother passed. She sat towards the middle of the bus with her back turned and her face to the window losing the fight against her tears. She cared about Slade so much, but his nasty words showed what he really felt. The fuel that propelled her life had suddenly burned out. She didn't know why she was being punished for saving her friend's life, but perhaps she didn't deserve happiness. Not after killing her mother, as her grandmother so often reminded. She wasn't even supposed to be here. *I should have died a long time ago.* This was a thought that she only spoke aloud once in her life with a simple "Yes," as her grandmother's response. She promised herself to never speak it or think it again – if not for herself, then just to spite her grandmother. However, this night gave life to her buried feelings.

As the bus came to its stop, Gisela left in hurry. She went into her hotel room to gather her things, left, and hailed the nearest cab. Slade watched from the hallway window as it sped off to the skyport where she would find the earliest flight back to the Northern Third. Douglassaire went back to his nearly unused room and waited. He would never admit it, but he feared Slade's rejection should he go to him once more. He sat in silence waiting for a knock on the door that never came.

CHAPTER FIFTEEN

Burrow University felt its warmest days yet. With spring break a thing of the past and final exams shortly ahead, the mixture of academic pressure and excitement for a long summer break was contagious. For some, this time in life meant even more. Some would graduate, and with that came the mark of the end of an era. For Gisela, that end came earlier than expected.

She saw Slade in their one class together from time to time, but no words were ever exchanged. They no longer sat next to each other and Gisela always tried to avoid the awkward situation of noticing him on campus by focusing on whatever book she had in front of her. She hadn't seen Douglassaire at all, not that she was looking for him. Lesech had even once asked her (though she felt more cornered) "Where's Douglassaire?" She supposed he stayed behind in the Southern Third.

She often wondered if Slade ever thought of her – if she ever meant anything to him in the first place. Those thoughts would sadden her, but, try as she might, she couldn't ferret them away. If only she could have read Slade's mind she would know that he often wondered the same. She couldn't, however, and settled on the most practical explanation she could come up with: he didn't. The incident at the Incaen Forest – those words and his face as he said them – would be one she knew she'd never forget.

Everything looked so bland to her now. Her home, Burrow University, even the people in it. Many who have traveled said that the North just cannot compare. After seeing such wonders in the Middle and Southern Third, the North was very mellow by comparison. Gisela was glad to have seen some of those places, but knew she would never see them again. She hated being back home. She could never do anything right for her grandmother and she began to accept that she was more of a burden on both her family and friends. All she had left was her mother in the lake.

She sat there now, at Lake Maesus, in her usual pose with her arms wrapped around her knees. She looked around as well as she could in the darkness to make sure she was the only one there. She was, and she began to converse with the only one who would give her comfort. "Mama, I'm tired. I tried so hard to do the right thing, but I can't do it anymore. Nothing is good enough. Everyone I love goes away – you and now Slade. I don't think I'll ever be happy." She began to wipe away her tears. "It should have been me who died, not you. I wish I had."

She could feel her body tighten. It ached badly for release. She felt a tugging in her heart towards the lake and subconsciously accepted the faint voice in her head as a symptom of her despair. "Come, Gisela…be with mother," it said. Had it been one of her own thoughts? Whatever it was, it was enough to convince her to go. She no longer needed to think about it. She had no one and desperately wanted to be with her mother again.

She got up to her feet and began to walk to the lake. The grass squished with each step she took until the toe of her sneaker first touched the water. Whether the water was warm or cold Gisela did not know. She had become numb to all senses. The water gathered around her ankles, then up to her knees, and finally to her waist when she stopped. She heard something again.

"That's right, Gisela…mother is waiting."

The voice!

Gisela's depression turned to fear. What spoke was definitely not her mother. She turned to make her way back to dry land, but it was too late. She couldn't move as the current became strong and tugged on her body. Small spouts of water rose from the lake; they twisted and formed arms that grabbed and wrapped around Gisela. And before she could scream for help, a watery hand covered her mouth. She could feel its frigid squeeze against her nose and mouth as it pulled her head below.

PART TWO

CHAPTER SIXTEEN

I

Septentrion City was a wonder to behold on the night of the Leaders Ball. The Northern Third played host this year to a party that celebrated the signing of the Nomiso Agreement, and its capital city was extravagantly decorated for the occasion.

White buildings, colored with lights for the occasion, lined either side of the main street that led to the Presidents' Manse at the top of the hill in the distance. A long pedestrians-only walkway was paved at the center of the street, and on either side lie the roadway for vehicles to come and go in opposite directions. The traffic was light that night as only invited guests were permitted there in their wheelers and limousines. Bystanders gawked at the luxurious parade of wheelers with tinted windows only dreaming of who was inside and lucky enough to be invited to the big event. All of the vehicles were on their way to the top of the hill where a red carpet led to the open doors of the Presidents' Manse with its tall white columns towering high over the crowd.

A black limo pulled up to the edge of the carpet and from either side came a man and a woman. They were instantly bombarded with the blinding white lights of cameras. The man, with short, wavy blonde hair, wore a black tuxedo and waved at

137

the mass of cameras with a big-toothed grin. He walked over to the other side of the limo and took his lady's gloved hand. The wheeler pulled off as they slowly walked the carpet and paused in front of the step-and-repeat for glamorous photos that would end up in the national news the next day. People would see a handsome man with a beautiful woman at his side with long, brown hair and a green dress to bring out the color of her eyes, and the envy in her audience. They would envy her sense of style – she, with her black princess gloves and black fur shawl to barely protect from the cold. They would envy her riches and wonder what life must be like to afford diamond earrings, a bracelet, a ring, and a necklace big enough to cover the entirety of her bare upper chest. Most of all, they would envy how that girl from the sticks of Ankor managed to start dating the most powerful businessman in the Northern Third. Gisela knew this, and with every flash of the camera she reveled in the words of tomorrow.

That was her name now. Gisela, or Gigi, as her boyfriend called her. The water spirit from Lake Maesus finally took control of a vessel and had to constantly remind herself of her new identity. She had been stuck in that lake ever since leaving Ether and got the sense that she was the only one of her brethren who hadn't experienced Elao's Pangaea. Well, her time had finally come. For millennia, she promised herself that once she walked the earth she would experience only the best of what humans could provide. Her first act at the lake was to throw away her vessel's old glasses. The human body contained more than enough water for her to control its natural healing process. There was no need for glasses now, for now her eyesight was fine. Now, as she stood at the Presidents' Manse in front of the flashing lights, she found the best of humanity quite enjoyable. Still, she was learning more and more about humans every day, and one theory she had about them was never disproven: humans are strange creatures. For example, their obsession with status fractured them. It was one of the first lessons she learned. In order to experience what humans saw as the best in life, she would have to be a rich non-Etherean – preferably from the Middle Third. The girl she inhabited was a Northerner, so she would have to do, but she could still hide her powers well enough to be thought of as non-Etherean. However, becoming rich was an obstacle she had to tackle. After meeting Wellesley and seeing that he could provide the wealth, she manipulated her way into his life, and wrapped him around her finger in the form of an engagement ring. Now, all that was left was to make the money permanent and then take Wellesley out of the equation. Everything was going according to plan.

She could stay in front of the cameras all night, but her fiancé had had enough, and with a polite nod to the press and a tug at her elbow, they moved closer to the door. Before entering, they approached their last stop where a woman in a simple yellow gown with a microphone in her hand waited. She greeted the couple warmly before speaking into the nearby camera. "I'm here with Wellesley van der Borea and Septentrion City's new it girl, Gigi, who is just dazzling tonight. I have to ask you, Wellesley, what does it mean to be invited to the Leaders Ball?"

Wellesley flashed a grin and ran his fingers through his golden hair. "It's always an honor to be invited to the Leaders Ball. I've gone for the past two years when the Southern and then Middle Third hosted, and I can already tell that the Northern Third will have the best one yet."

"I wonder why! Could it be a result of having a date with you for the first time?"

Wellesley chuckled. "Septentrion City is my hometown, so I'm extremely biased, but having my fiancé by my side is definitely the cherry on top." He looked into Gigi's eyes and said, "And as important as this occasion is it won't top our wedding just a week away."

Gigi returned a huge smile. *Just keep playing the part*, she told herself.

The interview continued. "There's talk that Commander Azure could announce his retirement tonight. What do you think will happen?"

"I doubt anyone would give up their seat of power so easily, but his retirement does mean a new Power Battle! Who isn't excited for that?"

"Wellesley, thank you. You both have a great time tonight."

The woman bid them both farewell and announced into the camera over a loud outburst of cheers, "I can see all the way down the red carpet and it looks like Lesech has finally arrived!"

Gigi paused and looked behind her at the mention of his name. She could make out Lesech's signature hairstyle and skinny frame among the crowded red carpet. He smiled and waved at his fans and paused for pictures of his outfit. He was one of the few men that dressed in color that night with a dark red tuxedo jacket and necktie. A memory briefly flashed through her head – a memory belonging to the vessel she controlled, the old Gisela. It had been four years since she last saw him face to face. She wondered if he'd remember her at all.

Wellesley and Gigi finally entered the Presidents' Manse where the carpet led them directly to the expansive ballroom. Wide white ribbons trimmed in gold hung from the ceiling and were attached to the great chandelier overseeing the whole room at the center. The white and gold tables and chairs completed the exquisite theme. They greeted, smiled, and hugged their way through the crowd of celebrities and government officials as they were ushered to their table. The rest of the seats at the small round table were empty except for the one next to Gigi where an older lady sat. She had grey hair, wrinkles at the corners of her eyes, and wore a simple black dress with only a small necklace.

Gigi and Wellesley sat down, trying to acknowledge the lady, but received no warmth or greetings from her. Wellesley leaned back in his chair with his arm rested on the back of Gigi's, behind her head. Gigi removed her shawl and sat it on her lap, then turned and kissed her man on the cheek.

"What was that for?" Wellesley asked.

She patted his thigh with her hand and said, "Thanks for bringing me this year. This is amazing."

He leaned over and kissed her on the forehead. "Glad I could make it happen." Something caught Wellesley's eye. "I'll be right back." He got up and waved at someone. Gisela craned her neck to see who and saw it was one of his business partners. She turned away from the sight of her fiancé's chat and saw the lady next to her giving her a strange look. Gigi didn't know what the woman's problem was, so she put her elbow on the table and used her arm as a stem as she rested her chin on the back of her hand and stared back.

The old woman next to her looked at the garish, over-accessorized Gigi and said, "First time here?"

"Yes. Is this your last?"

"Hmph. I may be mature, but I've still many years left and many of these events to attend in the years ahead. This may be your last, however. Wellesley is very experienced in marriages."

Gigi focused her water control on the woman's glass of wine until small bubbles foamed at the top. Unbeknownst to the woman, her wine turned into bitter vinegar. Gigi said, "Well, you know what they say, Third time's a charm." She pretended to turn her attention away from the woman, but continued watching out of the corner of her eye. The woman picked up her glass, took a sip, and immediately coughed and spit out the spoiled wine onto the table and her dress. Gigi feigned surprise, giggled, and scooted her chair a few inches away from the woman to complete her embarrassment.

The people standing around with their wine glasses all began to finish their quick introductions and catch-ups and find their seats. The remaining spaces at Gigi's table slowly became occupied by other couples and noteworthy individuals – including Lesech who had a seat directly across from her. He paid her no mind as he turned in his seat to face the main table that was raised on a platform. Wellesley came back and sat in his seat.

"Enjoy your conversation?" Gigi asked. A man appeared at the podium next to the main table on the platform. As two servers poured red wine into the goblets and perfected the placement of the plates and silverware, he raised his hands to quiet the audience. The remaining stragglers quickly got to their seats and the room began to hush.

"Very much," said Wellesley.

The man began his announcement. "Ladies and gentlemen, thank you for joining us on such a special occasion. Tonight we celebrate the unity of our nations and continue to work towards an everlasting peace. So, without further ado, please stand as I introduce to you our esteemed triumvirate: from the Southern

Third, Commander Azure!"

Everyone rose to their feet and applauded as the Southern leader appeared on the stage. His neatly cut hair was white with age and he held on to a long, wooden cane to support his painfully slow and careful walk across the stage. He wore a broadsword at his hip and framed his tuxedo with an ornate, deep red cape with black epaulets. His wrinkled face remained solemn as he waved to his audience. As strong as he tried to appear, most everyone knew this would probably be his last time at a Leaders Ball. He shook the announcer's hand and took his seat at the far end of the table.

"And from the Middle Third, please welcome Queen Aeothesca!"

Queen Aeothesca came out wearing an extravagant, bejeweled, forest green dress. Her red hair was pulled into a long ponytail that stayed as poised as her steady walk across the stage. Her lady-in-waiting, Catherine, wore a simple black pantsuit and followed her, holding the train of her dress. The queen stopped midway and bowed a curtsy to the audience, then gave her hand to the announcer for a kiss. Once she settled in her seat in the middle of the table, Catherine stood only a few feet away behind her.

"And last, but certainly not least, from the Northern Third, please welcome President Yu!"

The president stepped out with a big smile and soaked in all of the applause. His black tux was accented by a golden sash over one shoulder and his short black hair was slicked to the side. He shook the announcer's hand and gestured for his audience to sit as he took his place at the podium.

He began, "Queen Aeothesca, Commander Azure, and esteemed guests…thank you for joining us in what marks the twenty-sixth anniversary of the Nomiso Agreement. We've come a long way in so short a time and the peace we've achieved really is cause for celebration. Thanks to the support our great nations have shown each other, we have progressed farther than we ever imagined. However, now is not the time to stop. We in the Northern Third still have much to do in order to catch up to our peers. It's a well-known joke that the Northern Third is stuck in the past, but I believe that with help we can step into the future. That's why I'm proud to announce a partnership with Queen Aeothesca on the betterment of our daily travel. The Middle Third is a beacon of technological advances that is rivaled by the Southern Third. Now, with this new partnership, our nation will soon enjoy the luxuries of the rest of the world and finally join today's Pangaea." He ended his brief speech and mouthed the words "thank you" as he took in the applause with a look of satisfaction on his face.

The announcer returned to the podium as the president took his seat at the other side of the queen. "Thank you, Mr. President. Now, I believe Commander Azure has a special announcement to make and then we'll follow with a dinner prayer by the queen."

The Commander pressed down on his cane and slowly got to his feet. The crowd watched all of this silently, unbeknownst to each other that they shared the same uneasiness at the idea that the Commander could fall over at any second. He took his time making it to the podium on which he was visibly relieved that he could lean, and all at once the room's tension was released as well. He cleared his throat and began: "I've served and protected the people of my country to the best of my ability over the years, and I've seen it all – war and peace. President Yu had many years before he would become president, but Queen Aeothesca remembers. She was there just as I was. The war dealt a blow to all of us – especially the Southern Third. The earth broke open at just the right time to devour my men. I will never forget. I vowed then that I would never allow such a tragedy to happen again. I want to keep true to that promise, and so I've decided, contrary to what you all may have heard, to continue serving as Commander." He stole a glance over his shoulder at the queen. "There are certain people among us with devilish powers and evil intent, and they must be rooted out before I allow my seat to be taken by one of them. The much anticipated Power Battle will have to wait, but I know this in my heart to be the best for the Southern Third."

Every eye in the room was fixed on the Commander as he made this revelation. Everyone's eyes except Gigi's.

143

Unimpressed, she sipped on her wine and glanced across the table at Lesech. He looked even more intense than usual. The vessel's memories of his training flashed through her head and suddenly she knew that he would attempt to take part in this...Power Battle, whatever it was. She also got a vision of a man, jumping off of a cliff and becoming the vessel for the air spirit. *Douglassaire, was it? Would he participate as well?* As the Commander continued to speak she noticed she wasn't the only one paying him little mind. She felt another pair of eyes on her. The queen sat still, perched in her middle chair on the stage, giving her a cold glare. *Is she looking at me?* Gigi wondered. And then she felt stunned. How had she not noticed before? Her body felt heavy and she caught a glimpse of recognition in the queen. *So that's where you've been,* she thought to herself. Then, she felt a tinge of jealousy. The earth spirit was a queen! Suddenly her idea of the best of humanity did not seem to compare with the station of a queen.

Commander Azure continued, "As Commander I swear to continue this legacy of peace and protection for our country. Thank you." Everyone applauded politely, but most were disappointed in not receiving the news they expected. They'd have to wait a little longer for the start of such a momentous occasion as the Power Battle.

As the Commander struggled to make his way back to his seat, Queen Aeothesca stood and immediately Commander Azure went down. Clapping turned to gasps and screams of horror as the Commander's body dropped to the floor with a loud thud. Warriors from the Southern Army immediately rushed the stage to see if he was okay. After a moment, one of them flipped him over and began CPR.

Gigi stood at her table while trying to hide a nervous smile. Everyone around her was shaken. She heard a woman crying in the distance and people praying for the Commander's health. The crowd was noisy with worry and everyone wondered if the Commander would be okay. However, Gigi began to wonder something else: How did the Commander's cane suddenly fly out across the room? To her, the whole scene was fascinating.

CPR didn't seem to work. The warrior kept pumping his

leader's chest while the others stood by, unsure of what to do next. Finally, another warrior, seeing that his comrade's efforts were futile, touched his shoulder and repeated something that wasn't clear until he raised his voice. "That's enough!"

The crowd went silent. Queen Aeothesca stood still at the table, her heart racing as she braced herself for what she knew was likely to come next.

The warrior who was desperately trying to resuscitate Commander Azure stood, pointed at her over the table and screamed, "She did this! His walking stick flew out of his hands. You all saw it. Only an Etherean could do such an unnatural thing."

Catherine came from her post behind the queen and stood next to her. "Hold your tongue, Southerner! You are addressing the queen!"

"She is no queen of mine," the warrior said as he withdrew his sword. He paid no mind to his comrades' calls to calm down. The temperature in the room seemed to rise for everyone. The queen stood still with a sword in her face. Something was bound to happen. Some of the onlookers disappeared through the doors of the ballroom, desperate for calm and safety. Others couldn't draw their eyes away from the commotion. Unbeknownst to the soldier, Catherine slowly reached for the goblet of red wine at the table. The soldier concluded with a swift strike at the queen, yelling, "She is a murderer!"

Catherine was quick. While holding the goblet, she threw the wine at the warrior and froze the liquid that came out, creating a sharp sword with which she used to slice a deep opening at his neck. A smattering of blood sprayed out from the wound as the soldier fell on his back, and with her free hand, she redirected it to the soldiers standing by, soaking them in red. "His blood is on your hands, alone!" She threw down the goblet and grabbed the queen's train, urging, "Shall we go, Your Majesty?"

As everyone began rushing toward the exit, Gigi kept her eye on the queen's servant thinking, *That girl is very talented.* She then felt her arm being pulled by Wellesley.

"Let's go. Now!" he commanded. She shook her arm free from his grasp and calmly walked behind him toward the exit, smiling at the spectacle. She took a last look at the stage and watched the queen who in turn took a final glimpse at her. Queen Aeothesca briefly spoke to a man and then disappeared through the door in the back. Gigi instinctively rubbed the black, upside-down triangle mark on her neck, obscured by her hair, and continued with Wellesley to safely find her way to the exit.

II

The queen's supertrop, the *Guardian*, was one-of-a-kind. The whole craft was an emerald green color from the nose to its rounded body and elegant, flowing wings. It would use the lights on its exterior to be seen by the world as the queen made a dramatic entrance or exit. Tonight, the queen decided her exit from the Leaders Ball was dramatic enough and it flew through the air with stealth.

Catherine paced back and forth in front of Queen Aeothesca who sat in the big chair. Her footsteps sounded heavy against the carpeted floor. The cabin was designed to look similar to the throne room so it was natural for them to resume their places. Everything that had just happened churned Catherine's adrenaline and she began exercising the freedoms of a now four-year-old friendship with the queen by speaking all that was on her mind.

"Those Southern dogs! How dare they? Accusing you of assassination? They have lost their leader and now they have lost their heads. I am just glad I was there to defend you, my lady."

Calmly the queen responded, "I am grateful for your actions, but I assure you that I did not need defending."

Catherine bowed her head. "I know that, my queen. But...might I ask, why are you so calm? Have you not been shaken by what transpired?"

Queen Aeothesca stood and slowly walked to the window, gazing out at the swiftly passing night sky. "Shaken? No. To be honest, Commander Azure's death pleases me." She looked at the reflection on the window and saw Catherine's puzzled expression. "Please, dear. If I wanted to kill the man, I would have stuck that cane through his heart, not thrown it away like a mischievous child. No, that was not my doing, and I am not shaken. I am angry. You heard what the Commander said: ...*devilish powers and evil intent*. That was directed at me! These people pretend to accept me – accept us – and when anything happens, they look at us like we're monsters. I have been called *that* enough in my lifetime, but to be called a murderer! I have never been so insulted in my life! I grow tired of trying to fit in with these lesser beings. After all this time, after all of my protections and all I have done for them, I still do not have their trust. I have not told you this, Catherine, but often I wonder if Elao even exists."

Catherine gasped, "My lady! That's blasphemy."

"I care not! It is as though God himself has left my side long ago. All I have is myself. All we have is each other."

"You are angry, Your Majesty. Surely, you don't believe that. However, the Nomiso Agreement is all but burned. What will you do?"

"I will ruin them. The Southern Third has not seen real battle in over twenty years. I could, perhaps, strike when they find their new, inexperienced Commander."

A faint smile appeared on Catherine's face. Seeing the queen lash out was most enjoyable. It was even more fun to be a part of her wickedness. "You will go to war? Can I help? I could be a most valuable asset."

"You are of no use to me on the battlefield."

"You have trained me—"

"Only for using your ether," the queen responded with a furrowed brow. "Not for combat."

"Is that not quite similar? Also, I have been trained—"

"This is not up for debate!"

Catherine stopped lest the queen's anger turn to her. She settled in her mind that she would show the queen just how useful she could be. That would be for another day. Back on topic, she asked, "Will you speak with the advisory board?"

"The board is but a scale for me to weigh my decisions. After tonight, there is no need for them. I've never been so clear in all my life."

"And what of the North?"

"President Yu will not interfere. We are already too much a part of their lives. Perhaps we shall bring them into the new world by force after the South is handled. I do not know how, but whatever the method, I will control them both. I will make this world show respect for real power."

CHAPTER SEVENTEEN

I

The offices of M.3.A.N. were buzzing with talk about what happened at the Leaders Ball. The usually muted screens on the walls were alive with sound and many were standing and watching with disbelief. The newscast was rolling a repeated recording of Commander Azure's final moments.

"He slipped!" someone said.

"That's not just a slip. His cane practically ended up on the other side of the room," said another. "I think it *is* murder."

Ceiling lights illuminated the thirty-seventh floor of the high rise. The windows were tinted to keep the sun's glare off of the screens as all of the workers watched from their cubicles in anticipation of what came next.

"Everyone, I need your attention," announced a man as he turned the corner into the room. The screens were turned off and everyone stood up to listen. Slade, known to his colleagues as Director Maxwell, wore a fitted navy blue suit with a white shirt. As usual garb for department heads, the jacket was long and stopped just above the knee, giving it a small bounce with each step he took. The signature white flame logo of the Middle Third was stitched on the breast. With his chin up and shoulders back, he began to speak: "As you all know, the events at the Leaders

Ball and the death of Commander Azure are currently being investigated by the Southern Third. They believe, as well as many others, that our queen had something to do with it. Now, I've been in meetings with the other directors all day and communicating with the queen, and she asks us to do an investigation of our own. We've all agreed that this was indeed an assassination. Based on the physical evidence we have, Commander Azure's cane ended up an unnatural distance away from where he fell. This was no accident. This was the work of an Etherean with the ability to remove his cane without being noticed. The Southern Third is in an uproar and will no doubt try to come up with some evidence against the queen. It's our job to find out who the culprit really is and bring them to justice. The list of attendees has been uploaded to your stations as well as photos and video of the event. I expect a solid list of suspects by the end of the day. This is a special case where the queen, herself, has taken authority. Our orders are to take no action in apprehending the suspect without consulting her first. I'm sure I don't have to outline the implications of this case, but to be clear – the Nomiso Agreement, our queen, and our era of peace in Pangaea is now under enormous threat. Let's do our best to keep the peace." He brought his right fist to his heart and rallied his colleagues. "For the queen!"

They all did the same and chanted, "For the queen!"

The mood of decorum broke and everyone sat in their seats and went straight to work on their new task. Slade walked away to his own office and let the door slide shut as he put his hands on the window sill, hunched over and breathed a sigh of relief. Addressing his coworkers like that would take some getting used to. Just a week ago, he was sitting in there with all of them, and now he was in charge. He wasn't prepared for an assassination to fall on his lap, but then again, who was? He looked out into the darkening sky of Reor and saw constant movement. Civilian vehicles hovering inches off the ground zipped through the city, while official government air cars took the literal, less-congested, high road and flew to and fro. Lights from the entertainment district began flashing, beckoning for a night of fun. For Slade, everything in life had been moving so fast that past week that he hardly had a moment to think until then. *So, this is what power feels like?* he thought. *A mixture of awe and stress.* He realized his new position as Director had only given him a taste of this power. He remembered standing in this same spot and speaking with the man he replaced. Looking out the window, the man said to him in great pomposity, "In this city, what you see is what you own." Slade thought he was delusional then, but now found the draw to that conclusion very alluring. He could see a great deal of Reor and with the authority he'd been granted, he had to be careful not to fall into the same state of mind as his predecessor. He had a method, and it was to wonder what the view was like from the grounds of Lorelei Castle. One could probably see the world from there. He could hardly imagine the magnetic pull toward corruption for those who looked down from that great height.

A chime from the monitor on his desk pulled him away from his deep thinking. He checked a message that came in:

> *Mission success. Now tracking the VIP target.*
> *Icarus*

Slade studied the small portrait of the agent that appeared next to the heading of the message. Whoever Agent Icarus was, Slade had no idea. He wondered what their mission was and who they were tracking, but eased his mind and settled on the fact that it was none of his concern. In top secret cases like these, his only job was to forward any messages to the higher-ups in the castle. As he did, he immediately received a ring through his work comm. which sat on the edge of his desk. It was too early for any answer on the new case he just presented, so he had an idea who was trying to reach him. He pressed the flashing button on the comm. and put it on speaker. "Director Maxwell," he said.

"Yes, Director, there is a call from a Regina Maxwell."

As he expected. "Yes, put her through." He waited a moment. "Hey. Mom?"

"Hey, Director," she teased. "How is everything?"

He sighed. "Crazy."

"Oh, I know, honey. Your timing is perfect for an international scandal. But hey, at least you got the job. I know I keep saying this, but I'm so proud of you, Slade."

"Yeah," Slade said nonchalantly. "If it weren't for you and Dad, I wouldn't be here right now."

"You'd be like your sister. She's still trying to figure out her life. Now, I like a little adventure here and there, but she's been trying to get her little fashion line noticed for far too long now. That's just too much. Aren't you happy you're stable?"

Slade reluctantly nodded to himself, and tried to restrain himself from vocally affirming his mother's thoughts.

"Slade?"

The comm. was silent for an awkward moment while he really thought this through. He supposed he was stable; but happy? He took his mother's advice and gave up his college fantasies for a normal life. He had a respectable career for these last four years and, as always, his family was supportive and loving. However, somewhere deep inside he couldn't help but feel that he was becoming a simple link in somebody else's chain. Maybe that was something he had to accept. Some people are born to be at the top and the rest just work to fulfill that prophecy. "Uh-huh. Yeah, Mom, I'm happy," he said.

"What time are you coming over?"

"I should be home around eight unless something comes up."

"Good. I'm ordering out tonight. It should be here when you arrive. See you later."

"Bye."

II

Slade came into the office the next morning feeling agitated. A surprise visit from his sister last night wore on his nerves. As Slade walked through the halls of M.3.A.N. with a coffee in one hand and his briefcase in the other, he recalled his conversation with Samantha: "What happened to you, Slade?" she had asked. "You wanted something different, I thought."

"Some people can jump, Sam. There are people like you who can risk everything and not give it a second thought. Then, there are people like me who, as much as we may want to, we just can't do that. I can't do that."

"So, you're just gonna give up?"

"Give up what? I thought about doing something different, but I moved on. I grew up. I'm just accepting who I am. I'm just a regular guy."

"Well, Slade, if you truly believe that, then you're right."

Slade tried to forget the conversation as he sat his briefcase on the ground next to his desk. He sat in his chair, took a big swig of coffee, and took a deep breath. He finally felt at ease for the first time in days. Then, the desk comm. rang.

"Yes?" Slade said, answering the call.

"Director Maxwell, we've looked at everything you gave us, and we think we have a suspect."

"Great. Meet in the conference room in ten minutes."

***

Slade sat in the first tiered row of chairs in the dark conference room while his team manager explained their findings. The rest of the team sat in the rows behind their director, listening to their manager and watching as images flashed on the wall in the front.

"There were roughly 300 attendees at this year's Leaders Ball and out of all of them, only three were Ethereans...as far as we know. Queen Aeothesca, of course; Catherine Barthelomie, her lady-in-waiting; and the famous actor, Lesech. Our queen, we've obviously ruled out. Catherine we can also rule out as a suspect – she's a water user. Aside from the warrior's blood she spilled, there was no liquid on the stage for the Commander to slip or to drag the cane away that far. That leaves us with Lesech, an air Etherean."

"He's a citizen of the Southern Third. Why would Lesech do this?" Slade asked.

"Lesech has publicly stated his desire to take the Commander's spot and win the Power Battles. This is just speculation, but he may have anticipated the Commander's retirement even more than the rest of us, and when he didn't give it, Lesech took matters into his own hands."

Slade nodded. He could feel his team's anticipation of a big reaction like they all must have had, but he wasn't surprised. The man was a lunatic. His fame may have blinded the masses, but Slade never forgot who he really was. "Then, that is what we give Her Majesty," he said. "Thanks everyone. Dismissed."

III

Lorelei Castle grew closer and closer as the air car in which Slade was sitting lifted off the ground and took him to his destination. Slade grew nervous for two reasons. For one, he was going to have a talk with the queen face to face. Then there was the fact that he was up so high! He wondered how anyone could get used to traveling between Reor and the castle. There was no road beneath them and the roof of the car had been retracted which meant he could fall out at any minute. He thanked Elao that he had a seatbelt. He was strapped in and held on to the belt tightly as the car made its way up to the ominous rock.

Slade only ever saw the castle from the ground below and through binoculars. Aside from that, the only close views of the castle available were in magazines and on screen. To see it in person was an entirely different experience. The driver came to a slow stop and hovered a few inches off the castle grounds. Lorelei Castle was a beautiful work of art. Its white stone towers stretched high and framed high walls that spanned the length of the land. Slade stepped onto the main courtyard where there were perfectly manicured trees, grass, and paved pathways to anywhere. It was busy with some people who were working and others who were taking their break. The scene was purely magical. He dared to look at the world below him and saw an expanse of land stretching as far as the eye could see. The sense of wonder overcame him and his jaw dropped.

"I had the same reaction my first time, Director," said a voice from behind. Slade turned quickly to see the queen's lady-in-waiting walking his way. She was outfitted in tight, white body armor that bulged with extra padding on her legs, chest, and arms. She also had the hilt of a collapsible sword with a dark blue handle attached to her waist. She stuck out her hand and introduced herself. "I am Catherine."

"Yes. Catherine. It's nice to meet you." Slade shook her hand and looked at her attire with a confused expression. "Excuse me, but aren't you the queen's lady-in-waiting?"

Catherine smirked. "A bit overdressed for that role, am I? Since working with Her Majesty, I have become more of a bodyguard, as I am sure you have seen. Come with me." She turned and strolled across the front path to a side door in the castle.

"Yes, I have seen," said Slade as he followed along. He'd seen the video of her defense of the queen at the Leaders Ball. "You're very talented, Catherine."

"That is an unusual compliment. Thank you."

"Why is that?"

She turned her head and shared a kind smile with Slade. "It is not common for an Etherean to be recognized for their abilities – especially from one who has none. It is a nice change."

They made their way into the castle and Slade marveled at the high white walls, and pristine marble floor. The castle was busy with activity. Guards milled about, as well as other government workers including the maids and servants. The guards were outfitted like Catherine with the hilt of their collapsible swords at their sides. The only exception was that their armor had a chrome finish. Catherine's presence made everyone step out of her path as she led the way, allowing her and Slade an uninterrupted trek to the queen.

"How did you get that much control over your power?"

Catherine paused almost causing Slade to walk into her. "Am I a suspect, Director?"

"My apologies, but my insights on the case are for the queen's ears only."

Catherine huffed, "Very well," and continued to walk on. "Ethereans hardly use their power for battle, but I was determined to be of even greater use to the queen. So she trained me, herself, over the past four years."

"So, the queen can use her powers for battle?"

"The queen can use her powers for anything. Never underestimate her. You are lucky."

"Why?"

"You are a citizen of the Middle Third."

Catherine approached a door and it swung open revealing the throne room, illuminated in a kaleidoscope of colors from the massive stained-glass window on its far side. The room was wide with a great amount of floor space between the door and the few steps up to the throne in the back. Slade looked over Catherine's shoulder and saw that the room's pristine white walls and marble floor gradually gave way to a more natural environment. Grass and shrubbery met the marble floor halfway through and a tree sat on either side of the room. Even the throne looked as though it were forged in some otherworldly construction of tree roots. Slade felt a strange presence amongst all of the greenery. Technically all plant life was *living*, but these natural fixtures seemed to have eyes. And they were watching Slade's every move. The queen was well protected here, even without the guards.

"Your Majesty, I present to you Director Maxwell of M.3.A.N.," Catherine announced.

Slade came in behind her and immediately felt the queen's cold glare. He stepped into the center of the room before the throne and saw the queen sitting, as she always did, a few steps above him.

Slade bowed and said, "Your Majesty."

"Welcome, Director Maxwell. I take it you have information for me regarding the Commander's death?"

"Yes, Your Majesty." He tried to stop his voice from quaking. He thought it best not to appear intimidated, but he couldn't push that feeling away.

"And what are your findings?"

"It would be best if I could discuss this with you alone."

"Say no more. Catherine, please excuse us."

Catherine walked to the other side of the door and stood with her back to the room. The automatic door swung closed shortly thereafter.

"Go on, Director. Continue," the queen said.

"There's no way to prove it, Your Majesty, but based on what information we do have, we have reason to believe that Lesech is the assassin. It is our recommendation that he be brought in for questioning."

"Lesech? The actor? And what sense would that make?"

"He is an air Etherean and could have flung the Commander's cane away without anyone else's notice. He's also been training for the Power Battle, and now he has a definitive date."

"He is a citizen of the Southern Third and the Middle Third made him famous. Certainly he could have waited for the old man to die himself."

"Correct, Your Majesty, but I know Lesech...or, at least, I know of him. We went to university together. He lives to fight and he believes Ethereans are on a higher level than everyone else."

"And what do you think?"

Slade paused. This question caught him off guard. "I think we're all equal. We're no better than Ethereans." Slade waited for a shared moment of understanding, but soon got the sense that somehow his response was less than what the queen desired.

"Perhaps the Commander's little speech sparked his anger. I know it did mine." The queen went silent with a thoughtful gaze somewhere to the side of the room. "Where is Lesech now?"

"Working on a new film in the entertainment district."

"Very well, Director. I'd like to speak to Lesech as soon as possible. Dispatch a team to pick him up."

Today, the queen was full of surprises. Slade was positive that an order for Lesech's arrest was imminent, so why did she want to speak to him instead? Slade dared not speak his thoughts freely and opted for a bow. "Yes, Your Majesty."

"In the meantime, I have another mission for your team. I need you to find my sister."

"Princess Annonymn?"

"She gave up that title long ago, Director. She is a traitor and a threat to our nation. Please refrain from giving her such acknowledgement from this moment on."

"Sorry, Your Majesty. And we accept the mission."

"Good. See one of the guards outside to take a tour of the

castle. You are dismissed." And with that, she was done with him. "Catherine!" she called.

Catherine came into the room right away as Slade passed by. "Yes, my lady?" The door closed behind Slade and Catherine could speak freely. "How did it go?"

"Splendidly. I feel we may be in an advantageous position. If we can find my sister, Annonymn, and remove her potential for influence, we can start moving against the South or the North and control the message."

"That sounds wonderful. And what of the suspect for the Commander's death? Who is it?"

"It is Lesech."

"Oh, my."

"Who would have guessed? And in my pursuit for control of this world, I have a sense that he would make a very powerful ally."

CHAPTER EIGHTEEN

I

It was the day she had worked so hard for. Gigi's wedding to Wellesley. She sat in the private parlor of a country club along with her two bridesmaids – wives of Wellesley's business partners and friends – as they all chatted happily. The air was thick with the scents of perfume and hairspray, but they paid it no mind. Their assistants worked on their hair and makeup, expertly avoiding any stains on their matching white robes. Gigi smiled and laughed and went through the motions. She was so happy. Not because she was marrying Wellesley, but because of what she would inherit soon after. The ladies around her couldn't tell the difference, nor could her new butler, Garren, who was sitting on the other end of the room. He always insisted that he stay by her side. All the while she thought of how stupid they were. And to a greater extent, all humans. They were so trusting. So easily manipulated. This was child's play. They each had bottles of water sitting nearby. She toyed with the idea of using the water and killing them all right then and there and watching the aftermath, but she stopped herself. *Just one death tonight will do*, she thought. *Perhaps I'll start a war if the money fails to excite me. That would be fun.*

The thought triggered a pain in her chest. She clutched her

chest and let out a sharp shriek that startled the ladies around her. "Stop this, stop!" She lost control of what had escaped her lips.

"Are you okay?" one of her bridesmaids asked.

"Sorry. I'm fine. Just a stomach pain. Excuse me." She got up and maneuvered around the chairs, people, and clutter in the room and entered the bathroom. She took a quick look under the stall doors. When she saw she was alone, she looked in the mirror with a disgusted look on her face. "What the hell do you think you're doing?"

She saw herself speak back. It was the girl she took over, Gisela. "I'm not letting you use me anymore."

"Use you? You accepted this. You wanted all of this."

"You're wrong. You can't treat people like this. This isn't how I want to live."

She couldn't help but laugh at this. "'...*you*... want to *live?*' Listen to yourself, little girl. You desired death and you got what you wanted. Stay down and shut up. This is my life now."

Gigi successfully quieted the girl inside. That was a close call. She shook her head, vexed that of all times now would be when her vessel tried to take control. Gigi exhaled, smiled, and returned to her guests, ready to complete what she started.

II

All of the invited guests congratulated the newly married couple and remarked that the ceremony was beautiful. The event took place outside on the lawn of the country club and Wellesley and Gigi spoke their vows to the backdrop of a pond and the open blue sky. After the exhaustion of the pictures and kicking off the reception in her bridal gown, Gigi changed into a shorter white dress for what she would call the grand finale.

It wouldn't be easy, however. The vessel was reacting to her plans, trying to make her stop. As she walked from the private parlor to the large, white reception tent on the lawn, she felt a pain in her chest once again. *Damn, this girl*, she thought. Gigi kept walking trying to quiet Gisela within.

Gisela's voice sounded in her head. "What are you doing?"

"Don't interfere," she replied.

"I won't let you—"

"Shut up!"

The spirit successfully suppressed her vessel once again and entered the reception. She focused on her new husband who was all smiles and seated at the main table. She almost felt sorry for him. He was so happy. So in love. So stupid. All eyes were on her as she entered the tent and revealed her new dress. Then she took the open seat next to her husband. All she needed now was the right moment.

Wellesley's comm. rang and distracted him for a moment. He leaned over and kissed Gigi. "Sorry, babe. Business call. I'll make it quick."

"No worries," she replied. This was it. She hoped he hadn't noticed her glee for him to leave the table. The day had already

163

turned to night and she watched as Wellesley left the tent to answer his call outside. It was perfect. Nobody would notice a thing.

The party turned from dinner to dancing and as Gigi made her way to the crowd she stole a quick glance outside. Wellesley stood in front of the pond. With little effort, she focused her power on the pond and its level began to grow. She giggled to herself remembering the oddest thing she needed to repeat as a part of her wedding vows: *May no force but death separate us.* Gigi was the only one who knew how close death was.

She took a final glimpse at Wellesley, who spotted her, smiled, and waved. She waved goodbye, too. The music playing was excellent and she turned her back on her husband to join the party. Now it was *really* time for celebration. She controlled the water of the pond as she danced, feeling all that it covered. She could feel the blades of grass moistening from the rising water level. Soon after, she could feel the rubber sole of Wellesley's shoe. Her smile was uncontrollable.

***

The water running underneath Wellesley's feet wrapped itself around his ankles and pulled him down fast. His comm. fell a few feet away and he felt as though a carpet had been pulled from under him. He grabbed the back of his head in pain after knocking it hard against the ground. Wellesley groaned and tried lifting himself up, but something was seriously wrong. His back was drenched and the water surrounding him twisted and formed into hands and arms that clutched at his clothes. His breath got shorter and couldn't believe what was happening. He turned on his stomach and looked to the reception tent. His attempted scream for help was cut short as a watery hand gripped his throat. Face reddened, he still fought. His comm. was still functioning so he reached for it, but his body began to slide against the wet grass toward the pond. His fingers scratched at the earth, but he couldn't grab a hold of anything. More hands covered his body and pulled his arms to his side. He slid away in a cocoon of water with his eye on the reception, hoping his beloved wife would come checking on him. She never showed.

***

Gigi continued to dance, but her movements became stiff as Wellesley struggled. She was frustrated that he wouldn't just die, but on some level she respected him for his fight. Even as his body was pulled below the surface of the pond, he still shook with all his might to free himself. It was enough to make her shake and exert extra ether just to stabilize herself. The triangle at the back of her neck flashed blue for a moment, but only the most astute eye would notice as it was covered by her hair. She could feel Wellesley weakening. Almost done. Everything of Wellesley's would be hers very soon.

Suddenly, her movements froze. The pain in her chest grew sharp and she let out a scream. The people closest to her stopped dancing to look and it had a ripple effect on the rest of the party. Soon everybody stopped dancing to see if the bride was okay.

"Gigi! Gigi, what's wrong?" one of the bridesmaids asked.

Gigi was hunched over in pain and her lips began to move, but her voice was too low.

"Somebody cut the music! Cut the music!" The music stopped and the silence filled its place. "Gigi, what's wrong? Do you need a doctor?" Gigi didn't respond and so the bridesmaid called out, "Where's Wellesley? Somebody get Wellesley!"

Nobody could find him, but Gigi's butler appeared. He leaned in and put his hand on her back. "What's the matter? Are you ill?"

Not now, Gigi told herself. *Not now, Gisela. I've worked too hard for this! Get back in your cage.* She fought for control, but her vessel was trying everything to ruin her plan. She could feel the water weaken its grasp on Wellesley. Her whole body shook as Gisela spoke through her own lips. Her voice was a pained whisper. She looked into her butler's eyes and said, "Stop...me..."

The sound of her body hitting the floor startled everyone. Gisela could feel the water spirit's control on her lessening, but not before hearing her last words. *It's too late for him.* She was right. She could feel Wellesley's lifeless body drifting in the pond.

As the spirit's power weakened, so did her control of the water, until she felt him no longer. *I'll always be here, Gisela. I'm a patient spirit. And I'll be back.* Everything around Gisela went black.

III

Moments later, Gisela opened her eyes and lifted herself off the floor. She looked at her hands and felt her body, unsure of the sensation she was feeling. *I'm back?* she wondered to herself. It took her a moment to trust the voice inside her head, but she soon understood that it was her. She had done it. She came back.

She turned her eyes to the commotion around her. Only Garren, her butler, stayed by her side while her guests rushed outside to screams of horror.

"Garren," she said. She knew the man's name and remembered his short white hair and salt and pepper goatee, but it felt like her first time meeting him. She found herself thrust into a charade and had to keep the act going by pretending to know him. Her concern for the man she tried to save, however, was real. "Where's Wellesley? Garren, where's Wellesley? Tell me he's okay!"

"I don't know, Mrs. Van der Borea. You need to lie still. The ambulance is on its way."

Her new last name came as a shock, but it quickly subsided as her bridesmaid came in. Her face was flushed and she was wiping her eyes. "Gigi…" she said. She couldn't find the right words to deliver.

"No," said Gisela. "No! No!" It couldn't be. She didn't really know Wellesley like Gigi did, but she just couldn't have another life taken on her account. Not like her mother. She'd never forgive herself. She got up, pushing away Garren as he pleaded with her to lie still, and walked outside. Her guests were all crowded on the lawn and when they saw her, they made room. She neared the center of the crowd unimpeded and took in the scene. The groomsmen were kneeled over Wellesley. They were tired from pulling him out and tired from pumping his chest with their hands. Gisela felt everyone's eyes on her as they waited for the inevitable outburst. It never came. When she saw this man who was lying lifeless on the ground, she did not see her husband. She didn't see the tragedy of a new bride who had lost the love of her life, as everyone else must have. All she saw was her failure. She came back into the world with the same reason she wanted to leave staring her in the face.

CHAPTER NINETEEN

Queen Aeothesca sat on her throne and looked down on the handsome, wiry man in front of her. Lesech had been brought to her just as ordered. The prideful look on his face revealed all she needed to know about who was really guilty for the Southern Commander's death. His eyes darted around the room and the queen had a good idea what was going on in his head. "There is no escape, Lesech. And I assure you, you are much too weak to take me on."

"Why am I here?" he asked. His piercing hazel eyes bored into hers with rage. He had just been taken from his apartment against his will for reasons unknown. He didn't appreciate that and he didn't like being trapped.

She didn't much care. "You tell me. I am sure you can come up with an adequate guess."

He kept his eyes locked on hers and remained silent.

"Very well," Aeothesca said as she stood up from her throne. "You are here because of your attempt to frame me for the assassination of Commander Azure."

"Frame you?"

She chuckled, "Oh, dear. Is that the first question that comes to mind when I accuse you of being the true assassin? So you are, indeed, the one who killed the Commander?"

169

Lesech said nothing. His hair began to bounce along with the slight breeze he summoned as he readied himself for an attack.

"Stop it. That would only end badly for you."

"I won't let you take me without a fight."

"I have no reason to fight you, Lesech. In fact, I would like to thank you." She descended the few steps and stood with Lesech at eye level. "Commander Azure has been a thorn in my side for decades. Why did you take action against him?"

Lesech let go of the air around him. He didn't know where this was going, but he wanted to find out. "He was a tyrant and a bigot. He used us Ethereans for his own means, but never gave us the respect and support we rightfully deserve. Surely, you understand that. I want to become the new Commander and put Ethereans in their rightful place as the rulers of this world."

"A noble cause. Our feelings are mutual," said the queen. What she omitted was that she had no intention of sharing power with anyone – Etherean or not. But it was better now to play to his wants. "The truth is, Lesech, I did not call you here to execute you or anything of the sort. I believe we can make a deal."

"And what would that be?"

"Win the Power Battle and become the new Commander, then join me in a campaign against the Northern Third. We can then place Ethereans in all positions of power and have a world truly of our own. I will need your signed confession for the Commander's death, but it will never be spoken of again. What do you say to that?" The queen offered her soft hand.

Lesech smiled. He never expected to step foot in Lorelei Castle, let alone strike an alliance with the queen. He could see a vision unfolding in his mind. This was a win-win. Once he controlled the strongest army in the world, he would join the queen in collapsing the Northern Third, then he would take the Middle Third for himself when she least expected it. He grabbed the queen's hand and they shook. "It would be an honor to join you, Your Majesty."

CHAPTER TWENTY

I

It was the beginning of a heat wave in Pelagus, the Southern Third's capital city. The streets were crowded with citizens who made their way to work with a sense of mourning that had not left since the death of their Commander. Deputy-Commander Albion Rain rose to the temporary spot left open and decided to take some precautionary measures. Pelagus's celebrated warriors were a normal sight on the streets of the city. This time, however, their numbers were increased and they were highly visible with the dual purpose to quell the threat of instability and give the people a sense of security. Many people walked or drove to their jobs with a grim anticipation of what was to come next, holding on to hope that all would be set right once a new Commander was revealed after the Power Battle just a few weeks away.

The landscape of the city was very spread out with vast patches of well-manicured park grounds that softened the otherwise tough impression of the small sandstone buildings scattered about. The city's few skyscrapers surrounded the massive glass pyramid at the center, which symbolized the seat of power in Pelagus.

Miles away, Douglassaire stood on the rooftop of a house and stared at Pelagus Pyramid as he wiped his sweat-beaded brow. All of the training he had undergone, the years of service, and the years of waiting led up to this: the threshold to a new life…or an untimely death. The Southern Third's forty best warriors would soon participate in a free-for-all at the coliseum for the title of Commander. As much as he thought he was ready for the Power Battle, the specter of doubt lingered somewhere in the recesses of his mind. Doug qualified as one of the forty, but keeping his air spirit at bay and just using its power was a hard job. If he lost focus, the air spirit could take complete control, and who knows what would happen then? He had come so close to his dream, but he could not ignore the reality that he might lose himself and die in the process of reaching for it.   The sound of a door closing behind him shook him from his thoughtful daze. He looked back and saw a blue-eyed teenage boy staring back at him. His brown hair swayed in the breeze and he had a sword in his hand at his side. He charged Douglassaire without notice, but was too slow to land a strike. In the short period between the boy's steps and his attempt at a strike, Doug unsheathed the sword at his back and blocked the attack. He smiled. "Nice try, Isidro."

"I wasn't going for the kill."

"Oh, I know, but why don't you show me what that looks like?" Doug pushed him away and crouched into a battle-ready stance. As Isidro got his balance back, he reached into his pocket and pulled out a lighter. He held his sword in front of him horizontally and struck a flame from the lighter underneath. Instantly, the blade of the sword was enveloped in flames. He dropped his hand to put his lighter back in his pocket, but Douglassaire jumped at the opportunity. Isidro was caught off guard and sloppily blocked a number of Doug's attacks. He managed to place the lighter in his pocket and finally got out an offensive swing, but Doug dodged and knocked the sword out of his hand. As the sword fell to the ground, the flames disappeared, and Doug ended the little spar with a pointed blade to Isidro's neck.

"That's no fair!" Isidro protested.

"You think somebody's gonna wait for you to use your power on your sword before they strike?" Doug returned his sword to the sheath at his back. "Nothing is fair in combat. Remember that."

"What am I supposed to do then?"

"Find a faster way. Keep working at it. You'll get it."

"Yes, sir." He grabbed his sword off the ground and watched as his teacher folded his arms and went back to studying Pelagus Pyramid in the distance. "So, are you ready? The Power Battle is only a few weeks away."

"As ready as I'll ever be."

"What if you win? That would be so cool! What would you do?"

"The Middle Third needs to feel the consequences of taking down our Commander…among other things."

"Yeah. Queen Aeothesca is pretty scary, but if anyone can take her, it's you. And you'd have the best army there is." Isidro stood beside Doug, put his hands on his hips and looked at the pyramid with him. He never felt any freer than when he was next to his teacher.

Doug looked at Isidro and thought about all that transpired to get this point. He noticed a change in his student from the first time he'd met him. Doug remembered one of the hardest times in his life four years ago when he was feeling emotions that he kept hidden since childhood. He showed his true self to someone special and, yet again, he had been abandoned. He wished things with Slade had turned out differently. Instead, he poured himself into his training to get away from those feelings and ended up training a group of young wannabe warriors. This is where he met Isidro.

II

Slade had left an indelible mark on Douglassaire. Perhaps it was even deeper than the scar of his non-existent family. Never before had he shared so much with another human being. It was freeing. At least that's what he thought it felt like at first. In reality, he figured it was a trap. He knew there was a slim chance Slade would discard him, but he never suspected it would happen so soon. Still, he took the chance with his heart and when Slade left without a word, he decided to protect what was left.

He supposed he deserved it. He knew better. People hurt. He much preferred the pain of exercise and training to the torture of his feelings. At least that pain he could manage. He knew when to expect a muscle ache and if he ever was expected to fight, he could easily dodge the slice of a sword. And if he were ever cut, he knew at least the pain would subside with his death. He couldn't, however, anticipate the deep wounds caused by a relationship – any relationship. Even worse, these wounds did not kill. One is forced to live with these wounds, and Douglassaire was determined to never feel this pain again.

After his failed spring break trip, he settled in the Southern Third's capital, Pelagus, and never returned to Burrow University. He didn't want to face Slade, but he also wanted to completely focus on his goal of winning the Power Battle. If only he could become the Commander, he could set some things right in the world. And with access to unlimited power and freedom, he would become immune to the pain of emotions. This would end all of his problems.

Douglassaire needed to be at his best in order to win. He had seen an opening for a junior war instructor at a local training school. It was an opportunity to train himself and make some money at the same time. Places like this were all over the Southern Third. The respect earned by those in the military was the highest in the nation and many young ones looked up to their heroes and wanted to join them someday. So, it was a natural occurrence that people opened up shop and advertised their training school as the best to hone their skills. He had approached the school, but when he came upon it, he was taken aback by its appearance.

From the outside, it looked like somebody's home. It was a three-story residential structure with an angled roof and a wooden porch that led to a screen door. It badly needed some paint and the tall grass in the front yard was begging to be mowed down. Doug stood in front of the structure and looked at his surroundings, unsure if he was in the right place.

"Hello? Can I help you?" a rough voice called. Doug hadn't known where the voice was coming from and was getting really tired of this happening to him.

"I'm here for the instructor job," Doug spoke into the air.

The front door of the place opened and a man appeared on the porch. His short grey hair was thinning towards the front of his scalp while a healthy portion remained further back. He was almost as tall as Doug and a little more stout, but still solid. "Can you fight?" he asked.

"I'm part of the military, sir." Doug walked up and handed over his identification.

The man looked it over and rubbed his graying stubble. "Good enough for me. 'Name's Locke."

They shook hands. "I'm Doug…Heuresyt." Knowing his own last name had been a gift of which he'd never tire. It was the missing piece to an identity he'd long struggled to find and spoke it with pride.

"Come on in, Doug. I don't have time for a whole bunch of interviews and shit. Let's go over your pay and get you started. I got kids coming in a little bit."

Doug followed the man inside and eyed the vicinity as they talked about his terms. The whole first floor was like a dojo. Nothing was on the floor and the walls were scantily decorated with certificates and various photos of what looked like a younger Locke with other warriors. He remembered noticing the faint smell of cigarette smoke lingering in the room as he gazed straight into the backyard, which was surprisingly big. Unlike the front, the grass in this yard was perfectly maintained. The greenery lined the perimeter of a wide concrete court. A locked glass case of swords stood by the court signaling to Doug that this was where the more intense weapons training took place.

Doug had accepted the terms of his employment and started that day as the instructor of a group of eleven teenagers who hoped to someday be a part of the military. He would train the kids in the day and train himself at night, making sure to conceal his newfound ethereal ability. He was instinctively secretive, so this was no problem for him. Being a normal human his whole life, however, had left him oblivious to just how cruel the world could be for people who were different. He never knew the sting of being an Etherean until he met Isidro.

***

Isidro was among the eleven students. He started when he was thirteen years old, and he was bright and enthusiastic about beginning his training, but this didn't last long. Isidro came to class early one day and saw he was alone. So, he ventured into the backyard and grabbed a sword from the nearby case. It was unlocked as the case was something Douglassaire routinely forgot to check.

Douglassaire stood on the roof of the house and peered down, unbeknownst to Isidro. His student waved his sword back and forth with all the floundering of an amateur. Doug shook his head realizing how far he had to go to give his students' parents their money's worth. Then, something happened that made Doug pay even greater attention. He had begun to walk back to his room, but stopped in his tracks as a bright light from the yard caught his eye. Isidro held on to the sword as it burned alight with a red flame.

Doug hadn't the time to marvel at the spectacle, for he heard the closing of wheeler doors and the arrival of the other students in the front. "Isidro!" he called.

The boy froze from shock hearing his name bellowed in his teacher's deep voice. He looked up and saw Doug standing there.

Doug warned, "Put it out!" but it was too late. Isidro looked towards the back of the house and saw his classmates lined up outside with their eyes and mouths wide open as they gazed at the burning sword in his hands. Isidro quickly dropped the sword and the flames disappeared. He had hoped this last ditch attempt at hiding what was already seen would make them think it was an illusion or a dream of some sort, but the looks of horror and disgust never left their faces. They stood there in silence that seemed to stretch forever for Isidro. Ten against one. Douglassaire rushed down the stairs to try to salvage the situation, but as he approached the backyard, he heard one of the kids mutter, "Freak." Almost as visibly as the flames dissipating from the dropped sword, Doug saw the life leave Isidro. He stood there broken and looking through the ground into some unknown dimension where only despair existed. Doug knew that look very well as much as he tried to hide it, but it was then that he realized that Ethereans must have visited that place often. He hadn't realized it before, but now that he had some powers of his own, he could only imagine that many people would look at him the same way those kids did Isidro. And instead of standing up for Isidro he had done something he would regret for the rest of his life.

Nothing.

"Come on, guys, let's get started," he said. Isidro was slow to join them, but after only a few minutes of exercises, he left alone through the front door.

III

That night, Douglassaire knocked on the door of Isidro's home. It was nighttime and all was quiet except for the occasional wheeler rolling past. The creak of the wooden porch grew louder as he shifted his weight and waited for an answer. The door opened and a woman looked up at him with a concerned look on her face. "Mr. Heuresyt," she said, "please come in."

The woman stepped aside and Doug stepped in looking for the boy. A man sat silently at a small round table further in with a cross expression and his arms folded. "He's upstairs," the woman said. "He's been up there all day."

"I told that kid to keep it to himself," the man said.

The woman slowly closed her eyes and tried her best not to respond to this. She spoke softly to Douglassaire and said, "First door on the left."

"Thanks," said Doug. He traveled up the stairs and felt his hands begin to shake. His breathing grew a little heavier and he began to think about what he was going to say. He was surprised at his fear. How could jumping off of a cliff be less scary than talking to a kid? As strong as he was, opening up and having tough conversations was not one his skills. He hadn't felt this uneasy since...he shoved the thought of Slade away as he got to the top step. He didn't know what to expect from his pupil, but he steeled himself to accept whatever hatred and judgment would come his way. But as he opened the door to Isidro's room, he saw the same look of fear in his eyes. At least they had that in common.

Isidro sat on the far side of his bed and turned away from his teacher as Doug closed the door. Douglassaire walked over and he wanted to sit next to him – put his arm around him and apologize, but he couldn't bring himself to do it. Instead, he stood against wall and crossed his arms. The loud chirping of crickets outside was the only thing that broke the silence until Isidro glared at Doug and asked, "What do you want?"

"I want to show you something." He had persuaded Isidro to come outside with him to the nearest park. Isidro's parents made no objection. It was still warm outside but cooler than it had been during the day. When they got to the park, which was well-lit at night, Doug made sure they were alone.

"Okay, we're here. I don't see anything," Isidro said.

"What do you feel?" Doug asked.

"Nothing."

"How about now?" Doug lowered his arms and opened the palms of his hands and the air around the both of them had begun to swirl in a fast circular motion.

Isidro's expression had changed from annoyed, to amused, to shocked. "How are you...? Are you...?" He couldn't quite get the words out of his mouth.

Doug said nothing and let the wind subside and become still again.

"Does everyone else know?"

Doug shook his head. "No. Honestly, I don't even know how to control it just yet, but maybe that's where we can help each other out."

Isidro agreed to private training with Doug on the condition that he come back to the group and deal with his classmates. From then on, Doug saw firsthand how people ostracized others who were different. He saw the pain Isidro had to go through with the others, but he also saw him grow stronger in the face of it all. Over the years, Douglassaire's control over his power grew as did Isidro's, and soon enough, as old students left and new students joined, Isidro gained their respect. Some even thought what Isidro could do was cool and secretly wished they could do the same.

Now, as Isidro stood next to Doug on the rooftop of the house turned training facility, for a brief moment, Doug marveled at how far Isidro had come. Doug wished he had had someone to force him to deal with people despite the pain they caused. Maybe then he would be as strong as his pupil. Isidro taught him to open up, but he was still a work in progress. Perhaps winning the Power Battle would be enough, for he would be forced to deal with the world then.

IV

"Douglassaire! I finally found you," said Lesech as he slammed the door to the rooftop behind him.

Doug and Isidro both turned to face the man with alarm. When Lesech removed his gold-rimmed sunglasses, Doug's cold expression did not change.

When Isidro realized who it was and it became much too difficult for him to hold back his smile, he looked at Lesech, then at Doug, then back and Lesech. "Holy shit."

"At least *somebody* is happy to see me," Lesech said. He smiled and cocked back his head in a reverse nod and asked, "What's your name?"

"Isidro."

"Izzy. Nice to meet you." He gave Isidro's unprepared hand a firm pump which caused his whole arm to shake like a rubber band.

"Can I get your autograph?"

"Uh…sure."

"Okay, I'll be right back." Isidro hurried back inside the house.

"Oh, my, the world really has gone mad, Douglassaire. They left you in charge of our youth!"

"What do you want?" asked Doug.

"Now, is that any way to greet an old friend? I wanted to come see how you were – what you were up to. You never came back to school, and it worried me so. Tell me. How are things?"

"You'll see how things are when we fight."

"So you *do* intend on participating in our nation's great tradition." Lesech sucked his teeth and made a clicking sound.

"Such a shame."

"For you. The fact you came here shows me you're scared. And you should be."

Lesech chuckled, "Oh, Douglassaire. Scared? Unlike you, I make the effort to at least give my friends a proper goodbye. That's all I'm here for. Unlike the Power Battles of the past, this one is sure to be a bloodbath. The list of the fallen will be long and I'll make sure you're on it."

Isidro trotted back onto the roof and stood next to Lesech with a notebook and pen. He looked up at him smiling and Lesech took the materials out of the hands of his adoring fan. He spoke aloud the words he wrote to him, "To… Izzy. Keep… the… S-3… strong. Lesech." He handed the notebook back to him and said, "Here you go."

Isidro read and reread the message as though it were scripture. "Thank you!" he said. He looked at Doug and said cheerfully, "You have to call me Izzy now, Teacher."

Lesech patted Isidro on the back and looked at his rival one last time. "Goodbye…Teacher." He muffled his laugh with closed lips. The shadow of the inside of the house slowly swallowed his frame as he opened the door and left.

CHAPTER TWENTY-ONE

I

The coliseum in the western part of the city was repainted and decorated like new for the Power Battle. Banners hung on the outside of the walls welcoming spectators and the traffic around the place was heavy and slow with excited patrons making their way to their seats. The big day had finally come, and the world was watching.

The forty warriors who were participating all waited in silence at various places inside the coliseum. The ground level of the coliseum looked like a big circular locker room. It was dim and had the musky smell of a gym. Half of the circle was occupied by the warriors who would soon battle it out. Each of them was dressed in personalized versions of their armor sans helmet. The armor was a form-fitting obsidian that added a thick layer of protection over the warriors' bodies. Instead of the Southern Third's normal black coloring, many had painted their armor in festive colors for the occasion.

The other half of the circular room was walled off and inaccessible to anyone. Some warriors got close to the wall and could hear the grunts and snarls of the other competitors they would be facing – the lusae. These new additions, added to the unspoken insanity it took to participate in such a ritual, made

183

most of the warriors nervous. The decision to use the creatures in this Power Battle was one already made by the late Commander Azure and was welcome by his stand-in. Should all the warriors perish, Deputy-Commander Rain would have a permanent seat.

Many of the warriors sat still, meditating in front of their individual door from which they would emerge on the field. Others, like Lesech, were pumped and enthusiastic. They were the ones who were standing, stretching, hopping in place, or swinging their swords in rehearsed movements. Douglassaire was among these forty warriors, yet he could not place himself in the company of the nervous or enthusiastic. He sat on the bench in front of his door and felt nothing. His mind was blank. Here was the moment he had prepared for his whole life and he couldn't bring himself to feel anything but indifferent at its approach. He started to wonder why, and came to the conclusion that it was because he had no one cheering him on. Without anyone's support, there was no fun and nothing to prove. Like all the other events in his life the Power Battle seemed like just another objective – a means to an end.

But this wasn't true. He began to think about who possibly in this world would look at him fight and hope for his safety and success. He had to remind himself that he was not alone. Isidro promised he would be in the stands cheering him on the loudest. He was also sure some of his other students would be watching and supporting him. Even his boss, Locke, who stood to get a huge boost in business because of Doug, would be watching. He knew Editra, the only mother he'd ever known, would not be watching. She was too kindhearted for such savagery, but he was sure she would be thrilled at his success. As he thought about all of these people, he finally started to feel the butterflies in his stomach and tightness in his neck and shoulders. He couldn't let these people down.

Then, he thought about Slade. His face always appeared in his mind at the most unexpected moments usually followed by a pang of woe. *Would he be watching?* he wondered. Despite his attempts to dismiss these thoughts and accept that Slade didn't care, he knew the answer was yes. Slade knew Lesech and Doug, and he wouldn't dare miss out on the possible display of ethereal powers. Doug finally decided to stop wrestling with that reality and accepted it. Once he did, he felt the enthusiasm. He was going to show Slade what he was missing out on.

II

The music sounded and the people in the stands cheered. All at once, all of the warriors waiting patiently inside silenced themselves. This was it. They were about to take part in a battle of which they had very little practical knowledge. They heard old stories of past Power Battles, watched old recordings, and practiced as best as they could, but they all suddenly got a feeling of walking blindly into the place of their doom. Commander Azure was in power for a long time and none of these warriors had seen the action of a Power Battle for themselves.

The announcers began running down the list of fighters, and as they did, each warrior's door would open up allowing for a grand entrance. One by one, each warrior's name was called and they stepped out onto the sandy, barren field and into the bright sun, receiving a round of applause and cheers.

Outside, Isidro and a few of the other warriors-in-training finally got to their seats in one of the middle rows. Isidro peered down at the warriors who were already announced and got a closer look by gazing at the big screen on the adjacent side of the field. "I don't think he came out yet, guys," he said to his crew.

"Ladies and gentlemen," the announcer began with much enthusiasm and affect, "we have a *very* special fighter joining the warriors today." He crescendoed and the crowd got restless with anticipation. "You may know him from his role as Stratos, defender of the Southern Third, or as Alex Zephyr the secret agent. Warrior number twenty-nine - he goes by one name. You know it folks! Lesech!"

The cries from the stands were loud, but nothing compared to the deafening cheers when the door opened and their hero stepped out. Lesech slowly walked onto the field in pristine white armor and a matching cape. He smiled and spread out his arms wide as if hugging his entire audience. He kicked up the wind around him making his curly hair bounce and his majestic cape flow.

Isidro was saving his loudest cheer for his mentor, but Lesech's dramatic entrance brought him close. He and his friends cheered, but awaited the announcement of one of their own.

Still in the dark locker room, Douglassaire rolled his eyes at the audible increase in cheers after Lesech entered the field. He thought about a request Isidro made earlier in the day: "Please don't kill Lesech. If he dies, I'll never speak to you again." He meant this partly in jest, but Doug responded, "I won't kill anyone, but with him, I can't make any promises."

Warrior number thirty-four was just announced and she stepped out into the sunlight to a big cheer from the audience. Doug stood up from his bench, took a deep breath, and cleared his mind. He thought of nothing when he was ready to fight. He waited patiently as his introduction to the world was announced.

"Our next fighter hails from Probuston. His name bears an uncanny resemblance to that of a famous explorer. Mystery has entered the arena. Let the shiver of recognition run, everyone. It's number thirty-five, Douglassaire Heuresyt!"

Isidro and his gang led the crowd with ecstatic cheers, but the rest of the crowd did not follow. There was plenty of polite noise, but no raucous hollering or whistling. "Heuresyt?" a woman behind Isidro asked.

As the door opened and Douglassaire trotted out, his face shown big on the large screen in the stands and the noise began to grow. "Oh, my god, look!" the woman behind Isidro pointed at the screen. Douglassaire raised his hand and slowly turned in a circle as he waved at the crowd. Suddenly, all at once, it was as if his audience came to the same conclusion – this was somebody related to the late Douglass Heuresyt whose death sparked the last war. With revenge fresh in the Southern citizens' minds, this added an extra spice. Isidro's energy was finally matched by the rest of the audience in a roar of sound and applause that rivaled only Lesech's greeting. Douglassaire was surprised by the attention he got from the crowd, but loved it all the same.

The last five warriors were announced and appeared on the battlefield. The energy was palpable. "The rules are simple," the announcer began. "Eliminate your opposition by removing both pauldrons…"

The announcer was interrupted by Lesech's grandstanding. He grabbed his right pauldron and threw it on the ground. This caused another round of raucous cheering, swooning, and bloodthirsty yells.

As the crowd quieted, the announcer continued. "There's a chance that some of our warriors won't make it by the end of the day, but it won't matter if it's not you. Be the last one standing and receive the title of Southern Commander! Begin when you hear the horns of battle! Are… you… ready?" The cheers were deafening as the warriors drew their swords and readied themselves for battle. Douglassaire bent his knees and drew his sword in front of him. And then the horns blared.

The warriors rushed either to their left or right to attack their prey. Some took a defensive stance and let their attackers come to them. What was once a joyful scene had turned into an arena of pandemonium as the swords of bloodthirsty warriors clashed. Douglassaire was immediately flanked by warrior thirty-four. He was able to dodge a charging strike, but he was caught off-guard and forced to be on the defensive. She aimed for his shoulders and would have pierced one and removed a pauldron if perhaps she weren't screaming a battle cry on her way over. She was persistent and she frowned with the deepest concentration. The point of her blade jabbed at Douglassaire's shoulders. He supposed this was what it felt like to be in a fencing match. The woman was so close that if she could just tear off one pauldron, she could go to the other and finish this man, but he was so fast. Doug saw a change in his enemy. She bared her teeth and the look in her eyes sent a jolt through his body. She was frustrated and ready to kill.

She changed tactics – instead of poking at his shoulders, she began to swing her sword, going for any limb she could. The sound of metal hitting metal exploded as Douglassaire blocked her attacks. Douglassaire blocked a deadly strike at his neck and his opponent let out a scratchy yelp as she endured a hard kick to her side. Doug's sword came down at a perfect angle and her first pauldron was sliced off. Doug resisted the temptation to celebrate as he saw another warrior slowly coming up behind his enemy. She noticed the same thing happening behind Doug and they both instinctively turned their backs to one another to defend.

Behind the man sneaking up on him, Douglassaire saw a group of three warriors, two women and one man, skulking off the field with their pauldrons removed. As he prepared for a new fight, he felt thankful someone handled a few of them because that meant less work for him. Also because that meant they would get out with their lives intact. He knew that on the other side of the field, things weren't going quite as nicely.

***

Lesech found himself surrounded by three enemies. He hadn't moved since the horns sounded the beginning of the battle and his back was still to the door from which he emerged. He remained still, legs in an 'A' shape, with his hands folded over the hilt of his sword, and the point of the blade stuck straight in the ground. He smiled as the three warriors stood still, cautiously waiting to see who would act first. His stance was peculiar – too easy to strike him down. He must be up to something. "I'm deeply sorry for these circumstances," he said, speaking over the loud cheers and clangs of swords, "but unfortunately you will all die." As he spoke, none of them noticed the churning of air at their feet. The sand on the ground billowed like smoke and barely made their boots visible.

The rightmost warrior lost his patience with Lesech's arrogance. He dashed for the first strike, but lost his balance to a hard gust of wind that enveloped all four of them in a cloud of dust. Everyone in the stands watched in surprise as their beloved actor disappeared from view. All that could be heard was the tearing of flesh, the breaking of bone, and the screams of defeat. Lesech took full advantage of the immunity of his celebrity. He'd used his powers openly in the movies. While other Ethereans were generally disliked, he became one of the good ones. He learned early that as long as he used his ether for regular people's entertainment, he would be fine. But he wasn't satisfied living life like a caged animal to be gawked at and patted on the head. He wanted to be truly respected. And if cutting down every non-Etherean that got in his way was what it took, then he'd gladly take that on.

The dust was whisked away in a flamboyant gesture and only Lesech remained standing. His white armor was stained and spattered with blood. He had a sword in each hand, one of which he had to shake free of a dismembered arm. The audience audibly approved and some even noticed that his own sword remained untouched and still sticking out of the ground. They continued their celebration as they viewed a close-up of his face on the big screen. Lesech channeled pieces of the characters he'd played over the years and used his acting skills now to play the hero. He turned his face to the sky and his eyes were flooded with sorrow. He respectfully knelt beside his fallen opponents as they lie dead in a pool of blood. "We love you, Lesech!" a woman screamed from the stands closest to him. As he stood, he saw the woman and blew her a kiss. Then, he covered his face with his forearm to wipe his eyes dry. He took the moment to laugh to himself. He almost broke into hysterics, but successfully held it in. People were so gullible, and he loved the manipulation.

He scanned the field to see who his next victim would be and spotted Douglassaire swinging, blocking, and dodging.

Doug finally defeated his opponent by removing his last pauldron and took a moment to catch his breath. He caught Lesech's glare and briefly stared back. Lesech wished he could send his threatening thoughts from across the field.

***

The big screens at the top of the field noted how many warriors were left standing. Douglassaire glanced upward and saw that out of forty only twenty-three remained. Two men approached him – one in front, the other behind with only one pauldron remaining. Douglassaire was hitting his stride and smiled confidently. He kept his eyes on the man in front and heard the footsteps of the warrior charging him from behind. As the footsteps became louder and more intense, Douglassaire perfectly timed a daring backflip and ripped the man's last pauldron from his shoulder. Doug landed and threw the pauldron, letting it sail out of his hands and into the face of the other warrior like a bullet. The man screamed as he held his face in pain, allowing Doug enough time to charge and quickly slice away his pauldrons. The crowd screamed in approval and Doug looked at the screen once again. The number dropped to twenty. He looked over his shoulder and felt his stomach turn at the sight of Lesech pulling a sword out of the back of a dead warrior.

The horns blared once more signaling an even more terrifying threat than the people with swords. The fighters all paused, waiting to see what monstrosity came through the gate on the blocked-off half of the arena. A large glass wall slowly slid up high in front of the audience for protection, and when this was done, the iron bars that covered half the arena walls dropped with a loud clicking sound that made almost everyone start.

"Ah, yes, the lusae," the announcer said. "Fearsome creatures of the wild with unspeakable power. It is time for our warriors to kick it up a notch. Will they work together and take them down or will they all be defeated?"

From the darkness of the cages emerged a flash of light. Nobody saw the rasaji coming. The lion with burning mane and a tail of fire pounced on the nearest warrior it could. The man was lit aflame, but the rasaji silenced his screams with a ferocious bite to his neck. Behind it emerged a creature quite the opposite in both element and ferocity. The ceffyl slowly trotted out on its four hooves searching for its prey with a regal presence. Its silky white hair dripped as though the horse were a pure embodiment of rain.

The nineteen remaining warriors in an unspoken agreement decided to deal with the lusae first. Two of them charged the rasaji as it stood atop its fallen victim snarling and roaring. Douglassaire braced himself as the ceffyl sputtered, set its sights on him, and dashed in his direction. As the ceffyl made its way to Doug, other warriors swung their swords at it in an attempt to stop it in its tracks. One lost his balance and another fell over, face first, into the dirt, mystified at the ceffyl's ability to liquefy itself and escape harm.

Doug saw what it did, and what's more, he saw the ceffyl grow horns and harden its body into a coat of ice. On the edge of panic, Douglassaire thought back to what his father wrote in his journal about taming the lusae, but didn't want to use his power so early. He was saving it as a surprise attack against Lesech, but he saw the danger he was up against and he wasn't going to die here. He quickly sheathed his sword and held both hands open, palms up, to his side.

A few people in the crowd protested, thinking he was crazy not to attack, but Isidro held his breath knowing what Doug was about to do.

Doug felt the air around him grow stronger and slide through his fingers. When the ceffyl got close enough, his arms pulsated as he pushed the heavy air in its direction. The ceffyl flew back from the force of the powerful blast and landed hard on its back. Its icy form shattered into pieces and Douglassaire sighed in relief.

Lesech was further down the field among a group of five trying to rid themselves of the third lusus to be released: a halo. It was a brown, hawk-like bird with a sharp tail and a ring of air surrounding its body that could only be seen by the dirt that entered its orbit. Its broad wings flapped keeping it in midair while its tail lashed like a whip over and over sending rings of air that sliced through its opponents. Lesech allowed the rest of his group to get cut down while he attacked the halo from behind. Whether it was a cunning or cowardly move was a point sure to be debated in the months after. He jumped and sailed, assisted by air, to his target and stabbed it in the back, pinning him down to the earth. He did all of this just in time to see Douglassaire's victory against the ceffyl, but just as Doug let his guard down, Lesech could see the creature's broken pieces liquefy and reform. In only a matter of seconds, the ceffyl stood once more.

Nearby, soldiers were falling one by one to the rasaji's flames. It killed four warriors before facing its first real threat. The woman who first came after Doug managed to cut into the creature, but not deep enough to exact any critical wounds. The lion swiped a fiery paw at her face, but she turned just in time to receive a finishing blow to her pride as her last remaining pauldron flew off. Lesech decided to let the other warriors continue their losing fight to the rasaji and ran over to the ceffyl. He yelled, "You've been holding back, Douglassaire! Since when are you an Etherean?"

"Are you here to help me or fight me?" Doug asked with his eyes on the reborn creature. The ceffyl just stood there, docile and staring blankly back at Doug.

Lesech, still armed with two swords, stood beside his rival and said, "Our fight will be so much more interesting one-on-one, don't you think? Let's dispatch of this vermin first."

The ceffyl's calm demeanor suddenly changed as Lesech came into its view. Its wet white coat glistened in the sun as it stood on its hind legs and neighed loudly. The dripping of water from its back stopped as it turned to ice once again and the ceffyl charged ahead as soon as its front hooves landed. It came straight for Lesech and tried to ram him with its frozen horns, but Lesech dodged to the side and swiped at it with his sword. Of course, the ceffyl remained unharmed, liquefying itself as the sword went through what would have been its flesh. The horse turned quick and raised its frozen hooves at Lesech who successfully blocked its kicks that sent a painful shock wave through his arms. "Why isn't it coming after you, Douglassaire?" he commanded.

Doug smiled, realizing that what his father said was true. "Don't worry about it."

"How do we kill this thing?"

Doug saw the lion down the field and said, "The rasaji."

Lesech frowned in disgust, but knew this was the only way. "Enjoy the *only* time you call the shots on me." He ran towards the rasaji with the ceffyl close at his back. He yelled at the warriors fighting the lion, "Everyone move!" He threw one sword at the rasaji and provoked it to come after him. As he got close, the rasaji jumped at Lesech's face with its white fangs wide open. Lesech jumped sideways at the last possible second and the rasaji slammed into the ceffyl. The ceffyl turned to water, but the rasaji's flames were too hot and all that was left was a cloud of steam. Douglassaire took advantage of the rasaji's blindness and struck it down with a deep cut to its back. Its flames disappeared and the rasaji clawed at the ground where it lay until it lost all strength.

The ten remaining warriors stood still, numb to the screams and cheers from the crowd. An air of suspicion passed between all of them as they wondered who would be the first to strike and begin the last phase of the battle. Douglassaire saw the cages had not yet closed and said, "Wait. It's not over." As if waiting for its cue an atlas slowly stepped out from the dark cage and into the sun. Seeing the monstrosity – how it towered over all of them with its rough brown fur and snarling fangs – the audience felt uneasy, but some of the fighters began to feel panic set in. Each step it took made the ground shake, and the atlas roared as its fur exploded and stood upright into countless quills. One of the warriors dropped to his knees and quivered in fear. The atlas swiped his paw at the warrior, resulting in his instant death as he crashed into the wall of the stadium.

Douglassaire summoned all the power he could and launched a full blast of wind at the atlas. The big bear lifted itself on its hind legs to shield itself and landed on the ground, quaking the entire stadium. It roared again and returned the attack for one of its own. The atlas turned its back to its enemies and shot a barrage of quills through the air. The wooden missiles tore through five of the warriors while the remaining four were able to dodge. Douglassaire and Lesech used their powers of wind to change the course of the quills and knock them away with their swords. "Looks like your little trick isn't working, Douglassaire," said Lesech. "I'll take care of this one."

Lesech negated the air resistance around him and charged the beast with great speed, grabbing his tossed sword in the process. He jumped and sailed through the air aiming for its back and landed a hard strike. Chunks of wood shattered and flew around Lesech as he tore some of the quills, but the atlas didn't even flinch. Lesech remained airborne after his first strike and dodged the atlas's quilled counterattacks by flying through the air. The audience screamed its approval of their hero. Douglassaire shared in that moment of awe as he realized just how far Lesech had come since his days in college. His experience using his ether was well beyond Doug's. Doug began to worry about that. He would have to figure out a way to remove Lesech's last pauldron before they began to fight.

Lesech dodged and attacked again and again, but his only result was angering the monster even more. Saliva erupted from its wide jaw as it roared and swung a paw at the annoying fly. Douglassaire yelled a command at the warriors, "Go for the underbelly!" He ran and slid under the atlas on his shin guards in demonstration and attacked from below. The atlas cried out in pain as Doug came through, and the other two warriors on the ground followed his lead. As they began to run and slide under the atlas, Lesech, hovering a few feet in the air, saw an opportunity. He flew below the atlas and zigzagged to each leg, delivering hard blows and throwing the atlas off-balance. The two remaining warriors delivered the final blow as they slid underneath, but fell victim to Lesech's trickery as the dying atlas came falling down quickly on top of them.

"Ladies and gentlemen, what an amazing battle this has been!" The announcer was especially excited now. "Lesech brings down the atlas and we're down to only two combatants!"

If Doug wasn't on the battlefield, he would have seriously been annoyed by that claim. Isidro handled all of the annoyance for the both of them. "Oh, come on! Really? That was all Doug!" he cried, drowned out by the cheers.

The announcer hyped the audience for one last time. "Who will win? Who is our next Commander? Lesech, the superstar, or Douglassaire Heuresyt, the legacy?"

Lesech landed on his feet with a sinister grin on his face. "Finally, we get to the good part. Ready to die, Douglassaire?"

"Don't talk so big, Lesech. You've only got one pauldron left. I haven't been hit yet."

As he spoke, the atlas's back began rising and falling like it was breathing again. Doug remembered reading about the atlas's parting gift.

Lesech said, "Well, *I* haven't come after you, yet. And I'm not going for pauldrons."

The atlas suddenly sprayed its quills into the air. Doug made his move and redirected them all in Lesech's direction with a powerful gale. Lesech was blinded by hundreds of large wooden needles but easily blocked them all with a force of wind of his own. As the last quill was removed, he saw Douglassaire inches away aiming for his last pauldron and swinging down with his sword. Lesech made a last-second block with one sword and said, "Ah-ah-ah, Douglassaire. It won't be that easy."

Lesech used his free sword and swung for Doug's legs. Doug jumped and flipped behind Lesech going for another strike but was unsuccessful. They went after each other with a ferocity that intensified with each unsuccessful attempt at a win. Douglassaire could taste the end of his journey and his success, if only he could bring down this lunatic. The air spirit inside of him beckoned, *Now, Douglassaire! This fight is too much for you. It was meant for me.*

I'm not letting you take over, Doug responded inwardly. *This is my body.*

Lesech wanted this win more than ever. Despite how good he was at it, he was done being the side-show for non-Ethereans. It was an important first step to real power, especially with his alliance to the queen. There was no way he was going to let Douglassaire win.

Lesech held on to his two swords and unleashed a barrage of attacks that put Doug on the defensive. He was being pushed back further and further, closer to the door in the coliseum where Lesech emerged. Lesech suddenly stopped and Doug could sense he was using his ether for something. The wind picked up from behind Doug and Lesech smiled and said, "Game over, Douglassaire." The sword he stuck in the ground when the battle began flew out from the force of the wind. The sword spun in the air and the point came soaring at Douglassaire's back. Doug looked behind him at the last second. His eyes widened with a fear he'd never known. And the world suddenly went pitch black.

Lesech's smug expression changed when he saw Doug's free hand holding on to the sword's hilt. It was as if he switched places with the bladed missile. Lesech's hair bounced and swayed with the fierce wind that emanated from his opponent. He looked into Doug's eyes and frowned sensing that something had changed. "What happened to you, Douglassaire?"

"You dare address a king with the name of a peon? I am not Douglassaire!"

Lesech could certainly see that he was not. As he blocked each swing of Doug's swords, he noticed he was faster...stronger. The mark on the back of his neck glowed a bright white, and he was using his ether to a degree even Lesech could not match. Lesech's determination to win grew even more serious. Somebody was going to die here, and if he had any say, it would not be him.

Lesech parried an attack and went for the kill, but was too slow and got kicked into the air. The air spirit flew after his target and punched him back to the ground. Lesech landed and gasped desperately for the air escaping his lungs. He lie still and watched as the possessed Douglassaire hovered over him. He could see Doug was clearly out of his mind.

The air spirit let go of the swords in his hands and let the air carry them at his side. The audience went silent, watching in a mix of excitement and horror at the power of this man. Some gasped as they noticed movement around the field. Suddenly, all of the swords on the ground left behind by the fallen were hoisted up into the air and pointed at the grounded Lesech.

The air spirit felt a nagging from its vessel. *That's enough*, Doug exclaimed.

Hardly, the spirit replied. *You knew it was over and gave up at the last second. If I hadn't taken over, you'd be dead. Accept your place as my vessel and I'll take the place of Commander. This worm dies.*

No!

Lesech closed his eyes and accepted defeat as he saw all of the swords flying fast in his direction. A moment passed, but he felt no pain. He opened his eyes to see the blades just inches from his face and Douglassaire trudging toward him in pain with just one sword in hand.

His voice was labored, and the air spirit spoke through Doug's lips one last time as Doug started to regain control. "For whatever reason...my vessel strongly desires your life remain unharmed. Go live the life of a knave... That is all you are suited for." He swiftly cut off Lesech's last pauldron. And the Power Battle was over.

III

One by one, the airborne swords began to fall as if being cut off from their invisible puppet strings. The spirit's hold over Douglassaire slowly slipped away, leaving the true Doug to enjoy the feeling of achieving his dream. The sound of people cheering him on and the announcement of his victory made it official, "All hail the winner and new leader of the Southern Third, Commander Heuresyt!"

Isidro screamed in delight, jumping and cheering along with his fellow students, some teary-eyed, and all in shock at their teacher who had just become the most powerful man in the nation.

There was one man who did not share in the jubilation. He did not hear the cheers, he did not hear the announcement, and he didn't even see anything but a cloud of red and the silhouette of his rival who may or may not have been smiling and waving at the crowd. Everything he had worked for and everything he had done to get to this point shattered in an instant. He hadn't even died an honorable death as the famous actor, Lesech. He probably wouldn't even be able to act anymore. Now, he would only be remembered as the man who lost to Douglassaire…and that was simply unbearable.

Lesech grabbed one of his swords and slowly lifted himself up. First to his knees, then to his feet, and finally he regained his balance.

A few people screamed in the audience and the crowd's mood suddenly changed. Lesech charged after Doug with his sword pointed out in front of him and screamed from the depths of his soul. Douglassaire, unarmed, looked behind him and saw the

199

man taking his last cowardly stand against him. As the air spirit's control faded, he swung out his arm and used every ounce of power he had left to draw the remaining airborne swords straight through Lesech's back. Lesech stopped in his tracks as blood began dripping from his mouth. They looked each other in the eye – the sight of Douglassaire's frowning expression of pity, Lesech's last.

CHAPTER TWENTY-TWO

I

Queen Aeothesca watched the Power Battle on the screen in her private quarters. Her face was cross with disappointment at Lesech's failure. As the battle took place, her posture changed from straight, to leaning forward, to deflated by the end.

Catherine, ever nearby, watched along with her and was just as disgusted. "That swine! We should have known he would lose...and to a nobody. Who is this Douglassaire, anyway?"

The queen raised her hand and said, "Shut up, Catherine. I am thinking." The plan to use the Southern Third's army through Lesech was no longer an option. Now that they had their new leader they would no doubt call for her head. She would have to do something drastic. This new Commander was certainly interesting. "Catherine, this man, Heuresyt, if he is who he says he is, his father was the cause of the Pangaean Conflict twenty-five years ago."

"What?"

"I have told you the story of my mother's attempt to cover up my abilities...how she had a man killed on Southern soil? Apparently the man had a son, and somehow he survived."

"He is an Etherean. Do you think we could use him in Lesech's stead?"

"Absolutely not! For him to even mention his last name…why, I am tempted to think of it as a declaration of war, itself. No, he cannot be trusted. He is likely well aware of his lineage."

"Well, then what will you do, my lady?"

"We will have to attack the Southern Third as soon as possible."

"Can we succeed against such a powerful enemy?"

"Now is the best chance we have. An army is only as strong as its morale, and right now, that is something they have to build. Getting a new Commander is one thing, but crowning one who is an Etherean is entirely different. No matter how strong he is, he needs to show that they can trust him, and we need to strike before he gets the chance." Aeothesca silently mulled this over for a moment. "But perhaps things have worked out for the better. Did you notice anything strange about the new Commander, Catherine?"

She hesitated. "I was not going to mention it, Your Majesty. You have been quite secretive about the mark on your neck, even to me. However, I did notice that he had a similar mark on his."

"And because of that he would be much more valuable alive."

"Why is that?"

Aeothesca held her hair away from the back of her neck and allowed Catherine to see. "This triangle is the symbol of earth. When I was little, Mother took us on a trip to Sabulton, where I was forced to walk the desert in search of a mirage where people were said to sink into the earth and disappear. I nearly had the same fate until I heard its voice – the earth spirit. She made me take a chance on my life for greater power. She never liked that I was an Etherean, but I suppose since I was one already she would make me the most powerful. And had I died it would only be one less burden for her. Whether she welcomed the fact that I survived I will never know, but the point is, I got this symbol as an agreement to become a vessel for the spirit of earth."

"Okay…what?"

Aeothesca chuckled as she let her hair drop and veil the mark like before. "Dear, simple Catherine. You do know the legend of Ether, do you not?"

"Of course I do. Every true follower of Elao knows the story of Pangaea's creation."

"Then you know of the four spirits of war that escaped Ether during the holy fight. And a true follower of Elao such as you should know of the stories thereafter that told of the legendary Ethereans – normal people who were the vessels of those spirits."

"Yes, Your Majesty, but what are you saying?"

"What if I told you that everything was true? That there are eternal, powerful elemental spirits who, from time to time, inhabit us humans in order to experience the world as it is? And that I am such a human?"

Catherine was breathless. "…Your Majesty…but you were born Etherean; were you not?"

"Yes, dear. The new Commander and I share a similar trait. It would seem we are both vessels of ethereal spirits. But as an Etherean by birth, becoming a vessel for the earth spirit has only doubled my power. The Commander has the air spirit, which is quite interesting. I remember reading logs from my mother's time that mentioned a man with the air spirit stored his ether into the crystals outside and lifted this very castle into the sky. He must have died. That could be the only explanation."

"My queen! We live in holy times, indeed!"

"Remember the line in the old story, 'Three of four to open the door'? What I would desire most is to step through that door. To Ether, to the Djed Key. The power of God. It would make my mission all the more successful. This world would be mine. I could control everything. Everyone's fear of me would no longer be a bother. They call me a devil, a witch, a monster – well – I'll show them a monster. And this monster they would have to obey."

"So, you would need this man and one other, but where would you find such another vessel?"

"That is what makes this plan more than mere fantasy. I already know of one other – a water Etherean like you, Catherine."

"Your Majesty, I must show you something. Please allow me."

II

A few moments later in the middle of the knights' sparring room, Catherine stood across from a knight, both dressed in stretchy pants and a tank top. With the hilt of her collapsible sword in hand, she pressed a button for a royal blue blade to quickly fall through and snap into place. She looked to the room's stone wall where the queen was standing, eager to show her what she had learned. The knight across from Catherine drew his sword – its snap creating an echo in the musky room. At once, they sparred.

The knight lunged at Catherine, and her objective was to defend against every attack. The deafening sound of clashing swords rang through the room as the knight tried to break through her defense. He was unsuccessful. Catherine blocked overhead strikes, pushed back, dodged, and blocked some more. She had plenty of openings to mock a lethal strike and end the session. The knight felt she was toying with him and for good reason. She hoped the queen would recognize the same.

Strange things happen when in the midst of battle, sparring or not. The knight's ego took more hits than anything, and it showed in his increased intensity. He couldn't let the lady-in-waiting beat him in front of the queen. However, that is just what he did. His anger overrode his focus and he soon found himself in the role of defender. One hard strike from Catherine and his arms flew back, leaving his chest widely unguarded. Catherine got carried away and readied herself to spear the man's heart. She took one step forward–

"Stop!" yelled the queen. "That's enough."

Catherine froze. It took a moment for her to register that the fight was over, but she lowered her sword.

"Leave us," the queen said to the knight.

He brought his arm over his chest in a salute, bowed, and left the room.

"My, my, Catherine. I must say I am impressed."

Catherine's smile was wide. She was overjoyed to hear it. "Thank you, my queen. He and I have been training together for some time now."

"Oh, I know, dear, but I had no idea you had made such progress."

"Your Majesty, I could be of use to you. This war – let me be a part. My combat skill alone…and I haven't even used my abilities yet… I just know–"

"Calm down, Catherine. I am well aware. I have a proposition for you that I believe will satisfy the both of us."

"Say it, my queen, and it is done."

"For being the most loyal of my subjects, and as skilled as you have proven, from this moment forth, you will take charge of our knights. You will be General. When we begin our fight, bring Douglassaire here. Then, the world will be ours for the taking."

Catherine felt her heart pulse with joy and purpose. Her years of being one of the world's outsiders finally meant something. She had finally made it and it was all thanks to her beloved queen. She thrust her arm in front of her and bowed. "Your Majesty, it would be an honor. Thank you. I will not let you down."

CHAPTER TWENTY-THREE

I

Douglassaire was everywhere. He was the new face of the Southern Third, the new hope, the hero who could take down the queen, and the villain who took down Lesech…or so the headlines read. Slade only knew him as the dreamer – the kind-hearted, yet fearsome man who flew like a bullet to his ambition, crashing through any obstacle in his way. It was the crashing that had scared Slade all those years ago. Even now, a few days after the Power Battle, Slade sat at the desk in his office worried about what lies ahead for his old friend. The room was dark, and the halls of M.3.A.N. were quiet. All that was on was the small desk lamp and a big screen on the wall depicting scenes of Doug's victory. Commentators were devouring every bit of information they could find on this handsome mystery man. The segment was titled *Friend or Foe?* – a sly allusion to the danger of his ethereal powers.

Slade grabbed the remote control sitting in between his cup of wine and his comm. and turned the voices and pictures off. When the Power Battle took place, he could barely watch Doug perform without jumping and shuddering. The rush was not for him. And now, every time he saw him, he felt a pang of melancholy. He quickly picked up his comm., flicked the screen on, and searched for Douglassaire's number. He was going to call him now. *Don't think – just do it,* he said to himself. Then, he wondered if his number was still the same. Probably not, he's the Southern Commander now, and even if it was…would he answer? Slade put his comm. to sleep and sat it back down on the desk. He crossed his arms on his desk and used them as a pillow while he lamented the inability to congratulate his friend on such a big achievement. He wanted to say, *Way to go, Doug. I knew you could do it.* He wanted to tell him how inspiring he was…and ask forgiveness for abandoning him. His heart screamed, *Take me back!* but he knew Doug would only question his motives, now he'd made it big.

Slade didn't care; he had to try. Suddenly, his courage surged. He sat up straight in his chair and grabbed his comm. He got back to the screen showing Doug's number and pressed *CALL.* His heart accelerated as he pressed the comm. to his ear. Then, it slowed as he heard the delightful voice of a dreadful pre-recorded message, "Sorry, we can no longer make this connection." Slade hung up, flung his comm. across the desk, and sank back into his swivel chair. He swung left to right, left to right, waiting for some interruption to his despair.

He couldn't even call Gisela. He already knew she hated him, and he understood. He would hate him too if he had been treated the way he treated Gisela. He had been so immature and wished he had handled things better. Now even she was in the news grieving over her dead husband. He wanted nothing other than to call and offer his condolences, and would have had he not half-expected her response to be a boisterous "Fuck you!" It was as if she had snapped after that trip they took. Everything about Gisela had changed, including her tolerance for Slade.

Slade was startled by the sound of his desk comm.'s ring. For a brief moment, he had the hope that one of his friends caught his waves of depression from the universe but was pulled back to reality when he reminded himself that only work associates knew how to reach him at his job. He answered the call saying, "Please tell me you found the princess. I need some good news."

The man on the other end spoke apologetically. "Director, we still don't know her precise whereabouts."

Slade exhaled. "Any leads at least?"

"We have reason to believe she's somewhere around Probuston, in the Southern Third, sir."

"Probuston?" Slade was surprised at the hiding place. It was the last place he expected a former princess would go.

"Yes, sir. We're still working to see what we can find, but she's done a pretty good job of disappearing."

"All right, keep working." He ended the call. What more could he say? He continued to reflect on his life and became even more depressed. This was what his life had become – an endless string of calls and waiting. He took a sip of his wine and sat back in his chair.

So, what are you gonna do about it? he thought. Thoughts like this, relics of the old Slade, would wander into his mind from time to time. He was now well-practiced at shooing them away. However, after seeing Douglassaire's victory, the thoughts began to linger. So he toyed with the idea – what could he do? He was a director at M.3.A.N. in the middle of an assassination case and trying to locate the lost princess. *Not much.* But that wasn't entirely true. There was still one thing he could do. He lost a spark for life when he left Douglassaire. Perhaps by seeing him again, he could get it back. As crazy as it was and as awkward as their meeting might be, Slade knew as soon as he had the time that's what he needed to do.

II

"Mr. President!" Doug called as he entered the Presidents' Manse. Isidro, acting as his new personal assistant, followed closely behind. Douglassaire extended his hand for a polite shake with President Yu who was surrounded by a political entourage. After winning the Power Battle, Doug wanted to hold the Middle Third accountable for the deaths of his parents. He came to his senses, however, once he realized how many other people's lives he'd been entrusted with. He couldn't start a military conflict for a personal vendetta. Plus, it wasn't Queen Aeothesca who was to blame; it was her mother. Yet, despite her actions, a Heuresyt had still rose to power and stood on the same level as a world leader. His victory at the Power Battle had been revenge enough. Still, after the assassination of his country's previous Commander, the peace treaty was under enormous threat. His citizens were accusing the queen of being the killer. He didn't trust that she would not retaliate in some fashion. He also knew there was a chance that some of his people might start conflict. He was here to make sure that neither of those things happened.

"Commander," President Yu replied, "how great to have you. Is this your first time here?"

"In Septentrion City? Yeah, but I did go to school at Burrow for a time."

"Fabulous. Let's take a walk."

The Manse was clean, yet had the musky smell of an old library. The press was waiting in an area that was roped off to the side of the big hall. Their cameras went clicking away and captured the president standing with the new Southern Commander in front of the cherrywood walls of the room.

Douglassaire felt nervous. He'd never met another country's leader before. Weeks after winning the Power Battle, he still couldn't believe how much his life had changed. The deep crimson cape he wore over his black suit made him feel imposing, but deep down he didn't mind the ability to intimidate.

As they began to walk ahead of their staff, the president said, "I'd like to congratulate you on your victory in the Power Battle. Your skill is amazing."

Doug sensed the forced nature of President Yu's words. He'd heard the same ever since the Power Battle. When people said he was *amazing* what they really meant was *terrifying*, so he constantly had to placate their fears. "Thank you. It is only in battle when I use my power. I hardly meant to go that far."

"Certainly. Fighting brings out the worst in all of us, but I must say that you showed honorable restraint. Even while facing a madman you tried to spare his life. You learned a valuable lesson in leadership very early, my friend."

"And what is that?"

"Unfortunately, some deaths can't be helped."

They reached the wooden double doors of a private room and stepped in alone. The theme of dark cherrywood continued but was balanced by the sunlight that came through the big window in the back. In the center was a big table and a seat on either side. The two men each took a seat.

"So, what brings you up north, Commander? The brief conversation we had lets me know it's important."

"Mr. President, tensions are high. Ever since what happened at the Leaders Ball, my people are angry. They want the Middle Third to pay."

"There's no hard evidence that the queen is responsible for Commander Azure's death."

"I know that and they know that. But a lack of evidence doesn't stop paranoia. I don't want the Nomiso Agreement broken because we're angry. War is the last thing we need, but my people need to feel heard."

"So, what are you proposing?"

"We need something stronger than the Nomiso Agreement. We can build a coalition, so that all of us are held accountable for actions taken against another nation. North, Middle, and South can come together and make deals on trade, better travel, and we can hold each other accountable for any cross-national conflicts like this one. If the Middle Third attacks the South, they then have a problem with the North *and* the South. And the same any other way. If I show my people that I put pressure on the queen to agree to this, I think that could save the peace."

"And what if she disagrees?"

"She won't. Not if I have the North's support."

President Yu chuckled. "I like how you're so sure." He stood and paced to the window. "Let me remind you that this is Queen Jacqueline's daughter you're talking about. The apple never falls far from the tree. Allow me to blunt, Commander. You're asking us to pick sides between yourself and Aeothesca – two Etherean gods of war. The North has no dog in this fight."

"I'm not asking you to pick a side–"

"Of course you are. If I agree with you and the queen says no, then we'd have no choice but to step into war against her."

Douglassaire stood and said, "Mr. President, the only side I'm asking you to pick is the side of peace." He felt a flash of anger inside of him, but calmed himself down. He'd been poor before, but he wasn't used to begging. "I'm trying to stop a war here. Just agree, so we can see where it goes. Whatever decision the North decides to make if she disagrees, we'll deal with it, but I need to be able to force her hand."

***

Douglassaire appeared through the double doors with a confident stride and rejoined Isidro. They walked toward the exit with the undivided attention of the press while the President's staff flooded the room Doug had left.

"How did it go?" Isidro asked.

Doug smiled, no longer able to keep a straight face. "We got it."

III

"Commander! To what do I owe this pleasure?" Queen Aeothesca answered her desk comm. in the study. She sat at the big desk in front of the window overlooking the water. The desk was cleared of books and papers for once. There was nothing to distract her from this important call. What happened right now could be the first step to attaining absolute power.

Douglassaire's deep voice was heard clearly through the speaker. "Good evening, Your Majesty. I'm calling to offer you the chance to come back into the fold. Yesterday, the Northern and Southern Thirds have agreed to a coalition and we need your involvement. This is a way to strengthen the peace between us."

"Well, we certainly would not want an end to peace, Commander; would we? But we already have the Nomiso Agreement in place. Why the need for something else now?"

"I'm sure you've noticed a change in attitudes between our nations after the previous Commander's death."

"Yes, an event you have caused."

Silence.

Aeothesca waited for his response. It was time to push his buttons and see how easy it would be to anger him.

"What do you mean, 'an event we have caused'?"

"Well, *I* certainly did not kill him. Surely, you agree." She sat up in her chair and leaned over the speaker. "It is a strange thing, Commander, this...peace you are trying to protect. The only threats to the world's peace seem to come from your people. In fact, the Pangaean Conflict arose from the actions of your own father."

Douglassaire's voice grew louder. "How can you possibly

place the blame elsewhere? On my father? Really? That's offensive."

"Then, please enlighten me as to who you think is responsible for our world's troubles."

"The Middle Third killed my family! And, now, I'm damn near convinced that you killed the Commander."

The queen smiled and sat back in her chair. "Well, now I know where you truly stand. And if that is your unshakeable position, you have left me no peaceful solution but to join your coalition. However, you understand that we would need something in return. Please allow me three days to figure out what that might be."

"Two days. And you won't get much."

"Very well. In forty-eight hours, you will hear from me again. Take care, Commander." The line went silent. Queen Aeothesca looked across the room. "Did you get that?"

Catherine was nearby the whole time. She was sitting by a recorder attached to the comm. by a long cord. "Yes. Everything," she replied.

"Good. Have it doctored and send it to the press. We are going to war."

CHAPTER TWENTY-FOUR

I

The temperature began to drop as night fell in Probuston. All was quiet as a light rain touched down on the city. The usual thugs and ruffians that roamed the territory, threatening their hard-working neighbors, seemed to find shelter elsewhere. The streets of Probuston were dangerous, but tonight seemed to be an off night. The only movement taking place was a man running down a back alley. He slipped and lost his balance on the brick path that led to the street, but stopped himself from falling by reaching out and scraping his hand against the outside wall of a building. He glanced behind him and saw a dark cloaked figure continue to chase him. It was so dark, he felt lucky to have noticed the figure in the first place. In his split-second glance he also saw something new. The figure was holding something long and metallic, but it wasn't a sword. A BAC! As his hunter raised the gun for a shot, he ducked his head and quickly turned the corner.

***

"Shit," the cloaked figure muttered.

"What's wrong, Anna? Getting rusty?" One of the men on the

rooftops teased through his radio.

The one who started this little chase and missed her shot wanted to say, "Don't let my royal blood fool you," but needed to hold on to her secret of being the queen's sister. Instead, she responded, "Don't test me. I could shoot you dead from here if we weren't under orders to keep it as quiet as possible."

He laughed. "I'm no criminal like this guy. We both know you'd give me a fair swordfight."

Another man cut in on the conversation. "Stay focused, team. We need this guy alive for the big money. He's an Etherean, so we have to be extremely careful. Shoot only if necessary."

"Right, Libra," said Anna. She ran after the man and spotted him as she turned the corner. "He's on his way," she warned to her two teammates at the end of the alleyway. "Be ready to apprehend."

They awaited the man around the corners of the buildings. As the splash of puddles and footsteps grew nearer, the two of them popped out from behind opposite ends with their hoods on and swords drawn from their sides. "Stop! You're under arrest," yelled one of them to their target. "Put your hands up, nice and slow...there ya go."

Anna, a far distance away, could see the man slide to a halt under the streetlamp and comply. Thunder could be heard in the distance and the rain began to fall harder. Just as everything seemed to draw to a close, Anna noticed something strange. The rain around the man began to fall away from him as if he held an umbrella. Anna lifted her rifle at the target and yelled into her radio, "Heads up! He's up to something!"

One of the figures on the rooftops yelled, "Stop or we'll shoot!"

The man didn't listen. His wet, wiry dark hair clung to his face and his thin lips twisted into a grin revealing a pattern of brown and missing teeth. The falling rain around him halted and froze to ice in midair.

"Get back!" Anna yelled.

The two men darted back to their opposite covers dodging the frozen beads of rain as they shot past them at breakneck speed. The man turned and saw Anna gaining ground behind him. She looked down the barrel of her gun and shot. The unlaunched frozen beads of rain at the target's back melted away as the man clutched his injured right arm and fell. Anna bolted down the alleyway while reaching in her pocket. The crystal bullet caught and refracted the single light in the alleyway as she reloaded her weapon. Her target tried lifting himself back up to his feet, but the pain of Anna's boot to his chest knocked him back down.

"Son of a bitch."

Her teammates came out from hiding. "Good work," one said.

"Yeah, Libra," the one from the rooftop chimed in as he jumped down the fire escape. He removed his hood revealing his dark eyes and long black hair, which was now getting soaked. "Your girl's a great shot."

"Do you want this guy knowing who we are? Don't say my name, and put your hood back on," Libra commanded.

"Doesn't look like he's listening to much of what we're saying, anyway."

Their last teammate came down the opposite fire escape and joined the four of them as they surrounded their target. The man they caught was in a fetal position with his bleeding arm to his chest and groaning.

"Let's go get our bounty," Libra said. With the help of another teammate, he lifted the man to his feet. The criminal's spirit was crushed and he offered no struggle as his arms were placed over the shoulders of his captors. The long-haired one removed a can of spray paint from the pocket of his cloak and drew a symbol in the small pool of light. An 'A' enclosed in a circle – a reminder to all that they existed in the shadows.

As Anna walked with them through the rain she marveled at how after years of running she was able to find stability and security. She was happy. She remembered that it was a night just like this when she was first introduced to these people. Soon, the memories of her first time in Probuston, and subsequent joining of this group, flashed through her mind.

II

Probuston wasn't the ritziest of locales, but after being recognized almost everywhere else she went, Annonymn decided her change needed to be more drastic. It had been eleven years since she ran away from royalty – away from her cruel sister who was more like their mother than she'd ever admit. When she started, she never expected the difficulty that came with keeping a low profile. She knew she couldn't stay in the Middle Third for long. So, she headed south.

Finally, six years ago, after years of hopping from small town to small town, she settled in Probuston, but not before making that agonizing decision to cut her hair. She did this realizing her vanity was the final piece of being a princess that she had to let go. Her beautiful, straight auburn mane was no more, replaced by blonde dye and an angled haircut that covered almost half of her face. She had finally become Anna.

Adjusting to Probuston proved to be almost impossible. What once was probably a beautiful cityscape was now an ugly, broken-down cluster of rusted, abandoned architecture with missing windows. Some people tried their best to make do with what they had, but most were just out for themselves. She found it hard to find work as everyone was either too suspicious or too poor to hire her. She tried to fit in, and while no one suspected her of being the princess, they still knew she was an outsider.

The same could be said for the Auctorati, the small band of mercenaries that gave her shelter for the night. Really, it had only been the decision of the man they called Libra. Apparently, he was in charge. That's the only reason they went along with it.

Anna first met Libra on a night like this – dark, damp, and

miserable. She couldn't find a place to stay in this rotten city and had used her only blanket as a shield from the heavy rain. She shivered, cursing her fate and cursing her decision to ever leave Lorelei Castle in the first place. She missed the castle. It was home. Then, she remembered her sister, and the feelings of nostalgia were always overshadowed by the memories of what she did. The queen stole Anna's fiancé, Orleone. There was more than this, however. Her sister had changed more and more over the years. As a queen, she became a tyrant just like their mother. Lorelei Castle became an insufferable place to live and losing Orleone was the breaking point.

As she sat there in the rain, huddling with her head bent over, she heard the wet steps of a pair of boots stop in front of her. She slowly looked up and saw a man with a sword on his hip and a rifle strapped around his shoulder. He had on a dark, foreboding hooded cloak that barely revealed his face. His expression was fierce and her fearful heart quickened. She flinched as the man extended his hand.

"This is no place for a princess," he said.

"I'm no princess," she replied. *How does he know?* she wondered.

"Come on, get out of the rain."

She fought through her hesitation and grabbed his hand. She usually never trusted anyone this heavily armed, but she didn't know how long she could last in the cold rain. She popped up feeling as light as a feather. He was strong. Water-logged, she followed Libra back to a warehouse a few blocks away.

As she entered, she couldn't hide the look of surprise from her face. What she had expected to be a larger version of a hut turned out to be surprisingly cozy. Faux walls made of curtains were erected to make space for different rooms, all of which were furnished with mattresses that lay on the floor covered in a quilt. There was a small kitchen area – nothing fancy, just a stove, sink, and a countertop. The folding table a few steps away was surrounded by four plain, wooden chairs – one of which was occupied by a particularly surly looking young man with a shaved head. Tattoos covered his arms and colored what was once a canvas of pale, pinkish skin. He was attacking his soup in the most undignified way. The table was covered in small dark and light brown squares – places where game pieces called home when people weren't eating their dinner. The wooden figurines had been pushed to the opposite side of where the man sat.

Libra noticed the look on his guest's face. As he pulled off his hood he said, "It's not Lorelei Castle, but it'll do for tonight." When the light hit his face, Anna could see he was actually quite handsome. His tousled brown hair fell back into place framing his square jaw and covering his ears after being tugged by the hood.

"I have never been to Lorelei Castle, so I wouldn't know," she responded.

Libra chuckled, "Yeah...okay."

"I was actually expecting worse than this."

"...Who the fuck is this?" inquired the man at the table. His voice was hard and tough, just like his exterior.

Libra looked at Anna through the corner of his eye. "This is uh…" Libra started.

Anna had almost winced at what looked to be a revelation of who she really was, but when she looked at Libra, she saw a gaze that was more imploring than threatening. "Anna. My name is Anna."

"Anna. Her name is Anna. Anna, this is Jack. Jack, get her some soup. Anna, take a seat."

Without a moment's delay, Anna walked over and sat in the seat next to Jack and looked him square in the face. She knew the game of intimidation well – she was a princess after all. Jack frowned defiantly, then puffed out a chest full of air and rolled his eyes. He got up and headed over to the stove where a hot pot of soup sat. As he lifted the pot cover, the aroma of fresh, hot beef, onions, carrots, and what she thought was rosemary delighted Anna's nose. She felt her mouth moisten with anticipation and watched as Jack lifted out a few ladlefuls of soup into a bowl. After throwing in a spoon, he returned and placed the bowl of soup in front of Anna, allowing a few drops to spill over. He stood over her and crossed his arms and watched as she grabbed the spoon for her first taste. She hadn't had much food lately and what she did have was bland. This had been a welcome change of pace for her. The soup's beef broth warmed her cheeks and the mixture of vegetables and chunks of meat filled her. She became ravenous, but refused to show it. "It is good. Quite good," was all she could manage.

Jack grunted his appreciation and sat back in his seat.

Libra disappeared somewhere leaving the two of them to eat in silence. Once Anna was done, Jack took the bowls off the table and sat them in the sink. "Libra, your stray's done," he called. Out popped Libra from behind one of the curtain walls, shirtless, displaying the scars of past battles on his arms and chest. It had occurred to Anna that he had a story of his own. He remained undefeated, for he was still here – alive. She wondered what that story was.

"Anna, you're in the room with Kandyce tonight," he said, pointing his thumb to the other side of the room. She saw another woman with dark features and hair in a long, messy ponytail standing in that direction. Her arms were crossed and she shifted her weight as she waited for Anna to join her.

Anna got up from her seat and began to walk over, but before she got past Libra, he put out his arm and the same fierce look he gave her outside had reappeared. He said in a low voice, "No funny business. She sleeps with a candle the same way we sleep with our swords."

It took her a moment to digest what that meant. Then, she wondered whether she was a guest or a hostage. She measured the distance between her and the door with her eyes, but Libra caught her.

"Like I said, don't try anything. We'll talk tomorrow," he concluded. He retired to his room.

Anna took more cautious steps toward the woman after that. Kandyce disappeared behind her curtain and Anna followed. A space to sleep had been set up next to Kandyce's mattress and in between was an unlit white candle held by a bronze candle holder. Sitting beside the candle was a small crystal, glowing red.

"We don't have another mattress," Kandyce said in a deep alto. "It might be uncomfortable, but it's better than being outside." There were just two quilts. One sat on the floor and the other on top. Kandyce handed her a towel and some soft, dry clothes.

"Thank you."

"Thank Libra. I would never bring you here. In fact, I don't think even he would if he didn't have something on you. What we do is too important to let just anyone in." Kandyce lay down and pulled the cover over herself. "Go on, Anna. Get some rest," she said as she touched the crystal, sparking the candle's wick to life with flame.

Anna never expected such a mundane item to appear as fearsome as it did right then. She kept her eye on the flickering flame as she made her way to the opposite side of the small room. She had begun to dry herself and change and asked, "What do you all do?"

"We're bounty hunters." A slight grin appeared on her face at Anna's distress. "For Libra to let you in here must mean you're a big catch. I don't know what you did, but I can't wait to find out. Just don't try anything – bounties are usually more if we bring you in alive. Good night." Kandyce closed her eyes.

As Anna pulled the top cover back and lay down between the quilts, she worried about what the next day brought. She couldn't run, for fear she would be burned alive by Kandyce. If Libra told the rest of the Auctorati who she really was, she would probably see Lorelei Castle very soon, and most likely her death. She tried her best to get some rest, but between the hard floor and her worries, it wasn't much. She brainstormed ways to get herself out of this predicament, but kept coming up short.

***

Sleep left as fleeting as it came, and when Anna awoke, she saw she was alone. The candle between the beds was snuffed out and the light of morning broke through the small windows at the ceiling. She got up, leaving a pile of covers on the floor, and pulled back the curtained entryway just enough to peek at her new surroundings.

"Get a good sleep, Princess?" It was Libra. He sat back in his seat at the small checkered table with his booted feet on top, crossed and lying on the corner. The apple in his hands was his current project as he carved it with a small dagger. He cut a piece and brought it up to his lips, but stopped when he saw the look on Anna's face. "Don't worry, it's just us this morning." He ate his slice.

Anna felt her cheeks get hot and she crossed her arms as she walked toward the table. "I suppose you find it amusing to tease me like that?"

Libra looked up at Anna who tried her best to be the intimidating presence she once was and smiled. "Kinda," he said. He removed his feet from the table and kicked out the chair next to him and said, "Have a seat."

This man was infuriating. He knew who she was, despite her attempts to blend in. Now having that information did not daunt him in the least. And he kept doling out orders. She sat down, eyes fixed on his. "How do you know who I am?"

"It's my job to know."

"Whatever does that mean?"

"It means that I listen to the streets. The Auctorati wouldn't be successful if we didn't. Rumors of a girl resembling the princess began to circulate in other villages. Last I heard she was headed west to Probuston, and then you appear. Anyone in town with two eyes can see that you're not from here. It was probably the hair that threw everyone off." He cut another slice of apple and offered it to Anna. She declined with a steady silence.

"So, what now? Will you take me back to the Middle Third? Tell all of your friends? Make some money?"

Libra shrugged. "That's up to you. Usually the guys we catch would be in jail by now, but I get the sense that you must have had a good reason to leave home. As far as I can tell there's really no crime in that."

"Then, what do you want with me?"

"You'd make a good insurance policy. If we lose all our money or have to disband the group, you go back to the queen, we get paid, and either rebuild or go our separate ways. In the meantime, your secret is kept, you get a job, and a place to stay and eat. You can stop running."

"You make it sound all so appetizing. I suppose I do not have much choice in the matter." She had feigned annoyance, but in truth she was relieved. She wouldn't have much to fear as long as the group stayed intact. By then she could come up with an exit strategy. Until then, she decided she'd enjoy the small comforts the Auctorati could provide. She watched the man sitting in front of her devour another slice of his apple, unable to pinpoint what it was that mesmerized her just then.

Libra lifted his hand to his mouth as a drop of juice ran down the side. He caught Anna's gaze for just a moment and his eyebrows twitched as he awkwardly looked away. She did the same. He noticed that her face was less serious than a moment ago. The expressive eyes and pout of the princess were features he'd secretly pined after for years. Him and every other man. "If you're gonna stay here, you need to act less princessy and more tough. Otherwise you won't be able to keep your secret for long."

"How do you propose I go about doing that?"

"For starters, stop talking so proper." He paused and dared to look at her once more. "If you hang around us, you'll get it eventually."

III

That was how she joined the Auctorati. She started out doing simple chores around the group's hideout and stayed out of the way. At first, the rest of them weren't too thrilled to have a maid who knew all their secrets hanging around, but they trusted Libra, and for some strange reason, Libra trusted Anna. After a while they grew to trust her too.

Anna hated being left behind while the rest of them went on missions and began pestering Libra to train her. He finally gave in, giving Vinzant, the talkative one with the long black hair, the role of trainer. Over the years, she became proficient with the use of a sword, but she found that her specialty was with aim. The BAC was her weapon of choice. It was light enough to swing around her shoulder quickly, but had enough weight to make her feel powerful. Her fingertips became familiar with its rough metal edges. Armed with both the BAC and a sword, she joined the Auctorati on the streets of Probuston to bring in its criminals and reap the cash rewards.

The rewards got bigger after an idea she proposed. It was the day that moved the group from being a minor annoyance to an urban legend amongst the city's criminals. Libra had called a group meeting and they all sat around the small checkered table with the exception of Jack who was leaning against the kitchen counter. As they arrived, Libra pulled out the seat next to him for Anna. She ignored this gesture, just one of many, and pulled out a seat for herself across from him.

"We're not going to be able to keep this up, guys," Libra said. "There's too many of us to support and our pay isn't getting any better. These small-fry criminals aren't going to do it anymore."

Anna's chest tightened as she remembered the talk they had when she first joined. Over the past two years, she'd come to like all of them, but she knew that money came first in their mind. She hadn't realized that money was becoming an issue. Libra kept a tight lid on the group's finances from everyone. It was his way of easing their worry, but only now served to worry everyone greatly all at once – especially Anna. Just when she was feeling safe, this problem came along. Maybe they would turn on her.

"It would help if we could bring in more of those fuckin' Ethereans," Jack said. He saw Kandyce shoot him a cutting look. "Sorry, Kandyce, but they *do* have a higher bounty."

"It's okay," she replied. "You're right. We are more dangerous if we know how to use our ether."

Vinzant had his arms crossed on the table supporting his head. "Why don't we just make Kandyce the leader and fight magic with magic?"

"Because I'm not enough to take on every Etherean we come across."

"And I'm the leader, in case you forgot," Libra said.

"With the way things are going, you won't be leading anything for long," Vinzant replied.

"They do have a weakness," Anna said. She sat there in silence until now, desperately brainstorming a way to take Libra's insurance option off the table. Everyone looked at Anna with an intensified focus.

"What do you mean, 'they have a weakness'?" Kandyce inquired.

"Crystals."

"Crystals are only a way for us to store our energy."

"They can also be used as a way to suck the energy out."

"Really. And how do you do that?"

"Embed a crystal in an Etherean's body. It'll redirect their ether to the crystal and stop them from using their power."

Everyone paused and stared at Anna, contemplating the obvious question.

"Crystal swords, anyone?" Vinzant added. This was not the question. This was just Vinzant.

"It would probably be best as something that wouldn't kill

them," Anna corrected, "or at least something they couldn't easily pull out. A bullet, for instance."

Kandyce huffed, "Crystal bullets?" She jokingly added, "For God's sake, we aren't vampires, we're Ethereans."

"Nobody said you were. If you want a way to bring in Ethereans, that's it."

Jack finally asked the question on all of their minds aloud: "How do you know all this?"

Anna hesitated. The use of crystals against Ethereans had been a secret only the Middle Third found out through a series of tests done during the reign of her mother, Jacqueline. If there was one good thing Aeothesca did, it was ending that atrocity. There was only one use of crystal bullets that Anna had heard mentioned, but she forgot exactly what she heard. She glanced at Libra for help. "Um–"

"That doesn't matter," said Libra. "If there's a way to bring in more money, we should check it out."

His assistance made her feel grateful. As the group meeting came to a close she thought about what she came to learn about Libra. He loved Probuston more than anyone and fought to keep its streets as safe as possible. And he always protected her secret. Libra was a good man and she admired him. She always felt the possibility of a deeper bond between them, but up until then, she feared that at any moment she would have to move on from the group. So, Anna never opened herself up to his flirtations. Perhaps it was time for a change.

It was a lot of effort finding crystals, having them cut, then made into bullets, but once Libra said "go" they got it done. The bullets were forged, and after a successful test run with a bounty, they soon added at-large Ethereans to their list of bad guys to turn into the authorities.

Anna had averted the crisis of the group breaking up and they were able to make an even bigger name for themselves. With all of the money they made they could afford sprucing up their hideout and even go to the bar and have some fun once in a while.

IV

With their pockets fat from catching the water Etherean they chased down in the rain, the Auctorati decided to do the same to their bellies. Jack promised a good meal in celebration of their catch and everyone agreed that he made good on that promise after tasting what he whipped up. After dinner, Anna and Libra sat snuggled together on the floor in his room facing the painting on the wall and listening to the comforting music that played through the small speakers at his bedside table.

Anna suddenly stood up and reached out her hand for Libra to take hold and hoist himself up. They began to move their bodies in rhythm to the music and Anna asked, "Remember the first time we danced?"

"How could I forget?"

***

It had been a celebration much like this one, but at a local bar instead. Years of pent-up angst and frustration finally came to a head until Anna and Libra had to admit that they both liked each other as more than acquaintances. Jack and Vinzant were chatting by the bar. Kandyce was entertaining the conversation of a young woman with the courage to approach her. Anna sat silently at a table with Libra, mesmerized by the difference in dancing between the parties held at Lorelei Castle and the Southern Third. Had they danced like this in Reor? She had never realized how disconnected from the real world she was until then. There was still so much she didn't know.

Suddenly, a hand was in front of her face. She looked up and saw Libra. She was reminded of when he first came to her on the street in the same manner, but this time his expression was not intimidating – in fact she noticed a bit of nervousness. "Come on, Anna. Dance with me." She thought he was so adorable with the tough guy act – how could she not? He was a man who took chances, and this time it paid off. She grabbed his hand and allowed herself to be led to the center of the room.

She held on to Libra's hand and put her other on top of his shoulder, just as she had always done. Libra surprised her and let go of her hand, opting for wrapping his arms around her waist. Anna felt her cheeks flushed with heat as Libra pulled her close. The music here was different, rhythmic…even a bit tribal. And the dance was salacious. There was no rise and fall, no turn, no footwork… just a swaying of the hips. Anna felt embarrassed until she realized she had finally blended in like she wanted. Nobody looked at her strangely or even batted an eye, for they all were dancing the same way. After a while, she fell into the groove of the music and was hypnotized by Libra's touch and rocking back and forth. She didn't notice Jack and Kandyce's eyes staring at them in disbelief, nor Vinzant's whistling in their direction. She almost didn't notice Libra's lips as they touched hers, but a few seconds later she did, and she closed her eyes.

***

Anna and Libra recreated that night now in his bedroom. They rocked back and forth to the music as Libra placed his lips on Anna's. Then, they fell into an embrace so warm there was no need for exchanged words.

She placed the side of her head on his shoulder and thought about all it took for her to get to this point. Her happiness hadn't reached this level since she played with her sister as a little girl. Anna briefly thought about Orleone and immediately saw the difference between him and Libra. She knew for a fact that the man she was with now would never leave her side. She was safe and comfortable once more.

Then, the wall exploded.

CHAPTER TWENTY-FIVE

I

A full moon loomed in the sky with its radiance dimmed by the bitter lights of the city of Reor. The city's streets were filled with onlookers who craned their necks to see their queen speak at Crystal Park. Only an ornate railing protecting a small patch of land with a few crystals jutting from underground was what was left of Reor's main landmark. Queen Aeothesca stood at a podium flooded with lights and cameras that had been set up behind the railing. Behind her stood a few armored knights and other government workers for support. Among them sat Slade in his navy blue ceremonial suit. He marveled at the sight of Reor, a city that was always on, always moving, but was now still by comparison. He wondered what the announcement would bring. Neither he nor the other governors or government workers knew what they had been called to sit and watch at so late an hour. He looked around with the feeling of something missing, and then noticed the absence of the newly-named general, Catherine. Her presence was alarming enough, but he found the lack of it an omen of something even worse. With Lorelei Castle hanging overhead in the background, the queen made her speech:

"Loyal citizens of the Middle Third, dark times have fallen upon us. The Nomiso Agreement is no more. Commander Azure has fallen and the Southern Third, in all of their hatred and envy, seeks to pin his death on us when in reality, it was none other than one of their own. You have heard the reports, and they are true. The Southerner, built up by the people of the Middle Third, held in such high regard, Lesech, is to blame. We have been betrayed. Commander Heuresyt has already exacted revenge upon the culprit, yet, true to Southern form, he does not heed common sense and evidence. I have here Lesech's signed confession of guilt, but instead they have chosen to slander your queen, and in turn, defile the name of the Middle Third. You have heard the tapes! The Commander has deluded himself into believing that I killed their leader. And he has held on to a grudge that the world has long put behind. Our latest beacon of hope, the new Commander, has swiftly burned out. What we hoped could be a return to peace between our nations has evaporated, for Commander Heuresyt has fanned the flames of ignorance. We cannot stand by and let the Southern Third be whipped into a frenzy. For if we do, they will no doubt turn against us. It is for our safety, it is for our good name, it is for Elao that we must fight and bring down those that wish us ill. As we speak, our brave knights have landed in Probuston and Pelagus for a battle that will end their threat. I know you want peace, I know you want freedom. So, fight for it! This is it! This is your time! Elao be with us!" The crowd clapped as they always did after an address from the queen. Some even cheered, convinced that this was the right move. Most, however, were scared of the unknown ramifications of war with the Southern Third. That fear was reflected in a sea of faces as Aeothesca looked out among them. She didn't care. She had done all that she could to prove why war was necessary and she was proud of her performance.

Slade's heart skipped a beat, and as he looked to his right, he could see he wasn't alone. As surprised as they were, he was sure the Southern Third would feel the shock even more. He thought of the lives that would be taken; children who would no longer have parents; parents who would no longer have children; and many of them without homes. He thought of the beauty of the Southern Third, and the rest that he did not yet get to experience. He knew it would no longer appear the same as it did and that his chance had passed. Then, he thought about Douglassaire. Would he really have done the same if the queen hadn't struck first? Slade didn't believe it, but it really didn't matter now. The move had been made. It was a selfish, even treasonous thought, but he hoped that Doug would survive. He needed to see him one more time.

The crowd continued its appreciation and the queen looked back at the governors' seats. All of the governors at once shook off the weight of their shock and stood and applauded Even Director Maxwell, who felt more like a fraud now than ever.

II

Anna could see the red hue of a bright light behind her closed eyelids. There was an explosion and her first thought was, *They found us.* She thought the Auctorati had been exposed to some of the criminals they sought and had been attacked. She tried slowly peeling open her heavy eyes and groaned at the blunt pain at her side. She moved her hands around and felt dust and rubble all around her as she tried picking herself up. She brought her legs up below her torso and managed to sit up, all the while catching the sight of blood below her. She quickly touched her side – she wasn't bleeding there; it would just be a bruise. A drop of blood fell from her head and landed on her other hand. She lifted her hand and felt a sharp pain at the gash in the hairline at her forehead. All at once, all of her senses came back in a rush. Her heart raced as she looked around at the devastation, the fire raging in the bedroom, the hole in the wall, Libra. She watched in horror as a chrome-armored knight pulled his bloodied sword out of Libra's limp body.

"Libra!" she screamed.

Anna looked over as another knight appeared from the street through the hole in the wall with the hilt of a sword in hand. Anna shook at the sound of his blade falling and snapping into place. She saw her first assumption was wrong. As she looked past the knight and into the street, she could see the building across from theirs was destroyed, too. People were running, screaming, and being hunted by knights. *What is the Middle Third doing here?* Her eyes spotted Libra's sword and BAC hanging on the wall. The knight was only a few feet away, so dodging him would be almost impossible, but she had to give it a try. If she were fast enough, she could use Libra's sword to defend herself. She sprang to her feet and ran for the weapons. The knight took a giant step towards her and swung, intending for the length of his sword to finish her off.

Anna couldn't see how close she was to death. When she felt a sudden wave of heat behind her, she ducked, spun around, and watched as the knights screamed while burning alive.

"Anna, let's go!" It was Kandyce.

"But Libra—"

"Libra's dead! Get your ass in gear and let's go."

Anna recoiled at the words, the matter-of-factness at which Kandyce spoke. It was cruel and Anna hated her for it. However, she knew what Kandyce was telling her was true. So, she grabbed Libra's gun and sword from the wall and took one last look at his face – dead with silence, yet alive with pain.

She didn't know what was going on, but she knew who was to blame: her dear old sister, the queen. The more she thought about it, the more rage she felt building up inside. Her lips pursed and she spoke through gritted teeth, "Aeothesca." She made a promise to herself right then and there. "I'm gonna kill that bitch."

III

They fell from the sky in the dead of night. Soldiers clad in chrome, with their heads hidden by ornate helmets, slid down their winged transports onto the border of Pelagus at the top of a hill. They could see Pelagus Pyramid in the distance. Nobody expected their arrival, and their plan went perfectly.

Countless rows of knights from the Middle Third would soon march their way to the capital city. They awaited their orders from the general. Catherine removed her helmet before her arrival. It would only be a nuisance, and she wanted no hindrance to the sight of what she promised would be a successful mission. She stood in front of her army and gazed upon them all with pride. "Knights!" She yelled. "We are here on behalf of the Middle Third's legacy, on behalf of our queen, and Elao himself. We have but one mission – destroy that which means us harm. We do not have the cloaking on our armor that M.3.A.N. does due to expense, but we do not hide! We do not have a leader whose tactic is to 'wait and see' like the North, because we do not cower! We are the Middle Third and we shape our own destiny!" She raised her hilt to the sky and out popped her sword, dyed as royal a blue as her cape. With the weapon raised in the air and pointed at their destination, she let out a scream of words that roused her audience. "The Southern Third must fall! For the queen!" The knights of the Middle Third erupted into a frenzy of noise and charged the quiet city. Catherine stood still in that pose, allowing her men and women to swarm around her and, too, began her trek at the backlines.

She couldn't help but smile. Catherine had trained with the queen to get as powerful with her ether as she did, but even that did not compare to the limitless power she felt now. However, her excitement was tempered with a dose of reality. This was war and it was her first time controlling an army. One false move and she could lose their faith and her life. She continually drove doubt from her mind. She was ready. Catherine strutted confidently behind her army to Pelagus.

***

A man decided to take a stroll through the northern park in the wee hours of the black morning. His peace was obliterated as he saw knights from nowhere enter homes, burn whatever they came across, and even kill the few Southern warriors who patrolled the streets. His heart raced with shock and adrenaline. He made up his mind to run as far as he could, but he didn't get far before feeling the slice of cold steel down his back. He closed his eyes to the burning city – his home. The last sounds he ever heard were the sirens of war.

***

"What the hell is going on?" Douglassaire growled. He exited the clear elevator to the top level of his new home at Pelagus Pyramid. He was awakened by Isidro rushing into his room and frantically telling him about an assault on a nearby city and the sight of a fleet of supertrops hovering by the border of Pelagus. Doug felt a flash of anger, but managed to throw on his black robe and not direct it at Isidro. His living quarters were just below the pinnacle of the pyramid, but his ride in the elevator to the top felt much too long.

The large room was hardly ever used at night. The four slanted walls were made of glass, so natural sunlight was usually enough. Doug usually liked it when the artificial lighting was used. Their dim reflection against the black marble floor gave the room an imposing feeling, and each time, he treated the space as something to conquer. He succeeded every time he took his seat and reminded himself that he was finally in charge.

This time was different, though. The news of the Middle

Third's attack made the room seem almost insurmountable. As he approached his chair, he had to fight the feeling of being swallowed whole. The view of the land was magnificent. Each window, despite a portion being utilized as a screen for surveillance, revealed an expansive view of a specific part of the capital. The cityscape was now dotted with lights. Douglassaire steadied his mind, determined to not see those lights go out.

In the center of the room, a woman and a man occupied two out of three seats at a small triangular table plated in gold. The only spot left was marked by a large black chair with a high back and a black wooden border with a design that twisted and turned. Doug plopped down hard in his seat with a predatory energy he hadn't felt since the Power Battle. Isidro gave him and the others their space and watched the northern end of the city with deep concentration.

"Looks like the queen gave us her response to your proposal, Commander," the woman said. "The Middle Third has attacked Probuston and looks ready to make their move on this city at any moment." She sat there in her perfectly tailored pantsuit as part of the triad that helped make the big decisions in the country.

Across from her sat Deputy-Commander Rain who expressed his concern. "We need to send all of our troops in now and stop them at the border."

"For once, I agree with him, Commander. We can reserve some of our people for the evacuation of civilians, but it's imperative that we attack now. They've already overrun Probuston. The queen obviously has no interest in diplomacy."

Isidro jumped at the sight of the first fire erupting on the horizon. The sirens sounded, giving Douglassaire's gut a turn. As Commander, it fell on him to make the final decision of how to move forward. He lowered his head in disgust. He had been foolish. How could he have ever thought that a coalition with the Middle Third was possible? His enemy got the jump on him at a time he least expected. He first spoke to the woman. "Lieutenant, take a small group and have them usher the civilians as far south as possible. Rain, have our forces launch a full-scale attack on our enemy – now! Push them back!"

"Sir!" they both said as they stood up and accepted their

orders. As they left through the elevator, Isidro walked over to Doug.

"I'll have someone send up your armor, just in case."

Douglassaire shook his head. "No need. I'll get suited up downstairs. I'm fighting now."

"What? No Commander fights on the front lines. You have to stay safe."

Doug paid Isidro no mind as he got out of the chair and headed toward the elevator. Isidro stayed with him every step of the way and stepped in front of him just before reaching the door.

Isidro spread out his arms and said, "I can't let you go."

"Move, Isidro; that's an order."

"Look, as much as I want you out there and as much as you want to be out there, you can't go right now. You're not a warrior anymore, Teacher. Let your army do their job. You're the Commander. You *are* the Southern Third right now. We just lost one Commander. If you die, that's it for us."

Doug released air from his nostrils like a bull. He frowned and contemplated knocking over his former student and leaving by force, but he knew he was right. Instead, he walked over to the glass wall and watched the northern section of the city which was now in complete disarray. "If we can't stop them where they are now, I'm going out there. Screw the rules."

He could see multiple fires burning now with military vehicles making their way in and civilian wheelers trying to make their way out.

Isidro lifted a comm. to his ear and spoke into it, saying, "Bring up the Commander's armor."

IV

The lives left in the Auctorati's wake weighed heavy on their spirits. Even in their missions if they saw no other alternative than to kill a criminal for a bounty, Libra treated that mission as a failure. If only he saw what was happening now as the knights of the Middle Third stormed Probuston. Anna didn't think of this, however. Libra's death had made killing easier. These scumbags had to pay, and so did her sister.

The group fought their way to safety, and as day broke, they finally made their way to Lotus Valley. As they walked down the main road, they could see the old tourist town was nearly deserted. Hungry and tired from hours of running and fighting off knights, they hadn't had a chance to think, much less mourn the loss of their leader. It was time to catch a breather.

A few stragglers were left behind looting from stores on the main street before they made their way out of town. Anna felt her temperature rise as she watched a man nimbly climb out of a window with a smile on his face, a bag of food in his hand, and not so much as a scratch on him. He looked only a few years older than she and was certainly able-bodied. Why was he able to enjoy free food when she had to fight her way here? Where was the sense in that? She found it infuriating. She unsheathed her sword and charged the man before he had the time to run off and pinned him against the front door of the establishment. She pointed the sword at his face and yelled, "This is what you do? Your country is in crisis and you start tearing it apart?"

The man looked back in horror at the crazed woman with the blade as she bared her teeth at him. He tried, but couldn't muster up the strength to respond to her questions or plead for her forgiveness.

"Whoa, Anna, take it easy," Vinzant said, placing a hand on her shoulder. "You're gonna feel silly when we go in here for the same thing. I know I'm hungry."

Anna grabbed the man by his shirt and threw him out of the way. He stumbled, tripped, and fell skinning his hands in the process. He then ran off with surprising speed. Anna violently swung open the door to the store and walked in, taking a seat on the floor. She used the first shelf column she saw as back support. The shelves were nearly empty and only a little merchandise remained untouched. The rest walked in behind her, stepping over the few cans and bags lying on the floor, and watched as she buried her head in her hands. They didn't question her anger. They felt it, too. Libra was dead, their home was in ruins, and they didn't know what to do next.

Vinzant sat on the ground next to Anna and put his head back, exhausted, while Kandyce stood in front of them. She was still and looking through every object in the room to some unknown place in her mind. Jack leaned against the pane of the broken window looking outside and said, "Fuckin' Middlers."

"What do we do now? Join the army?" Vinzant asked.

"No. The army is for fools," said Kandyce. Her voice was distant and her eyes were wide and still looking into space. "I won't throw away my life. I fight to win."

"Well, if there was ever a no-win situation, this is it."

"They killed Libra?" Jack asked himself aloud.

"They're killing everyone," Anna said. She finally spoke, snapping her teammates to attention. "That's what they're doing. They're beating us into submission." Her face was red with a mix of anger and dried tears. "I'm sorry, everyone."

Jack's face revealed a puzzled expression. "Sorry for what? There's nothing you coulda done."

"Maybe not," she said, "but there's something I can do now. I can keep you guys safe. It's the least I can do after accepting me into the group."

"What are you talking about?" said Kandyce.

Anna exhaled, unsure of exactly how to say it. She knew they would be angry at her for this, but she was prepared to bear it.

"My name is Annonymn – Princess of the Middle Third."

Kandyce and Jack stared at her, unsure of how to take her words. Vinzant studied her face for a moment and suddenly dissolved into a fit of giggling. His shoulders began to quiver, his head snapped upward, and out bellowed an even more boisterous laugh. Kandyce and Jack looked at each other and soon joined the laughter, unable to contain themselves.

Kandyce saw Anna's confused expression and her laughter subsided. She began to shake her head, thinking the poor girl must have lost her mind. "Anna…"

"You can't be serious, right?" Jack asked.

Anna's eyes burned into Vinzant and he quickly quieted down. She looked at Jack and said, "Yes," as she pulled back the hair covering her face. Her team's expressions changed as they studied her face and realized she was telling the truth.

"Wait. So, we were living with our biggest bounty this whole time?" Kandyce asked.

"Wow," said Vinzant. "If only Libra knew."

"He did know," Anna corrected. "And I promise you, I will avenge him, but for now, if you offer me, you will get safe passage to the Middle Third and away from this war. He wouldn't want to see any of you hurt."

"Least of all you," Jack said. "Offer you? Are you kidding?"

"Now, wait a minute, Jack, I don't like being lied to," Kandyce said.

"And that's no reason to turn on our own. She's telling the truth now and offered us safety. Even she hasn't turned her back on us."

Vinzant chimed in, "And if Libra knew and didn't do anything about it, why should we? He'd want us to stay together."

Kandyce exhaled and turned her gaze toward Anna. "You're right. So, what's next?"

Jack said, "Well, Anna, if you're gonna avenge Libra, we wanna see it go down. Hell, I'd like to give the queen a piece of my fist, myself." He caught himself and realized he was talking to the queen's sister. "Sorry."

Anna shook her head, "Don't apologize. I don't even know who she is anymore. It's why I left. All she wants is power. All she does is take. Now, she took Libra." She looked at her team with a renewed sense of appreciation. She nodded her head and said, "Let's put her down."

V

From Pelagus's center came a mass of warriors from the Southern Third to meet the Middle Third's knights head on. The Lieutenant's group of warriors successfully evacuated most of the people to the southern end of the city, leaving the north as the battleground between each nation's forces. The chrome-armored knights clashed with the Southern Third's obsidian-clad warriors with the deafening sounds of swords crossing.

Day broke, and as the sounds of warfare and the smell of hopelessness filled the sky, Catherine made her way through the main street. Her blue sword sliced the backs of many unaware warriors who were already in conflict with one of her knights. "Good job!" she screamed. "Push! Push to the pyramid! The Commander must fall!" Her entourage of knights grew as the numbers of warriors dwindled. She already commanded a group to begin their conquest of the eastern sector, and the Southern Third's army responded just as she expected.

"The auxiliary team will defend the east," Deputy-Commander Rain said, screaming over the yells and cracks and bangs of metal. "Keep your post here! Kill these Middler bast—"

The cold steel of Catherine's blue sword stung the heart of Rain, cutting his words short. The knights by her side cut down the warriors who attempted a quick revenge as she pushed him to the ground and withdrew her blade.

"Knights, onward!"

***

"Deputy-Commander Rain is dead," said a voice from the

speaker on the triangular table. Douglassaire, now dressed in obsidian armor with deep red epaulets and a red cape, winced at this news. He stood next to Isidro and studied the video that appeared on the screen portion of the glass wall. He recognized the woman in charge of the knights as the same who killed one of his people at the Leaders Ball. She was dangerous. Simultaneously, he viewed the cityscape from the window and could see the chaos growing closer and fires starting in the eastern end of the city.

"Where's Lieutenant Kaltrop? Put her through."

"Right away, sir," said the voice.

Another voice came through on the speakers, yelling over the discord. "Commander!"

"What's your status, Lieutenant?"

"We've got a few casualties, but we're holding the east. There aren't a lot who have infiltrated."

"Rain is dead."

"Thanks for that. What are our orders?"

"Clear out the enemies in the east and then come to Central." He continued watching the video on the screen showing the knights' leader heading the march to his part of town unchallenged. "We'll have to stop them here."

"Roger," she said. The line went silent.

"That's it. I'm going," he told Isidro.

Isidro groaned.

"Stop it, Isidro. That woman is an Etherean," he said, pointing to the window. "I need to be out there."

Isidro looked at his teacher's determined expression and relented. He lowered his head and said, "I'm sorry. I'm just worried."

Douglassaire placed his hands on Isidro's shoulders. "No need. I got this. And if I don't come back, I just wanna say thank you…for being a true friend."

Those last words sent a shiver up Isidro's spine. As Doug walked past him to the elevator, he said, "I'm going with you."

"No. Go find your parents."

Isidro opened his mouth to protest, but stopped himself and nodded instead. The elevator door opened and Doug stepped on.

Isidro watched as the door closed and his teacher descended from the highest point in the nation to the murky depths of war.

***

The knights reached Central en masse with Catherine in the lead. Pelagus Pyramid stood high in the background and Catherine stopped in her tracks seeing the wall of southern warriors headed by Commander Heuresyt, himself. The city was oddly quiet and only the boots of countless soldiers could be heard. No one spoke. It was a standoff and everyone waited with bated breath for their order to attack.

"This is the end, Commander," Catherine yelled. "Surrender now and yield to the queen."

"The Southern Third will never surrender. And the Middle Third will pay for their crimes," Douglassaire replied. He unsheathed a sword as red as his cape and outlined in black.

"We tried mercy, but if you still desire war that is what you will receive. Knights, charge!"

Douglassaire ordered his men, "Go!"

The two sides crashed into one another as the silence was broken by screams of conquer and wails of defeat. The once scenic and quiet courtyard of the pyramid became a graveyard of fallen fighters. Douglassaire put a gale of wind behind the swing of his arm, knocking down the front most line of enemies. Catherine grabbed one of her own men as a shield and discarded him just in time to meet Douglassaire at the center of the conflict. She smiled at the spectacle of it all. She was enjoying herself. Not only did she have the chance to bring down the leader of the South, but she anticipated the glory of Queen Aeothesca and the Middle Third crowning her with the title of hero.

Douglassaire had her on the defensive. He was fast, but she still managed to block his attacks. "You're skilled, Commander," she said, her sword still in action, "but two can play that game." She blocked another attack and Doug felt the hard thud of her fist in his face. He closed his eyes as he staggered over and grabbed the side of his head in pain. When he opened them,

Catherine was behind him with two of her own knights by her side running toward the pyramid. Doug took off with a few warriors following him.

"Stay back," he said. "This one's mine."

"But, Commander, we can help," one of the warriors said.

"I don't need your help. None of you are any match for her. Fight off the knights. I'll take care of her."

Hesitant, his warriors followed their orders and went back into the fray. Douglassaire continued his pursuit, leaving his army far behind. He caught up to her and saw she stopped just at the edge of the bridge that connected Pelagus Pyramid to the north end of the city. The two knights stood at either side, but her sword was retracted and sitting by her hip. He slowed his run to a walk as she turned around to speak.

"Commander Heuresyt. As we speak, your people are dying. Why? Because you are too foolhardy to admit defeat. We have destroyed one part of town, and your precious pyramid is next unless you surrender immediately."

"You'd need your army to take that thing down, and I don't see them anywhere."

Catherine smiled. "Would I?" She planted her feet in ground and brought her hands to her sides. Her face was strained as though she were lifting the heaviest weight in the world.

Douglassaire tightened and looked around, alert, as the ground began to tremor. He could do nothing but stare at the wall of water that shot into the air destroying the bridge behind Catherine. A heavy rain fell upon them from the water, soaking all of them. Doug watched as water from all sides of the pyramid erupted into the sky.

He began to charge Catherine, but was met by resistance from her two knights. One of them kept their place and raised a weapon that caused Doug's stomach to turn. A BAC! He had no time to think as the knight shot at him. Doug's air-assisted speed allowed him to dodge the bullet. The other knight blocked his charge head-on with a sword, but didn't last long before feeling the sting of Doug's blade through his chest. He hadn't noticed until now, but this knight had a gun, too. They were playing dirty with these old weapons. *But why?* he wondered. "Stop this,"

Doug yelled to Catherine. She just smiled and shook her head. Her arms were lifted high as the water twisted and turned into a perfect dome over the pyramid. Another shot whizzed by Doug's ear – the gunner's last before being pushed off the side of the cliff by a gale of wind as Doug surged his hand in that direction. He was aiming for Catherine, but saw that her legs were wrapped in ice up to the knee. By then it was too late. Catherine had already brought her hands together in a thunderous clap and the water responded in kind, collapsing on the pyramid from all sides.

The sight of the destruction and the sound of the glass pyramid shattering was experienced throughout the city. The city's citizens, all evacuated to the south, watched in horror as the end of their civilization came into being. The warriors, fighting off their enemies, felt a weakening in their cause. Some had even begun to question if their Commander was still alive.

Douglassaire didn't let the destruction of their nation's symbol stop his charge toward Catherine. If anyone was going to stop this war, it would be him.

The wet ground beneath his feet turned to ice and Catherine laughed at his tumble to the ground. "How about some more wind, Commander?" she said. The ice thawed back to water.

He quickly recovered and swung his sword haphazardly in her direction. He hated the humiliation. She snapped out her sword once again and blocked his attacks.

"Surrender now–" her words were cut short as her head flew back at the force of his punch, but she didn't stumble.

"That was for earlier," Doug said. Catherine looked back at Doug with a veil of hatred. As she did, Doug noticed something strange about her face. Her cheek had turned snow white and jagged cracks formed from the center out. It was as if he had punched glass. The crack on her cheek grew and spread to her hairline and an icy shell fell from her face revealing perfectly unharmed skin.

"And this is for the queen!" She collected water from the ground to form into ice on the back of her hand and struck Douglassaire in the face. He fell over, dropping his sword. He reached for it on his knees, but failed as his arms were forced together by water and bound by ice. Catherine grabbed the BAC of the fallen knight, pointed it at her prey, and pulled the trigger.

PART THREE

CHAPTER TWENTY-SIX

I

White puffy clouds whisked past the large window of the private supertrop as it flew to its destination. Next to the window was a large, cushioned seat where Gisela lounged. Her heeled shoes rested askew on the floor below her stocking-covered feet which were resting on another cushion just above. She enjoyed the solitude of having her own aircraft as much as she could. As she lay down on her back in the seat with her dark hair spread out behind her like wings, she stared at the ceiling. Heavy questions floated in her mind: What had her life been up to this point? And was she doing the right thing now? She turned to her side, sure to reposition the flimsy blanket over her shoulder and paid no mind to the stories on the screen in the front of the cabin that played at low volume. She had been absent for so long that once she returned, she barely made it through living the life that her water spirit had provided for her. She hated that it had taken the death of another person to come back. She knew Wellesley hadn't fallen in love with her, but with the water spirit. If she came back soon enough, maybe she would have found a way to explain to him what was really going on.

The fear of being found out had lessened over time. There was no proof of Wellesley doing anything other than falling and drowning, and nobody knew of her ethereal abilities. Regardless, she felt she would never be able to forgive herself for taking another person's life, but hopefully there was a way to do some good.

She could feel the presence of her butler who softly made his way down the wide aisle of the cabin to her seat. "Anything I can do for you, Mrs. Van der Borea?"

Without looking, Gisela raised her hand and waved, "No, Garren." She almost requested once that he use her original surname, Benitez, but figured it best not to alarm anyone. She wouldn't want people to get the wrong idea – *take the man's money, but leave his name* – no, besides it was a well-respected name. Despite the discomfort of portraying herself of being his loving, grieving widow to the public, she figured she could use the name to do some real good for the world – especially during this time of war. She used the money and influence of the Van der Borea name to start a safe place for the refugees of the war. She was headed there now.

Garren said, "Very well," and left back to his quarters.

Gisela glanced at the screen and saw images flashing of the destruction of the Southern Third, the separation of families, and even those who had escaped north to the Middle Third. She had a moment of déjà vu. In the weeks since the war began, she found herself in a similar position in a chair in front of a screen watching the news outlets' continuous coverage of misery, so it was no surprise. She sat there now almost numb to its effect until a black and white picture of Douglassaire appeared on the screen. Then, she thought back to when she first heard the news.

It was back home in Septentrion City. Gisela lounged on her living room couch and the same black and white picture of Douglassaire appeared on-screen for the first time. Garren was close by and as she sat up with alarm, she said, "Garren, turn this up, please."

He did and the words of the reporter hit her unexpectedly hard: "…we have confirmed with forces from the Middle Third that Commander Heuresyt has died as a prisoner in Lorelei Castle due to severe battle-related injuries."

Her heart seized. She looked at Garren who seemed

unphased, then back at the screen, when she realized she'd have to experience her moment of terror alone. The Southern Third had fallen and the Middle Third became even more powerful. "Garren?"

"Yes?"

"What are the chances that we're next?"

"Oh, you mustn't worry yourself about that. Queen Aeothesca has no reason to come after the Northern Third. We've done nothing wrong. We're her allies."

"Right. Thanks." His words had been comforting enough, but there was an innate fear in her breast of which she could not rid herself.

She shook off the memory of that dreadful day. As she flew from Septentrion City to her next destination, she looked at the Commander's picture again while the news anchors spoke of what his death meant for the Southern Third. She remembered the silent war between them for Slade's attention. Ultimately, neither of them had won, but seeing the report of his death only reconfirmed her idea that if Slade had followed Douglassaire he, too, would have been drawn into his chaos. She exhaled in a psychic pat on her own back. She did well. She did her job as a friend. Slade was safe. But was he happy?

She wondered if Slade had been hurt by the news, or whether he'd emotionally moved past Doug enough to not feel anything. What if she made a mistake? She was safe, too, but her life was in shambles. What's the point of being safe if you're not happy? Doug was happy. He took risks, he achieved his goals, and even though his life was cut short, she could bet he was happy. A thought suddenly struck her: *Perhaps it's better to be happy and vulnerable than safe and sad.*

Well, if that were true, she was glad she was headed where she was. She couldn't stand the people around her – rich, comfortable, and completely unattached to the world around them. They were worried about the latest in entertainment and fashion while people were losing their lives and livelihood in the Southern Third. There were people who needed help. She badly wanted to atone for her sins and this war gave her an opportunity.

II

The hours-long flight finally came to an end as Gisela's private aircraft touched down some miles away from the Reorian Crater. The site of the end of the previous war between the Middle and Southern Thirds had become a tourist attraction over the years, but the breakout of more fighting changed it to a refugee camp for people escaping the war-ravaged South.

Gisela managed a change of clothes before her landing and opted out of the expensive fashions with which she had become accustomed. She emerged from the supertrop wearing sneakers, jeans, and a red T-shirt. This was no time for flash. She arrived to the camp in a private hover car that sat waiting for her on the tarmac. The drive over was as silent as the ride through the air, and she was struck at the differing sights of a peaceful, functioning Reor and a melancholy, half-chaotic refugee camp just at the nation's border. Faded green tents stretched out along the horizon and with signs designating their operation. *Food and Bedding* were some of the more repeated signs while the biggest and busiest tent had a sign attached to it that read *Infirmary*. As Gisela came onto the camp grounds, she saw that the medical professionals stayed inside, dutifully completing their services. Volunteers in their red T-shirts moved about, ushering hurt and healed alike from one place to another. Despite the camp's overwhelming sensation of sadness, anger, and shock, she also felt a sense of pride as she walked into the tent closest to the border labeled *The Van der Borea Foundation*. It had a sign on the front that read *Administration & Entry*. She walked past the large line of refugees and made her way to her seat at the big table in the back, all the while greeting and shaking hands with some of her volunteers.

Setting up camp in the Middle Third had been easier than she first expected. The Foundation needed authorization from the Middle Third, which was received without delay. Of course, they had to agree to the government's terms. As long as their refugees swore an oath of loyalty to the queen, they could grant asylum. Gisela wasn't fond of the idea of forcefully converting people's loyalties, but she decided to agree. She also knew most would not truly align with the Middle Third. Sometimes words were just that. If she wanted to help these people, there was no other choice.

But there was another choice – not for her, but for her country. The North could fight. Gisela found whether or not her country should fight a hard question to answer. She hated that her country sat idly by and did nothing while the Middle Third moved in on the South, hurting innocent civilians. *Casualties of war* is what they called it, but she knew better. The queen only gave her foundation and others the swift authorization to help refugees as a way to communicate that their fight was with the Southern Third government alone. But how does one destroy a system without destroying lives? On the other hand, if the Northern Third did lend their aid, what would that yield? More bloodshed? Loss of some of the Northerners' lives? And it was this debate that kept the North stagnant.

As she sat there checking in new refugees, Gisela saw firsthand just how quickly the world could change. The war only started a few weeks ago, but it seemed things were deteriorating quickly. Skirmishes and battles still erupted and died out in the Southern Third, even after the loss of their Commander, as its people tried desperately to cling to their way of life. It was only a matter of time before the queen's knights brought the Southern Third's sovereignty to a close.

CHAPTER TWENTY-SEVEN

I

The days seemed longer for Slade. What was once a daily routine peppered with some happy moments turned into empty sequences of sights, movements, and sounds. Douglassaire was dead and with it any hope he had of reaching out. When the news first came, he was unaware that he'd react with tears. What if he could have helped or even prevented this? What if he had the courage to literally go through the fire that miserable day? Would Doug still be alive today?

He remembered a conversation with his co-worker who, upon hearing the news, said, "Good! It's about time somebody put him down."

He also remembered something his mother said when speaking about the war: "I'm just happy the worst is over. We don't have to worry about the Southern Third anymore."

With Doug's death, Slade began to feel a distance between himself and the rest of his people. Douglassaire wasn't a monster and he wouldn't have attacked the Middle Third the way the queen fooled everyone into believing. Slade knew that without a doubt, but the queen's words were too strong, and so, too, was the paranoia of the Middle Third. And now, there was surely nothing he could do, but fall in line.

Slade rode the elevator up to the thirty-seventh floor to M.3.A.N. headquarters. Upon approaching his desk, he saw a new light flashing on his monitor. He put down his briefcase and leaned over the desk, not caring to remove his jacket. As he switched on the screen, he saw that the light signaled an update to an already-existing assignment to one of the field agents in M.3.A.N. Apparently, Agent Icarus finally had an update on his VIP target:

Target and I arrived just outside Reorian Crater. Mission complete. Awaiting further orders.
Icarus

Slade closed the message. He would soon forward the message to the queen's people at Lorelei Castle, but he still had a few minutes before his workday officially started and wanted to enjoy every last moment. He exhaled and gazed out of his window while removing his jacket and slinging it over his seat. He stretched his arms over his head and thought about grabbing a cup of coffee. As with every time he received a message from Agent Icarus, his mind also worked to unravel the mystery of the VIP target's identity. Then one thought led to another: *Wasn't the Van der Borea Foundation one of the refugee camps down there? I wonder if Gisela is there.* He glanced at the digital inbox on his monitor and frowned. *Wouldn't she be considered a VIP?* He chuckled and shook off his small bout of paranoia. There was no way she could be the target. She never gave the Middle Third any reason to spy on her, nor would she ever set foot near a warzone.

He exited his office and walked through the bare hallway to the small kitchen area. The aroma of fresh coffee warmed his nose and he began to pour a cup. *What if she was?* The thought wouldn't leave him alone. One of his past friends already fell victim to his country's actions. Would another? If she did, what could he do about it? Besides, if she were the VIP target, he'd been instructed not to go near her. Then, he thought about his missed chance at making things right with Doug. He knew it would haunt him for the rest of his life.

He stood over his coffee and shook his head. If she were at

257

the camp, he had to see Gisela – there was no choice. It was a risk he had to take. If anybody said anything about his going against orders, he could just explain it away as meeting an old friend. Hopefully that would work, anyway. He didn't really care. He now knew from experience how important it was to tie up loose ends.

II

About an hour after work, Slade arrived. He began to feel nervous when stepping out of his hover car. It was a bit too much. He saw the lines of people at the refugee camp and was reminded of how his country had changed the lives of people forever. These people who lost their homes in the Southern Third probably looked at him as an enemy, and if Gisela were here, he wouldn't blame her if she did, too. He closed the door behind him and walked toward the entrance. His crisp black suit and sunglasses made him feel even more out of place than he already was. *Maybe this was a bad idea*, he thought. He hesitated and almost turned around back to the car to take off, but then he saw her. At least he thought it was Gisela. A woman with a red T-shirt and jeans was walking around and talking with some of the other volunteers. Her dark brown hair revealed her green eyes and a face with no makeup – just a natural beauty. She looked at lot like her, but she didn't look like she was in charge. Perhaps she was just better at fitting in.

As if to confirm his thought, she looked over at him. She squinted slightly and began to walk over, and as she did, Slade smiled. It *was* her.

"Hello, sir, can I help—" she began. "Slade?"

"Hey, Gisela."

"Slade!" She almost tackled him in a huge hug.

He didn't expect the enthusiasm, but welcomed it all the same. He hugged her back.

"How have you been? You have to fill me in. What's going on with you these days?"

"I've been okay. I'm working for the queen. Mom pulled

259

through for a job right after college..." he said nervously. He remembered a tactic he'd learned mixing it up with the higher ups in the government when he wanted to change the subject – ask them about themselves. "How are you?"

"Oh, it's been a crazy year. I've been better."

"Sorry about your husband."

She lowered her eyes and nodded. "Yeah." His tactic worked. Now, she was the one who was nervous. "Would you like to sit down? Let's go chat."

"Sure," he said.

He began to follow his old friend through the busy camp of Southerners and volunteers. She led him to a trailer that sat isolated from the rest of the camp. She stepped up the three short stairs to the door, opened it, and walked in. Slade came in behind her, closed the door, and took in the sight of the small room. A couch was to his immediate right which sat across from the kitchenette, and the bed was further in the back.

Gisela saw him looking at everything and immediately remembered his extravagant lifestyle. She swung out a hand inviting Slade to take a seat on the couch as she sat along with him. "You might not see it from this trailer, but believe it or not, I actually caught up with you, Slade."

"Oh, I believe it all right. Both you *and*..." Slade looked away and let his voice trail off.

"Have you spoken to him? Before everything, I mean?"

Slade shook his head. He felt Gisela's warm hand cover the back of his own and looked into her concerned eyes.

"How are you holding up?"

"I'm better. That's actually why I came to see you. When I heard the news, I felt horrible. I still do. I just wish I said something to him. Even if it was just a congratulations – anything. Now he's gone and left with the impression that I just left and never thought about him or cared. I didn't want that to happen with you. I'm sorry. I know you hated me after that trip and I don't blame–"

"Stop, Slade. It's okay. It's forgiven. We all had a part in the breakdown."

Slade fought to stay stoic as the weight of the past began to drop from his shoulders. He looked at Gisela and saw that whatever change he noticed in her after their trip was gone.

"I should show you something," she said.

She pulled her hair over her left shoulder and turned her back to Slade.

Slade's mouth opened as he drew in a breath of surprise. On the back of her neck he saw a black upside-down triangle with a line of skin separating the lowest point from its broad top – the symbol of water. Slade shook his head in disbelief. "Gisela...when did you...?"

She released her grip on her hair and turned back to face Slade. "Not too long after we got back. It's a long story, but this thing completely took over. If it weren't for her, I probably would have talked to you sooner. She turned me into a complete...witch."

Slade was amused at her restraint, but felt that the word was oddly more accurate. Then, he noticed something he hadn't before and asked, "She?"

Gisela nodded, "Yeah. That's what these things are. They're like having a completely different person inside of you fighting for control."

"And you lost the fight at first?"

"More like I didn't try," she sighed. "It's been horrible, Slade. I was only recently able to come back. I feel like a hypocrite. I became exactly what I was trying to stop you from becoming. I just want to get rid of this thing."

Suddenly the door to the trailer a few feet behind Slade swung open and a man called in. "Is everything okay here, Mrs. Van der Borea?"

"Everything's okay, Garren," said Gisela.

Slade didn't react at first, but turned to view the man after hearing his name. It sounded familiar, and it clicked once he saw the man standing there. His short-cropped hair and goatee looked like a mix of salt and pepper. His red T-shirt was layered on top of a crisp white button-up shirt just the way a snooty butler would do. But he was no butler, and his eyes betrayed his cover for a brief moment when they locked with Slade's in an unspoken recognition between Agent Icarus and Director

Maxwell. Slade felt his pulse quicken. *What's going on?* he thought. Garren kept his eyes on Slade as he left the trailer and Slade knew that he'd soon have some explaining to do. He looked at Gisela with an alarmed expression, perhaps too long because her face returned the favor. "What's wrong?" she said.

Something was going on, and Slade couldn't put his finger on it. *What does the queen want with Gisela?* He wondered what she could possibly have that was of value to Queen Aeothesca. He knew now that she was a vessel for the water spirit, just as Doug had – *That must be it*, he thought.

Gisela started at the sight of Slade jumping to his feet. "Slade."

He grabbed her as she stood up and hugged her. As he did, he whispered in her ear, "Be careful of the queen." He felt a slight shiver from her and she pulled away confused.

"Slade, what's going on?"

He spoke low, fearing they may be overheard. "I gotta go. I won't let anything happen to you, I promise. Just stay away from the castle as long as you can. Just remember what I said. Be careful."

"Slade–"

The door of the trailer slammed shut as he left in a hurry. He stepped down the stairs to the trailer and walked back towards his hover car, avoiding bumping into the volunteers and others who were milling around. As he got to his car, his swift stride came to a halt. Garren stood next to it with his arms crossed. "Director Maxwell," he said.

Slade proceeded closer to his car and gave the man a firm nod. "Agent Icarus."

"With all due respect, sir, you're not supposed to be here."

"I was just visiting an old friend, Icarus. I had no idea she was the VIP target."

"And I have no choice but to report this to the queen." He stood still blocking Slade's entry into the driver's side door.

Slade felt the tiny tremors of fury building from within. He wanted nothing more than to shove this man away. "Don't forget your place, Icarus. I'm *your* boss."

Agent Icarus took a few steps away allowing Slade to make his way into the car. He was just about to close the door when he heard Icarus respond, "Yes, sir, that is true, but the queen rules over us all."

Slade looked back at Gisela's trailer. In the window, he thought he caught the final moments of a curtain being put back into place. Then, he looked at Garren straight in the eye. "Do what you must." He closed the door and sped off eyeing Agent Icarus from his rear-view mirror who just stood there, still, with his hands in his pockets.

III

Slade raced into his office and sat down at his desk. He remembered what Douglassaire told him once about the queen being a vessel. That information meant nothing at the time, but right now he felt it could mean everything. He tried calming himself down, but something told him he was on the verge of something big. *Okay,* he thought, *so what? What does she want with Gisela?*

The waning light of the afternoon highlighted the room and his fingers went to work as he searched for something he remembered seeing long ago during his first search for information about Ethereans. He retraced his old footsteps and did a quick search for the term *Etherean* which led to a screen that was very familiar. It displayed the whole creation story, line by line, stanza by stanza. Slade frowned as he reread the story, wondering which part pertained to the spirits of Ether. Then he saw it:

> *Elao and Calamity both enraged*
> *Fought and fought for 40 days.*
> *And after each 10th day had passed*
> *A spirit of Ether escaped their grasp.*

> *Each spirit announced, nay, they swore*
> *"Three of four to open the door."*

"Three of four to open the door," he said to himself. *Open the door to what? To Ether?*

Suddenly, a memory came to him. Gisela sat next to him in

class and told everyone, "It's said to house the Djed Key at its center which, if removed, would grant its holder the power of God."

"The power of God…is that what she's after?" he thought aloud. He shuddered at the thought. What would the queen do with the power of God? She was already winning the war in the South. Was she planning to take over the North, too? Slade slouched back in his seat, exhausted with the stress of what this all meant. After a moment, he gripped the arm handles of his chair and shot up straight. *If she's after the Djed Key and she only needs three spirits to go to Ether, who would the three be? Herself, for one, Gisela, and…*but it couldn't be. Douglassaire was dead. Was there somebody else?

Slade leaned forward on his desk and typed in the words 'Commander Heuresyt death' into a search. The headlines were just as he had remembered: END OF AN ERA – COMMANDER HEURESYT'S FINAL FLIGHT and POW HEURESYT DIES IN LORELEI CASTLE. He hadn't died on the battlefield. There were no witnesses. No reports came from the Southern Third, only the Middle Third's news outlets. If Doug was in the castle, that meant he was away from the public, and surrounded by only the queen's most loyal subjects. The queen twisted plenty already. She could have her people tell the press anything. Slade's heart beat faster with hope. *He's alive – no, he might be alive.* Slade desperately wanted it to be true, but he fought against the possibility of future disappointment. The stories might be true and Douglassaire dead just as they reported. Still, his excitement grew as he sat there, elbows on the table, facing the monitor while resting his nose on the back of his folded hands. If he was alive, there had to be a way to find out.

A sound chimed as a graphic flashed on his monitor. He received a new message marked 'URGENT'. He opened the message and read with a mild sense of worry and when he read its contents he saw that he was right:

Director Maxwell:
Due to recent notification of failure to follow mission protocol, the queen requests your audience at the castle. Your arrival is expected immediately

after your opening of this message. Speak to no one and come now. Your failure to appear will result in your arrest.

Her Majesty's Office

For The Queen

There was no getting out of it. Once Slade opened the message, the sender was notified. His time was ticking. He turned everything off at his desk and looked out of the window. The castle hung high above the city. He hoped it wouldn't be his final trip.

CHAPTER TWENTY-EIGHT

I

Lorelei Castle's throne room glowed with an amber hue from the room's lights. As Slade stepped in behind Catherine, the pleasantries were skipped and Queen Aeothesca demanded, "Tell me what you know about Gisela Van der Borea." Catherine bowed and left the room.

Slade felt a sudden surge of hate for the queen. He hated this room as well. The grassy platform where the throne sat was picturesque, but the most unnatural thing he'd ever seen. Sometimes the trees and grass gave sway where there was no wind. It was as if everything there was alive. "She is an old friend."

"Certainly you know more than that, dear. Please..."

Slade took a moment, searching for what to say. Just like the last time he visited the queen, he fought for control over his nerves. "She grew up in Ankor. She lost her mother very young and was raised by her grandmother. We went to university together at Burrow, and since then, she married Wellesley Van der Borea who died not too long ago."

"You compromised a mission, Director. Typically, this would not require a visit, but this is a special case. We have been following Mrs. Van der Borea for quite some time now and I received word that you made contact with her today. Why?"

"As I said, Your Majesty, she is an old friend. I had no idea she was being followed by us."

"But you certainly could have guessed, could you not, Director?"

"Your Majesty, in all our years of service, has my family ever given you a reason to distrust us? I am a Maxwell and you have my word that this mistake goes no further."

"Well, Director, you see, my hands are tied. For your indiscretion I must now deal out an appropriate punishment." She saw the worried look on Slade's face. "Oh, do not fret, dear. I only ask that you accompany your field team to apprehend Annonymn once she is found."

Slade's facial expression had not changed. He was relieved he wouldn't be imprisoned, but he feared a warzone just as much.

The queen continued, "You have been trained, Director. You are well prepared to fight should the need arise. It is a good time for you to step up as the leader and example you are. Any injury you face was brought about by you, alone. No further discussion."

Catherine reappeared through the door and traded spots with Slade for what he thought would no doubt be the discussion of what just transpired. He left the ladies to themselves and stood in the great hallway with its constant activity. He hated that he'd been called up to Lorelei Castle for a reprimand, but he was prepared to make the best of it. If there was a chance Douglassaire was alive, he had to see for himself.

Despite his role as Director, he still felt like an intruder in the castle. He did his best to hide that and held his head high as he walked through the hallway. A few of the people acknowledged his presence with a polite, "Hello, Director," and "Good evening, Director," to which he nodded and replied in kind. As he made his way toward the dungeons, he found that the crowd grew more and more sparse. He missed his camouflage amongst the castle-dwellers, for now he knew that he would stick out like a sore thumb. He didn't belong in this part of the castle. Nobody did.

He descended a flight of stairs that led to the dungeons and saw the only people who roamed free were a few guards. Judging by their faces, their freedom could be questioned just as much as the prisoners they watched. He found the scene of the dark quiet room of cells jarring to the bright and busy hallways of the rest of the castle. As he walked in, a guard stepped in his path with a hardened expression. Slade dug in his pocket and flashed his badge. The guard nodded and acknowledged his position as he stepped out of his way. Slade was happy he hadn't been flagged from visiting certain areas. The last thing he needed was to notify the queen that he was snooping around the dungeon.

He walked slowly down the narrow hall of cells and looked to his right and his left with each one he passed. He'd seen it all before – the glass floors, the loose nooses around the prisoners' necks reminding them each second of their imminent demise. He wasted no time pondering the ethics of such a confinement as he did in his previous tour. He had a more serious task. Unfortunately, it looked as though it would end in failure, for none of the cells held Douglassaire, nor anyone that even looked like him. Would he even be here?

He walked to the very end of the hall where the torch with white flame sat dancing in the dark. With his head hung low, he turned to leave. He knew it was a long shot, but the feeling of hope evaporating once again struck him harder than he expected. Leaning back on the brick wall behind him, he let out a long breath and banged his fist on the wall in frustration.

"Hey, guard," said a deep voice, "I need food."

Slade jumped at the sound of the voice. He looked for its source in the nearby cells, but saw no occupants. It sounded close but faint.

The voice spoke up again. "If I die on your watch, you'll be in here next. Trust me."

Slade turned to look at the brick wall. Was it a false? How could he get in? He opened his palms and pressed against the wall. Nothing shook. He wouldn't be able to open it that way.

"Okay, I got it," the voice said. "Shut up, right? Whatever. It's your funeral." He chuckled. "Mine, too."

Slade couldn't believe what he was hearing. He felt hope claw its way back into his system, but he didn't want it. He couldn't bear the thought of losing it again. He almost didn't say the man's name out loud, but risked calling him anyway. "Doug?"

The silence was dreadful. Too long. What was only seconds stretched on for an eternity as he awaited a reply. He started to think he was going crazy until–

"Who's there?"

Slade's heart beat faster as he kneeled on the ground to match where he heard the voice coming from. "Doug! Doug, it's me. It's Slade."

"Go away."

Slade withdrew from the wall. He stopped a surge of emotions from rushing in too quickly – a mix of rage and sadness – as he asked, "Doug...you don't want me here?"

"What is this, a joke?"

"No."

"Listen, whoever you are, just go away."

Slade took a deep breath. "Doug, it's really me. I'm right here. I'm here." Slade waited in a silence even longer than before.

"Slade, is that really you?"

Slade exhaled and smiled, "Yes, Doug. It's really me."

"What are you *doing* here?" Douglassaire asked.

Slade laughed, "I could ask you the same thing. I work for the queen."

"Oh..."

"Don't *oh* me."

"Well, what else do you want, Slade? Really, what are you doing here?"

"I had to see if you were alive. And I wanted to say... I'm sorry."

"Well, a lotta good that does now."

Slade took the hit. He knew he deserved it, but even more than hurt he felt courage. It was a strange thing that always seemed to come to him when he was with Doug. He knew this wasn't right – nothing was right. Douglassaire wasn't a prisoner, the Southern Third shouldn't be in shambles, and the queen shouldn't be able to take over the world, but that's what was happening. Slade knew right then as he sat walled off from Doug what the queen's true plan was. He didn't want to let such an evil woman have such power. "You wanna do something about it?" he asked Doug.

"What are you gonna do, Slade? You're on the wrong side."

"No, I'm not. I'm on your side. I'm getting you out of here, Doug."

"Yeah? And how you gonna do that? Open the bottom of this dungeon? Let me hang?"

"If I have to." Slade waited patiently for the response to which Doug was slow.

"Don't give me false hope, Slade, not again. There's no way I'm leaving here alive."

"Listen. I know my word doesn't mean much right now, but don't give up. You needed me to believe in you back then, Doug. Now I need you to believe in me. Wait for me, Doug. I'm coming back for you. I promise, I'm coming back." He left without notice to escape the chance of hearing another word of protest from Doug. Little did he know that if he stayed, he would have heard no such thing. He left the Commander sitting there smiling for the first time in weeks.

***

Shortly after Director Maxwell's departure from the throne room, Catherine spoke through a laugh, "He is to go with a field team to retrieve your sister? You are not one for mercy, my queen."

"Our dear Director must experience the repercussions of his actions. I had no other choice."

"But is he really suited for battle?"

Aeothesca stood and folded her hands behind her back as she walked to take a look at the night sky through the stained-glass window. The view was partially obstructed by one of the big white crystals – its base firmly planted in the field in the distance. "I doubt the playtime that M.3.A.N. calls basic training is enough to prepare anyone for war, but it will have to do for him. He is expendable. All of these nobles throw their name around like it means something."

"He could use the M.3.A.N. armor's cloaking ability to hide," Catherine laughed.

"Yes. It is a shame how expensive it is, for all my knights could benefit. But a half-hour's use is hardly enough time for a war."

Catherine changed the subject. "And what is your plan, Your Majesty? The Djed Key? Your target has reached Reor and we have the Commander in our grasp. When shall we get started?"

The queen smiled at the prospect. Everything was coming together. "Tomorrow."

II

The activity at the refugee camp was beginning to quiet down. Lights surrounding the area illuminated the grounds at night and more people settled into their quarters for the evening. Gisela sat at the small table in her trailer staring at her small mobile monitor while Garren helped himself to a beverage at the miniature refrigerator. Gisela was tired and ready to go to sleep. The stress of Slade's visit wore her down and she almost wished he never said anything. His words continued to ring through her head: *Be careful of the queen.* She began to close the top of the machine and put an end to her day when she heard a chime. After lifting the monitor to its former position, she drew in a nervous breath.

Garren noticed her in a state of alarm and asked "Is everything all right?"

"Oh, it's nothing, Garren."

"Nonsense. Let me have a look." He walked over and took a peek over her shoulder at what she read. "Ah! Well, this is great news! The queen wants to meet you. I know a very many people would love to be in your shoes."

"I don't know. I don't think I'm gonna go."

"Mrs. Van der Borea, you would miss an appointment with the queen? It's unheard of." He began to laugh. "For a moment I thought you serious. Very good, Madam."

"I'm not joking, Garren."

"I see. I apologize. Is something bothering you?"

"No."

"Some*one*?" He waited for a response that never came. "Well. I don't mean to pry. I am sure you will feel better in the morning and you have most of the day tomorrow to think about it." He

273

walked to the trailer door and held it open. "Why don't you get some rest? In the meantime, I'll pick something for you to wear that's fit for a visit with the queen."

And with that, Gisela was alone. She closed her mobile monitor and prepared for bed. For a butler, Garren was being extra pushy tonight. Gisela didn't care how he felt about it. Slade told her to be careful of the queen, so she wasn't going.

CHAPTER TWENTY-NINE

I

The objective was to arrest the former Middle Third princess, Annonymn, for treason. In the wee hours of the morning, one of the knights stationed in the Southern Third was patched through to Slade. He revealed that he and a few other knights had fought a woman closely resembling the princess, and that she got away.

"Where is she headed?" Slade asked.

"She's with a small group and they're headed up north," the knight replied.

"Are they trying to reach the border?"

"I don't know sir, but we can pursue and try to stop them now. The Incaen Forest is on the way and they have a fire Etherean with them. I'd hate to see what would happen if they reach it."

Slade understood. The flaming forest he'd visited years ago would be the perfect place of protection if the princess linked up with a fire user. Under normal circumstances he would have told the knight to stop them immediately, but he needed a way to save Douglassaire and Gisela. The fire spirit in the Incaen Forest spoke to Slade once, and if he was going to help his friends he needed to speak to it again and take its power for himself. It was a long shot, but Slade saw an opportunity and he was going to make the best of his punishment.

"No," he said. "Just lie low and trail them for now. Contact us when you're close to the forest. My team will deal with them there."

Now, sitting inside of a small supertrop with its few windows and dark interior, Slade could barely feel any movement as it flew through the sky. In fact, despite the digital information at the visor on the inside of his helmet, he barely noticed anything. The battery for his armor's cloaking ability was displayed as full. He could have tapped the side of his helmet to read the current information about the mission, but he already knew the information and needed no time to review. Instead, he bounced his leg and fidgeted with his hands in anticipation of events that he knew would be life risking.

The M.3.A.N. agents around him, a small team of six, were suited up in the same gunmetal gray body armor with sword hilts at their sides, BACs hung around their shoulders, and daggers embedded within the bumpy fabric at the upper arm. Another latch at their chest provided storage for their small, personal effects – IDs, comms., and things of that nature. They sat in their seats lined against the wall facing each other while reviewing the information of the mission. Not much was there except a few photos one of the knights on the ground took of Annonymn in battle. They showed a woman with blonde hair and a BAC slung over her shoulder swinging her sword at Middle Third knights. In one picture, half of her face was obscured by hair, but in another they could see there was a definite resemblance. The other photos showed some people who appeared to be on her side. Two men and one woman. The gravity of this mission did not escape some. They were really going to bring in the princess. Their success would shape history.

The mission objectives were overlaid on the photos as the agents flipped through:

- Main target wanted alive.
- All other targets may be eliminated upon resistance.
- Female target is a fire Etherean. Approach with extreme caution.

Slade's body surged forward as the aircraft lowered its altitude and slowed down. He snapped to attention and stood as the leader of the group, holding on to the bar just above his head. Whenever a director joined their field team, they outranked the captain, but usually deferred to them for combat. Slade saw no reason to change tradition. He said, "Listen up, everyone. We're taking in a high value target, so there can't be any mistakes. Force will only be used if absolutely necessary. There are only four of them and seven of us. As long as you stay cloaked, you stay alive. Let's make this easy and get in and get out. Captain Hettic, we're following your lead."

Slade and the agents tightened their grip on the bars as the small supertrop landed safely on the ground. The disorienting light of day flashed into the aircraft as the back opened. Slade stood by as his agents ran down the ramp, disappearing one-by-one as each of them made sure to punch the button at their chest to activate their suit's cloaking ability. Slade ran after the last agent and hit the button on his chest. A timer appeared on the screen of his helmet, the visor; he had thirty minutes before the cloaking would dissipate and need a recharge.

The visor noted their targets were camped about a mile away. As the team walked towards their destination, the supertrop lifted itself off the ground and disappeared in the clouds above. Slade stayed towards the back of the group. Doing a mission where the whole team was invisible was always strange. As one of M.3.A.N.'s office workers, Slade only practiced this a couple of times. Still, he managed to keep in step with his teammates while eyeing their location marked by a red dot on his visor.

The Southern Third was cast in a cloudy gray. The open field of hills and tall grass stretched on in all directions as far as the eye could see. Slade recognized the terrain and fought against painful memories that would distract him from his mission. He had no time to think about how he lost his friends here because this is where he would fight to get them back. As the team trekked on and on to the top of a steep hill, the Incaen Forest came into view. It was nestled deep in the valley where the only trees around were ablaze and the heat could be felt from where they stood.

"I've got a visual," one of the agents said. "Southwest, towards the opening."

Everyone else turned their heads to look and zoomed in their view on the helmet. They took in the scene of a ruined campsite and saw that some of their fellow knights were in combat with the two male targets. The female stayed back towards the forest. "She must be the Etherean," Slade said.

"But where's the princess?" an agent thought aloud.

"No visual on the princess, yet," replied the other.

"She's gotta be in there somewhere," Slade said.

Captain Hettic spoke up. "If she's hiding, we'll make her team tell us where. Be careful, guys. We have to get in close without being detected. Let's move out."

They all moved in around the surrounding ridge of the Incaen Forest to its opening. They got closer to their targets who were fighting off more knights of the Middle Third and still unaware of their presence. Slade stopped just before they got to the fighting and let his team move in while he surveyed the land. Princess Annonymn had to be around here somewhere.

Slade watched as the woman in the back went down, her face hitting the ground, tackled by two agents. She yelled in pain as she was restrained. The knights and targets alike were struck by the strangeness of seeing her fall to the ground by some invisible force. This gave the other four agents ample time to take down the big bald man and the skinny guy with the long hair. They didn't fight back. Slade sighed in relief seeing that their mission was almost complete, but as he looked to the ground, he saw a fallen knight and looked at his wound. He'd been shot through the heart!

Slade looked up and saw a couple of agents release their camouflage and come into full view. As the rest of them followed suit he yelled, "No! Don't—"

The shot of a rifle coincided with the explosion of blood from one of the agents' backs. He was holding on to the woman, but now she had a hand free. "Don't do it, Etherean!" yelled the captain as he held down one arm and snapped out his blade to her neck.

Slade realized he was the only one left who hadn't blown his cover to the shooter. The timer on his suit's cloaking counted down from three minutes. "Nobody move," Slade said as softly as he could through his suit's radio. His visor showed that the shot came from his left. She must have been up on the ridge lying low. He knew he only had a little time left before she reloaded and took another shot.

He bolted up the hill in that direction. One of the targets must have sensed something was wrong, for as Slade approached the top of the hill, the woman yelled, "Anna, run!"

Slade scanned the field as he ran and spotted a figure popping up from the tall grass. As she turned and looked in Slade's direction, Slade finally saw that it was her: Princess Annonymn. She began to turn and run, but before she could get to full speed, Slade tackled her to the ground. After shackling her arms at her back, his suit's cloaking device powered down, and he declared, "Princess Annonymn, you are under arrest for treason."

II

Slade held a tight grip on the black round shackles that bound Anna's hands behind her. They both took hard, awkward steps downhill on their way to the rest of the agents. Slade wasn't prepared to speak with the princess, but she began to speak everything on her mind.

"You're just another of the queen's pawns. Is the Middle Third full of mindless slaves?"

"That's enough," Slade said, unsure of whether to tack on a "Your Majesty" to the end of that.

"Don't you have a conscience? Don't you see what's happening? She let the power get to her head, and now she's using it to suit herself – damn anyone else. You know as well as I that the Southern Third is just the beginning. And we had no intention of taking the Middle Third."

We? Slade thought. She showed no allegiance to the Middle Third. Had she truly turned her back on her own country? "I said, that's enough. Even if you're a traitor, she'll probably let you off a lot easier than anyone else."

"Ha! She, go easy? You don't know her well, do you? She had better not. I'd gladly take…" *her life* is what she almost said, but thought better of revealing her feelings and just huffed herself silent.

Slade was struck by the rage in her words and realized that something big must have happened between them.

"Somebody needs to be brave," she continued. "Not *everyone* in the Middle Third can be a mindless fool, can they? What's your name, Agent?"

Slade felt the princess pulling her weight and bent to the

pressure of respect for royalty. "Slade Maxwell. Director of Intelligence."

"Oh, a Maxwell. And a director? What is a director of M.3.A.N. doing here? Oh… I see. Somebody did something the queen didn't like. Tell me, how does it feel to be thrown out with the wolves after undying loyalty to your leader? You could have been the agent with a bullet in his back."

"But I'm not. Please, Your Majesty, be quiet."

They neared the bottom and began to turn towards the opening of the forest. The heat emanating from that place was beginning to become unbearable. "Like I said," Anna continued, "Somebody needs to be brave. Deep down somewhere, you know she needs to go down before it's too late."

Slade pretended not to listen, but was surprised that they shared the same convictions. He caught up with his team who had the rest of Anna's allies secured in the same black, round handcuffs. The two remaining knights were bent over the M.3.A.N. agent who'd been shot. His helmet was removed and his face was twisted in pain as they applied pressure to his wound to hold off the bleeding. He wouldn't last long.

As Slade approached the group, he heard a familiar voice that stopped him in his tracks: "Slade Maxwell, the weakling," it teased in its raspy voice. The voice emanated from the forest. It was fire spirit once again – the chance Slade had been counting on.

Anna noticed the sudden shock in the agent holding onto her, but before she could say anything, he passed her off to the knights. "Don't hurt her," Slade said. "Follow the agents back to the 'trop and put her on. I'll catch up."

Anna incurred the knights' dirty looks as one grabbed her roughly by the arm and the other picked up the injured agent. The group started their walk back to the aircraft that hung in sky, leaving Slade behind.

CHAPTER THIRTY

I

The Incaen Forest stretched before Slade in an ominous red blaze. Slade took a deep breath and calmed himself from the slight fear that always came with the presence of something supernatural.

"It's been a while, Slade…" said the voice from within.

"It has."

"Go now before you find company with the bodies lying at your feet."

"I'm not weak."

"Oh? Are you calling me a liar? I want nothing more than to find a vessel worthy of my flame, to see the world burn by my hands, but I'm afraid you are not it."

"I am."

"You'll die."

"I won't." *Somebody has to be brave*, he thought. This was the moment he'd been waiting for, and the princess's words stuck with him.

The fire spirit sighed. "You are a fool! Very well, enter and be consumed."

Slade walked toward the edge of the forest and could feel its heat intensify. For the first time, the smell of burnt wood hit his nostrils. The fire that usually left the trees unharmed began to burn. He fought his mounting fear, knowing that if he let it, the fire would burn him, too. He thought of Gisela and Douglassaire who both endured the same experience and who needed his help now; the queen whose power would grow tremendously if not stopped; and he thought of himself, powerless to do anything unless he faced his fear right now. He stepped into the flaming grove determined to gain the power he needed to fight. He decided to be brave.

He felt the pain of his skin and blood boiling for only a split second before something amazing happened. The fire that enveloped him danced on his frame as it once did to the trees, doing no damage to him at all. He calmly removed his helmet and dropped it to the ground. He saw nothing in the distance but the orange flames surrounding him as his head was alight with flame that burned with the coolness of a summer breeze. He gazed at his arms and hands amazed at the sensation of power flowing through him.

"I underestimated you, Slade," said the fire spirit. "Do you agree to become my vessel?"

"I do."

And with that, the flames on the trees began to dissipate as Slade felt the fire spirit becoming a part of him. He began to feel his consciousness slip away as if falling into a deep sleep. It felt warm, cozy, and inviting. The spirit's raspy voice spoke through Slade's lips, "Surrender..."

Just as the last bit of light began to fade from view, Slade remembered what he was here for. Douglassaire and Gisela needed him. And the queen had to be stopped. He reined himself in and could feel his head pounding from the struggle. "No!" he said. "You surrender to me."

In an instant, the fire of the Incaen Forest disappeared and Slade closed his eyes, unaware of his fall to the ground.

II

Slade awoke to the sight of the ground moving beneath him. He felt the constant thump of a large shoulder in his chest as quick, hard footsteps moved along. He took slow, steady breaths and fought to open his eyelids.

"Director," a man exclaimed.

"Is he breathing?" another asked.

The steps came to a stop and Slade felt himself being cradled in someone's arms then placed down on a hard surface. He opened his eyes and saw the other M.3.A.N. agents, helmets removed, looking relieved that he was still alive. He looked around and saw he was in the supertrop, along with the prisoners they came to arrest. One of the agents must have recovered his helmet from the forest because it was sitting on the seat across from him next to his sword and BAC. The prisoners sat further back with their handcuffs attached to their seats, craning their necks to see the commotion.

"Director, what happened?" Captain Hettic asked.

Slade shook his head, unable to speak with his mind so jumbled. He felt a strange presence inside of him and felt fatigued, as though he'd been fighting. It was a fight he couldn't quite remember, but he must have won, for he was in complete control of himself.

The back ramp closed and the whole craft shook as it took off into the sky. Slade sat up and looked out of the window next to his seat as they flew high into the air. Everyone, even the prisoners, looked out in wonder. The Incaen Forest was nothing but a grove of trees now. No fire burned and not even a trace of embers was lit on the ground. As Slade gazed at the spectacle below, he felt eyes boring into the back of his neck. He turned and saw Anna staring at him with a severe expression. She looked down and away, pretending not to notice the black triangle that had appeared on his neck.

CHAPTER THIRTY-ONE

I

Lorelei Castle, bathed in sunlight, grew closer and closer as the supertrop landed. The hatch opened and the agents stepped off, one by one, the first four with one of their prisoners in tow. Jack, Kandyce, and Vinzant marveled at their surroundings for a brief moment before joining Anna in worrying about what horrors awaited them. Slade had gotten his wits about him by that point and hurried out of the aircraft last, by himself.

He let the rest of the agents handle their job from this point. Now that his punishment was over, he had a new objective. Saving the world wasn't going to be easy, though, and he knew the potential for blowback was huge. If he tried anything crazy, his mother could be in the queen's crosshairs.

The agents took the prisoners straight to the doors leading to the castle dungeon while Slade went in the opposite direction to the castle's front courtyard. He pounded the pavement with his feet in a speed just below a jog and maneuvered around the castle's busybodies with tunnel vision for entry into the main hall. It took him a few seconds to even notice that the person he'd been looking for was already calling his name.

"Slade! Slade!" a woman's voice called.

Slade stopped in his tracks and looked to his right and saw his mother standing there in a white blouse and navy pants grinning widely and waving her hand in the air.

Upon his approach, she hugged him and asked, "Hey, baby, what are you doing here?" She noticed something was wrong and ended her embrace with a frown. She held him back by the shoulders and looked him square in the eyes. "Slade? What is it?"

"Mom, I want you to go home."

"Go home? What are you talking about?"

"I can't explain it. I just want you safe."

"Safe? Slade, you've got to come better than that, now. What's going on? You're not in trouble are you?"

"No. Well, not yet."

"Whatever you're doing, if it's going to jeopardize your job, it's not worth it."

His frustration began to mount and he raised his voice. "It is, Mom!" She recoiled at his volume in surprise. Slade took a breath, trying to calm himself. "It is," he repeated. "Something big is gonna happen and I don't want you caught in the middle of it."

"What do you have to do with it?"

"Everything."

She waited for Slade to say he was joking, or something – anything to reassure her that her feeling of fright was misplaced. Slade expected more fight, more words between them, but when he opened his mouth to continue, he was cut short. His mother saw Slade's conviction and said, "And you've made up your mind?"

He nodded.

"You remind me of your sister right now. Well, if there's no stopping you, then I'll go. But, Slade, whatever you do, promise me you'll make me proud. And be careful."

"I will." He hugged her again and said, "Now, go. And stay home until it's all over."

As his mother pulled away from the embrace, Slade noticed a tear in one of her eyes begin to roll down her face. He figured she was just afraid for his wellbeing, and that was partly true, but what he didn't know was that somewhere deep inside, she was already proud of the man her son had become right before her eyes.

II

Slade waved at his mother as her car disappeared through the clouds below. He saw the worry in her face, and nearly relented his decision, but Douglassaire was waiting for him and he couldn't turn back now.

Slade moved through the busy courtyard of Lorelei Castle, taking deep breaths of distress at the thought of uprooting the calm scene. He did what he could to keep those thoughts at bay. All he kept in mind were the things that needed to be set right, no matter the cost. He ran back to the door leading to the dungeons, not too far from where he landed. The princess and the others were probably in their cells now. If he was going to free Doug, he knew he needed a big distraction. He entered the dungeons and looked for the newly imprisoned team and found them in the nearest cells; Anna and Jack on one side facing Kandyce and Vinzant. Anna was unusually quiet as Slade approached and she eyed him cautiously.

"Can I trust you?" he asked. He went around the corner to a console where he pressed his thumb against the small scanner. On the screen, he opened the four cells holding the Auctorati. He turned the corner again and saw them all emerging from their cells with a suspicious look on their face.

"Trust us?" Anna asked. "With what?"

"Information. You said you needed someone to be brave and stop the queen. Now that you're back home, how do you feel? Do you feel the same?"

"I can't say that being in a dungeon brings back any fond memories."

"But you are the princess. What if you're forgiven? What will you do? Run back to her side?"

"After what she's done? Never. I'm an Auctorati, now."

Slade felt the eyes of her cohorts on him. He knew he had their full and undivided attention. "All right. Commander Heuresyt is alive."

Kandyce gasped and Vinzant made a sound like he'd been punched in the gut. Jack just stood there nodding and Anna kept her unwavering eyes on Slade's. "And?" she asked.

"The queen wants to use his power to finish her conquest of Pangaea. I want to stop her. I'm breaking him out and getting him as far away from her as possible."

"And what do you want us to do?"

"Do what you want. Fight. Flee. I don't care. I'm letting you loose, so I just need you to free the Commander for me."

"Why don't you just free him now, yourself?"

"Because I have to help somebody else. I won't have time to do that if I'm fighting my way out up here." Slade opened the small latch on his body armor where he removed something and tossed it.

Anna caught it and saw it was his ID Card.

"I'm not flagged just yet, but I will be soon. There's not much time. You remember where the armory is?" Slade asked.

"Of course."

"Good. Give me about ten minutes before you drop the Commander. Then go get your weapons back. You'll need 'em."

"Where is he located?"

"He's at the far end of the dungeon behind a false wall. He might be guarded now. I don't even think the guards there know who he is."

Anna nodded.

Slade nodded and began to leave without a word, but stopped in his tracks at the sound of his name.

"Slade!" called Anna. She walked up and stuck out her hand. "Thank you. You are a brave man."

Slade smiled and gave her hand a quick shake. "Good luck, Princess." He turned and left through the doors leading outside.

***

Vinzant remarked, "Well, that went better than expected."

"It's just pure luck, but you're right," Kandyce replied. "This is much better than going through the camps on foot."

Anna turned to her team. "We do this for Libra…and for Pangaea. This is where we make our stand and tell that witch 'This is enough'!" She led the way further into the dungeon with Jack, Kandyce, and Vinzant following close behind.

III

Slade regretted the fact he left his helmet on the supertrop. His suit's cloaking ability would have been a great boon to him now. In his hurry, he'd forgotten to pick up his weapons, too. At least he wasn't completely unarmed. He still had a dagger embedded in his suit's arm.

Slade knew if he made one wrong step, he'd be in the dungeons himself. All of the castle's air cars were parked in an area just off to the side of the supertrops. He needed one, but only the drivers had the keys, and none of them were around here now. He walked to the main courtyard and saw an air car approaching close to its edge. This was his chance.

As the car's two passengers climbed out of their seats he ran after the vehicle as it turned to make its descent back to the mainland. He waved his hand and yelled, "Hey! Driver, wait."

The driver was an older man with a big grey mustache and a cigarette in his mouth – much against the rules for his position. He concealed the cigarette in the car's cup holder and frowned at the M.3.A.N. agent as he neared. "There's no need to rush. Another car will be up in a few minutes."

"No, sir, that's not it. The queen requests your presence in the throne room."

"What? She does? For what?"

"Don't worry about that sir, it's urgent. Our queen needs you."

"What are you trying to pull?"

Suddenly, the castle's sirens blared through the sky. The busy courtyard grew still with apprehension.

"Sir, there's no time." Slade turned his head to the sight of people making way for the flood of knights running toward his position. He looked back at the driver, ignored the commands of "Halt, Director," and instead reached up his arm and pulled out his dagger. "Get out of the car, now!" he yelled.

The driver froze and Slade grabbed the man by the arm and pulled him out of his seat. As the driver landed on the ground next to Slade, the unmanned car began to drift downwards. Slade took a quick glance behind him at the knights who were nearly at his back and even saw a knight stand still amongst the crowd and point his BAC. People began to scream and scatter away from the confrontation. Slade ducked his head as the gunshot rang out in the open air and jumped after the car, just before it was out of reach. Slade had his armored suit to thank for protecting against the thud from landing in the car on his side.

The car was losing altitude quickly and Slade sat up in the driver's seat. His heart raced as he pulled the emergency brake and tightly gripped the wheel. The car shook and stabilized to a fast midair halt. Slade breathed hard and fast, still unable to get his heart rate under control. His foot pressed into the brake pedal while he released the emergency brake and chanced a glance upward. As the knights began pointing their guns at him over the edge, he pressed the acceleration, hoping his head wouldn't explode in the process. He supposed he shouldn't be surprised to have guns pointed at him – he was considered a criminal now.

He turned the air car to the jagged bottom half of the floating landmass to where the dungeon floors would open. He waited looking for any sign of Douglassaire dropping through. He had a sick feeling in his stomach as the sirens continued their wail. He hoped he wasn't too late.

IV

Anna knew the way to the secret chamber like the back of her hand. It was funny how after years of absence everything came back to her. It was as if she never left. The Auctorati went undetected in the dungeons until they came upon Douglassaire's chamber.

As they approached, the castle sirens rang bringing the guard who stood watch to attention. He snapped his sword into place and looked around, freezing in surprise at the group of four coming at him. "Stop right there," he commanded.

Their trot came to a quick halt. Even though they outnumbered the one guard, they were still unarmed, and all of the knights in the castle would soon be at their position.

"How are we setting the big guy loose, now?" Vinzant asked.

Anna spied the lit torch of white flame behind the guard's head and looked at Kandyce.

"I was just thinking that," Kandyce said. She raised her hand and every inch of the dungeon was illuminated in white light as the torch erupted into a huge flame that covered the ceiling. The guard turned and ducked at the sudden burst then felt something crack as he landed hard on his face. He tightened the grasp on his sword but felt a shooting pain in his free hand as one of his fingers was twisted in some ungodly direction by the man on top of him. "You can let go the easy way or the hard way," Jack said. The knight relaxed his hand and let the sword clang to the ground. In an instant, the white flame shrunk down to a small sphere and danced in Kandyce's hand.

Vinzant picked up the dropped sword and said, "Well, that's one problem down, but you're still locked out of the system,

Princess."

"I don't need the Director's permission to do anything in my own home, Vinzant," Anna said as she stepped past them all to the wall. She reached up for the empty torch and turned it once clockwise on its side. A piece of the wall slid open to her left revealing a console with an all-white screen. She placed her hand over it and the console whirred and chimed, but the screen flashed red with an error message. Anna glanced at the stupid look on Vinzant's face and said, "Don't say anything," to which he simply raised hands.

"Heads up," called Jack.

Anna caught another ID card as it floated to her from Jack's toss. It was from the knight on the ground. "This should do it," she said, and she pressed the knight's badge against the screen. Words appeared on the screen that confirmed the knight's identity. Below, she tapped a few buttons until one appeared that read UNLOCK.

"Hey, Commander!" she called. "Hold on to your rope."

V

Each wail of the sirens slowed the beating of Slade's heart. He was a sitting duck here and he didn't know whether to wait or flee. Had the sirens come on because they found the Auctorati's cells empty or was the news even worse? Had Anna already released Doug and Slade had just been too slow to get him? Slade knew the knights would be in air cars pulling around the bend at any moment. This was his last chance at escape.

He braced himself for the inevitable – jail time, probably torture, death. He bounced his knee and darted his eyes looking for any sign of the knights or Doug. In the absence of sound between sirens, Slade heard a loud click and looked up. It was him.

Douglassaire was caught by surprise at the sudden drop. He was still in his tattered black armor and only a sliver of his red cape remained, off to one shoulder and flapping in the wind like a long scarf. He inhaled a panicked breath and reached up for the noose tied around his neck. The rope was long and he had only a quick second to grab hold, but he did, his hands burning from the slide downward. Had he been only a second later, the long rope attached to his weight would have killed him instantly. He secretly thanked the mystery woman who gave him the slightest of forewarning.

The rope dug into his neck and his breathing became more and more labored. He felt swallowed by the empty sky below him. He bought himself a few seconds, but still kicked his legs and shook the rope trying to free himself.

"Doug!" cried Slade. He looked around for something – anything to cut him loose. He grabbed his dagger, but threw it back down knowing he was out of reach. He looked all over and then a small red light caught his eye. It was the cigarette left by the driver and its end was still smoldering. Slade was still new to his ether, but it looked like this was his only hope. He lifted the cigarette out of the cup holder and held the burning end away from his face with another hand hovering over it like it was a crystal ball.

Just as he began to feel hopeless and stupid, a bright spark of light shot out to Douglassaire's rope, giving Slade a start. *Did I really just do that?* he thought. The rope caught fire and the flame traveled in both directions: up to the void of the dungeon and down towards Doug, inching ever closer to his hands. Slade concentrated on the flame, making it hotter until it turned blue and the rope snapped in two.

Doug relieved his lungs with a shallow breath and kicked his legs, aimlessly searching for some solid ground beneath him. Slade's air car slid beneath him and his back and buttocks exploded in pain.

"Doug!" Slade cried. He watched Doug clutch his leg. There was a bandage wrapped around his thigh soaked in a patchwork of dried and wet blood. He wondered what happened to him, but once Doug opened his eyes, he decided to leave the questions for later. Slade handed Doug his dagger and said, "Told you so."

After cutting the noose away and getting his first full breath, Douglassaire could only manage the faintest of smiles in response. That was enough for Slade. He knew they'd soon be followed if he didn't get moving. He hit the acceleration and sped down and away from Lorelei Castle.

VI

"Let's move," said Anna walking away from the hidden cell. Vinzant and Kandyce followed close behind while Jack put the knight in a chokehold until he fell asleep. He jogged up behind them and caught wind of a minor squabble.

"We're not going to the arms closet, are we?" asked Kandyce.

"Yes. I need my gun."

"There's no way. The guards'll be all over us."

"We'll make a way."

"Anna, that's dumb."

"We're already dumb, Kandyce, we're attempting a coup against Aeothesca. The only thing worse is going against her without a crystal bullet."

The pathways of the dungeon suddenly got crowded with knights as the sound of hard boots hitting the ground filled the air.

"Here," said Anna, pointing out the exit. The group quickened their pace, but came to a standstill at the sight of a group of knights blocking the doorway and brandishing their swords.

"We got it this time, Anna," Vinzant said.

Anna stood aside as Vinzant and Jack ran ahead to meet the knights head-on. Kandyce stood by her side ever ready to provide support.

Vinzant blocked the closest knight's first swing with his stolen sword and gave him a hard punch to the face with his free hand, knocking him down. Jack grabbed the downed knight's sword and joined the melee. The other knights were easy to take down without much bloodshed, but Vinzant sustained a hard kick to the ribs and fell on his back. As another chrome-armored knight stood above him and raised his sword for a final blow, his hands suddenly burst into white flames. His sword banged loudly against the concrete floor as he fell to his knees, screaming in pain.

"Go, go!" yelled Kandyce to everyone. The way was clear, but more knights were definitely on the way. Anna ran through the door followed by Jack and Vinzant who had picked himself up. Kandyce stole back the flame from her burn victim, sure he wouldn't follow them now.

They all ran and followed Anna down the bright castle corridor. She made a sudden stop and turned into a big room with shelves and drawers with weapons and even some armor hanging.

"This is a closet?" said Vinzant in awe. "I could live in this room, alone."

"Here," Anna said, opening a small cabinet door. She saw Libra's BAC and sword leaning against the wall of the cabinet and grabbed them with haste. "Hurry, everyone. Get your stuff."

As they reunited with their arms, they all felt a strange sense of relief in the midst of being hunted down. Anna checked the barrel of her gun. She unloaded the plain bullet and replaced it with one of the crystal bullets she found in the ammunition drawer. She grabbed a couple more just in case.

"Everyone ready?" she asked.

They all nodded and headed back out the door, ready to fight their way to the queen.

CHAPTER THIRTY-TWO

Gisela sat at the small table in her trailer poring over documents. The mass of people fleeing the Southern Third was almost becoming too much. She'd have to expand her base of operations and get more rations. With her elbows rested on the table she exhaled and sat her forehead in the palms of her hands. Managing the camp wasn't all that was bothering her. Her appointment with the queen came very near and she kept dismissing Garren who was eager for her to get dressed. She didn't know what the consequences would be for missing it. Her ability to manage the camp could be taken away, but she still couldn't ignore Slade's warning.

She got up and walked to her bed to see, once again, the outfit Garren pulled for her to wear. It was her green dress – the same one she wore at the Leaders Ball. She could only recall the events of that night in fragments, save for a few details. That was because she had been under the water spirit's control. There was Commander Azure's fall, of course – who could forget that? And she remembered, amongst the chaos, watching the queen leave her seat to speak with a man.

The door to the trailer slammed shut and she jumped, seeing Garren standing there where he once was not.

"Are you ready to go, Mrs. Van der Borea?"

"Garren, you scared me. What's the matter?"

"We need to hurry now or we'll be late."

Gisela looked at her dress and reconfirmed her decision. "I'm not going."

"Mrs. Van der Borea, enough of this. Get dressed and let's go!"

Gisela felt her chest tighten. She thought of Slade's warning and knew this was what he must have been talking about. "You're right, Garren," she said. "It must be the stress that's getting to me."

As she sat down on her bed and fiddled with the laces on her sneaker, her trailer began to feel more like a cage. She had to do something.

Gisela... the spirit inside of her beckoned. She ignored her. She didn't want to use her power...but was there any other way out? Holding on to her resolve to help people had been her way of keeping the spirit locked down, but now she began to feel desperate. *Garren has to go.* The voice inside of her rang loudly at the worst possible time. *No, no!* she thought, trying her best to fight it off, but...

Gigi smiled.

She pointed to the small couch next to Garren. "My shoes are over there. Could you grab them for me? Oh, and could you grab me a cup of water?"

Garren bent over and grabbed her high-heeled shoes then came down the small aisle and handed them to her, just as ordered.

"Thank you," said Gigi.

Garren turned his back to Gigi and went to the small kitchenette. "I'm sorry for my roughness, Madam. Missing an appointment with the queen has just never been done, you see. You made the right choice."

Gigi continued to pretend to untie her sneakers, all the while taking small glances over her shoulder at her butler. "It's all right, Garren. Sometimes we all need a little wake-up call."

Garren grabbed a small cup from the cupboard and picked a bottle of water from the group of them standing in the mini fridge. He twisted open the bottle of water and tilted it over the cup, but before anything spilled over, he stopped, remembering a strange event earlier in the year. He remembered being in the living room of the Van der Borea estate and standing beside Gisela who was standing alone and gazing out onto the landscape of Septentrion City. The day was horrible. It rained heavily and most everyone stayed indoors, but at that moment, the rain had died down some and just continued to lightly sprinkle. The glass wall where Gisela stood in silence was separated into squares and covered in raindrops, fragmenting the scenery beyond. Garren played his role as the dutiful butler to perfection. "Is there anything I can do for you?" he'd asked.

"No, Garren. Thank you." She had stepped away into her bedroom and left him standing there alone. In that moment to himself, Garren had stood where she stood and looked where she looked, trying to see if there was some way he could get her perspective on things. A strange feeling that he couldn't place took hold of him as he looked through the glass, and inexplicably haunted him ever since.

Now, standing in the trailer, about to serve Gisela her cup of water, he realized what bothered him so much. The view of Septentrion City was so crisp and clear as he stood in that spot. Had he not moved to Gisela's vantage point, he would have only seen the fragments of rain splashed upon the glass. But here, it was as if someone had gone outside and wiped the square of glass clean. Then, he remembered the strange death of Wellesley – a drowning in a pond while his wife doubled over in pain and looked into Garren's eyes. *"Stop... me..."* he remembered her pleading.

He looked over his shoulder and saw a smirk of confidence on his employer's face as she stood inches away. It had been a while since he'd seen *that* Gisela. It was only a split second before the water from the bottle covered his mouth and nose and pushed its way in. He dropped the bottle to the floor, but none of the water splashed. It hung, suspended in the air and attached to his face, slowly filling in the void. He stepped around Gisela in a futile attempt to flee, but fell to the ground. He reached his arm out to the door of the trailer, choking and coughing.

The door of the trailer flew open and all Garren could see of who walked in was a pair of armored legs and shoes. He lie there struggling and felt his body begin to shut down, paying no attention to what the man was yelling.

"Gisela, stop!"

Slade looked in horror at his changed friend. The trail of water fell to the ground at the sound of his voice and Gisela looked at Slade in bewilderment. She shook her head as if coming out of a trance and looked at the ground around her. "Oh, my God!" she exclaimed. She kneeled next to Garren, and looked up at Slade, shaking her head. "Slade, I didn't—"

"Help him!"

She snapped her attention back to Garren and flipped him on his back. She held her hand over his face and drew out the water that hadn't already entered his lungs. His eyes were closing and he was fading away. Slade sat next to her and nudged her out of the way and placed his hands on Garren's chest, one over the other, and pumped four times. Garren coughed up more water and after a moment began to sit up. He drew in big gasps of air and blinked as he tried to regain his composure.

Before Garren could say anything, Slade grabbed Gisela's hand and said, "Come on," lifting her up. Without thinking, Gisela followed as they ran out the trailer door. When they got to the stolen air car, Slade opened the back seat door and forced Gisela inside. "Slade—" she started, but was interrupted by the door's slam. Slade trudged his way around the car to the driver's side door and got in. As he started the car, he looked in the rear view mirror at Gisela whom he saw watching him. "Slade, I… I didn't mean to."

"He's fine, now, Gisela that's all that matters." He began to drive away.

"I'm not talking about him," she said choking up. "I mean Wellesley. I killed him. I killed him, but I didn't mean it, I swear." She could feel the tears welling up in her eyes and let them drop as she held her gaze on the floor.

"Gisela?" inquired a deep voice at the front. She looked up and saw Douglassaire staring back at her from the passenger seat.

"Doug! Oh, my God! Oh, my God, how?"

"The story was false," Slade said. "They never killed him."

Gisela came down from the shock. "It's good to see you,

Doug,"

"Yeah, you too," he said. He turned back and sat upright in his seat, out of Gisela's sight.

"What's going on?" she asked.

"She needed him. They didn't kill him because she needed him – and you."

"Wait. Who?"

"The queen."

"Need us for what?"

"She wants to get the Djed Key and use its power."

"For what?"

"Think about it. She's already taken the South. Your country's next."

She paused for a moment, taking it all in, then frowned and shook her head. "I still don't see how I figure into this."

"I'll explain it once we get out of here. Just hold on."

Slade, Douglassaire, and Gisela tried to wrap their minds around what was happening. They continued riding along as Slade drove to some place unknown to Doug and Gisela. A few minutes passed before Douglassaire decided to say, "You didn't kill him, Gisela. Your husband? That's not you." He heard her shift her weight behind him and knew he had her attention. "These spirits…they're constantly fighting us. They want control. I'm sure even Slade feels it."

Gisela shot Slade an intense look and locked on to his eyes through the rearview mirror. Slade shifted his view back to the road.

"So drop it. It takes a strong person to keep these spirits in check. I'd say you're plenty strong right now."

Gisela looked at the back of Doug's seat with a sense of wonder. She finally began to understand what Slade saw in this man. He made her acknowledge a truth she had been all too eager to deny. She wasn't at fault for Wellesley's death – that was the water spirit's doing. And her grandmother was wrong, too. She didn't kill her mother – the spirit did that. She helped a lot of people with the refugee camp, but it was time to help herself. No matter what, she would get rid of the water spirit so it couldn't do any more harm.

Slade slowed the car to a stop and got out. Gisela and Doug emerged from the car, unsure of what they were doing here. They were parked on the top of a hill that overlooked the city of Reor. The city's façade of peace remained, but the three of them knew the city was in turmoil. They caught up to Slade who stood still, studying the cityscape.

"All right, Slade," Doug said. "What's going on?"

Slade enjoyed the moment of calm and drew in a breath as he prepared to explain. "Do you remember the spirits of Ether from the old story? 'Three of four to open the door'? They're the spirits we've accepted. We have the spirits of Ether within us. And if three of them are together, that should open the door to Ether." He turned to Gisela and said, "That's why the queen had you followed and kept Doug alive – because she's got a spirit of Ether as well."

Doug shook his head. "If you had told me this stuff a few years ago, I would have looked at you like you were crazy."

"But it makes sense," Slade said. "Ether was never found, because it can't be reached any other way. Now she wants the Djed Key. With that much power, she'd be a god. She could do anything she wanted. She could take over Pangaea and stop any hope of the people fighting back."

"Why are we here?" Gisela asked.

"To stop her. Even if she doesn't have the key, it's almost certain that she'll start a war with the North. They're not prepared to defend against her."

Doug grunted, "They're too far up her ass."

"And then who knows what'll happen with her in complete control?" Slade continued. "You've seen it, Gisela. The Southerners already got a taste of her oppression. The Middle Third hasn't felt anything – *yet*."

"She wouldn't want you guys to know about this," Doug said.

"Right. There would be an uprising. As quiet as it's kept, even we like to get away from the queen's rule every once in a while. She'll probably come down harder on everyone if she no longer has the world to answer to. We've got to go to Ether and get the power for ourselves."

"And then what?" asked Gisela.

"And then we'll knock her down. Gisela, the Northern Third needs a hero, and after what you been through, you must want to get rid of the water spirit. This might be a way to do it. And, Doug, here's where you can get her back for everything...your family and your country."

Slade waited for an answer and turned to face the view of Reor. A thought occurred to him: he recalled his old vision of learning about magic and Ethereans, adventure, and having Douglassaire by his side. He realized he was in the middle of it right now. He didn't know it would be so intense at the time, but he knew he was exactly where he was supposed be. For the first time, things just felt right, and he was determined to make sure Queen Aeothesca did not turn things wrong.

"Okay," Gisela said. "If this is the only shot we've got, we have to take it."

Doug looked at her, surprised, then back at Slade and said, "No need to ask. You know I'm down. There's just one thing." He pointed at his bandaged leg. "I haven't been able to use my power since I was shot. Whatever it is, they left it in there."

"A crystal bullet," Slade said. "Shit, that is a problem."

"A crystal bullet?" asked Gisela.

"Yeah. It's what we use to take down Ethereans. Think we can take it out?"

Douglassaire gritted his teeth. "It's in there kinda deep." He opened the car door and limped his way into his seat with his legs out. After unwrapping the bandage, their faces all turned at the ugly scar. "They cleaned it and kept it fresh. Never let it heal."

"The queen wanted to take the bullet out eventually. You'd need your power to open the door," said Slade.

"I might be able to help," said Gisela as she knelt over the wound. "Anyone got any water?"

Slade and Doug both shook their heads.

"Okay..." she said. She watched blood drip from the wound and got an idea. "Doug, this might hurt." She spread her hands over the wound and focused on his blood. She could sense his blood wrap around something and begin to pull.

Douglassaire clutched the car cushion and cried out in agony. His leg pulsated and beads of sweat formed on his brow, but after a moment, the pain subsided and out dropped the crystal bullet in a small pool of blood. He took huge breaths of relief and wiped his forehead. "Thanks, Gisela." He winced as he tightly rewrapped the wound in the same dirty, bloody bandage.

"How do you feel?" asked Slade.

Doug lifted his hand and forced the wind to dance around his fingers. "I'm good."

"Good. You ready to give this Ether thing a try?"

Doug pulled himself up from the seat. "Let's do it."

Gisela grabbed Slade's hand and slowly reached for Doug's whose hand latched onto hers.

Slade looked down at Doug's big hand which was open and stretched in his direction. He grabbed it trying his best not to look Doug in the eye. He failed – and what a failure it was. A touch he thought he'd never feel again warmed his hand and his heart. He lowered his head and closed his eyes to concentrate, feeling the gravity of the earth pull down harder.

Douglassaire saw a pale red light emanating from the back of Slade's neck. Then, he saw a faint blue light coming from Gisela at the same place on her neck, darkened by her hair. His own mark glowed white as he closed his eyes and felt his once lost ethereal power flow through him.

They could all feel the presence of something nearby, but none of them opened their eyes until they heard a loud click, like the sound of an old lock. As they opened their eyes, they saw an enormous white gate stretched stories high close to the peak of the hill just a few feet behind Slade. Its ancient hinges creaked loudly as the gate's doors swung inward. They all let go of each other and stared in awe at what they called forth. All they could see through the gate was the same cityscape of Reor. Still, their spirits felt a pull inside. Ether beckoned.

"Okay," Slade said. "We get the Djed Key and we get out. Then, we can deal with the queen."

They all hoped it would be that easy. They would be the first humans to ever step foot into Ether and had no idea of what lie ahead. All they knew was that they had to do this, for if they didn't they would probably end up dead by the end of the day. The queen would grab the power of the Djed Key for herself and kill all three of them without hesitation. Then, she would begin her reign of terror over Pangaea. They couldn't let any of that happen.

Without a word, each of them stepped through, and the gate to Ether closed shut and disappeared.

CHAPTER THIRTY-THREE

The Auctorati's unhindered trek through the great hall of the castle came to a complete stop as they saw a wall of knights blocking their path. Even more closed the way behind them. The castle's sirens died down and Anna, Kandyce, Jack, and Vinzant pulled out their swords.

"Not so fast," yelled the woman in front of the knights. Her white armor and mere presence showed that she was in charge. "My, my, if it is not the traitor," said Catherine. "We have been ordered to keep you alive – for what, I have not the slightest, but our fair queen desires it so. You must be very special to her, Annonymn. You, who have caused the queen such pain and suffering. I would like nothing more than to deliver you to her in pieces, but I have my orders. Now, surrender like the peon you are and let your team go. It is over."

"Peon?" Anna said. "That's a laugh. You're nothing more than a glorified servant. Don't forget your place. Aeothesca will never love you."

Catherine's face twisted into rage. "I take it that you refuse to surrender. In that case, we have been ordered to take you into custody by force." Catherine commanded her army, "Everyone stay back! I shall take on these curs alone."

Catherine slowly grabbed her hilt from her side. The blue

blade briefly reflected the light of the room as it fell and snapped together. Everything happened in a flash. Vinzant was caught by surprise with a stab to the shoulder while Anna got a simultaneous kick to the gut. Jack swung down at Catherine in an effort to end it quickly, but in a backhand strike, the top of her sword's hilt came crashing into his face, knocking him away. Kandyce received a swift head-butt in response to throwing a ball of fire and hardly even burning a hair on Catherine's head.

Jack grabbed Catherine's arms from behind and yelled, "Go, Anna! We'll handle her." Catherine slipped out of his grasp and lunged after Anna, but was stopped by Vinzant. His bloody, injured arm hung by his side, but his other hand still had a hold on his sword.

Catherine yelled, "No! Don't let her escape!"

"Yes – let her come," commanded a voice that filled the room. A silent obedience took over and everyone froze for a moment as they turned and listened to the queen standing just down the hall. Dressed in an opulent, golden blouse and fitted navy pants, she commanded, "Do what you will with the others." She kept her eyes on Anna as she turned and entered her throne room.

Anna looked at her team. She felt the pressure of accepting an open invitation from Aeothesca, but she couldn't leave her team behind. They were already tired and beat up as it was.

"Go," said Jack again.

Anna sheathed her sword and turned her back, saddened and sure she would never see them again. "Thank you. For everything," she said. She began to walk towards the group of knights and they all stepped aside with their haughty looks and grunts of disapproval.

Catherine screamed in defiance and swung her sword wildly at Vinzant who deftly blocked each strike. "Get back here!" she yelled over his shoulder. "I'll kill you myself! Annonymn!"

Vinzant never felt such hatred for a person before and those feelings grew with each strike he blocked. His face reddened and shrank into a frown as he retaliated with a fatal blow straight through Catherine's heart. Her screams fell to silent mutterings as she clung madly to life.

For a brief moment, Vinzant just stood there watching the life fade from Catherine's eyes. He removed his bloody sword and let her drop to the ground. Catherine's fellow knights screamed in agony and swarmed the three of them, leaving Anna to walk alone to the throne room where her sister waited.

CHAPTER THIRTY-FOUR

Queen Aeothesca stood at the far side of the room looking through her stained-glass window. Her face reflected the sun and her hair shined the reddest of reds. She could tell by how Catherine's shouting was cut short that she had lost her. Her own feelings had surprised her. For a moment she almost grieved for Catherine, but kept in mind what was to come. It was fine. Another lady-in-waiting had to be replaced. Soon all would bow to her and show as much respect as Catherine. That damned Director Maxwell only delayed her plans to retrieve the Djed Key, but without a third spirit of Ether, there was nothing he could do. She would deal with him soon, but for now she had another loose end to tie up. Her hands were folded at her back and she took a deep breath preparing herself for the reunion. The queen heard the door of the throne room open and slide shut. Her long lost sister was here.

"Dear sister, what havoc have you brought upon our house?" the queen asked.

"I could ask you the same."

"I feel I am having the absolute worst of days, but to see your face…" Aeothesca turned and approached her sister with open arms. "Oh, Anna, these walls have missed your presence."

"Stay there," Anna said as she drew her sword.

Aeothesca paused and lowered her arms, taking in the full picture of her changed sister. "Oh, Anna...whatever have you done to your hair?"

"That's enough, Aeothesca. This room that you love so much will be your grave."

Aeothesca laughed, "And who then would be queen? You? Come now, dear sister, what do you know about being a queen – about being a ruler?"

"I know enough to not turn the monarchy into a vehicle for selfish means. We are supposed to help the people."

"*We? The people?* The same people who hate Ethereans so much that they would suspect their own queen of murder? No, dear, in this world there is only us and them, and you made it very clear which side you chose when you branded your own sister a demon. No one who renounces the crown is fit for a queen. Even if you did become queen, you would fare much worse than I."

"You don't know what I'm capable of–"

"And I wish not to find out! You do not know the nature of power – its temptations. I always had real power, then Mother died and I took the reins to control a whole nation. Any lesser human would have destroyed the Middle Third long ago. Trust me, dear, you would not be able to handle any of this."

"If you have all of this power and control, why aren't you happy? Isn't it enough? Aren't you satisfied? Why destroy the Southern Third?"

"Because even with all of that power, I am still a slave to the fear and expectations of...*the people*. *Your* people. If I wish to shake free of that – free all Ethereans of that, I must have control over all. I am no villain, Anna. You are." She ascended the steps to her throne and said, "You and your people will listen to us. And we will be free."

"You really have lost your mind. You've convinced yourself that this war is noble. You stole my life here and this war stole my life again! You will pay for that."

Aeothesca sat down in her chair, crossed her legs, and rested folded hands on her knees. "I would love to see you try."

For the first time in her life, Anna became acutely aware that

313

Lorelei Castle was indeed floating in midair. It had moved barely, but she could feel it. She could also sense the slight wavy movements in the grass and trees in the stairs above. This whole room – no – this whole castle had become an extension of her sister's power. She swallowed her anxiety and knew that if she struck, she better hit, or it would be all over for her. She stood there watching her pompous sister sit there amused while looking down on her. A second of time seemed to stretch forever until the queen blinked. Anna's sword dropped to the ground in a loud bang as she swung her rifle from over her shoulder. She aimed a perfect line at Aeothesca's forehead and shot. While lowering her gun, her eyes grew full of disbelief.

"A crystal bullet," said the queen from behind a vine that covered her face. It untwisted its end from around the bullet and allowed the projectile to drop to the ground with the sound of a small coin. As the vine snaked away, her face revealed her displeasure and shock as she remarked, "I am surprised. You really do mean to kill me. However, I will show you mercy if only you–"

Anna dropped the BAC, picked up her sword, and rushed up the stairs. If she couldn't shoot the queen, she'd have to cut her down. It was her only choice, but the queen was so powerful. Each platform was a small battle against the earth itself. Anna swung against the grass that suddenly grew and grabbed at her heels, defended against the leaves from the trees that flew at her like knives, and hacked at the vines from the walls that attempted to stabilize her. Even chunks of stone were broken and thrown at her arms and legs. It was looking bad for her.

All the while, the queen commanded, "Stop this at once! Stop this or you will die here."

CHAPTER THIRTY-FIVE

Ether was unlike any place Slade, Gisela, or Douglassaire had ever been before. There were no pathways or paved roads, just an expanse of moss-covered trees, vines, and tall plants sticking out of the brown jungle floor. The trickling of water against rocks signaled a nearby river and everywhere the golden light of the sun filtered through the shade of the trees. The island was alive with sound, but none of it familiar. No birds or crickets were chirping. In fact, they doubted that any normal animals even existed on this island. All they saw were lusae and that alone was terrifying. A group of jaculi passed in front of them unphased by their presence. Halos flew high above them, and yowies, with their flat faces and furry, short limbs moved about the trees. They stuck their hands out, forcing dangling vines to magically swing into their palms for their swing to any part of the jungle.

The three of them stood still, overwhelmed by the sights. Douglassaire stepped forward, but Slade grabbed his arm, stopped him, and shook his head – afraid of what the lusae might do. Douglassaire looked back and said, "I don't think they care. Come on." He continued limping ahead, and when the lusae made no moves against him, Slade and Gisela followed close behind.

"Why aren't they paying us any attention?" Gisela asked.

Douglassaire figured it out. His father wrote about this in his journal. The lusae respect those more powerful than them. The spirits they held within them gave them a presence of dominion over Ether, and this was their home. "'Cause we belong here," Doug said.

Just as he said that, Slade tripped and fell into a wall. He put his hand out and caught himself, but the strange brick-red color and scaly texture made the hair on his neck stand on end. The ground rumbled slightly and the wall shifted.

Gisela gasped and covered her mouth.

"Slade," Douglassaire warned.

Slade froze while touching the scales and he slowly turned his head to look over his arm at the big red eyes of a dragon. His stomach turned and he felt faint. The dragon blinked once, its menacing vertical pupils as tall as Slade. Slade felt its body expand as it inhaled, winced, and then fell over from the force of the hot air that escaped the dragon's nostrils. Slade's heart raced as he stared at the creature, but the dragon simply looked away with a grunt and sat its head back on the ground to continue its rest. Gisela offered her hands to Slade and helped him off the ground.

"Come on," said Douglassaire. "This way."

They didn't question him. There was no need. None of them had ever set foot on Ether, but they knew the way to the Djed Key as if it had been etched in their minds. Just as it had for Douglassaire, it became clear to Slade and Gisela that being vessels for their spirits gave them this knowledge.

A rasaji slept atop a large rock with its flames extinguished. They made sure not to disturb it as they traversed the bumpy ground. Spots of sun shone bright on their faces and dimmed as they passed under the trees. They finally happened upon where the river started – a large lake with the cleanest, bluest water they had ever seen. As they continued, just beyond the edge of the lake, the ground began to incline, and at the top of the hill was an object that resembled a sword. This was it. The Djed Key.

Its hilt was golden and its blade silver. It would have looked like any normal sword had it not been for its adornments. On each side of the blade sat two shards of crystal, one on top of the other, that resembled glass and greatly enhanced its width. Each shard was stained with the color of the elements: one red, below was green, another white, and finally, blue was below. The mythical sword with the power of Elao was real, stuck in the ground and leaning to the side, untouched by anyone. With power like that, they stood a chance at defeating the queen.

They all paused for a moment, and as Douglassaire stood between Slade and Gisela, he felt their eyes looking to him for the next step. Douglassaire stood still, contemplating whether he should nominate someone else to draw the Djed Key, but he knew as they did, that the task fell to him. He accepted his duty and began his climb to the Key alone.

When he reached the top of the hill, he felt the air spirit inside of him rattling its cage in excitement and fighting for control. Douglassaire reached out for the sword, his breathing growing deeper and longer. Sweat beaded his forehead and for a moment he thought he was making a mistake, but the Djed Key's power drew him so wildly that he couldn't have avoided grabbing it even if he wanted. When he put his hand around the golden hilt, the pain in his leg vanished and he felt a rush of supernatural power. The Djed Key looked like it weighed a ton, but in his hands, as he pulled it from its lifelong niche, it was as light as a feather.

"All right, Doug," called Slade from below, "let's go back. Doug?"

"What's wrong with him?" Gisela wondered aloud.

They gazed upward at their friend whose back was still turned with a posture that suddenly shifted. He stood hunched over with his broad shoulders extended into long arms that he held down as though they carried the weight of the world. His ruined scarf-like cape flapped furiously as the clouds grew dark and flew by in an alien speed. They were frightened when they heard a roar in the distance.

Slade and Gisela waited with bated breath to see just what it was that had made that horrific sound. All of the lusae scattered as the ground shook in steady, rhythmic pulses. Slade even spied the dragon fly away.

Slade looked back at Douglassaire who was still at the top of the hill with the Djed Key. He seemed unaffected by the sudden change in scenery. Slade wanted badly to run to him and see if he was all right, but his instincts told him it would be better if he stayed back. Slade could sense something was wrong with Douglassaire. He had changed as soon as he pulled the Djed Key from the ground. Douglassaire was far more powerful and dangerous than anyone or anything in this world. His power only seemed to increase as the Djed Key began to glow.

Doug lifted the sword into the sky and thin trails of white, green, red, and blue wisps sailed through the darkened sky and straight into the Key.

Gisela asked, "What's going on?"

Slade looked at the glowing mark on Gisela's neck and asked, "Is my mark glowing, too?"

She nodded, "Yeah."

"It's collecting power. It's taking it back. The spirits of Ether that the Djed Key released are returning."

Gisela lifted her hand toward the nearby lake and a stream of water flowed to her palm. "I can still use mine."

"I'm guessing not for long."

"Slade, look!" Gisela said, pointing in the distance behind them. The rumbling of the earth became more and more fierce and what they thought was the sound of thunder was clearly heard as gigantic footsteps getting closer and closer. Gisela felt sick at the sight of what appeared at the top of the trees.

A cloud of black smoke hovered there and made a ridiculous sound that was a mix of a man's cry and a lion's roar. The greenery of the trees and the grass all around it began to blacken, wilt, and die with each step it made forward. And as it finally made its way into the clearing where Slade, Gisela, and Douglassaire stood, they could see the complete picture of the monstrosity facing them. At the top of its head stuck out large sharp spikes – a crown of daggers. Its entire body and face was covered in black smoke, tightly wrapped around it, revealing only the creature's glowing yellow eyes and white, razor sharp teeth. The source of the thunderous sound was its black claws banging against the earth and dragging itself forward. Its legs were bound by a golden chain.

Slade shuddered as he spoke the creature's name, "Calamity."

It was already as tall as any monument in Reor – Slade couldn't imagine what it would be like if it were standing upright. As he and Gisela stood there looking up at Calamity, they shared a knowing look. This was their time to fight. Stopping the queen would have to wait. If they didn't stop Calamity here, it could destroy everything.

PART FOUR

CHAPTER THIRTY-SIX

I

The vines around Anna's arm, legs and neck grew tighter and her breath was cut short as she hung suspended in midair over the steps to Aeothesca's throne. Only her left arm was free, but it wasn't holding the sword. She looked down on her sister who was looking up at her with the eyes of a viper. Another vine began to slither out from behind the queen's throne, but Anna grabbed her sword out of her bound hand with her free arm and hacked it away just in time. Anna sliced at the vine wrapped around her neck, took in a huge gasps of air, and defended against another onslaught of them. While they occupied her enough to stop her from freeing her other arm and legs, she saw something else was happening. The ground began to shake and the stairs to the throne cracked and opened beneath her. Her sister was preparing the floor to be her literal burial ground. Anna couldn't let it end here, but she'd have to be quick. After one last successful defense against the vines, she sliced through the others that held her up in one sweeping, circular motion. She landed on her side next to the hole in the floor and the vines that had held her up slowly withered away. Anna hadn't expected a break in the attack, but then she looked up at her sister and saw her expression had changed.

The queen rubbed the triangular mark of her earth spirit on the back of her neck and looked confused. Her mouth opened as she stood up from her seat and Anna could see her mark was glowing green.

Had she lost her power? Anna wondered.

The room was deathly quiet and all that could be heard were the muffled shouts of horror and the rushing of feet in the hall. She didn't have time to ponder the question. Anna spied her BAC just an arm's length away. Now, while the queen was vulnerable, was the time to take her shot. She grabbed at the gun and reloaded another crystal bullet with great speed while her sister just stood there. Anna aimed and shot.

Again, she was too slow. The queen had a wall of concrete shoot up from the ground between them just in time to stop the bullet. She stepped from behind the wall with the same confused look on her face. Anna could see her sister's power wasn't gone, but what was the problem? She had one last crystal bullet, but as she reloaded, her sister ran.

The queen stepped down the ruins of the throne room, ran toward the stained-glass window, and pressed her hands against it. Pure, unfiltered sunlight broke through the cracks of a hidden door and she stepped through. Anna grabbed her sword off the ground, hung her BAC over her shoulder, and chased after her sister.

The sky was a perfect blue, the grass a majestic green, and the great crystal in the distance its usual pearl white. The two women ran. Past their memories as sisters and past the rays of their childhood. Anna's heart ached as she remembered the last time they ran together like this. Life was so simple then. It was just her and her sister. However, this time as she watched her sister's beautiful red hair swing back and forth, those feelings of innocent happiness were replaced with something sinister. Anna was here to kill her sister. How did things become so unhinged? She continued to follow her sister until she saw her stop in front of the crystal.

Queen Aeothesca studied the crystal and fell to her knees. "Anna. What did you do?"

Anna raised her gun, but knew that shooting her wouldn't

work – not now. She needed the perfect moment. "What do you mean?"

"The crystal is losing its power. The castle will fall!"

Anna looked to the top of the crystal and could see a trail of white streaming out to some unknown destination. Something was taking the ether it contained.

The queen continued, "And my earth spirit. It is weakening. Is this the Djed Key?"

"All I did was free the Commander—"

"I know you did!" she snapped. She began talking more to herself, trying to figure out why this was happening. "But even so, there were only three of us, unless… Who is the fire spirit?"

"Slade Maxwell, your Director. I was there when he got it."

The queen balled her hands into fists and the earth shook. "Slade! I will kill him my own bare hands for this!"

Anna saw a wisp of green trail from the queen's neck and into the atmosphere. The shaking ground became still once more. She was relieved. It felt like she finally had the upper hand. "Well, your bare hands are all you could use now," she said. "You're out of power. And you won't get anywhere near him because this ends now. Any last words?"

The queen stood up from the ground with fists balled at her sides and pivoted on her feet to glare at her gun-toting sister. "You have been away far too long. You, of all people, must have forgotten that I was born Etherean. And for that I am hurt beyond measure. I do not need the earth spirit's assistance. I am never powerless!"

She stomped her foot and the ground beneath them quaked once more. Anna lowered her gun and stepped back as chunks of the earth from all over the field broke off and flew towards the queen. She looked behind her and rolled to dodge a large piece of concrete that came straight for her head. Her gaze turned back to the queen who now stood on a newly raised platform high off the ground. After a moment, Anna could see an earthen body, legs, and arms form around her sister into a creature that completely enveloped her. Anna could feel her breathing quicken. *What the hell is that?*

The queen yelled from behind an opening in the golem's

chest. "Now I ask *you*, dear sister. Any last words?"

II

A blur passed between Slade and Gisela as Douglassaire charged ahead. He held the Djed Key in both hands to his side as he made his way toward Calamity. The creature made another ear-shattering scream and shook the earth as his claw came sliding across the field.

"Doug!" screamed Slade. He saw his friend disappear behind the smoky black claw. For a moment, he despaired but saw that the creature was struggling. He was eased at the sight of Douglassaire holding off its blow.

Doug pushed back the hand just enough to escape getting smashed against a tree. As he slid away, he swung his sword in the monster's direction, sending a blade of wind that cut straight through. Calamity roared loudly in pain, but more would be needed to stop his reign of destruction. It swung its arms in retaliation and Douglassaire blocked each swing as though the weight behind it was nothing more than a mere man with a sword.

Slade and Gisela watched in awe of Doug's sudden surge of power. He flew through the sky with the power of wind used the nearby body of water to stab Calamity with enormous sickles of ice. He threw boulders at the creature with the power of earth. The Djed Key was amazing. It granted him the ability to use all of the elements.

Yet, despite all of this, the monster still fought. It was unphased by the miraculous attacks of the Djed Key and fought back with the same intensity. It used its smoke to form black fireballs and vines in an attempt to kill its attacker. Doug deflected the black flame to a nearby bush, but then was knocked to the ground by smoke-covered vines that ripped through the air. He struggled to his feet and wielded the sword.

Slade looked at Gisela and said, "Come on. We have to help." He ran ahead and drew some black fire from the burning shrub. Gisela took a deep breath and settled in her mind that she would do anything to leave here alive. She ran to the lake and stood there with her arms spread out. The water swirled around her and she began a relentless assault against the monstrosity.

Slade stood a few steps behind Doug and shot fire from his hands to which Douglassaire turned and yelled, "Get back! This vile demon is mine!" Douglassaire's voice was completely changed, and with words like that, Slade knew that the air spirit was in complete control.

Slade ignored the command and continued his attack against Calamity.

Douglassaire towered over Slade with his face just inches away with a furious gaze. Slade was shaken by his presence, but found enough courage to speak.

"Doug," he said. He could feel his voice wavering. "You're strong enough. Fight it, Doug. Come back."

"You humans' definition of strong never ceases to amaze me. He can't handle the power of the Djed Key. The only reason I don't cut you down now is out of respect for my kin who resides within you." He grabbed Slade by the neck and lifted him off the ground. "Now go!" he said, throwing him away.

Slade flew back and landed with a hard thud. Not only did Doug have control over all of the elements, but his strength was incredible. Slade got up and Gisela yelled, "Are you okay?"

"I'm fine. We've got to bring him back, Gisela." He ran back to Douglassaire who hacked and slashed away at Calamity with minimal result. Black fire danced around in the palm of Slade's hand, and as he began to throw it at the beast, a smoke-covered spike came flying out of Calamity's back. All Slade had time to register was the surge of air flowing from behind him as he landed against a nearby tree. His flame was nearly gone. Just the final waning light of a candle sat in his hand. As Slade caught his breath, he looked down to see the spike jutting out of his abdomen. He touched the spot and looked at his hand in disbelief – it was covered in blood. The sound of his beating heart filled his head. When he finally realized what had happened, his ears clicked back to work and the first thing he noticed was the high-pitched scream of his name from Gisela. He looked up at his friend who rushed her way over with her eyebrows raised in panic.

Gisela knelt next to him. "Slade. Oh, God, Slade!"

Slade said nothing and looked down the way where Douglassaire was fighting. He saw the man standing still, dumbfounded, and staring at him. A wisp of white traveled from Doug's mark down his arm and into the Djed Key. Slade could see the real Doug was back. He was able to rid himself of the air spirit and push it into the Djed Key where it belonged. Doug turned back to Calamity who attempted another swipe with its big claw. The earth tremored as the claw dragged its way toward the warrior, and Doug screamed with every ounce of his body and lifted the Djed Key at just the right time to dislodge the claw at the wrist. It went flying into the air and both Douglassaire and Gisela attempted to catch their balance as it came crashing back down. Black smoke filled the air as the appendage disintegrated. Doug pointed the sword at Calamity and the surrounding trees and shrubbery regained their green color and came back to life. Vines from the monster's left and right stretched out from the jungle and wrapped around Calamity leaving only its hideous face uncovered. Calamity struggled, screaming and roaring, but he stayed put.

Douglassaire turned away from his enemy and ran to Slade, kneeling next to him upon his approach.

Slade was gasping for air and coughed up blood. "Doug?" Slade asked, his voice hushed by pain.

Doug nodded and grabbed his hand. "Yeah. It's me, Slade. I'm sorry."

"No, Doug–"

"Just hold on. Please. I don't want to lose you again."

"You never lost me. I'm just sorry we won't have more time."

"Don't talk like that, Slade. You're not going anywhere.'"

"Doug, please… I'm not getting up from this."

Gisela lowered her head at those words, not wanting to

believe what she was hearing. Calamity roared and shook more and more.

"Right now," Slade said, "we have to kill that thing."

"I'll take care of it–" Doug started.

"No. Trust us, Doug. We're a team. We're on your side."

Just then the Djed Key glowed once more and trails of blue and red flew into it from the triangle marks on Gisela and Slade. A trail of green came down from the sky and was collected by the Djed Key. Doug assessed the dire situation as only a Commander could. His friends' powers were being taken away, Calamity was shaking free of the vines, and Slade was barely holding on. There wasn't much time and he knew if there was any chance of coming out of this alive, he would need as much help as he could get. He looked Slade in the eyes and nodded. "Okay." As he got up and turned to face Calamity, he commanded, "Give it everything you've got! And Slade, you kept your promise and got me out of that prison. Thank you. This time I'm coming back for you."

Douglassaire ran after Calamity with great speed and jumped far into the sky, lifted with the power of air. He could see the horizon of water surrounding the island, all cast in a dark shadow. Below, Calamity's broken arm shook free of the vines and black smoke gathered at the stump to swiftly regenerate a new hand. Its newly formed claw lifted high behind Doug and prepared to swat him out of the sky.

Doug raised his sword above his head. The dark clouds twisted into a massive funnel that collected rock and trees as it formed.

Gisela knew it was her turn. It would be the biggest use of her power, and with it, she wanted to rid herself of the water spirit for good. The Djed Key was already drawing on her spirit, so that's where she focused her power. "Do some good for once, Gigi," she said, speaking aloud.

The water spirit spoke back, *I'm not finished with you, yet.*

"I know that, but I'm finished with you!" Gisela whisked the water of the lake into the funnel creating an airborne maelstrom. She made sure the stream passed through the Djed Key in Doug's hand. The water formed countless arms and hands that reached out to grab Gisela, but the Djed Key was too strong. She could hear Gigi's scream as it drew the spirit out of her body in a bright wisp of blue.

Slade lifted his hand and mustered as much power as he could into his small flame. The ball of fire grew into a substantial size and Slade launched it, engulfing the Djed Key in black flames. As he did, a trail of red left his body and was collected by the sword.

Those were Slade and Gisela's last uses of their spirits. Their powers were gone.

Douglassaire released the air holding him in the sky and fell fast toward Calamity, outpacing its falling claw close behind. The maelstrom touched down on Calamity, lifting it closer to Doug as it wailed in pain. Once Doug was close enough, a thunderous clap roared through the air as he struck with the Key. Slade and Gisela covered their eyes from the blinding white light that covered everything.

III

Anna's eyes widened at the sight of a rocky fist the size of a building coming straight at her. She scurried to her feet and dodged the punch at just the last second. Anna's legs worked hard to keep her balance after the resulting tremor and she continued to run. As she managed to barely dodge punch after punch, she knew she couldn't keep this up.

The golem's barrage of swings paused and Anna stopped to see what it was doing. Both of its hands were laced together overhead and began a descent right on top of her. A crash of the earth rumbled in front of her as she nimbly jumped back. The golem was hunched over and she saw a chance. She stepped on the creature's fist, ran up the arm, and lunged to its center with her sword pointed at the opening where her sister was. A jab at the queen's neck was unsuccessful as the opening sealed shut to block her swing. Anna fell to the ground and the seal reopened.

"Please," said the queen.

As the golem rose upright, Anna, tried to think quickly. She looked to the edge of the field and came up with an idea. As a child, she had only beaten her sister once in a race to the edge. If only she could do it now when it counted most, she could end this. It was a long shot, but it was her last and only chance. She bolted for the cliff.

"Bad idea," yelled the queen. "If that is what you want, I shall push you off!"

Anna could feel the tremors of the golem's steps grow stronger and faster as it ran after her. The cliff got nearer and she didn't look back. She felt a steady rumbling on the ground behind her as the golem dragged its hand to knock her off. She jumped the railing and disappeared over the side just before the hand connected. She speared the wall beside her with her sword and hung there as the golem smashed through the railing and tumbled over the side. As she reached for the edge of the cliff above her, she locked eyes with her sister inside the golem who was holding her head from the fall. The queen wasn't finished yet.

Anna grabbed at the edge of the cliff, stepped on the sword she'd lodged, and lifted herself back up to solid ground. All the while, she watched as the airborne golem was taken apart. The queen's arm was crossed over her, clutching her shoulder, and her other hand was placed over a wound beside her eye. Still, she used her ether to change the golem, piece by piece, into a staircase that led back to the castle. Her incline was labored and her injury distracted her. If Anna moved to her blind spot, there was no way she could see her and react.

Anna knelt on the ground with Libra's gun in her hands, aimed, and shot. The crystal bullet penetrated her sister's chest, shutting her power down.

Queen Aeothesca lost her footing and began to scream as the stairs fell away. Her screams were cut short. Anna had reloaded a regular bullet into her BAC and made contact with the queen's head.

Her sister's body fell, lifeless, through the sky, but Anna's rage took over. She pulled the trigger over and over but only heard the unsatisfying clicks of the empty chamber. Her cache of ammunition was depleted, but her senses hadn't yet returned. She felt no relief until the queen was but a speck in her eye.

Anna stood up as her ears popped. She swallowed to correct them. The castle was losing altitude and it was time for her to go.

IV

Anna ran through the stained glass door, through the throne room, and into the great hallway. As the door slid open, she saw her comrades slowly making their way down to the door.

"Did you get her?" Kandyce called. She and Vinzant tried their best to walk step by step through the hall with Jack's arms over their shoulders. He grimaced as he trudged along with a deep gash at his side.

Anna remembered that Vinzant's arm was injured and relieved him of Jack's weight. "Yeah," she said. "She's dead." She hoisted Jack up by his arm and placed a hand on his wound.

"'Atta girl," Jack managed.

"The knights all fled once they heard the news," Kandyce said. "We have to get out of here fast. The castle's—"

"I know," Anna replied. She tried to think of a way out. "The Guardian."

"What is that?"

"The queen's private aircraft."

***

The once-level ground had begun to tilt upward as the Auctorati made their exodus through the doors to the runway where the Guardian sat. The panoramic view of Pangaea had disappeared, and as they made their way to emerald green aircraft, it looked as though they were walking into the sky.

They spotted the pilot of the guardian, a young man suited in a navy blue coat. He stood next to the small staircase that led to its opening. He kept checking his wristwatch and looking at the horizon, obviously worried if he would ever depart safely. His task was to always wait for the queen, so the sight of four beat up ruffians approaching truly gave him a start. He raised his hand and said, "You can't come in here."

They paid him no mind and Kandyce led Jack up the stairs.

"I'll call the guards."

Vinzant swung his arm out in a sweeping gesture and said "What guards?" He ascended the stairs.

"This craft is for the queen's use only. I won't leave without her."

"The queen is dead," said Anna. "I'm in charge now."

The man tried to make sense of what she was saying. Once he studied her face, he understood. "Princess – Your Majesty," he stammered.

"Fly us off of this rock. That's an order."

He nodded, "Yes, yes, Your Majesty," and followed her up, closing the door behind them.

Anna followed the pilot halfway through the cabin and let him continue on his way to the cockpit. She was stopped by the memories this familiar setting brought up. Kandyce and Jack sat in the booth seats toward the middle, directly in front of the door they came in. Vinzant sat in the front most seat with his head rested in the corner where the wall and his seat met. Anna walked past all of them and wanted to sit in a similar seat, but felt the draw of something stronger. For a moment, she forgot she was on a supertrop and not in the throne room it replicated. The big chair sat further down, facing them. As her steps pulled her forward, she was reminded of how she always wondered what it would be like to sit there. She stepped up on the platform, turned, and sat on the throne for the first time.

Vinzant picked up his head and smiled. "Queen Anna."

V

Slade rested his head on the tree behind him and waited as his vision slowly came back. He saw Calamity's huge black claw hovering over the ground, but not moving. Suddenly, Calamity wailed horribly and its smoky exterior dissipated into thin air. When the claw disappeared, Slade saw Douglassaire with the Djed Key in his hands, down on bended knee. Slade held on long enough to see Doug lift himself off the ground. He smiled and closed his eyes.

Life began slipping away and Slade could barely make out the sound of Gisela yelling at him in defiance. "No, Slade. Don't you die on me!"

Gisela grabbed his face and gently slapped his cheeks. "Slade, come on. Slade!" She looked back at Douglassaire who was standing over the two of them, her eyes pleading for him to help. Douglassaire watched as the shadowy spike that pierced Slade disappeared into the air. Slade slid off the side of the tree and Doug fell to his knees to catch him. He stared at Slade and felt a tightening in his chest. What could he do? He always had a plan – always had a direction, but now he felt clueless. He'd rather face off against Calamity a second time than face this.

He saw Slade was losing a lot of blood and then the strangest memory flew through his mind. *His blood is on your hands, alone,* he remembered. That crazed woman he fought in Pelagus said that on the day Commander Azure died. He remembered she killed one of the Southern Third's warriors who threatened the queen and threw his blood at the other warriors who stood there. Then, he felt his leg and remembered how Gisela removed the crystal bullet using his own blood. He ripped off the bandage and saw that his wound was completely healed. Not even a scar was left. Douglassaire's thoughts were spinning in his head until he was struck with an idea. "Hold on, Slade. Stay with me, man; stay with me."

He lay Slade down on the ground and placed the Djed Key flat on top of him. He pressed down on the Djed Key and closed his eyes. The Key amplified his knowledge of water ether and he focused on Slade's blood to speed up its natural healing process. Gisela watched in amazement as the bleeding stopped. It wasn't long until the cavity that ravaged Slade's system was closed completely. Doug opened his eyes and saw that Slade hadn't yet opened his. He waited for a movement, a sound – anything, but got nothing. He rested his head on Slade's chest, defeated.

Gisela gasped. "Slade!"

Doug felt Slade's chest rise in a quick breath and quickly lifted his head to see. Slade opened his eyes and looked around, unaware for a moment. He saw Gisela leaning over him with tears in her eyes and settled his gaze on Doug's smiling face. He felt his body lifted off the ground in a surprising embrace. Gisela joined them, spreading her arms over the two of them, relieved that it was all over.

CHAPTER THIRTY-SEVEN

The gate to Ether reappeared back on the hilltop of Reor overlooking the city. As its gates swung open, out stepped Douglassaire with the Djed Key in hand and Slade and Gisela at either side. Douglassaire's armor had seen war, prison, and a fight with a demon. The once-polished black sheen was tarnished and cracked. Slade's grey armor had a chunk missing where he had been pierced through and the rest was almost as destroyed as Doug's. Gisela's jeans, sneakers, and red T-shirt were all blackened by dirt, smoke, and sweat. Doug used the Djed Key to call forth and unlock the gateway home. As they emerged from the portal, they looked as though they survived a trek through the underworld, but their spirits were lifted. They did what they set out to do and they survived.

Slade was still sore and tired from that fight with Calamity – a sentiment he was sure he shared with the others. He sat on the ground and Douglassaire took a seat next to him, finally enjoying a calm breath and the pink sky of the setting sun. Slade watched him as he looked out onto the horizon. Then something clicked in Slade's mind. He almost forgot. "We still have to stop the queen! Doug, we can't–"

"Slade," he said. "Look."

Slade looked at the city, unsure of what he was to make out, but then he noticed it wasn't something he was supposed to see, but something that was missing. Lorelei Castle was nowhere to be found. Slade wondered what it meant. "Do you think…" he started. He was interrupted by a ringing sound. He flipped open the latch on his armor and saw his comm. was ringing. Grabbing it, he looked at the screen and saw it was his mother calling. He answered it, "Mom?"

"Oh, God, Slade!" cried his mother's voice on the other side. "Where were you? I've been calling for the past hour! Oh, thank Elao. Are you okay? I thought you were still in that castle!"

"Yeah, Mom, I'm fine. What happened?"

"It just fell out of the sky! They're saying the queen was still in there. I don't know what's going on. Now there's some girl all over the news who claims to be the princess. What did you do, Slade?"

"I'll tell you all about it when I get home. And I got a couple friends coming with me…and somebody I want you to meet."

Gisela smiled at the conversation and anticipated some comfort and normalcy. She thought of her own mother, but this time, the fear and regret were gone. The water spirit was put away where it would cause no more harm. She was proud of herself, and she was sure her mother would be, too.

Slade ended the call and put the comm. away. They all turned their heads at the sound of the gate creaking to a close. The Djed Key lit up once more and began to levitate off the ground. Just as it began to fly back into the gate, Douglassaire caught it by the hilt. The sword tugged and tugged, and Douglassaire pulled back on it hard. The sword was being pulled home, but Doug didn't want to let it go. The power he had, the strength, the freedom he'd fought for – it was all his. He would retake his rightful place as Commander of the Southern Third, and the Djed Key would allow him to protect his nation against any threat. The gate soon closed and disappeared. The Djed Key was subdued and remained in Doug's grasp.

Slade studied Doug's eyes, his nose, his mouth; Doug was the most powerful man he'd ever met, even without the Djed Key. He wrapped his arms around him and said, "Doug, you don't really need that thing."

Doug thought about it. It wasn't the Key that made him the Commander – he did that. And it wasn't the key that saved him from a prison cell – Slade had. He looked back at Slade, raised his hand, and felt the smooth skin of his cheek under his thumb. "You're right," he responded. "I already have everything I need." Douglassaire put his rough hand on the back of Slade's neck and pulled him forward. As his lips pressed against Slade's, he knew everything would be all right.

Gisela smiled at the couple, finally able to be truly happy for her friend. And not just Slade, but Douglassaire as well, who had proven more than enough that he was worthy of the title. The thought of her old crush on Slade crossed her mind. As she watched him, she felt no jealousy, only pride. She learned that she was strong enough to handle anything on her own. Love would come, but she was going to enjoy being happy with herself in the process.

Slade knew he would forever remember this moment. The pink sky, the setting sun, and the feel of love coursing through his veins as his warrior, his man, Douglassaire, kissed him. His powers were gone, the queen was dead, and the Middle and Southern Third would forever be changed. He realized then that even though the Pangaea he knew no longer existed, there was still magic in the world.

ACKNOWLEDGMENTS

Thanks to my father, Jonathan King, who always believed in my skill as a writer. Without his belief, this book would not have been written. I also thank my mother, Terri King, who pulled me through more tough times than I can count. My gratitude goes out to my brothers, Jonathan King II and Justin King, for *getting* me. It means more than they'll ever know. Thanks to my amazing sister-in-law, Suleika King, for bringing love into my life in the form of three beautiful little ones: Joey, Jayson, and Jaylani. I also thank her for the use of her maiden name, Benitez, as Gisela's surname. And thanks to all of my extended family. When I say "I love you" I mean that with every ounce of my being. Your love and encouragement has made this accomplishment possible.

Thanks to my editor, Amelia Beamer, for her great wisdom and advice. You helped bring this novel up to the level I envisioned. Thanks to my proofreader, J.R. Scott, for the kind words and the *right* words. Thank you fellow author, Samuel Alexander, for your guidance.

Last but not least, thank you dear reader. You've made a dream come true.

ABOUT THE AUTHOR

Jarrod works in search engine optimization (SEO) and is a graduate of Temple University. When not writing stories or website copy, he writes, sings, and produces his own music. *Pangaea: Unsettled Land* is Jarrod's first novel. He currently lives in Philadelphia, PA.

Sign up to learn more and get notified of future releases by this author at www.jarrodking.com/subscribe